I

# Also by Jared McCann

*Marked for Judgment*

# READERS SPEAK OUT

"Make sure you keep your arms and legs inside this roller coaster the whole time, because it's gonna take you for a ride!"

"If Jared McCann isn't already on your bookshelf, then it's time you put him on it - two thumbs way up for *The Dead Will Rise!*"

"Just like *Marked for Judgment*, I couldn't put this book down. Another page-turner that has you begging for more! Mr. McCann's rising, new voice is a vibrant addition to fiction."

"*The Dead Will Rise* is a nail-biting, edge of your seat read that delivers with a heavy punch! A talented author who writes with genuine passion, Mr. McCann shines again in his second novel."

"One word: WOW! I'm not a reader, but even I haven't been able to turndown Jared McCann's *Marked for Judgment* and *The Dead Will Rise*. Keep writing young man, keep writing! The late nights you keep me up are so worth it!"

"After reading Mr. McCann's *The Dead Will Rise,* I'm left absolutely speechless. Not one page or one word is wasted. One of the best novels I've ever read. Ever! And I've read a ton."

# THE DEAD WILL RISE

THE DEAD WILL RISE
Copyright © 2017 by Jared McCann

Published by: JDM Books February 2017

ISBN-13: 978-0692849866
ISBN-10: 0692849866

Cover Design: Jared and Debi McCann

Printed in the United States of America

# A NOTE FROM THE AUTHOR

First and foremost, I would like to thank you for taking the time to read this book, whether that was purchasing it, borrowing it off of somebody, reading it on Amazon Prime, etc. Like *Marked for Judgment*, I put my whole heart into this novel with the hope that you will enjoy reading it as much as I enjoyed writing it. Any mistakes are mine and mine alone.

With that said, I want people to know where I come from as an author to correct a possible misconception. I am not a Christian author; however, I am an author who happens to be a Christian who makes his beliefs known in his writing. What I write is for both the believer and the nonbeliever. However, I'd be lying if I said I hoped my writing didn't bring the nonbeliever closer to God and a personal relationship with Him through His Son, Jesus Christ. I write with trying to make the Gospel attractive in every way, both to the believer and the nonbeliever. I write with my reader in mind, making them a part of the novel so they feel like they're right there with my fictional characters.

With writing, I attempt to use real life weaknesses, temptations, and other problems that we all as humans struggle with; but, with that said, I want my reader to also know that there is strength to get through those same weaknesses, power to overcome those temptations, and solutions to those various problems that we all go through in life, regardless of what they are. There is light, hope, positivity, and love through all the badness in life, but it's up to us to make it known. Some of the struggles I write about with my characters are also some of the same ones that I struggled with in life - ahem - and still do. There are characteristics that I share with my main fictional characters, and if I'm throwing anyone under the bus, then it's going to be me.

Thank you again for your support.

Now I say, walk with me, side by side, along with my leading character, Job McCants, into *The Dead Will Rise*.

With my gratitude,

*Jared McCann*

# THE DEAD WILL RISE

## JARED MCCANN

*[signature]*

Ed & Sue,

Hope You Love The Book!
God Bless!

6/2/2017

JDM BOOKS + OHIO

*For all those who I love*
*and*
*for all who love me*

"There is more joy in heaven over one lost sinner who repents and returns to God than over ninety-nine others who are righteous and haven't strayed away!"

-Jesus
*Luke 15:7*

There is a path before each person that seems right, but it ends in death.

*Proverbs 14:12*

# THE DEAD WILL RISE

# PROLOGUE

My name is Job McCants. And no, my first name isn't pronounced like the occupation one works, but J-O-H-B, like the guy from the Bible. You know, the one who goes through all those abhorrent and terrible trials?

If you don't know the Job who I'm referring to, then take a quick gander at the Bible. The book is in The Old Testament. Read the first two chapters of Job if you have time, and when you think you've had a bad day, then think again.

Between you and I, I've experienced my fair share of trials. As I sit here in prison, I'm writing to recount the details of the one trial that nearly claimed my life; it's the same one that ended the life of one who is dear to my heart, but you will come to know those details in the following pages.

I used to be a paramedic and help save lives, but now I seem far from that. Many names were buried in shame with this test that hung my life by a thread. It's worth mentioning and perhaps you can learn something I should've learned long ago.

Revenge is not the way to go, and I had to learn this concept the hard way; I'm now a witness of its consequences. For me, God played a major role throughout this ordeal and I wavered time and again; and although I'm imperfect and seem to fall short of His standard continuously, I try and stay the right path.

My prison home is dull and colorless: beige walls, and within these same walls are my cot, toilet, and a desk with the writing utensils I'm using to write my account of the gang I took head-on to avenge the love of one who was close to me. I'm able to look out through the small window in the door of my cell, but I don't care to look at the other prisoners, so I pretend it's not even there. I feel like Robinson Cruesoe stuck on an island inhabited with raging waves all about me.

No supplies to get me outta here. No SOS. No escape.

Forgive me for trailing off; it's just that I get so lonely and bored in this place. I spend my time reading, mostly the Bible, and I run around

1

The Yard daily to keep up with my cardio. It's not the same as running downtown or in my old neighborhood, but it does the job.

For a "white boy", as some of them call me, some of the other prisoners have taken me into their good graces, but that's mostly because I too was an enemy of their rival gang. I was the one who took down their rival leader: Rufus "D-Locks" Booker, who was the kingpin of the South Side Soldiers or SSS. The NEB's, also known as the North End Boyz, seem to have my back while I'm incarcerated and....

Sorry, there I go again trailing off.

I don't want you to get the wrong impression of me; first looks can be deceiving. If I seem laid back and easy, I'm not. And if this situation doesn't seem serious then you're wrong. This was the most serious and life-altering trial that I had ever been through, and I will probably most likely never face anything like this ever again.

Most likely.

Because of what I went through my heart turned black for a while; it was taken out of my chest and sandwiched between sidewalk and foot, and a large part of it cannot be replaced.

I found myself around people and places that I never dreamt possible of me being near. Some of those people were drug dealers, thugs, and murderers. And some of those places were the SSS's kingdom and a strip club. Trust me, the latter I wouldn't have gone to unless I absolutely had to. Ironic how we humans tend to think we'll never do something, or go somewhere, or be around a certain person in all our lives, but then we find our very thoughts pierce us, and the things we thought we'd never do somehow make their way into our lives.

Something like this found its way on my front doorstep and before I knew it, I was in a deadly game with no way out.

What I'm about to tell I've cried over many nights, I've punched many holes through walls, and I cursed the person who I had become; but, most of all, hatred had become me.

In the end, though, I like to think that I turned out all right, but that'll be for you to decide. As I sit in this cell, I want you to put your feet in my shoes and to try and comprehend my actions. Maybe you would've done things different, but no one truly knows what they're going to do until they're placed in that situation, right?

My name is Job McCants, and I want to tell you about my revenge against those who killed my wife.

2

# PART 1

"Don't be afraid of those who want to kill
your body;
they cannot do any more to you after that."

*Luke 12:4*

# 1

It all started like any other ordinary day. I awoke, had my regular morning cup of joe, and sat in the back screened-in porch area with my black lab Manny, short for Manhattan.

Living in Columbus, Ohio can take a toll on a person. It seems some sort of evil lurks its way into its city's gates and reaps havoc at some point everyday. There hasn't been a day that I haven't seen some sort of arson, or murder, or theft, or.... you get the point, during the evening news. It makes me so sick that I end up turning the tube off with anger rising into my eyes, turning them red.

I kinda have a temper problem, so bear with me when it comes to that.

But in contrast to the perils of the city, my wife Naomi, Manny, and I live in a quiet neighborhood that has a cul-de-sac at the end. One way in and one way out. It's a few miles outside the city, but far enough that there's peace and quiet. What makes sitting out on the back porch great is the picturesque wooded area. This end of the house faces east so I get to see the orange sun arise between the trees during autumn. During the summer it resembles a jungle with its vast greenness.

Our home isn't large, but is just right for the three of us. Naomi was deemed barren and unable to conceive years ago, but it didn't bother either of us really. We enjoy children and get to see our nieces and nephews often, but one thing Naomi and I agreed on was that we didn't need a child or children in life to give us absolute happiness. We were very content just to have one another.

My wife was raised Christian - quite unlike me - and she said not having children allowed her to focus more of her time on the Lord and what He wanted her to carry out in life. Naomi always was positive even when life short-stacked her; I admired her for that. She seemed to be at peace in life, and I oftentimes wondered what she thought of in that head of hers.

Guess I'll never get an answer to that.

It was a Saturday morning and we usually went for a morning run on Saturdays and made some type of Italian dish for supper that night. It was also the day we had date night and we'd stay up and watch a movie and have popcorn. I'd be lying if I said we didn't have a little Naomi-Job time on the couch afterwards. Manhattan staring at us would make me uncomfortable, so she had to be shut in behind the guest bathroom.

For some reason that morning though Naomi didn't want to go for a run, but said she instead just wanted to spend the entire day together at home. Thunderstorms were approaching anyway, so I said it sounded good to me. We sat outside and talked for hours. We talked about life in general, love, how thankful we'd been, God, and many other things; but the one thing that I truly remembered was when she said, "No matter what happens in life Job, I'm always with you and I love you always."

It was odd, but it was like she was foretelling some sort of prophecy that I had yet to witness. It made me shiver, but I held her hand and looked deep into her blue eyes and said what I often did when she said things like that, "Too me." It was kind of a dumb, childish thing that only her and I understood, but when we were first dating I once meant to reply "me too" to one of her comments, but instead it came out "too me."

That was also the night we shared our first kiss in my truck when I was dropping her off at home from a night out.

Thanks to my saintly wife, she helped me find God and little by little my faith had grown. From our earlier days I'd attend a Baptist church with her - we still attended church - and I came to find Jesus; and although I wasn't perfect - and still am not by far - I had a relationship with the One who gave me life. It was because of my wife that light shined into my heart.

It was because of me that darkness crept its way in.

Little by little.

My wife and I did a lot together and our jobs allowed us to have time to do things with one another. She worked helping troubled kids and I was employed by the city of Columbus as a paramedic. We weren't going to get rich by any means, but we had each other.

Relationships last, money doesn't.

I never raised my voice at Naomi and our arguments were few and far between, and I really was appreciative for a loving and gentle wife. One could say it was a match made in Heaven, and although our interests differed in many ways, we were one.

I guess opposites really do attract.

After we went to the grocery that day, we came back and double-teamed making chicken Alfredo with broccoli and mushrooms mixed in the sauce. Garlic bread and sweet red wine went hand and hand with it. Over a candlelit table we ate, savoring the moment together.

We didn't bother cleaning up afterwards. We headed straight for the sofa and I let her pick out the movie while I made a bag of popcorn. When I hopped onto the sofa she'd picked out *Ghost* starring Patrick Swayze. After the movie she said, "That's how life should be spent with your loved ones and friends. Cherishing everyday as if it's your last." Her words still ring in my ears, and I still quiver when I reminisce.

When we made love that night, the heat between us seemed to rise a few degrees higher than normal, like we were cherishing every moment as if it were our last.

As I held her in my arms that night against my hairy chest, I realized how blessed I truly had been in life and I felt, even if just for that moment, that no matter what could happen in life Naomi was right: we would always be with one another. Her soft, warm breath against my chest had its own tune as the moon hung high and bright.

That's when I heard glass shatter, and I arose to a sitting up position. Manny at the bottom of the bed barked loudly and jumped off, running downstairs.

"What was that?" Naomi tiredly asked.

"Someone's breaking in." The hair on the back of my neck felt like it rose one inch.

We heard Manny growl loudly and bark for what seemed like ten seconds, and then she let out a sharp and high-pitched yelp. The growling stopped. Upstairs, Naomi and I were frozen in bed, but I knew that I had to do something and do it quick.

Crime was low on our end of town and we didn't carry firearms, though I thought several times to purchase a home-defense shotgun for protection purposes.

Wish I had now.

"Job, I'm scared. I mean, really scared," Naomi whispered. She clung to my body like any separation from it would separate her from me forever.

I had to do something.

"I'm gonna try to scare him off. Call the police."

She moved toward her nightstand, but then she returned and squeezed me like a boa constrictor. "I left my phone downstairs."

I almost cursed but didn't. "Me too." We didn't have a home phone since iPhone's basically covered everything.

Great, I remembered thinking. I was going to have to bluff myself out of this one and hope it would work. I got out of bed, boxer briefs only, and made my way to the top of the staircase that overlooked our kitchen and living room areas.

I flipped the light switch on at the top of the stairs.

Silence filled the house.

The window to the right of the front door had been shattered and broken glass was on the hardwood floor. The door was open. Whoever had broken in must've taken what they wanted and left.

But where was Manhattan?

"If anybody's there, the police have been contacted and will be arriving any minute. I have my shotgun and I don't wanna use it, but this is your first and only warning!" I tried to sound authoritative and strong, but inside I was as shaky as someone trying to ice skate for the first time.

Too bad I really didn't have a shotgun so I could slide the forestock and make that *chit-chit* sound to really give it away.

The house remained silent.

"If anyone's there, speak now or I'm coming down!"

Nothing but silence.

At that time I wasn't sure what was the best move. I could've stayed up there having the intruder believing the police had been called and that I had a shotgun and that we were protected upstairs, but contacting the police wouldn't be possible then. If I went down I was taking a chance, but to protect my wife and get the authorities here ASAP also sounded more safe and worth the risk.

I chose the latter, but before making my way down I hit the lights off just in case so that if someone was down there they'd think I had a shotgun in my hands; and by turning off the lights they may not chance it by trying to come toward me since they couldn't see.

I also was hoping that if there was an intruder, he didn't have a gun.

Like I said, I was taking a chance.

Before I took the first step down I heard Naomi's voice in a whisper. "Job, everything all right?"

I returned hastily to the opening of our bedroom. "So far nothing. Maybe just some punk taking what he could get and then getting out quickly. I'm going down."

"Be safe, Job. I love you."

"Too me, babe." I tried a small smile, but good thing the room was mostly dark; I'm sure horror was written on my face. "Hide under the bed and don't come out unless you hear me say so."

She hurriedly, but quietly, removed herself from the bed to the bottom of it.

There wasn't any kind of weapon, so I went down armed only as myself. Now I'm not a very large man by any means, but I'm what my coworkers call "ripped" and I'm in excellent cardiovascular shape; but I would've felt more confident if I had a little more bulk going down with me.

After going down quietly, I came to the bottom of the stairs. I grabbed a fire poker by the fireplace in the living room, all in what seemed like total darkness. There, on the living room ottoman, with the light of the moon shining in, was my iPhone. I grabbed it and dialed 911 as fast as I could. I ran through quickly the situation with the dispatcher and she said she was sending units who'd be there soon.

Soon, for some reason, seemed forever.

I thought I heard an engine running, so I stepped to the open front door to see.

There, packed in like sardines in a later-looking Ford Expedition, were about four to five black men. I couldn't tell if there were any in the backmost seats, but it didn't seem so. The only way I could tell this and their color was because of the lamppost they were parked under. A couple had on sideways hats, some had gold teeth glinting from the lamppost light, others wore bling hung from their necks, and all of them had all-serious, bad business looks about them. One looked no older than fifteen, but one thing was certain: they all looked like trouble.

Especially the one who sat in the passenger seat that stood out more to me than all of the other ones. He seemed to have a commanding stature over the others in the truck. He looked more Jamaican than a street thug with long dreadlocks that probably went down to his mid-back. Of all the ones who looked like trouble, I remembered, he stood out more than all the rest.

His voice was also the first one to speak. "Hurry up, DJ. Make your bones!"

I didn't like the sound of that. Matter of fact, the only time I heard the saying "make your bones" was in reference to *The Godfather,* and it basically meant someone earning the respect of a crew by killing someone.

That's when it hit me like a ton of bricks: this was no break-in, this was an initiation!

The overhead lights in the kitchen and living rooms then turned on and shined brightly. I saw a couple of the faces inside the Expedition smile, but Jamaica kept a stern countenance. That's when I heard the voice behind me.

"Turn around mother...." the voice cursed and I seemed to be frozen in my tracks, but slowly I turned around to face my assailant. Like the younger-looking one in the Expedition, this kid couldn't have been over fifteen. "Look at this cat," DJ said more to himself than me. "I'm gonna cut you up real good." He smiled, a flash of gold, and he wore a white wife-beater with a large cross sporting on his chest that hung from a gold chain. DJ was far from religious, but to my fortune he held a knife in his hand instead of a gun. I wondered why, but I didn't care. It was better than a gun.

"Listen kid, you don't have to...." but DJ cut me off.

"Shut your mouth. I do the talkin'." He took a step closer to me before he spoke again. "You lied at first about calling the police and having a shotgun, and what're you gonna do with that stick in your hand boy." He smiled and I knew at any second he would come after me. I quickly turned around, but the others remained in the Expedition. DJ had to do this himself.

At that moment rage ignited within me. This gangster came into my house, has my wife fearing for her life, and on top of it all he's threatening to kill me. And, by the way, where's my dog? I didn't care if this was just a kid anymore. A burglar wasn't permitted inside a household, and if he did count the cost of his life before breaking in, then he shouldn't have entered in the first place.

Something must've changed in my eyes and face because DJ stuttered at coming toward me for a moment, like he saw a new spirit take a hold of me, and one that had him second guessing if he should mess with.

I went insane. "Come on then, do it! Kill me! What're you waiting for! Be a man! Come on!" My face flushed red with wrath and adrenaline pumped through my veins like blood. I really was trying to scare him off so he would change his mind; I wasn't trying to antagonize him, but unfortunately my attempt to get him to back down backfired.

DJ gripped the knife tight and ran toward me. With my back to the front door, I ducked his swipe for my face and with the poker in my hand I gave him a hard blow to the stomach with the base of the handle. He let out a long sigh; I'd knocked the wind out of him.

I didn't want this kid's blood on my hands, but he made it hard by swiping again for my face. I jumped back this time, missing his second attempt. "Kid, I'm telling you...." but that's when I yelled from the knife sweeping across my abdomen. Like a credit card, he swiped into my flesh as the knife had my blood and bits of flesh adhered to it after he pulled it back.

Cheering came from the Expedition behind me and I thought I vaguely heard someone say, "Thata boy, DJ!"

DJ tried an uppercut to my stomach, but with the poker held firmly in my hands, I hammered it down on his wrist, knocking the knife out of his hand onto the ground. With one hand holding the base of the poker and

10

the other holding the middle of it, I shoved the poker into DJ's chest in one quick upward motion, piercing him so that the poker went through to the other end of his body near his heart.

Standing still and blocking the crowds view from DJ, there I stood. DJ looked up at me with cold eyes; mine were filled with sadness, but I wanted none of this.

More cheering came from the crowd. They must've thought my standing still was my last stand on this earth, but when I turned around to face them and out of their views way, they saw DJ drop dead to the ground. Bewildered, the pack of onlookers had defeat written on their faces, all except Jamaica who stared me down like I had been sealed with a death sentence.

Sirens were approaching, but they were still a little ways off.

That's when I saw Manhattan. Somehow they had her in the Expedition with them and I wondered how they'd gotten her, but my wondering turned into diving and taking refuge on my stomach to the side of the front door as Mack-10's began spraying bullets into my house.

It didn't last long. The sirens stopped and soon the night sky was filled with red and blue from the light bars above the cop cruisers. I stood up checking my body to make sure I hadn't been shot. I hadn't. I stood in the doorway with my hands above my head as police spewed out of their cars and rushed toward me.

Naomi was running down the stairs ignoring DJ's body as she passed it. She threw her arms around me and I held her tightly. Her tears streamed down my back and everything seemed like a blur.

I had killed a kid, but what was I supposed to do? If I hadn't taken action it would've been the other way around and my wife would have become a widow. I loved her too much to allow that to happen.

A thin officer, clean-shaven with a friendly face said, "Mr. and Mrs. McCants, I assume?" His badge read Haver. "Are you all right?"

I didn't answer, but Naomi said she was all right. I only had one thing on my mind.

Jamaica and his gang had my dog, and I wanted her back.

# 2

That night at the hospital, the ER physician stitched my abdomen up before we went to the police station so I could give an accurate account of what happened. I explained the incident at our house, but proper police procedure required I come in and give a full detailed explanation. Still unable to believe what happened to my wife and I, and Manhattan - wherever she was - I ran through as best as I could with one of the detectives my unfortunate encounter with DJ whatever his last name was.

His name was Jehu (pronounced jay-who) Bridges. He looked younger than my thirty-three-year-old self. He had cornrows, but unlike the thugs earlier at my house he had a police attitude about him. Little did I know that he'd be the closest thing to a friend that I had when everything was said and done.

"We've been seeing this gang-related activity all too lately, Mr. and Mrs. McCants." Naomi and I sat across from him in his office. "The gang who was at your house this evening is who we call in this city the king of all gangs, that is, the South Side Soldiers, or more commonly referred to as SSS."

I'd heard of them, but gangs and that kinda activity took place on the other side of the train tracks, or at least I thought.

"Please, detective Bridges, call me Job." I looked at Naomi. "And she's Naomi."

"All right then." Detective Bridges gave a small smile. "You look like nice folks, and I'm very sorry this happened to you tonight." He cleared his throat. "I'm also sorry about your dog. We gave a description to the dog warden. Hopefully something will turn up."

We both nodded and thanked him for his kindness.

"We've been investigating SSS for a while now, me in particular." He gave what I thought a sad look, and looked sideways to a framed picture on a shelf of himself and an older boy. "They're trying to find worthy, loyal thugs for the chaos they do. Part of that is their initiation process."

12

Detective Bridges went on to say that in order to be a part of SSS one had to follow instructions to show that they were trustworthy and could be an abiding asset. He said that SSS "newbies" had been breaking into homes for the sole purpose of killing a member of that household to join the ranks - not small children, and sometimes the "newbies" wore masks while others didn't - and if one couldn't go through with the killing, they were left to fend for themselves. A couple of these "newbies" who couldn't go through with it ended up in jail for breaking and entering and passed along information to detectives such as Bridges about SSS.

The detective also told us that each "newbie" who followed through gave their signature at the home in the form of spray painting SSS onto a wall and putting the number '1' next to it. Bridges said this was to tell the police that another member had been accepted into the havoc-reaping gang. He also said that all the victims had been killed with a knife as being part of the initiation. In order to find the hardest of the hard, he told us, "newbies" had to prove to SSS they could use a knife before using a gun.

"Consider you and your wife fortunate, Mr. McCants.... I mean Job." Detective Bridges smiled.

"Trust us, detective," Naomi said taking my hand, "we've thanked God." She squeezed my hand with such sureness that I thought I might not get it back.

Bridges scratched at his goatee. "You've got nothing to worry about, Job. This was a matter of self-defense. We'll try and follow up on this investigation in addition to the other ones that are piling up with this gang." The detective shook his head and then turned it away from us. "It's like a flood with SSS. The crimes are coming in so fast that as soon as we investigate one, another follows and we can't keep up."

I felt compelled to offer a little encouragement. "You're doing what you can, detective Bridges. Hang in there."

The look on his face seemed to say he wasn't doing enough. "Can I offer either of you something to drink? Coffee, soda, water?"

Naomi said she could use coffee, but said she could get it herself. I refused anything. She left the room leaving Bridges and I alone. He leaned back in his chair. "Job, according to your description you've given us, do you know who the dreadlocked man sitting in the passenger seat was?"

I shrugged my shoulders. "Just another thug I figured." Jehu Bridges shook his head and filled me in on the man who would later become my number one enemy.

"That was Rufus Booker who goes by 'D-Locks.' According to our sources he's the leader of SSS, but authorities can't get close to him. His 'soldiers' protect him like he were the President himself, and a couple of times we got close to him from tips from some of the failed 'newbies'; but every time we get close he seems to get away."

The detective's face was earnest as he went on.

"Have you ever seen the movie *Brick Mansions* starring Paul Walker, Job?"

I shook my head. That was one Naomi and I had yet to see.

"Well then," Bridges said, "to make it short and not go into too much detail, there's a drug kingpin who basically controls his own part of a city and nobody can get to him. It's his world, his way, and he's got an army of followers. Cops can't touch him or his territory, so they form a bubble around their block and keep the peace in what they can control.

"That's the kinda deal that we're dealing with when it comes to Rufus 'D-Locks' Booker, Job."

I wasn't sure what to say, so I just sat there taking it all in; but it did interest me as to why the leader of this SSS gang would be waiting outside my house in a Ford Expedition while an initiation was taking place.

"Why then," I started to say, "would Booker risk being caught by being at my house for this particular initiation then?"

Detective Bridges raised his eyebrows with a I-know-but-you-don't look. "I'll get to that shortly."

Just then Naomi returned with a styrofoam cup in her hand that was steaming at the top. She didn't say anything, but sat back down.

"I don't want to instill fear in you, Job and Naomi, but we're going to, for a short time, station a cruiser outside your residence at all hours. This case is a little more...." he tried to find the right word, "sensitive than most, and we just want to go about it safe."

I figured this was just typical police procedure for folks who went through a devastating crime, but something was telling me there was more to this than that.

"This is my work number and I've written my personal cell phone number right below it. If you need anything or something comes up, you just go ahead and give me a ring. You got it?"

I took the card from his hand and nodded my head.

Naomi swallowed a gulp of coffee before speaking. "So, detective Bridges, why's this case more sensitive than the rest?"

"I'll let your husband fill you in on what you missed, but we're dealing with Rufus 'D-Locks' Booker who's the head of SSS, and we're going to take every precaution to keep you and your husband safe."

I sensed something was missing and I knew Jehu Bridges was slowly getting to it, but I wanted what was covered to now be revealed. "What aren't you telling us, Bridges?"

14

Detective Bridges' face looked slightly sullen, like he was getting ready to tell us bad news. "Booker doesn't care much for human life, but his only biological brother he's raised and has looked out for...." he stopped short.

I waved my right hand in a circle motion, suggesting to Bridges to keep going. "And?"

"And he wouldn't let nothing happen to this only brother of his. He would go against the world himself before letting anything happen to him...." again, Bridges stopped short.

My temper came to life. I'd had enough. "Get to the point Bridges and stop wasting our time! Out with it!"

The detective sighed and looked down before saying, "Rufus Booker had a brother named DJ, and he'll be looking to make amends against the man who killed him."

I almost missed what detective Bridges said in my anger, but now it all made sense. Now I understood why Rufus "D-Locks" Booker waited outside my house in a Ford Expedition, and now I also understood why our particular case was so sensitive.

"You mean...." I started to say, but Bridges cut me off.

"That's right, Job. Rufus Booker's brother was DJ Booker. The kid you killed tonight."

† † †

As we walked up our front door steps that morning, I must admit, a nameless fear crept its way into our home behind us when Naomi and I walked through the front door. For the first time in a long time I felt scared, like my wife and I were in death's crosshairs ready to be terminated.

Several cop cruisers were parked outside our house and a couple officers escorted us into our home. I noticed when we walked up to the front door that the window DJ shattered was replaced with a board. That was another thing I thought about on the drive home: our house would need worked on from the damage Rufus Booker and his goons had caused, but at least the window was patched up, leaving no free way for any intruders to make their way in easily.

"Officers," I said looking at them, "who boarded up the window?"

I couldn't tell at first, but one of the officers was Haver, who was one of the first arriving officers who made sure Naomi and I were all right.

15

"One of your neighbors, I believe he said his name was Mr. Greenley, came over while you were gone and boarded it up and cleaned up the broken glass."

Mr. Greenley was our next-door neighbor. He was a quiet man, but, all the same, he was also one who looked out for the neighborhood and was willing to tackle any home improvement project. I also thought, at any hour as well. Tomorrow I would stop by and personally thank him.

"Mr. McCants," officer Haver started to say, "the body's been taken away and we tried to cleanup as best we could for you." I appreciated their generosity. "Besides some bloodstains on the hardwood floor the rest should look all right."

Naomi spoke for both of us. "Thank you, officer Haver."

"If you need anything, we'll be out here." Haver made his way to his fellow officers as Naomi and I closed the front door behind us.

I stood in my house that morning stone cold and still, looking around our home that was a crime scene just hours earlier. My stomach upturned when I looked down and saw the maroon colored bloodstains where DJ fell to his death. I tried to erase the memory from my mind, but I knew it was one of those memories that could never be erased no matter how hard I tried.

Maybe in my later years dementia would take that all away.

Something didn't feel right, and it had nothing to do with DJ or the fact that I had killed him. The house was quieter, hollow, and that's when I knew what didn't feel right: Manhattan wasn't here. My poor dog, I thought. I hope she was all right. There was no reason for those thugs to harm our dog.

Or was there?

My brother Cyrus worked for the city we were raised in, but growing up he'd worked for a good home building company. I'd call him later today to help me with the home repair work. New siding would be needed for the bullet holes and a new window would be needed as well. Other than that it was just our peace of mind that would need worked on.

I looked at Naomi who appeared tired. Purple bags hung under her eyes. "Go get some sleep, babe. I'll take care of what needs done down here."

She wrapped her arm around my waist, looked up at me, and tried a smile. "We'll do it together and then get some sleep." Naomi, I thought, always positive and a ray of sunshine.

It didn't take long to clear the bloodstains and cleanup the rest of what was left of the mess. We sat down on the couch and just sat there silently. I don't think our minds, even after the fact, could make sense of the whole shebang of what happened under our roof. It was about this time when Manhattan would come over and rest her chin on my leg.

I desperately missed her. If she'd ran off I wouldn't have been so worried; she always came back, but she was in the possession of ruthless men who I wasn't so sure would be kind to her.

Naomi broke the silence. "So what do we do now, Job?"

I wasn't even so sure what to do, but I had to make her feel safe. "We trust detective Bridges and the police, my love. We let them do what they do best and we watch one another's backs in the meantime. And...." I started to say.

"And what?"

"We pray," I said, resting my hand on my wife's thigh. She put her hand on top of mine. We were together in this.

No matter what.

I'm not so sure what, but something seemed to arise in me just then. What started as a simmer was now on the verge of boiling. I was the man of this house, and I had to protect it. My wife depended on me and I couldn't let her down.

"There is one thing I know what to do."

"What's that honey?"

"I'm buying that shotgun I should've bought long ago."

# 3

The blood red, orange sun rose in all its glory Wednesday morning. Birds sang their songs perched on tree branches and a couple squirrels were bickering over a nut that the other thought belonged to it first. It was peaceful that morning as I sat out back and everything seemed the same.

That is, except Manhattan wasn't lying down at my side.

On a better note, my brother Cyrus and I finished the siding of the house and the repair of the broken window. Not a single bullet hole remained and it was as if no damage had touched my house at all.

My EMS (Emergency Medical Service) chief and coordinator gave me some time off that was well needed. It was spent with Naomi, and it was time we definitely both needed together given what we had been through.

Besides the police cruiser that was glued to our curb, we hadn't heard from detective Bridges since the other night, but I figured we wouldn't hear from him much at all anyway. According to him, the South Side Soldiers never stopped and a new case opened as soon as one was about to be investigated. He had a busy job, and I knew our case was only one of many.

For Naomi's and my own protection, I did purchase that shotgun I'd been talking about. I'm not well versed in guns but thanks to Jeff, the employee who helped me choose one and who sold it to me, I ended up buying a Mossberg 500 home-defense shotgun. Its pistol grip and smaller size compared to other shotguns allowed for easy maneuvering around corners inside a house, according to Jeff; and, he also said, it packed a "heavy punch" that would take care of any intruder.

Pops' Guns and Ammo, the name of the gun shop, had a shooting range out back and Jeff let me shoot slugs into a backstop area until I felt comfortable with it. I felt like someone with major stress buildup that had collected over a long time and, I had to admit, shooting bullets from the Mossberg and feeling the punch it packed made me feel good.

I want to say though, for the record, I never wanted to have to use it no matter how good it felt to shoot. After I got home from Pops' I kept it loaded, safety on, next to my side where I slept.

Just in case.

Something that didn't feel good were the nightmares that welcomed themselves into my life over the past couple of nights. One in particular had me standing on the edge of a cliff and far down below crashing waves broke into large rocks that stuck out of the sea. As I looked down it reminded me of the face of evil that was ready to swallow my life in its ensnaring teeth. Forcing me off the cliff were dark shadows who held what seemed like never-ending long swords in their hands. When the dark shadows finally got what they wanted, I was falling and I knew evil would consume me in its mouth of death; but, to my surprise, I kept falling and falling thinking I would hit the rocks and waves at any second. Instead, I kept falling into a dark bottomless pit that had no end.

When I awoke from the dream, I was in a sitting up position sweating bullets. They seemed like great drops of blood falling from my head onto the linen sheets. That night I couldn't fall back asleep, and when I was able to make some sense of the dream, I interpreted the dark shadows were Rufus Booker and his gang sending me to my death.

After killing his brother, I was sure that's exactly what "D-Locks" Booker had in store for me: sending me to my death. Not that I could blame him if the situation were different and I was in the wrong, but I hadn't been, and I thought any reasonable human being could understand that.

But, I wasn't dealing with reasonable human beings in this case.

I started thinking about Rufus Booker a lot ever since detective Bridges told me it was his brother whose life I ended. Would he follow me into town somehow and pull up alongside my vehicle and shoot me up? Was he waiting around a corner that I would soon turn into as I ran my morning jog? Were his eyes affixed on my house waiting for the police to leave so he could break in and avenge DJ's blood?

Questions like these and many others clouded my mind until I felt I was going insane. Like a hypochondriac, I was worrying about every little detail and things I had no control over. Since worrying couldn't add a single moment to my life and since I couldn't predict the future, what good was worrying doing me at all?

I decided I would do what was in my power and leave the rest in God's hands. As long as Naomi would be all right and left alone I didn't care what happened to me, but I knew that she would be so lost in this world without me. Not lost to the point of not being able to live and go on, but lost because I was her husband and best friend; I knew, as she told me

19

on a couple of occasions, she would never be with another. She always told me that nothing could disrupt what God had joined together.

As the morning drew to a close, Naomi eventually made her way out and sat on my lap. She usually read, cleaned something up, and worked out during the morning hours. "It's almost noon. You all right?"

I guess I hadn't realized how long I'd sat outside. I didn't have much to do today, but I also didn't plan on sitting out back for so long. "Yeah. I guess I just lost track of time."

"Whatcha thinkin'?"

I didn't want to bring up what I was really thinking; she'd already been through enough, and I didn't want to add any tension to the already tense time. "Nothing really." I scratched at my newly cut, short brown hair. "Just enjoying the day."

Just then the doorbell rang and it made the both of us sort of jump. We hadn't received any calls, so I had no clue who the unexpected company was. Naomi rose, but I placed my hand on her leg. "You stay. I got it." I made my way to the front door.

I opened to a brown uniformed UPS man whose back was to me as he made his way back to his truck. He turned his clean-shaven face around, waved, and smiled before he made his way into the truck.

Looking down, there was a small cardboard box placed on the front doorstep. I picked it up; it wasn't heavy, but whatever was inside felt unbalanced as it collided with whatever side I leaned it further to. I waved to the UPS man. "Thanks."

Closing the door behind me, I wondered what it could be. I hadn't ordered anything, but maybe Naomi had. The odd thing was that it had my name as the one who the package was to be sent to. Nobody had told me they were sending me something. I put it on the dining room table and took out a knife from a kitchen drawer to remove the tape. "Hey honey," I raised my voice so Naomi could hear me, "you order something?! That was UPS!"

The box reeked of something atrocious as I opened it. Tissue paper covered whatever was in there. I heard the partially closed sliding glass door being pushed open, so I knew Naomi would be coming in any second.

Looking back on that day, there was something sinister in the air that made its way into our home before I closed the door on the UPS man, but I definitely wasn't prepared for what the box held.

The dreadful smell grew as I removed the tissue paper. When I saw the content of the box I gagged and felt vomitus coming up from my stomach, but I swallowed it before it could protrude from my mouth. "Honey don't...." I started to say, but Naomi had already made her way in. I didn't want her to see what was in the box.

20

Tears filling my eyes, she made her way closer as I stepped back, keeping the box opened. "Job, what's the matter?" Her angelic face did a one-eighty as the mask of worry replaced it.

"Don't look in there....NO, Naomi!" It was too late. She looked inside.

I knew before her for only a short time, but now she saw the horrific truth. We now knew what happened to Manhattan.

I thought for sure she was going to scream, but she surprised me as she just covered her nose and mouth and stared down longer than I had. Physically I was stronger, but, emotionally speaking, she was by far the stronger of the two of us.

After a long minute she finally uncovered her nose and mouth and turned her head as tears streamed down her face onto her chin. I made my way to her, wiping away her tears and holding her for the longest time. We didn't speak for a few minutes, but when one of us did, Naomi spoke first.

Wiping her eyes and sniffing in strongly, she said, "Let's give our daughter a proper burial." I squeezed my wife tight to let her know that I agreed. I looked one last time into the box over Naomi's shoulder. I was still appalled and couldn't believe that any human being could do this.

Now hate is a strong word, and I never hated anybody, but I did now. I didn't like Rufus "D-Locks" Booker with what he wanted done to me, but now with what we just experienced in the box, an animosity came out of nowhere and crept into my heart.

I shut my eyes hard after looking into the box that last time. Even with shutting my eyes, I couldn't delete the picture from my head.

Sitting in the awful smelling, bloodstained tissue papered cardboard box was the head of our beloved dog. I let go of Naomi. With rage taking a hold of me, I punched a hole through our living room wall.

It would be one of many.

† † †

We buried what we had of Manhattan in the backyard. On top of her gravesite I placed rocks to form a small, sort of altar and wrapped twine around two pieces of wood I had in the garage, made a cross out of it, and stuck it into the ground. The sky was light blue and there wasn't a cloud to be seen as evening approached. Yellow, orange, red, and purple painted a beautiful portrait above us as if the hand of God prepared it specifically in contrast to our dark, gray, and colorless mood.

Naomi and I stood there, hand in hand, for a long time until the sun finally decided to set. "Boy, she sure was a good dog," I said staring down at her gravesite.

My wife was short and sweet. "The best."

I remember to this day when we picked Manhattan out of the bunch. One of our neighbors down the street was giving free black labs away after the mother, Bianca, gave birth to five. They stopped by our house first, I wasn't sure why, but I figured because they knew we were childless and had learned of our situation. I was reluctant and didn't want a dog, but, like most cases when it comes to women and pets, Naomi eventually talked me into it after a little whining and a frown I couldn't say "no" to.

Bianca had just got done feeding the puppies when we entered into the Walkers' garage. Their little girls, Evie and Gwyneth, were playing with them, but Ed and Georgia told them to go play inside for a while so we could pick out just the right one for us. The little girls pouted as they walked out of the garage. Evie, the older of the two children, stuck her tongue out at me before she left. I had to shake my head and smile.

I had no clue which dog was the right one for us. All of them were pretty funny and, I had to admit, cute. Ed and Georgia waited until the puppies were about five weeks old so we and whoever else might want one would have a personality to go along with it. One was chasing its tail, two were rough housing, one ran back to Bianca for more milk, and one ran up to my foot and then ran to the one who was playing with its tail. We all laughed as we watched them, trying to figure out which one we wanted.

The time came, and when it did, it was wet and yellow.

According to my wife, I apparently was zoned on the two puppies who were play fighting when the one who had recently walked up to my foot and ran back came my way again. I didn't see it, but when I felt something warm against my sock and sandal, I soon found out which puppy was coming home with us.

Already laughing before I had a chance to look down, Naomi and the Walker's stood there looking down and Georgia slapped her hand against her thigh not able to control her laughter. As I looked down Naomi said, "Well hubby, I guess we found out which is the right one," ending her comment in laughter.

I looked down and saw who would be called our Manhattan basically sitting on my foot, peeing yellow all over my left white sock and Adidas sandal. After she was done, she ran back to Bianca like she got away with something that nobody else saw.

Now, Naomi and I stood both grieving and softly laughing as we remembered that day. It seemed like it wasn't that long ago.

That night in bed, my hands rested behind my head as I looked up thinking about the past week. Never in my life did I think I'd experience anything like this, and now here it was happening.

In my house.

Rufus Booker and his clowns were monsters, the worst case of them I'd ever come across. They were heartless, cold-blooded, ruthless, inhuman, and I could've went on and on. It was people like him and SSS who made the world the evil and cruel place it was. It just made absolutely no sense to me how snakes like them could do the things they did and feel no remorse or penitence over it. Children of Satan instead of South Side Soldiers was a better name for them.

I wanted to get even with them, but what was I gonna do? Search around, inquiring about "D-Locks" Booker until it got me killed? I wasn't a violent man; I just had a bad temper at times that exploded in anger. Would I really be that ignorant to look around for a huge drug kingpin when even the cops couldn't take him down? Me. No way. Was I about to risk my life at the cost of death to make my wife a widow for life? I couldn't let that happen.

I just hoped and prayed that this would be the end of it. I prayed hard that this would be the end of it.

I didn't know at the time, but it wasn't unfortunately. Naomi turned on her side to face me. I looked over at her opened eyes. "Can't sleep, babe?" Instead of speaking, she just shook her head. "Me neither."

She moved over to my side, put her hand on my chest, and drew imaginary circles into it. She kissed me on the lips, but in that kiss, it was more than just a kiss. I'm not a psychiatrist, but love seems to penetrate even through life's most difficult times and trials. This was one of those times. She kissed me again, but this time she added a little tongue. I sensed her intensity and warmth and knew what she was wanting and, I had to admit, since we couldn't sleep, I was wanting it to.

She reached back behind my head and grasped one of my hands. "I love you, Job." She squeezed tighter with her other hand cupping my face. "I really love you."

"I really love you too, Naomi." I returned a kiss. "You're my everything."

She let go of my hand and moved her body on top of me. I loved every part of my wife's body and everything about her: her brown hair that hung down to her upper back, her sparkling blue eyes that resembled an angel, her luscious lips that belonged only to kissing me….again, I could go on.

23

There was nothing I wouldn't do for this woman; I loved her with my whole being. She completed me and we were one, and I knew it was the kind of love that would carry on even after this life. Naomi was my all.

We made love, and something struck me that I hadn't thought of before, as I rolled her over with me now being on top of her. Making love to Naomi felt as good as it did the first time. I never got tired of it and she never treated it like a chore. It was the most intimate feeling I ever felt, and I'm glad I felt it now.

Because that was the last night we ever made love.

# 4

A couple of days passed and in another couple I was due back to work. Naomi went back today and I felt a cool lonesomeness being in the house by myself. It was like the mute button had been hit, and it created a cemetery silence over the place.

I decided to go for a run since the nice day outside welcomed company. I put on some mesh shorts, a cut-off t-shirt, and laced my Brooks shoes before I locked the front door and closed it behind me. The warm weather seemed to rejuvenate me as I did a pre-stretch before I made my way to the street. I placed my Beats headphones on, turned up the volume full blast, and picked a song that pumped me up.

The cop cruiser was still there and a PD officer I hadn't seen before sat behind the steering wheel. I didn't want to seem unfriendly, but I wanted to get on my way, so I waved to the officer as I bolted past his car.

I didn't know how long a PD cruiser would remain outside my house. I guess, after all, it'd been a big deal with what happened at our house the evening DJ Booker was killed. The police must've figured I was marked for death with keeping eyes on our house for this long. Fear hadn't made its way into me yet. After all, if Rufus Booker came for my wife and I, the only thing we could do was prepare: lock the doors, turn outside lights on, keep a keen eye out, and use the Mossberg shotgun if I had to.

Which I didn't want to have to ever use, but I would if they came for us.

The light breeze felt good against my face as I made my way from our cul-de-sac into town. Back when I was younger, I used to run on wooded paths and a nearby bike path; but now I had to settle for downtown and urban running. It wasn't bad, but I didn't care for all the hustle and bustle of city driving, pedestrian stop and walk lights, and jerks who would holler something unwanted out their windows as they passed by.

My favorite street in the entire city was the current one I was running on: Duval Street. Old, but still in good shape fashioned homes clustered both sides of the street and tall trees formed a type of ceiling overhead. It reminded me of a homey neighborhood that is only seen in movies and not a thing ever goes wrong in it. The folks here seemed to have a quieter, independent demeanor about them than they did where Naomi and I lived; but, all the same, I enjoyed the change of visiting during my runs.

I ran further than I ever had that day. Maybe it was because I hadn't run in over a week. Maybe it was anger I was releasing. Maybe it was because it was a sunny, beautiful day and I wasn't in a rush to get back since Naomi wasn't home yet. Whatever it was, I felt good and felt like I could keep on going and going like the Energizer pink bunny.

On my way back, I entered once again into the city. It wasn't New York busy as when I first started, but it was still busy. I turned a corner, increasing my speed, and was approaching Walt's downtown liquor and drug store. Lecrae's *Don't Waste Your Life* bumped full bass in my ears, and I felt like a track star coming up to the finish line.

That's when this track star was struck on the side and I rolled over once, maybe twice on the sidewalk until I was looking up at the light blue, clouded sky. Quickly recovering my bearings, I looked up and saw a black male sprinting down the sidewalk with a book bag slung over his back. Overweight, bald-headed Walt ran outside hollering, "That's the last time you steal from me you punks! You hear me!" Walt raised his right arm in defiance and had an I'm-gonna-kill-you-if-you-come-around-here-again look. He looked down at me, but before he could ask if I was all right, I was back on my feet, running to catch up with the apparent thief.

As I ran, adrenaline overtook me and all I wanted to do was catch, put up against a wall, and yell at the person who shoved Walt's door right into my side, leaving me flying in the air and then lying in pain on the concrete sidewalk.

I really didn't know what I was gonna do, but I was beyond mad and wanted to discipline this jerk for what he did to me and Walt.

Closing the gap between us, Thief seemed to be a young black male, and when he turned around, his eyes widened as he saw me coming up strongly. He turned a corner, as did I, and the next thing I know he was pushing wooden containers from a mom and pops vegetable and fruit shop down onto the sidewalk to try and keep me from catching him. Apples and oranges decorated the sidewalk before me like a Christmas tree and a female's ear-piercing curses came from inside the mom and pops shop. It was going to take a lot more than fruit to stop me. I had to catch myself just once as I ran over the apples and oranges.

Thief looked behind him again, and if I thought he was surprised the first time he looked back, he doubled it this time; but this time I had the upper hand, because when he looked back this second time around, he ran

26

into a pedestrian ahead of him and fell down. He picked himself back up, but it was too late; I grabbed his book bag with one hand and the front of his shirt with the other and slammed him up against a concrete-blocked wall.

With his book bag torn off, I could see liquor bottles and various prescription drugs inside the now half-zipped bag. Thief went to grab for something near his waist, but I had already prepared myself and twisted his hand before I grabbed at the knife that was clipped near his left pocket. I tossed it angrily behind my back onto the ground, grasped Thief tightly by his collar with both of my hands, and stared him in the eyes.

I didn't speak at first, and when I turned to my right I saw Walt sure-stepping himself around the apples and oranges, making his way toward us.

"What were you thinking, kid!?" I asked Thief, shaking him a little. Now that I had him pinned, he looked to be around seventeen, maybe eighteen years old. Old enough to know better, but still a kid in my book. "Stealing this crap, causing other people damage, and to top it all off, thinking about pulling a knife on me?"

What surprised me about Thief is that he seemed to not have a care in the world. People and things were just objects to him; he didn't care about causing hurt or pain. "You got no idea who you're messing with homie," he said.

I didn't miss a beat. "Yeah, well, you can tell it to the cops partner." Walt made his way to us. With one hand I held Thief and with the other I bent down and picked up the book bag full of Walt's stolen supplies.

"Thank you so much, sir. What you did...." but Walt didn't have the words. He was amazed and just shook his head. "I already had one of my workers call the cops. They should be here any minute."

Walt grabbed and held onto Thief by the arm. "I got'em, sir. You take a breather." I let go and took a couple steps back. "Kids these days," Walt went on, "nothin' but trouble."

Thief tried to make a move, but Walt dropped the bag and held him still and firm like a vise grip. "You two are dead," Thief said, "you just don't get it."

"Get what?" said Walt.

I didn't like what Thief said next.

"SSS forever mother...." he went on to say what you already know, so I'll leave it out.

It was then that I saw it, and I thought for sure right there and then I was a dead man. Parked a little up the street facing me was a black, later-looking Ford Expedition, and packed in like sardines was a group of black men. I'm sure my face bled pale as I stood horrorstruck and stone cold still.

I looked back at Thief and then back again to the Expedition.

"That's my boys right there," said Thief.

This must've been where Thief was to meet up with them after he pulled off the heist. Too bad, this time. The Expedition, however, pulled onto the street and was making its way toward us on the opposite side of the street. The sidewalks weren't filled like fish in the sea, but they were crowded enough, so I figured nothing would happen; but, then I thought, SSS didn't care about nothing and would probably shoot up a crowd regardless of the body count or who the people were.

I could tell already who was sitting in the passenger seat. The dreadlocks stood out like thorns in a rose. I wasn't sure what to do or what I could do, so I just stood there awaiting my fate. My feet felt like they were permanently placed in concrete, and the world seemed to freeze in time; that is, except for the Ford Expedition making its way.

Maybe "D-Locks" wouldn't recognize me, after all, he had only seen me for a short time and that was a week ago. But would anyone ever forget the face of someone who had spilled his brother's blood? Or for that matter, would anyone ever forget the face of a person who spilled the blood of family?

Just when Rufus Booker and his cronies were almost to us, I heard a sound that couldn't have come at a greater time.

The sound of a PD's cruiser let out two quick squeals from the siren before stopping alongside the sidewalk in front of us. His lights were turned on as he got out of the vehicle and walked toward us.

The blood that came from the lacerations on my face and arms I didn't even know about until the police officer stood in front of me and said, "Sir, are you all right? Your face and arms are covered in blood."

I didn't hear him at first. My attention was behind him as I looked over his shoulder. He asked a second time and I nodded my head "yes." He walked past to the business behind me and all I could do was stare quietly ahead of me.

There, passing in front of me before they got to the intersection and made a right was Rufus Booker and members of his SSS gang. They stared me down with eyes of ice and their faces were as serious as someone's who had just received news that they had inoperable, terminal cancer. They stopped and parked for only a few seconds' time so we looked at one another on a straight level.

Rufus "D-Locks" Booker, with a thumb, sliced across his throat from one side to the other and gave me an eerie smirk. I got the point: he was letting me know I was a dead man. Another thing: he recognized and remembered me. They drove off and I just stood there.

My fists clenched so tight that I thought I might break my own hands.

# 5

After I gave my report to the police officer I made my way back home, only this time I didn't run but walked the rest of the way. I actually didn't have that far to go before Thief bolted me like a catapult onto the ground. The early evening was peaceful and bright in contrast to the pain I was feeling.

I'd refused EMS service because I knew they'd be guys I worked with, and I didn't feel like talking about what happened even though I trusted the guys I worked with with my life. While I gave my report, Walt sent one of his employees to cleanse and bandage my lacerations. Before I left the scene I looked in all directions to make sure a black Ford Expedition wasn't around to tail me home. I didn't bother telling the police officer about Rufus Booker because he was gone and I didn't see the point.

What did surprise me though was the substitute vehicle that was parked outside my house instead of the PD cruiser I'd grown accustomed to. I didn't recognize the car, but it was black with mid-tinted windows and I didn't like the looks of it. As I passed it, nobody was inside.

Now maybe it was just me, but lately I became sketchy of everyone and everything. Cars that passed outside our house, visitors that left me taking a double-look outside before I opened up, a nagging inner sensation. I felt like I had to be on guard every minute of every day since the night of what happened at my house. And this unknown vehicle parked outside my house only increased my sketchiness.

Instead of unlocking and going through the front door, I made my way out back, tiptoeing slowly up the wooden steps into the screened-in back porch. It was just getting slightly dark outside and the kitchen and living room lights beamed through the sliding glass door. I didn't hear anything from inside, but as I peeked into the kitchen, I now knew who the car belonged to outside, and there had been no need to be alarmed.

I tapped on the sliding glass door. Naomi came over, unlocked it, and let me in. We'd been on each other to make sure we always locked-up whether we were home or not. I came through, closed the door behind me, and said, "Evening, detective Bridges."

"Job, how are you....man, you all right?" He obviously saw where my wounds had been tended to.

Naomi must've not seen it at first either because she added, "Honey, what happened?"

I rewound to my recent episode and explained it all to them, that is, except the part about Rufus Booker because I didn't want to add anymore worry to my wife. I figured I'd tell detective Bridges if by some chance it were just him and I in the room.

"SSS," I said, "they're like a deadly cancer spread around the city."

"You're telling me," said Bridges. "That sure is something you did, Job. A lotta folks wouldn't have ever done such a thing." Naomi looked concerned, but I could tell she was just glad that I was all right and back home.

I wasn't sure how to respond. "Little dog messed with the big dog this time and thought he could get away with it." I paused. "He didn't." We all laughed a little.

I went on. "Bad people and bad things need to be stopped at times. I got caught up in the moment and acted on instinct, I guess."

Jehu Bridges smiled and removed the toothpick from his mouth. "Whatever it was, I hope I don't cross paths with you on a bad day." Again, we laughed.

Naomi tossed me a bottled water and offered detective Bridges a drink, which he refused. "Nah, but thanks ma'am."

I sat down on a stool at the kitchen island. "So, what brings you here, detective Bridges?"

A look changed on his face, I thought, and it wasn't for the good. "I got here just a few minutes before you did Job and I hadn't told your wife anything." He leaned against the countertop, crossed his legs, and folded his arms in front of him. "Mrs. McCants, you should have a seat too."

Naomi sat down beside me and placed her hand on top of my forearm. She also sensed that whatever was to be brought up cast a dark shadow about it. Jehu Bridges then said what he came to say.

"I'm not gonna waste your time, so I'm gonna be as brief as I can. We had to remove the cruiser from your house because we need all hands that we can possibly get with all that SSS is throwing our way. I don't feel comfortable doing so, just yet, but there's nothing I can do about it. The boss says we need every officer we have on the streets, and we can't leave one here anymore with all the chaos going on in the city."

I understood completely, and I was hoping Naomi would too. I totally got it. Keeping an officer babysitting our house was keeping him from other priorities, perhaps taking down an SSS member or some other Joe Shmoe reaping havoc in Columbus.

"I wanted to prepare the both of you," Bridges went on, "because I don't think you've heard the last of Rufus Booker." Naomi's hand seemed to crunch my forearm, and it caused me a little discomfort.

"Then why," Naomi said, "would you not leave some sort of eyes on us then? With all due respect, detective Bridges, my husband, in self-defense, killed Rufus Booker's only, and should I say, younger brother. He's just waiting for the right time to avenge his brother's blood." There was a hint of strain in my wife's voice and it made me sad for her.

Bridges looked down like he was in the wrong for something. "Trust me, Mrs. McCants…."

"Call me Naomi," said my wife.

"Sorry, Naomi, trust me, this wasn't my call and I went to bat for the both of you on this; but, like I said, it's outta my hands and there's nothing I can do about it." He opened up his hands like he was pleading for understanding.

"I know what I'm about to say the both of you already know; but, because I care, I'm gonna do it anyway." His arms dropped to his sides. "Lock your doors, keep your outside lights on at night, and try to keep a TV or radio playing when you're alone or outta the house. Have you thought about a home security system, and do you have a firearm handy?"

Naomi looked to me. "ADT's supposed to be coming next week and I just bought a home-defense shotgun."

"Good, good," detective Bridges said nodding his head. He looked both of us in the eye, longer with me. "You didn't hear this from me, but if something does come up and you fear for your life," he stressed "fear for your life", "don't hesitate to use that shotty, Mr. McCants." He didn't say Job, so I knew he was very serious with this last comment.

I nodded. "Lord knows I don't want to, detective Bridges, but I'll do what I got to in the event that something does come up." The detective nodded like he understood.

"You have my number," Bridges looked at both of us, "so please call if you need absolutely anything."

I walked Bridges outside to his vehicle and told him about my run-in with Rufus Booker that afternoon. With a look of disgust, the detective shook his head. "I gotta be honest with you, Job." He looked toward our house. "I didn't wanna say anything in front of your wife, but I'm not liking your situation with 'D-Locks' Booker."

"Me neither."

32

"I have a past with Rufus Booker. I know how he operates and he's not gonna let this slide. That scumbag needs brought down."

He got my attention. "What past?"

Detective Bridges looked unsure. "He," but then he paused. He didn't speak further about it, so we left it at that.

"I'll try and stop by every once in a while to make sure you and your wife are all right, okay Job." I nodded and we shook hands. "Like I said, call me if something comes up."

Jehu Bridges started his vehicle and I watched him drive away until he made a left out of view. I stood alone, looked at my house, turned, and looked out toward the empty, quiet neighborhood. There was something frightening in that silence as I stood there, and without the police here I felt sort of naked, like my wife and I were re-exposed to the world.

Now it was up to me and only me. For some reason, with a chill going down my spine, I totally agreed with detective Bridges. I didn't like our situation and I didn't think we had heard the last of Rufus "D-Locks" Booker. Standing alone, I thought hard on this.

Alone.

Like I said, I didn't like our current situation or the thought that we hadn't heard or seen the last of Rufus Booker. Looking back, I also wouldn't have thought it possible that we'd be seeing him again so soon.

That night.

† † †

Once again, I laid in bed with my hands folded behind my head looking up at the ceiling. Naomi walked out of the bathroom smelling of a sweet aroma from a shower, hit the lights, and got herself tucked in next to me. Laying her head on my chest and putting an arm around me, I rested an arm across her back and kissed her fragrant head.

"You all right, babe?" I asked her.

She sighed. "I'm not gonna lie, I'm scared; but I know we also can't live in fear everyday. Whatever might happen, God will take care of it all."

I rubbed my wife's back. "Yes He will." My mind was full of everything, like a collage with too much to make any sense of.

"Thanks, Job."

"For what?"

"For being an amazing husband." She squeezed me a little tighter. "I've been so blessed and even if my life were to end, I've lived a happy and faith-filled life." She paused and I'll never forget what she said next. "I know that even without me you'd be all right."

I thought different, but I wasn't going to tell her that. It was actually me who was more blessed to have such a wife who I often felt I wasn't worthy of having; but God works in mysterious ways, and for whatever reason, unknown to me, He brought us together.

I should've told her that night that I was the one who was more grateful, I should've spoke all those intimate and emotional words that men are uneasy about saying, I should've held her tighter, I should've made love to her even though we were physically exhausted, I should've....

But I didn't, and I regret it everyday.

I must say that, now that everything is said and done, I know that my wife sees me and knows the feelings that my heart holds. There's a peace in my heart where she resides and nobody, not even Rufus Booker himself, can ever rob me of. I've experienced firsthand that after someone does something to you physically, even if that's ending your life, they can't touch your soul.

My wife showed me this.

One thing I said to her that night though I'll never regret, and I don't have to worry that I never told her. "I love you Naomi, with all my heart. It's this same love that I know that lasts forever, and it lives on no matter what."

She gave me a long kiss before we closed our eyes and drifted off into sleep. "That's right, handsome. Too me." We laughed. "Seriously, Job, I love you too. So much." We kissed again and fell asleep in each other's arms.

It was the last time.

# 6

They say dreams can last anywhere from twenty seconds up to a half hour. I don't know how long mine was before I awoke, but it seemed really short.

I wasn't on the edge of a cliff this time, but the same dark shadows starred in this dream too. They had Naomi and were taking her away from me. In a fury, I fought back as hard as I could to bring her back to me, but it seemed the harder I tried, the further she was being separated from me. It was like an invisible wall was between us; her side seemed controlled to move back miles away while mine wouldn't allow me to push a single inch forward. Her ear-piercing screams shook me to the core. The dark shadows carried her away and I was left alone, broken on the other end.

Back in the real world, I felt something or someone forcing me to wake, but this dreamlike state wanted me to stay in its realm. Naomi's screams sounded so real, but at the same time they felt surreal. It was when I felt something hard against my head that I came to find out that her screams were real.

Semiconscious and not yet fully aware of my surrounding, I heard my name, "Job!" being shouted several times, which was then followed by screams.

"Shut her mouth!" I heard a man's voice say with authority.

The room was dark and lit only by the paleness of the moon. I turned to my left to see who I figured were two men holding Naomi. One of them held his hand over her mouth to keep her quiet.

Now fully aware and awake, an anger-filled rage took a hold of me. I arose to a sitting-up position and went to grab at the man who had my wife's mouth in his hand. Like the dream I just had, these real dark shadows were pulling my wife away from me. I couldn't get close to her, so I did the next best thing: I grabbed for my home-defense shotgun that stood to the side where I slept.

When I grabbed for it, I didn't feel it. That's weird, I thought. I grabbed farther back but still it wasn't there. That's when the bedroom

35

light shone bright and it blinded me until my eyes could adjust, but when they did, I didn't like the figure who my eyes beheld.

Standing tall with a serious look about him was the dreadlocked man who I absolutely despised: Rufus "D-Locks" Booker. His dark face boasted fright and his stature signified fear. He didn't quite dress like the members of his SSS gang; he looked more like a casually dressed Jamaican with a tinge of thug.

I looked over at Naomi. Tears were streaming down her face and she couldn't get out of the snare that the two SSS members had her in. I made a move, boxer briefs only, toward my wife, but the voice of the man I hated stopped me.

"Stop Job, or she dies!" Rufus Booker called me by my first name; I can't believe he actually had the nerve to use it.

Sweating from the anger building inside me, I sat on the bed motionless. I wanted to say something, but I didn't have an idea what.

Earnest in look and speech, Rufus Booker spoke again. "You killed my brother, so now I'm taking your wife." The two men holding Naomi started walking away with her toward Rufus. When she passed behind him to the hallway, I made my move.

I jumped out of bed to take on Rufus Booker, but all too quickly I saw something to my right side out of my peripheral vision.

The other member of SSS who was in the bedroom I hadn't seen the entire time since I awoke. When I looked to my right it was too late for me to try and save my wife, but I did find out for only a split second what happened to my shotgun.

Its butt end was coming toward me. Like a car crash, it collided with my head, and I knew no more.

$$\dagger \quad \dagger \quad \dagger$$

It took something wet and cold to hit my face before I woke from unconsciousness. When I opened my eyes, my head spun in circles and I didn't yet have my full bearings; but what was worse, I couldn't move. The only thing I knew for the moment was that we were in our living room.

My mind tried to recollect how I came to this position. Naomi's screams....lights turned on....Rufus Booker....my shotgun coming toward my head.

I remembered it all. My bearings came back quickly; I tried moving, but something kept me from doing so.

When my eyes cleared, I saw a sight that I hated.

There before my eyes was my wife sitting across from me with Rufus Booker standing behind her. I'd say about twelve or maybe fifteen feet separated us. Her eyes were red from filling with tears, but they hadn't streamed down her face yet.

I shook from right to left and then forward and backward, but still I couldn't move. When I looked down, still only in my boxer briefs, I then knew why: I was strapped down and two of Rufus Booker's thugs each had a hand resting firmly on one of my shoulders.

The other member of SSS, the one who knocked me out cold with the butt of my shotgun, tossed an empty water pitcher to the ground. It took my mind to do some remembering, but I recognized him as the younger looking one in the Expedition the night I killed DJ Booker; the one who looked no older than fifteen. He stood off to the side, but to my surprise he had a shaky look about him.

How in the world did they get in here, I thought? Naomi and I had been locking-up, and it wasn't like they had a key to get in. Then it hit me like a punch to the stomach when I looked toward the kitchen. The sliding glass door that led from the kitchen into our back porch was opened about a half a foot. I'd forgotten to lock it after I made my way in earlier when detective Bridges stopped by.

How could I have been so....but a voice stopped my thinking.

"It's about time you woke up," Rufus Booker said with a partial smile. I ignored him and kept my sight focused on my wife. To make anger erupt in me, Booker rested a hand on my wife's shoulder.

I sprang forward as best I could; I felt the legs of the chair move upwards. Apparently the two members of SSS weren't expecting my hasty move, but I didn't get far; they hurriedly grabbed my shoulders and sat me back down. They pushed down on my shoulders so hard that I couldn't move an inch, like I was permanently placed in concrete.

"Easy, Job, easy," Booker said. "We're all adults here. Relax."

"You all right, baby?" I said to Naomi. She didn't answer, but nodded her head nervously. I had to do something, but in my present position I wasn't sure what. I would attempt to talk Rufus Booker out of whatever he had prepared.

"Booker, listen...." I searched for something. "I don't know what you want, but she has nothing to do with it. Let her go."

Rufus Booker's face changed more into all-seriousness. "She doesn't have anything to do with this, but you do." He stopped shortly before speaking again. "You killed my brother."

I looked around praying that someone or something would rescue my wife and I from this horror film. There was nothing, and we just sat there, like two scuba divers who unfortunately found themselves in shark-infested water.

I'd play Rufus Booker's game, but I had no clue what its ending would be. "Your brother tried killing me. What was I supposed to do, just let it happen?"

"Yeah," Booker returned. "That's exactly what you shoulda done."

These really were people whose perspectives were upside down. There was no reasoning with them and they did what they wanted to; their right was wrong and their wrong was right. I met their kind on many squad calls I'd taken in the city of Columbus, but not to this lowly of an extent.

What was worse, I found out, it didn't matter what I said. They were gonna do whatever they had come here to do, and I knew what that was: kill Naomi and I. Perhaps Naomi knew this as well as I, but I knew that once the victims saw the faces of those who were doing them harm, they wouldn't allow them to live. There could be no witnesses. I knew our fate was sealed by these ruthless human beings, and I knew that moment was going to come at any minute.

Sweat started dripping down from my forehead and I could feel my body temperature rapidly increasing. As I stared at my wife, I wondered what her final thoughts were. It was odd, but I felt that my wife knew what was coming. Her eyes seemed to whiten and there was an unexpected peace about her, like she knew she was going to be in a better place within a few minutes.

It made my eyes start to water, and a tear, maybe two, started to make its way down my face. She knew what was coming, and so did I.

Rufus Booker looked around and affixed his eyes on a cross decoration we had mounted on the living room wall. It was something I had made for Naomi, sanded and stained, while I was out in the garage woodworking. The Scripture *John 11:25* was etched into it, which reads: *"I am the resurrection and the life. Anyone who believes in me will live, even after dying."*

Not that Rufus Booker or his gang would know that, but Naomi and I did. Looking back, I thought how ironic it was that specific Scripture that happened to come up at that time.

Booker studied the cross for a few seconds and then turned to me. "So you're Christians, huh? Then you should have no fear with what is about to happen."

He patted Naomi on the shoulder, made his way in front of her, and walked toward me. Good, I thought, he was going to end my life first. I wouldn't be able to bear seeing my wife go before me.

Booker knelt down some so only a couple of feet separated us. Our faces were on the same level. His face was dark and it looked to be filled with a lifestyle of crookedness and immorality. His dreadlocks rested on his chest and he kinda reminded me of the Predator, which starred Arnold Schwarzenegger, only there was no mask to hide behind.

He said aloud, "Doesn't the Bible also say something like 'the punishment must match the injury: a life for a life?'" The answer to this question he already knew; his arrogant smile I wanted to wipe off. To my surprise, this psychotic man actually knew something about the Bible.

I'll never forget what Rufus Booker whispered to me next. He made sure it was only me who could hear it. "You killed my brother, so now I'm taking your wife away from you."

Again, I made a lunge forward, but the two SSS members were expecting this time and I moved nowhere.

I pleaded. "Kill me! Leave her alone! I'll do anything! Just let her go!" The tears started coming down like a rainstorm. "Please, let her go! Just take me!"

I looked across to my wife with blurry eyes. Her eyes were closed and her head was bowed. She knew what was coming. Like a prisoner who is given his last meal, so my wife was saying one final prayer.

"Naomi! I love you! I love you so much! I'm....I'm sorry!" Something spiritual took a hold of me just then and my voice lessened. "My wife, here soon we will meet again, and when we do, nothing will be able to ever separate us."

Rufus Booker gave a short laugh and shook his head, sending his dreadlocks waving from side to side. "Yeah, right," he mockingly said.

The young one holding my shotgun held it out for Booker to take, but Booker shook his head and said to him, "You dumb? It'll be too loud." The kid lowered the gun and stood there quietly.

Rufus Booker then took out a handgun that was tucked behind his waist and just stood there looking at me. He turned to face Naomi, but I continued to plead. "Booker, stop! Take me...." but he cut me short.

He pointed the gun at my head and said, "Shut up, Job. Your turn is coming soon."

I tried moving out of my snare, but it was useless; I wasn't going anywhere. My wife sat there across from me and I knew that my moments of seeing her alive were dwindling down to their final seconds.

Naomi, after sitting there for the longest time in silence, finally spoke. They would be my wife's last words in this world. "We will be together, but not yet. I love you, Job." She looked up and closed her eyes. Maybe inside she was saying, "I love you, God," or maybe she was thanking Him for the time she was given on this earth, or maybe....or maybe I had absolutely no idea.

Either way, I would never know.

Rufus Booker turned again to face my wife, and he raised the gun in her direction, only this time he had removed a pillow from our sofa and held it in front of his handgun. He started making his way to her and I tensed in rage. The gun was aimed toward her heart and I knew he was only a second or two from pulling the trigger.

"Booker, stop! Naomi, I love you! Naomi! Booker....NOOO!"

The blast was muffled but still loud, and my whole world froze like ice. My wife just stared at me with what seemed like idle eyes; her look was lost in some time that I couldn't perceive. Her eyes stared into mine for a brief moment, and then she fell to her side on the ground, motionless.

With an unknown, abrupt sweep of strength, I stood up, forcing the two SSS members up with me. All four legs of the chair were in the air and, like a ram racing toward its rival with horns out in front, I headed toward Rufus Booker.

Just when I came within a foot of him, a heavy arm struck me on the left shoulder, sending me on my side onto the floor next to Naomi. She hadn't been tied up but I had, and I couldn't reach out to her. We stared at each other for what seemed like the longest time. After what was probably only about ten seconds, she closed her eyes.

She seemed to have breathed her last.

Usually I would have exploded in extreme anger, but all I could do was lie there in a quiet, sorrowful silence. I had a lot I wanted to say to Rufus Booker, but I also didn't want my last words in this world before God to be any kind of curse or vulgar word.

All I could do was cry as I looked at my dead wife, mumbling her name as I did. Snot ran down my nose and my tears mixed in with it. Like a severe asthmatic, I felt like I couldn't even breathe.

I could hear laughter as I laid there. Booker said, "Nice hit, K-Dogg." When I turned to look at them, I noticed it was one of the SSS members who was holding me down who'd sent me onto the floor.

I wasn't going to forget his face.

The young one just stood back, like he was unsure of what was taking place before his eyes. Maybe it was just me, but for some reason I felt within me that he wanted no part of this. The other member slapped hands with K-Dogg and Rufus Booker stared down at me like I was the lowliest of the lowly.

What took place next was monstrous and, humanly speaking, insanely gruesome and something I didn't have the word for.

Each of the other three members took turns using the gun Booker had just used, held up the same pillow in front of the handgun, and shot my wife three more times in the chest. I prayed that she was already dead after

40

Booker's initial shot. With my voice gone, all I could do was lie on my side and cry in disbelief. I did notice though that when it came time to the young one's turn, he couldn't do it and Booker took it upon himself to place his finger over his and pull the trigger for him. The young one took many steps back, horror-filled with what he just abetted in.

Now many people wonder what the last thoughts are of someone who is about to die. Let me tell you, everything happened so fast that I didn't even have time to think. In a quick flash of whatever amount of time my life had left, I thought of my wife who was lying dead before me, I thought about God and said a quiet inner, "I love you," and lastly I thought to myself that this life is almost over.

I took one last look at my wife before I heard Rufus Booker say, "Hey, Job." I looked Rufus Booker in the eye; he had the gun pointing at my head, for some reason no pillow in front this time. "Say good night." My head twitched in expectation of the kill shot.

I didn't feel it; I only vaguely heard the sound of the earsplitting gunshot. In that very short-lived moment, something red was washing over my eyes and my sight was slowly constricting into darkness. Death was covering me like snow covers the ground during winter.

Even though my eyes were open, all I could see was a deep, dark blackness. My spirit breathed its last, and I knew nothing more. This earthly life was actually over. I would awake no more.

But I did.

Three months later.

# PART 2

When Jesus arrived at Bethany, he was told that Lazarus had already been in his grave for four days. Then Jesus shouted, "Lazarus, come out!" And the dead man came out, his hands and feet bound in graveclothes, his face wrapped in a headcloth.

*John 11:17, 43-44*

# 7

## THREE MONTHS LATER

Blackness.

For a long time I resided in a world of blackness. There were voices speaking to me; some I could make out the words, and others it seemed like a language that was unknown to man.

I would walk and walk in every direction, but every way I turned just kept going, like a spider's web of roads that had no end. It felt like I was going in continuous circles, and every time I would come back to where I had started.

Both physical and spiritual is how I would say my existence was in this otherworldly realm. Nothing was how it had been on earth and it seemed I had been birthed into this world that only the dead know.

When I walked there was no foundation under my feet, where my hands would reach out to there was nothing to touch, and why I was here I had not the slightest notion.

But I will say there was a calming sense of peace and tranquility in this place. The voices that spoke to me brought no fear. Some of them were mellifluous voices, others were soft, but for some reason there wasn't any need to be afraid of them. It was like the further I walked, the greater they sounded.

I had no thought of my past, earthly life. Everything was new and unexplored in this place that I didn't have a name for. It was the darkest black I had ever seen; but, as weird as it might sound, there was a nameless serenity in this land.

Looking back on this experience, *Psalm 23* couldn't have been more real: *Even when I walk through the darkest valley, I will not be afraid.* I didn't hear any kind of water movement that signified a valley, but you get my point.

If you don't, then you don't.

Everything was so new but so real. This world had no thought of my former life; it was like history that had no part in this new chapter. I didn't know if this was my new home or a temporary one like the one I had just came from.

All that changed when I heard a loud trumpet sound and an unmistakable voice that roared like a lion after it. I didn't know the meaning of what the commanding and authoritative voice said. To me, it was a foreign language that I had never ever heard; but one thing was certain, there was truth and a refreshing newness in this divine voice.

Just then, like scales falling from my eyes or them being no longer blinded, I saw a light. The nearer I came to it, the more intense it was. The colors of my past life were nothing compared to these strange and radiant colors. An instilling warmth filled my being and I was given a foretaste of what this new body felt like.

Like a man walking the tracks of a dark train tunnel, this brilliant light was growing and coming closer to me with what seemed faster than the speed of light. What started as a baseball-sized light was now enlarging into something that would soon overtake me; but in difference to the earthly fear of being run over by a train, I was ready for this light to become one with me.

Like the largest tidal wave of light I had ever seen, this wave was about to collide with me. The warmth in my being grew and I was fully convinced that if I believed in this light, I would never have to walk in darkness again.

The light came even closer, and soon it would wash over me. I heard the divine voice that resembled a roaring lion say very quickly, but slowly at the same time, *"When you have repented, return to me."*

I didn't know what that meant at the time, but after I awoke and where I am now, it all made sense.

Like two becoming one, the light overtook me. It was the most dazzling white I have ever experienced. In that moment, everything changed.

I felt different, like I was brought back to a more familiar territory. Blackness was what I saw again, but there was something different about it.

My fingers rubbed together and then my toes flexed back and forth. I remembered something about this world, but for some reason it was all coming back at snail's pace, like an epileptic who came out of their seizure, slowly regaining their surrounding.

I was lying on some type of bed and thin sheets covered me. Chirping sounds from a machine filled the room and I could feel fluid running through a vein in my left arm.

Another person's voice, not the divine voice of a lion, said, "Mr. McCants, can you hear me? If you can, open your eyes."

The blackness that I was seeing was the back of my eyelids. It took an effort, but slowly, and together, I lifted them up.

My eyes were open.

It had taken three months, but here I was.

Back in the earthly world.

# 8

Like many books and movies, certain points of writing or scenes in a film or show aren't always necessarily true, but they are told or shown so that the reader or viewer can relate to it.

Let me explain.

If you've ever watched the show *ER* or a similar show, you often see the patient's heart rate go into what many call "flat-line" and the physician or attending nurses shock or "defibrillate" this rhythm. In contrast to this, this isn't how it is in the real world; that is, it won't help your patient at all. It would be similar in trying to jump a dead battery with a charger that's not plugged in: it won't do anything.

Asystole, or "flat-line", was a rhythm I later found out I went into several times; but with the help of medications and CPR I was brought back into "v-fib," a rhythm that can be shocked, and was brought back each time.

Three times I laid dead on a hospital bed, but all three times I was brought back to life by the grace of God.

Why The Almighty brought me back each time is beyond me, but He chose to and I don't question His ways.

I can say, though, that the reason He brought me back - I know and believe - wasn't because of the things I would soon do after I walked out of the hospital. Many of those things were wrong, and I wondered why God brought me back to life knowing I would do such things; but, like I said, He has His ways and I don't question them.

Those things I would carry out were of my own accord; under no circumstance am I saying God agreed with the things I did and that's why He brought me back. On the contrary, I'm a believer that God allows His creation to go through with something whether the individual can see the good or bad in it.

We aren't robots. He has given us the opportunity to think and do as we like whether it be according to His ways or against them.

But in the end all bad will be done away with, and only the good will stand.

† † †

Coma.

By definition a coma is a state of prolonged unconsciousness, including a lack of response to stimuli, from which it is impossible to rouse a person.

I had been in one for three months or about ninety days, depending on the perspective you want to look at it from. Although that's a long time, it felt shorter to me. Why? I don't know. Not that I would know anyway; I was unconscious and out-of-it.

My coma was caused by Rufus Booker's gunshot to my head that resulted in hypoxia, or lack of oxygen getting to my brain.

According to Dr. Turner, one of the docs who cared for me, I spent a lot of time in the intensive care unit. For the longest time I was intubated and had my ventilations assisted.

From procedures rendered, to taking care of me nutritionally, and to a lot of other things that I won't bore you with mentioning took place.

I awoke several other times before I fully woke up from my coma. It's common for coma patients to not regain consciousness instantly. The first few times I awoke I was only awake for a matter of minutes before I returned to unconsciousness.

There are two real-life reports where two men suffered a coma but woke up nineteen - that's right, I said nineteen - years later, and another one where a brain-damaged man slept for six years, but was miraculously brought back to consciousness after doctors had implanted electrodes into his brain.

Three months doesn't seem so long now, does it?

Another thing that I was blessed to regain was all of my memories. It's not that it all came back quickly, but everyday it seemed I remembered more and more about my life prior to the coma. Certain things I didn't recall just instantaneously, but it came after some time, even days. Amnesia attacks many people, but thanks be to God it didn't get me.

The worst memory I recalled was you already know what: the murder of my wife and the horrific scene that also almost ended my life. I cried a lot during those first return-to-consciousness weeks. Emotions swept through me: anger, depression, frustration, denial, you name it; but the one emotion, maybe more so a craving, I felt more than anything else: revenge.

It ate at me like cancer eats away its victim. I thought about Rufus Booker, "K-Dogg", and whoever else the other two were for days. A hate that started out the size of a pea grew and grew in my heart until it consumed it. Like Edmond Dantes from *The Count of Monte Cristo*, I thirsted and hungered for revenge.

At first, I wasn't sure if by revenge I meant putting Rufus Booker and the rest of them behind bars or by me going against them in some other way. It didn't matter to me at the time which of these, but the answer came not too long after my leave from the hospital.

I was going to have my revenge. Whether I lived through it or would die trying to claim it, I would have my revenge. It was against my Christian beliefs, but there were many Christian things that I threw out after I got out of the hospital.

The Bible says, "*I will take revenge; I will pay them back,*" says the Lord. I know in the end that evildoers will perish; but, wrong of me as it was, I wanted to speed the process of my revenge up knowing that it wasn't right in the eyes of God.

That was the one thing I wanted more than anything when I walked out of the hospital.

Revenge.

† † †

I had many docs and nurses care for me, but the one nurse in particular who cared for me the most I was grateful for. Her name was Debi and she had curly, reddish brown hair that hung down past her shoulders. The few freckles she had looked good on her and she was, I thought, very attractive.

She reminded me of Naomi, but I looked at Debi no more than what she was to me: a nurse who was there doing her job to care for and tend to me. We talked about a lot of things and she was married to a "sexy" fireman - her words - and she seemed very satisfied in life. I was glad for her. In contrast, my old satisfied world was in shambles. With the rest of the time I was in the hospital, she became a temporary friend.

There was a bandage applied to the left side of my head where the bullet entered. Apparently Rufus Booker's shot traveled away from the center of my brain, just slightly grazing the left side of my skull, but passing mostly through flesh.

I wasn't sure if it was a blessing or a curse. Blessing because I was alive, but curse because I longed to be with Naomi.

Besides some lacerations that were mostly healed and some scars, I was a rather healed-up man. Nurse Debi said the wound to my head was basically cured, but she also said I would have a daily reminder for the rest of my life when I touched my head in that spot.

A scar didn't bother me. Rufus Booker and his posse did.

My brother visited me often and my parents, Dave and Renee, came in from out of state. I was told they spent a lot of time at my bedside while I was in my coma. Once I fully awoke, I told them to get back to their routines of life. My father had already taken off enough time from work and I told my mother, against her protests of course, that she could visit once I got out of the hospital.

Family, including some church family, and friends visited me. My coworkers also visited and kept me company as well and my EMS chief and coordinator was giving me an extended period of time off.

To me, there still seemed a lot that needed done. No police authority had visited me yet, but I had a lot of thoughts on my mind. Now that I survived, would I be placed in some kind of protection with being able to recall my wife's and almost my killers? How would the process go with me knowing who killed my wife and getting them placed in prison? Was prison the choice I really wanted, or could I figure something else out? It wasn't a matter if he would, but when would Rufus Booker come for me when word got to him that I was alive? Too many questions filled my mind like a massive flood. Where was I to go from here?

But then something else just hit me: how could the authorities bring a thug-king in when, according to the words of Jehu Bridges, nobody could get to Rufus Booker? Even his right and left hand men seemed untouchable, like someone was helping them so they could never get caught.

So you can see, I was lost in a world of unknowns, like a freshman who was entering his first day into the big high school.

I needed to take my mind off of these thoughts.

Forgetting that it was even there, I grabbed the remote controller and turned on the television that was about fifteen feet in front of me.

Flipping through the channels, there wasn't much to grab my immediate attention. *ESPN* was boasting their sports, *Law and Order SVU* was dealing with their next special victim, and the cast of *Burn Notice* was trying to track down who burned Michael Westen. All of these shows I liked, but I was wanting something that spoke more personally to me.

49

The next channel I changed it to showed a slightly overweight minister who seemed to be preaching the Gospel. With being in a crummy state of mind, I wasn't much for hearing about God at the time either; but whether it was the batteries going dead in the remote, or, as I look back, God's intervention, I couldn't change the channel.

Mad, I tossed the remote to the floor. I closed my eyes, but the minister's words began speaking more loudly to me. Opening my eyes, I focused my sight on the white minister who was wiping away beads of sweat from his forehead with a red handkerchief.

"And the day will come my brothers and sisters," he was really getting into it now, "when Jesus will return coming on the clouds of Heaven! Those who have believed in Him will be vindicated, and the wicked will perish! The Son of Man will shepherd His people into the Kingdom of Heaven, and all those who have done evil and haven't repented will be destroyed!" He loosened the collar of his shirt and rolled his sleeves up.

"Remember when the Lord Jesus raised Lazarus from the dead when the man had already been four days in his grave!? Remember the words, '*Lazarus, come out*'!? And how the dead man came out and then Jesus told those standing nearby to unwrap him of his graveclothes and let him go!?" His voice dialed down a few levels, but he kept going. "So that's how it'll be for all who have believed in His name, all the way from times past, to the time right now, until the future present. The Bible says that God will not fail nor forsake you, and God will not do that if you trust in Him." The minister grabbed a glass of ice water and took a long gulp before continuing on. When he did, conviction filled every word he spoke.

"When Jesus returns, everything will be new. Those who thought He wasn't real will see, things will not be as we know here in this present world, and there will be a new Heaven and a new earth." His voice rose again with his next words.

"When Jesus comes back," he said aloud pointing upwards, "He Himself will come down from Heaven with a commanding shout! The sound of the trumpet will blast! Those who remain on the earth will meet the Lord in the air!" He then said something I'll never forget, and he said it louder than all the rest of his words. "THE DEAD WILL RISE!" He paused and then said, "Then all believers will be with the Lord forever!"

I was filled with a feeling I had not the words for, like something deeply spiritual had awakened in me. This minister who others probably looked at oddly, but who nonetheless spoke the truth, ignited a burning fire within me. I muted out his voice for a minute and thought hard.

Lazarus had been dead for four days before Jesus raised him back to life. I knew the story about Lazarus being raised, but it had way more of an impact on me now.

I may not have been dead for four days, but I died several times on a hospital bed and each time the Lord chose to raise me back to life.

Why? I still wasn't fully sure.

In a sense, Lazarus and I had something in common. Lazarus had been raised while Jesus walked this earth; I had been raised while I laid dead on a hospital bed.

The dead had been raised back then, and the dead were still coming back alive today. That minister on TV certainly spoke the truth.

The dead will rise.

✝     ✝     ✝

After another couple of days I finally felt it was time for me to be released. The hospital staff thought different though; they said another week of testing and rest would ensure that I'd be one hundred percent before being discharged.

I had a lot to do and I still wasn't quite sure how the process would go after I left this place.

Sitting on the side of the hospital bed so that my feet touched the ground, I looked over to a pile of clothes that my brother had dropped off for me whenever it was time for me to leave.

The longer I stared at them, the easier the decision to leave this place was for me.

Today was the day.

Certain words that the minister on TV said reverberated in my ears since watching him the other day. To me, it was an inner drive to get going.

"*Lazarus, come out!*" These graveclothes needed to go. "*Unwrap him and let him go!*"

The door to my room opened, but I had already started the process. Some lady was rebuking me; I didn't hear a single word she said.

In order, I did the following: ripped out the IV from my left arm, tore off the stickers from my chest that were reading my heart rate and rhythm, and lastly I removed the bandage that covered the bullet wound from the left side of my head.

The nurse, one who I hadn't seen before, yelled in protest. "Mr. McCants! That's enough!" She was older-looking and looked to be the type that didn't take attitude well.

I looked up into her eyes. "It's time for me to go, ma'am."

Standing up, I walked over to the clothes my brother had left for me. I'd walked around my room and the hospital for quite a while now and everything felt normal. Besides the IV pole I wheeled around like a dog, I got around good and all my sensations felt great.

"It isn't yet." Her voice subtracted a few decibels. "You have another week as far as I've been told."

I ignored her and grabbed for my socks and underwear.

"Mr. McCants, you can't go!"

"Watch me."

"Do you even know what today is or where you're at, sir?"

I didn't miss a beat. "Today's the seventh. I'm in room number three. And I'm in the presence of a yelling nurse here at Capernaum Medical Center."

Her eyes bore holes through me. "I don't find that last part humorous, Mr. McCants."

I relented some. "I'm sorry nurse….?"

"Jones."

"Nurse Jones," I nodded my head, "I apologize for my words, but honestly, I'm fine. This room can be used for someone in worse shape than I am."

"That's besides the point, Mr. McCants. The doctor has orders, and you're to stay another week."

She wasn't making this easy. "Okay, well, I'm not. Sorry."

"You know what leaving AMA," that's short for Against Medical Advice, "means, don't you?"

"I do. You don't have to explain."

"Mr. McCants…." but I cut her off.

I was just getting ready to remove my gown. "Unless you wanna see me naked here in about two seconds, I suggest you either turn away or turn around, ma'am."

Her face got red and she walked out of the room, talking and arguing to herself like she was a psych patient off of her meds.

She yelled back, "You have to sign a form before you can leave!"

"With pleasure!" I hollered back. It wasn't like me to act this way, but this place was driving me mad.

I got dressed and nurse Jones came in shortly after. She brought along a physician, but I ignored them both; I was leaving no matter what they said.

The physician, a younger-looking man, said, "Another reason we were wanting you to stay, Mr. McCants, was because a detective Bridges was coming in to visit you today."

That made me stop in my tracks, but I still wasn't staying. "He knows how and where to reach me."

Finally, I was going to get some insight into how I was to go about life outside this hospital. Specifically speaking, the steps to take now that I was a man alive and the knower of my wife's killers.

The air outside the double glass motion censored doors filled my lungs with life. Oxygen filled me with a freshness that didn't exist in the hospital.

Outside, it was a hot sunny day. The sun blinded my sight for a long minute before my eyes could adjust. The sound of the city and beeping horns filled my ears, and life didn't lose its pace the entire time I was in my coma.

What do I do and where do I go from here? Many questions still clouded my mind.

Home. That's where I was going first.

Something in my mood had changed when I stood up out of that hospital bed. It was like I was the same person, but a different demeanor had been birthed in me. I looked at life different with what happened, and I was more forthcoming in action and in speech.

A taxi happened to be parked near the front entrance off to my left side. I whistled and waved the taxi driver over. Good thing my brother Cyrus had stashed some money into one of my pockets.

I looked back at Capernaum Medical Center, my home for the past three months. There was something shadowy and eerie about it, like a haunted house during Halloween. I was definitely glad to be departing from it.

For some reason unknown to me, the divine-lion voice from that other world spoke to me. *"When you have repented, return to me."*

Little did I know I'd be entering into a dark, earthly world that I would've never thought possible of me entering into. Before too long, my world would be turning upside down.

I was going to do some bad things.

# 9

Many studies have been performed on individuals who have encountered a near-death experience (NDE). Some may go through psychological changes, others may be more appreciative of life and show it, and still there are those who were unaffected by their NDE.

In one study, an atheist had a NDE at a hospital in Paris and converted to Christianity after he said he called out to Jesus and was saved by a being of light that he believed to be Jesus. Another case dealt with a young boy who had drowned and was revived fifteen minutes later. He said he saw his younger brother on the other side. And there are studies where others deny the existence of aftereffects.

Whether survivors of NDE's have gained or lost something psychological, emotional, or spiritual, I don't know; but I can say I gained something that accompanied me most of the time since I walked out of Capernaum Medical Center.

Some may call it a guardian angel, others an inner voice, another a helper. Call it what you want, but I found out it stuck with me like white on rice. He, it, whatever you want to name it, I didn't give a name to, but I like to think of it more as my counselor/buddy/guide/I-got-your-back-bro kinda being.

It spoke to me shortly after I shut the door of the taxi behind me. I stood on the sidewalk and looked up at my house, like it was something familiar but yet something so ancient at the same time. Taking my first step toward my house, I felt a sense of lightheadedness come over me and I nearly blacked out and fell down.

*Say brother, guess those docs and nurses knew what they were talking about when they told you that you shoulda stayed for another week.*

What was that? I regained my bearings.

*It's me. I'm inside you, Job.*

Why'd you decide to show up now when you could've earlier during my life?

*It wasn't the time. You need me now though.*

54

Maybe, maybe not.

*You say the word and I can go whenever.*

Really?

*HaHa, nah, just joking Job. I'm here to stay. But I'll give you your time when you need it.*

I need some now.

*Got it buddy. Talk to you later.*

That was weird, I thought, as I removed my keys from my pocket to unlock the front door. Maybe something in my brain shifted, or maybe I inherited an extra proton while in my coma, I don't know, but for some reason I was blessed or cursed, I wasn't sure at the time, with this new being within me.

The door swung open and the first thing that hit me were broken pieces of my last conscious memory before entering into that world of darkness, like an amnesiac trying to put the past back together.

My parents and brother had kept the place tidied up the past few months. It looked the same, but the blood of my innocent wife had been poured on this ground.

Manhattan had been taken from me, Naomi had been taken from me, and now it was just me in this graveyard silent house.

I was mad at God. How could He let what happened to my wife and I and Manhattan take place? We lived how He wanted us to and still this dreadful page was turned. Just like a puppet master having authority over his creation, so I was a firm believer that God could create and take away whatever He wanted to whenever He wanted to. Enough said. He could do what He wanted and still it would be righteous and fair; but this truth pierced my lungs to the point where I felt I couldn't breathe, and it was then that I felt tears starting to coast down my cheeks.

Like Job from the Bible, I didn't curse God or blame Him. It was His creation I blamed and was furious with, but still there was a madness in my heart at God for letting all these terrible things befall me, and now I had to go through it all alone.

Alone.

There were drug dealers, murderers, thieves, and the such in this world and still they were able to get away with so much. And here I had been, a most-of-the-time pretty good Christian who, though not perfect, was getting what so many others deserved.

The hatred in my heart against Rufus Booker and his gang grew within me, like a small balloon that gets big after being blown up by the human breath.

55

I wanted answers from God, but I knew I wouldn't get them. I wanted to know why, but still the air around me was silent. I burned with an anger so red it came out with strong force.

Marching over to the wall in the living room that already had a hole in it from when I punched it when Manhattan had been taken away from us, I treated it like it was a punching bag that had Rufus Booker's face all over it.

I went to town. I don't know how big or small they were or how many more holes I put in that wall, but it was a lot. I thought about Naomi, our marriage, our life, our oneness....all of it broken.

I screamed her name with tears now rolling down my face and I threw punch after punch until I could punch no more. My arms became cement blocks, perspiration wetted me like morning dew on green grass, and I felt like I had just survived ten rounds against Rocky Balboa.

Not to mention my hands hurt really bad.

My counselor came back alive and spoke to me just then.

*Hey, J, that wasn't very smart guy.*

I thought I told you to go away for now.

*I had all intentions, but your hands look real bad.*

I looked down at my hands. They were painted with blood and it was dripping down into the carpet. Some cuts were deep, but I flexed my hands back and forth. Nothing felt broken, but my hands would be out of commission for the remainder of the week.

*You should probably....*

I'm a paramedic. I'll be all right. Now scat for a while, would you.

*All right J.* J seemed to be his new favorite name for me. *See ya.*

There was a voice. I thought it was my new friend speaking again, but I then realized it was a human's voice.

"Job, you all right?"

My face felt like plastic with the drying of my tears and I was exhausted to the point where I could barely stand.

Turning around, Jehu Bridges stood in the open doorway staring at me. He looked at me, the wall, and back to me.

Detective Bridges' face turned sad, like the view before him was too much strain. With emotion in his face, he said, "Why don't you have a seat. We have some things to talk about."

He looked down at my hands. "But first, let's get those hands cleaned up."

† † †

56

After patching up my hands, detective Bridges and I sat on the sofa and he told me what happened after I had been shot.

To make a long story short, Mr. Greenley, my next-door neighbor, awoke from sleep after hearing a loud "blast", and when he got up to look outside, he said he saw a large vehicle peel out quickly and make a right out of our street. He said it was too dark to identify the suspects, but that didn't matter, we knew who did it and I specifically knew who was involved.

Bridges had been upset with the deputy chief of his department for removing the police cruiser from our house, and he said he received a reprimand from the deputy chief when they broke out in an argument over what happened to Naomi and I.

"You gotta believe me, Job," he had said earlier in our conversation, "I did everything I could to keep a cop posted here."

I believed Jehu Bridges. He was a good cop, and he had been good to Naomi and I.

He then went on to say that there'd been no further progress into the investigation and that the case went cold about a month ago since there had been no witnesses and nothing much to go on. Regardless, Bridges said they weren't any closer to stopping Rufus Booker and SSS from their long streak of pandemonium.

"That all changes now," he had said, "that is, as long as you can remember who did this to you and your wife."

I slowly nodded my head "yes" and told him that two of the four members were Rufus Booker and some thug called "K-Dogg."

Bridges went on to explain "K-Dogg." "K-Dogg's real name is Kevin Durgess and he's nothing but trouble. He's Rufus Booker's wingman and they do everything together, like husband and wife if you know what I mean."

He said he had met my folks and that they were very nice people. Detective Bridges also said he stopped in every once in a while to check in on my family and house. "I would've been in contact with you at the hospital earlier, Job," he said at one point, "but we wanted you to get your rest and let your mind slowly get back to reality."

So now we sat quietly for a few long moments so my mind could take all of this in. I looked outside to see the fading orange sun lower behind the house across from ours, like it was slowly sinking into quicksand. The neighbors a couple houses down from ours were walking their golden retriever and Miss Goldstein was pulling her Range Rover into her garage, returning from work.

"So what happens now?" I said to detective Bridges.

"In all truthfulness, Job," he said following my eyes outdoors, "at some point Booker's gonna come for you; it's just the way the maniac operates. You probably should find another place to stay as well."

"I've thought the same thing," agreeing that Booker would come for me eventually and, "that won't happen," to Bridges saying I should find somewhere else to stay.

He changed the subject. "As long as we can bring the bad guys in you'll be on witness protection, if you choose, so you'd be well protected. For now, we'll do what we can. Certain states are different, but your life is threatened as we speak, whether you've received something from SSS or not. Here in Columbus we do things a little different. You're a victim of a terrible crime and the only witness of it. Plus, we know how SSS operates." He looked back my way. "We'll go through some photos down at the police station so you can point out all your assailants. The trouble will be...." but I cut him off.

"Bringing them in, I know," I said, "nobody has been able to touch Rufus Booker or his heavy-hitters."

Bridges' face softened, like he knew it was a long shot. "Maybe we'll catch a break."

"Yeah, right," I returned.

A couple of other thoughts came to my mind just then. "I was a victim of a crime and am now the only witness, Bridges, and I've heard of people getting less time because of that. And, not to mention, I was in a coma for three months, so I could see how others would think I've lost my mind and I was just making things up." The more I talked, the more agitated I got. "Plus, if things don't fall through, what other dirt do you have on these guys to get them put away?"

By his look, I don't think even detective Bridges knew about things for sure. "One step at a time Job," is all he said.

I put my hands together as if in prayer and rested them on my lap. "Say all goes well, how does witness protection work?"

"Basically," Bridges started, "we, that is, law enforcement, will be deeply involved and you'd be given a new name and place to live. The FBI would be involved." He scratched the back of his head and went on. "You'd have to find a new job after a while but," he paused before going on, "none of this matters unless we can bring the bad guys in."

My iPhone just then sang its text tune. It was my brother Cyrus: *Doing alright Bro?* I'd text him back later.

"What else would I have to do with witness protection?"

Detective Bridges sighed, like he knew I wasn't going to like what he was about to say. "There are restrictions along with it, Job. You won't be able to return home and you can't get a hold of former friends or acquaintances."

He was right. I hated what he had just said.

"I don't think I could do that, Bridges."

"I must warn you," Bridges met my eyes, "failing to comply and breaking the rules could result in your death, that is, if we catch the bad guys and you accept witness protection."

I ignored his comment, but I understood completely. However, how could I leave the only home that felt like home to me? I just couldn't walk away from this home that Naomi and I and Manhattan had so many memories in. And how could I just leave my family, and friends, and job? The ones I loved lived here in Columbus or around here - except for my parents - and I truly enjoyed my profession as a public-serving paramedic. I knew changes with witness protection would have to be made, but right now there was no way I was going to enter into it.

But it didn't matter right now anyway. The bad guys were still out there.

He could sense I wanted to end the subject. "We can talk about this later, but we'll most likely be placing another cruiser here for awhile, even if it has to be myself. For now, let's go down to the station and pick out your assailants."

I arose feeling weak. Detective Bridges walked out before me. I started closing the front door, but stopped halfway short.

Manhattan's bark knowing daddy was home when I got off shift rang in my ears. Naomi running into my arms as if she hadn't seen me in a week placed a warm feeling within my heart. The happy home that was filled with faith and joy I wish I could relive.

But I couldn't, and all that had been taken away from me. My heart bled black and I was slowly making plans in my head. Some of which I wasn't fully sure I'd be able to carry out.

Everything was happening too fast and seemed a blur. In the blink of an eye it seemed, my whole life had changed. I wasn't suicidal, but right now life meant little to me.

I slammed the door shut behind me, startling Jehu Bridges who slightly jumped in front of me.

# 10

Sitting in detective Bridges' office, I turned page after page of a photograph book in hopes of putting a name to my other two attackers, which included the younger-looking one who looked no older than fifteen.

I never did find him, but the other one I did. He had a hardcore I'm-the-man kinda look that I wanted to punch right off of his face.

"The young one isn't in here, but this was one of them." I turned the photograph book toward detective Bridges who was seated behind his desk and glued my forefinger just above my attacker's picture.

"Tyrese 'TT' Taylor," Bridges said shaking his head, "doesn't surprise me." He turned the photograph book back to me and said, "Another piece of work who earned his way up SSS's ranks. Let me put it this way," the detective said leaning back in his chair, "if Rufus is the chief and Kevin Durgess is the captain, Tyrese 'TT' Taylor is the lieutenant."

Although I was confused in how SSS was run, I at least knew who the top dogs were. I also knew if one wanted to cause mass chaos for an organization, there was no better way than to eliminate the in-charges.

Remember that.

"That's the third of the three musketeers," Bridges said. "Durgess is Rufus's right hand man, and you can look at Taylor as his left. They're three turds I've been trying to flush down the toilet for a while now, but somehow they keep clogging our city."

I laughed. It was something in the way Bridges had said it. It was also the first time I had laughed since walking out of the hospital.

Bridges smiled and laughed along with me.

Without knocking, a man opened the door behind me and made his way off to the right between Bridges and I. He wore a white police shirt that was different from the others. His shirt boasted a bright gold badge; he had a black mustache and thick black eyebrows on top of a white face. Embroidered on his right chest was Dep. Chief Haman.

"Bridges, where have you been all day?"

The detective's face looked agitated. "I've been doing my job, chief."

Deputy Chief Haman looked over at me with a hard look, like he was upset at my even being here. In what I thought a snotty tone, he said, "And who's this?"

Bridges sat up more straight in his chair. "This is Job McCants." The detective let that sink in a little bit. "You remember, chief, the man whose house you removed the cop cruiser from and that night Rufus Booker did his wife and almost him in?"

DC Haman's face flushed red. I couldn't tell if it was because he wanted to kill Jehu Bridges right there and then for his bold comment, or if it was more so from finding out who I was and wanting to take back his snotty comment he had just spoke a moment earlier.

The chief looked at Bridges first and pointed a finger his way. "I'll talk to you later." Then he turned to me. "Mr. McCants, I apologize for my previous comment; it's been a busy day and as you can see, I'm growing grumpy. I'm sorry for your loss and what you went through. I'm glad to see you back on your feet."

For some reason, and maybe it was just me, but his apology seemed empty and his attempted niceness was phony, but I said, "Thank you."

He came over and shook my hand softly, quite different from how real men shake hands.

Bridges filled him in on my visit and how I'd been able to identify three of my wife's and my four perps. He also filled him in on some of our conversation at my house earlier that day.

"For now," DC Haman said, "there'll be another cop cruiser outside your residence and we'll do all in our power to keep you protected until we figure out our next step."

Haman went on. "You'll have to forgive my thinking because it's getting late, but why don't you stay somewhere else for now, that way," he said rubbing his mustache, "you'd be safer and we wouldn't have to keep a cruiser at your house."

Detective Bridges cleared his throat, which caused the chief to look his way. When he turned to Bridges, the detective shook his head.

"I see," the chief said. "Then, like I said Mr. McCants, we'll keep a cruiser outside your residence until we figure out our next step. But do know," he went on, "everything will be coming quick and we'll need to make some decisions soon."

I simply said, "Understood."

DC Haman turned to Bridges and looked through the window to the night outside. "Very well. It's getting late gents and I'm calling it a night." He looked over at me. "Do get some rest Mr. McCants and think hard into what you would like to do. We can encourage, but you have the final say."

And with that, Haman walked out leaving Bridges and I alone.

After the door closed behind me, I said, "Looks like you got yourself into some trouble." I rewound back to when Deputy Chief Haman first walked in.

Detective Bridges again leaned back in his chair, but this time he leaned further back and rested his feet up on his desk. "Seems like he's always on my case. He's arrogant and thinks he's all this-and-that because he's got some au-thor-i-ty," he drew this last part out like he was a drill instructor.

"Either way," I said, "seems like you're on thin ice pal."

"Who's not?" the detective said, shrugging his shoulders. "It seems like he's been harder on me since...." he looked at that same framed picture on his shelf of him and that older boy the night Naomi and I were in his office when I killed DJ Booker.

He didn't go on and I could tell he was saddened by something. "What is it, Bridges?"

"Nothing," he sadly said, shaking his head, "forget about it."

I didn't press further.

"Well," the detective said, "we got three out of four identified. You said the fourth one was younger-looking right?" I nodded my head. "I'd say he's a 'newbie' learning the ropes from the big boys. He's probably not in the system, yet."

I wouldn't forget his face though. He was in on it, but I didn't forget his unsure look, like he wanted no part of what was happening moments before Rufus Booker pulled the trigger on me.

But he was in on it, and I wanted him put away too.

It was getting late and I'd had enough of the police department. "Mind driving me back home?" I said to Bridges.

"Not at all. Just let me put the finishing touches on a report, then we'll go." He removed his feet from his desk, sat up straight, shook the mouse of his computer to waken the screen, and started typing away.

"I'm gonna go outside and get some fresh air."

"Sounds good, Job. Be out in a few."

Going outside, the night sky was filled with pillows of white clouds and stars were flaunting their beauty for the world to marvel at. A comforting breeze blew in my face, and I was filled with peace at the present moment.

A voice broke my peace just then. It was the voice of the man walking toward his vehicle and I heard him say, speaking into his cell phone, "I don't know what we're gonna do now, just give me some time."

I tried to hold back a sneeze, but I couldn't. "ACHOO!" After the tiny sparks in front of my face disappeared - I never understood why that sometimes happened after a sneeze - the man speaking into his cell phone was turned around, staring at me.

It was DC Haman. I didn't recognize him from changing into street clothes. He stood in front of his white Cadillac Escalade EXT and smiled at me.

I nodded. Police chiefs must make pretty good money to have a vehicle like that, I thought.

"Like I said, honey," he said speaking back into his cell phone, "I don't know what we're gonna do about it just now. Please give me some time. We'll get a new one if we have to. I'll be home soon." He ended the call.

"The wife," he said to me. "Can't live with her, can't live without her." He realized the mistake of his comment pretty quick. "I'm sorry, Mr. McCants, I didn't mean anything by it."

My wife immediately came to memory and a tear started to form in my right eye.

Embarrassed, DC Haman got into his vehicle, started the engine up, and waved to me as he passed by.

There was something I didn't like about that guy.

# 11

The following morning, I sat out back watching the new day dawn with its radiant colors. It was humid, but the porch fan above me kept me cool. I thought about Naomi and Manhattan a lot, and instead of doing something productive, I engrossed myself in my sorrows.

I tried to pray but I was still mad at God, and for some reason I wasn't in the mood for prayer.

Though, I know now, it's better to pray, trust me, you'll feel a lot better afterwards. Regardless if you're mad, up, down, sad, or whatever, God will always listen.

*Good morning, J. You doing all right?*

Not really.

*Maybe say a short prayer, you'll feel better. You can't go this alone you know.*

I tried. Just not in the mood. I'll be fine on my own.

*That's what a lot of you humans say.*

How would you know? You only talk to me.

*You'd be surprised how many friends I got, pal.*

Sorry, my bad.

*It's okay. I'm only here to help J.*

I know, but I'm gonna be cantankerous for a while, just so you know.

*That's all right. I'm still sticking with you.*

What would you do if you were me?

*I'd delete some of those thoughts you've been thinking of, I can tell you that. It's not worth it J.*

But I can't just do nothing you....

*Like I said, it's not worth it.*

What do you know? You only showed up when my world came crashing down.

*Because this is when you needed me the most.*

What a good friend you are, I chuckled to myself.

64

*Don't forget about God in all this. Even though you're struggling, pushing Him away won't help, it's not....*

It's not worth it, I heard you the first two times.

*Gee, somebody woke up on the wrong side of the pillow on this glorious morning.*

You know, you're starting to tick me off now. Buzz off for a while again, will you.

*All right J. Just one last thing, please.*

Shoot.

*Knock knock.*

Are you kiddin' me. If it makes you go away, I'll play. Who's there?

*I woke up.*

I woke up who? I rolled my eyes and was annoyed.

*I woke up grumpy on the wrong side of the pillow this morning. HaHa!*

I shook my head, but my buddy actually made me smile.

*You look good smiling J.*

Thanks. Talk to you later.

*All right, peace brother.*

I stayed sitting outside all morning until my brother Cyrus stopped by around noon with lunch in his hand. He stayed a couple of hours; his emotional support was much appreciated. I went for a short run - maybe not the best idea but so what - after he left and when I returned, another police cruiser was camped outside my residence.

Decisions, decisions were on my mind. I knew they couldn't keep a cop babysitting my house forever, and I knew it was on me in certain areas where we went from here; but I just couldn't come to grips with all that witness protection would want from me in the event Rufus Booker and his cronies were found.

My EMS chief and coordinator checked in on me often. I had so much sick time built up and I rarely took vacation time unless Naomi and I went somewhere, but between bereavement and some sick leave, I had some time before I decided to go back to work. Probably the best thing was for me to get back to work to get my mind off of things and my attention on others, but I still needed my time of mourning.

And I still had decisions to make.

I updated my parents on my leave from the hospital, but told them there was no need to come up. Much against my mother's wishes, I begged her to stay home, for now, so I could get my mind and life somewhat back together.

I loved my mother, but mothers can sure weigh on their children with all their worry and over-concerned ways.

It was later in the afternoon when I decided to start up my laptop and search through the *Columbus Dispatch* to see what I had missed over the past three months.

The news hadn't been much different before my coma. Firefighters battled flames that were started by arsonists, drug dealers were put behind bars, theft and homicide were on the rise, and SSS was still making headlines.

There was something different, though. A new gang was making their presence known, and they were supposedly the rivals of SSS. They were known as NEB, or the North End Boyz. One of the articles mentioned gang wars between the two; however, according to another article, NEB had waited to make themselves known so they could increase their numbers. Their reason: SSS had taken over parts of their territory and they'd had enough.

According to other pieces of newspapers I'd read, NEB wasn't as vicious or savage as SSS. They only wanted to run their own territory, but animosity was created against SSS for them trying to bulldog them out. To me it sounded like NEB had beef with SSS and only SSS, and looked to knock them out, like a boxer winning by T.K.O.

In contrast to SSS, NEB didn't commit home invasions, murders against innocent people, or some of the inhuman things that SSS did.

Don't get me wrong, I'm not sticking up for them; I'm sure NEB had their drugs, fights, and other immoral ways, but it was nice to see they had beef with only those who committed wrong against them.

Who knows, I thought at the time, maybe the enemy of my enemy would be my friend.

I then did a more extensive search on SSS, their upbringing, their ways, and their madness. I learned a lot about them. Rufus Booker had been able to get away with a lot, that is, he and his gang; but it seemed nobody wanted to rat him or his heavy-hitters out. Much bad had been done by them, but it seemed someone else always took the fall for Rufus and his upper-class.

Rufus Booker was both a tyrant and a coward to me. By letting someone take the fall for him, he proved to me to be anything but a man; and he ruled with a harsh rod that nobody dared to override.

The worst thing about it is that he seemed untouchable. He always got away with everything, nobody ever pointed the finger at him, and, worst of all, he had yet to be caught, which didn't seem to matter, because he'd be let off it seemed to me anyway.

Basically speaking, he was an underground ghost, and I don't think he would ever be caught. I then thought, but how? I never knew of someone being able to get away with all of the things he did and never get caught. Even some of the most wicked criminals got caught, but somehow this thug-king escaped every time without a trace. Nobody was this good, I thought. So who was helping him?

My mind played games with theories until I felt my head was going to pop. I finally stopped thinking and was just getting ready to shut my laptop when another headline caught my immediate attention.

In black bold letters was the headline:

## Slain Victim Brother of Columbus Detective

It was an article from a couple years ago and it read:

Friday, July 16, 2015 6:46 A.M

Authorities are still searching for the suspects wanted in the fatal stabbing of a young man in the Columbus area.

Multiple hour manhunts performed by authorities are still taking place as detectives interview residents of the area and try to collect tips in hopes of finding the perpetrators.

Challenging to the authorities is there are no witnesses; however, according to a source, signs at the murder scene suggest this was committed by the hands of the South Side Soldiers, better known as SSS.

Jerome Bridges, 18, of Columbus, Ohio was stabbed multiple times late Wednesday evening in his mother's home. He was found when his mother returned home from work later that morning.

Franklin County Major Crimes Task Force Commander Bishop Allen said the scene implied another initiation by SSS. Authorities are looking further into this.

Detective Jehu Bridges, brother of the slain victim, spoke to reporters yesterday and said, "Today has been one of the worst days of my life. I won't stop investigating until I bring my brother's killers to justice."

Deputy Chief Charles Haman backed his detective by saying, "We are going to find this young man's killers, and when we do, they will have to answer to the law."

A vigil and prayer service is planned next week at the victim's home.

Jerome Bridges' death is one of seven deaths that appears to be committed by the brutal gang SSS.

I closed the laptop.

Now I understood why Jehu Bridges didn't like to speak about the framed picture on his shelf in his office. I now understood why he had a past with Rufus Booker. And I now knew that I had to have a talk with him.

I grabbed the keys to my truck and locked the front door behind me before I made my way back to the police station.

† † †

Jehu Bridges had his back to me when I barged into his office. He was standing up, looking outside.

"When were you gonna tell me?" I said with I'm sure a not-so-nice look on my face.

*You might want to be a little nicer there, guy.*

Not the time.

*Just saying.*

Bridges turned around to face me. "What are you talking about?" He looked puzzled.

I pointed to the picture of he and his brother. "Him. Your brother. Jerome."

The detective's face transformed into a world of hurt, like a painful past just came back alive. He turned back around to face the window.

"SSS kills your brother, which we both know was Rufus Booker's call," I started to say, "and then they kill my wife and you never thought to tell me?" I stretched my arms wide, palms up, and waited for Bridges to turn back around toward me to give me some kind of explanation.

But he didn't turn around. He just stayed still like a stone statue and his office was so quiet that the drop of a pin would've been heard.

*I told you J that you shoulda been easier. You lost Naomi, and he lost Jerome. He's going through pain too, you know.*

Point taken. Thanks.

Still without turning around, the detective broke the silence of the room. "I didn't want to bring it up because you and your wife had enough on your plate at the time. And I didn't think it appropriate just now with all that you've been going through."

When he turned around to face me, he wiped a couple of tears away from his face. "I'm sorry I didn't tell you, Job, but it still hurts real bad for me to talk about it, you know?"

68

Inside, I felt bad with how I just barged into his office and acted so aggressively.

*Tried to warn you.*

Shut it pal.

"Who told you?" asked Bridges.

I calmed my manner and said softly, "An old newspaper article." The detective simply nodded his head.

"Sit down," were Bridges' next words.

I took a seat as he made his way to his chair behind his desk. He wore black jeans and a white t-shirt underneath a black, un-tucked flannel shirt. After he sat down, he removed the toothpick from his mouth and put it on his desk.

"My brother, Jerome, was a good kid, but he got caught up in the wrong crowd for a little while." He leaned back in his chair and sighed. "That crowd happened to be Rufus Booker and SSS."

I had a feeling I knew where Bridges was going with this, but there was no way I was going to interrupt. Sitting still and like a sponge, I soaked in every word he spoke.

"I didn't know until my mom brought it to my attention, but Jerome was making small strides toward the gang life. Of course, being the older brother and a cop, I wasn't going to let him walk down that dark and treacherous road."

Ringing phones, numerous voices, and phone handsets being slammed back into their hook filled the atmosphere in the open area behind us. Although the door to Bridges' office was closed, one couldn't ignore all the racket on the other side.

"I had a heart to heart with him one evening and he opened up," the detective said shaking his head, "and he'd seen and done some things that he shouldn't have." He got quiet for a few moments. "My little brother, I couldn't believe it, Job. Anyway, I told him if he traveled this road long enough, he was either going to end up in jail or six feet under."

I continued to listen as Jehu Bridges went on.

"The most important of all he'd seen was being a witness to a homicide committed by none other than Rufus Booker himself." He fingered his goatee and thin mustache. "We were in the process of cracking down on Booker, but...."

Bridges arose from his chair, placed both hands on his desk, and leaned his head in my direction.

"It wasn't long after my heart to heart with my brother that he decided to change his ways and realize what lifestyle he was getting himself into. My thinking, Rufus thought Jerome got cold feet and was gonna somehow get him turned in. So, I ask you, Job, if you're Rufus

69

Booker, how do you make sure someone who witnessed you commit murder doesn't talk and get you in trouble with the law?"

I looked the detective in his eyes; they were red and the beginning of tears started to form in them. Of course, I knew: if you killed off a witness, then they couldn't talk, and with no witness, well, you get the point. But I didn't need to tell Jehu Bridges that.

I just nodded my head in understanding.

"Plus," detective Bridges started to say, "my brother would've known where Rufus hangs out, but with him dead nobody would have any leads."

"So," I said, "in your brother's case, this wasn't an initiation."

Detective Bridges shook his head. "No. It was to make sure he didn't talk."

A question came to me just then. "Did you think at the time that Rufus knew you were a cop?"

Bridges stood up straight. "I have no doubt about it."

Jehu Bridges was in the same seat I was; only it was his brother who was taken away from him. We both shared a past that cut like a knife, and it had changed us as men.

"Jerome received several calls on his cell phone the evening he was murdered from a stolen cell phone," Bridges started to say, "and a text message asking to meet with him. It's speculation, but I believe they, Rufus and SSS, sweet-talked and made sure Jerome was home alone before they did him in."

The detective dropped his head and held it there for the longest time. "And my mother," he shook his head, "she had to find her youngest son dead at home when she got back from work that morning." He got quiet, then said, "She took it real hard as you can imagine, but it's made her a stronger woman."

Puzzle pieces were filled in, and what was secret had been brought to light. "And that's why you've been hard at it investigating SSS and Rufus Booker."

"You got it Job."

Detective Bridges walked over to the bookshelf in his office and stood to the side of the framed picture of he and Jerome. "And just like I said two years ago, I won't stop investigating until I bring my brother's killers to justice."

Jehu Bridges said this with such conviction that I believed it was just a matter of time before this truth became reality.

Just then, without knocking, a man who had long sideburns and spiked-up hair burst his way into Bridges' office. To me, he looked like a fan of punk rock who'd forgotten to carry in with him his skateboard.

Excitedly and hurriedly, he said, "Hey Bridges...." but then he stopped because he saw me in the room. "Who's this?"

Both Bridges and I could tell that the man was uncomfortable saying what he had intended for only Bridges.

"This is Job McCants," said Bridges, motioning his hand toward me. "Job, this is detective Goodwin," then motioning his hand toward his fellow detective. We both nodded to each other after I turned around to face him.

Detective Goodwin must've heard of me before because he stood more at ease. "In that case, you'll both want to hear this."

Outside Bridges' office, the clamor seemed to rise and many stood up from their seats and started walking around. Some shook hands and some high-fived one another.

Something was going on.

Goodwin looked at Bridges in a way that made more sense to them than it did me. "We caught a break?" Bridges said raising his eyebrows.

"A huge one," said Goodwin. The detective then looked to me. "You remember that later-looking, black Ford Expedition from your witness report you had told us about, Mr. McCants?"

I looked at Bridges, surprised. "Yeah."

Bridges and I then looked to detective Goodwin. "Yeah, well," Goodwin started to say, "we found it." But for some reason the detective wasn't done as a smile on his face widened. "And guess who was inside of it?"

No way, I remember thinking.

I arose from my chair, my ears as opened as they had ever been.

Detective Goodwin's words came out of his mouth to me like a slow motion, deep voiced part from a movie.

"Kevin 'K-Dogg' Durgess, Tyrese 'TT' Taylor, and someone else we're not sure about just yet, but we're hoping it's Booker."

Paralysis infected my legs just then and I couldn't stand. I dropped back down into the chair.

No way, I remember thinking.

# 12

Through a one-way mirror, I stared at Kevin "K-Dogg" Durgess, Tyrese "TT" Taylor, and the younger member of SSS, the one who looked no older than fifteen, from a back room in the police station so they couldn't see me.

I came to find out that his name was Derek Westbrook and he was indeed fifteen years of age.

Unfortunately Booker wasn't the third member found, but at least three of the four had been had.

I felt like I was in an episode of *Law and Order*. Only it wasn't detectives Stabler and Benson in the room with me; it was Jehu Bridges.

When I was finally able to stand back up in the detective's office, I still couldn't believe that these three had been found. How? I thought. They had been like ghosts, so how was it possible that they just happened to get caught on this day? I felt something just wasn't adding up, but I was elated that they were in police custody.

I was told later that someone called in a suspicious looking black Ford Expedition that appeared to be making a drug trade-off in a downtown alley. Who called it in I had absolutely no idea, but at the same time I didn't care.

Three scumbags of SSS were off the streets and were where they deserved to be. Plus, two of them were higher members of SSS: Durgess and Taylor.

Although it was considered valid identification when I picked them out of the photograph book the other night in detective Bridges' office, the police still wanted me to pick them out of a lineup now that they were in their custody.

Let me explain a police lineup in a short way.

The suspects are blended in with what police call "fillers" or "foils", which are people who may be other prisoners or even volunteers. They are people of similar complexion and height. This is done because a police lineup must be conducted fairly, otherwise the evidence of identification won't be admissible in the court of law.

Six black males stared at the one-way mirror with earnest faces, but I only had my eyes on the three who were guilty as sin.

Jehu Bridges stood to the side of me with a toothpick in his mouth. It seemed that he always had a toothpick in his mouth.

The detective told me before going into the back room that he wouldn't say a word until I chose the perp or perps who were at my house the night my wife was murdered. Bridges said he couldn't do or say anything that would persuade me to pick the suspect or suspects who he preferred.

I knew that. Law shows and movies always harped that.

For some reason my palms were sweating and my heart was pounding, like I was just getting ready to jump out of a plane to skydive. I stood still but inside I felt like my body was moving all about. I scanned over all those in the room before me who held up numbers one through six in front of them.

"K-Dogg" held number one, "TT" held number six, and Derek Westbrook held number four.

Without looking at Bridges, I said, "Numbers one, four, and six."

"Are you sure, Mr. McCants?" The detective sounded professional, no doubt because what was said in this room was being recorded.

I nodded my head and confirmed for the recording, "Numbers one, four, and six."

"Thank you, Mr. McCants," said Bridges. He knocked on the one-way mirror one time, paused, knocked four times, paused again, and lastly knocked six times. This was to let the officer inside with the lineup crew know who the guilty party members were.

A door was opened inside of the lineup room and all the members started making their way out, but not before I stared each of the three SSS members down with eyes of hate.

I turned around and walked out of the back room with detective Bridges following behind me.

† † †

"So what happens next?" I asked detective Bridges as we sat outside on a park bench.

73

We decided to get away from the police station for a change and take in some fresh air that was much needed. Foundation Park was nearby, so that's where we went.

Detective Bridges wiped his lip of some mustard from the pretzel he was eating. After taking a swig of his bottled water, he said, "You'll hear from me tomorrow about meeting with an attorney, and then we'll have a hearing, that is, a pre-trial hearing probably the day after that."

That was fine with me. I was glad I had a day to clear my head; plus, I had something important I wanted to do tomorrow. It was something I stalled doing because I knew it would crush my heart; but, nonetheless, it was time that I went.

"Speaking of," the detective carried on, "do you have an attorney, Job?"

I shook my head. I never needed one until now.

"I know a couple of good ones. We'll take care of it later, all right?"

I nodded.

I found out, to my surprise, that Kevin Durgess and Tyrese Taylor - though they had records - had no warrants out for their arrests, and besides some minor misdemeanors, Derek Westbrook had no other issues with the law. I wasn't sure what kind of lawyers they'd have, but I hoped that they weren't good ones.

The day was radiant as the sun shined on its podium up high. Small wakes from the wind on the ponds of the park flaunted gold from the sun's beaming rays, and the park was filled with all kinds of people: bicyclists, couples holding hands, owners playing fetch with their dogs, runners, and people sitting down on blankets enjoying the beauty of the day. This park reminded me of Hillside Park, which was a park in my hometown of Mount Vernon, Ohio.

Though Naomi and I had lived in Columbus for ten years, we both grew up in Mount Vernon. It was a small, historical city that had a lot going for it, and in time its population eventually grew and became the home of many. I loved my hometown, but I was offered a job being a paramedic in Columbus that I couldn't refuse. Plus, I had a little home woodworking business that kept me busy on the side.

Naomi and I had been high school sweet hearts. Though I hadn't been prom king, she had been prom queen; however, she saved the last dance for me. I knew on that night that she was going to be the one who I was going to marry.

Bridges awoke me from my daydreaming. "With a possible trial approaching, have you given anymore thought on witness protection? Booker will be gunning, literally, for you if it goes that route."

I hadn't thought about it much, but with a trial possibly in the works, I definitely had to give it some more thought, and soon.

I shrugged my shoulders. "Not really."

"Job." Bridges gave me a serious look.

"I know." And I did.

Bridges stood up to throw away the foil wrapping from his pretzel and recycle his bottled water into the container that stood to the side of the trash container.

I looked to a younger couple who was sprawled out on a blanket in the middle of a grass section in the park. I'd say they were in their thirties, like Naomi and I were. Sorry, had been, for my wife's sake.

The man laid on his side with his elbow resting on the ground, supporting his head with his hand. He smiled and kissed his wife or girlfriend, I wasn't sure, several times, and then she wrapped her arms around him and pulled him into her. After a few moments, he laid on his back and the woman rested her head on his chest, just like Naomi and I used to do.

Love.

It was such a beautiful thing. And I'm not just talking about a marriage kinda love, but the love for family, a friend, a coworker, a stranger, that kinda love. Love was something all people wanted to feel. It was something that couldn't be explained in words, but it was an emotion human beings hungered and thirsted and died for.

Love had been ripped out of my heart and thrown into a pit of despair. Love had been taken from me and replaced with lonesomeness. Love was something that seemed dead to me.

But I was happy for that couple as I stared at them. If it wasn't for Jehu Bridges making his way back, I might of shed a tear.

"What are you staring at Job?" said Bridges who sat back down.

"Just that couple over there." I pointed toward them.

"I got my eyes on that little hottie over there," Bridges returned. He pointed to a female, probably in her upper twenties, who I thought didn't wear enough clothes.

I looked away. "Aren't you a married man, Bridges?" I glanced at his wedding ring.

If Jehu Bridges could blush, I'm sure he would've just then. "Yeah, but what's the hurt in looking?" He said it more like a question instead of being sure about it.

"Forget it," I said.

"No really, Job, I wanna hear your take on it." To me he said this with sincerity.

75

He wanted it, so he got it. "You may not be cheating on your wife physically right now, but inside your heart you are. Trust me, I used to be the same way man; it's not worth it. I struggled with it time and again, but it's the same body part, just on a different woman." I sat up more straight. "Stick with your wife. It's better," and then I said amusingly, "and it's safer too."

Bridges smiled and laughed.

My inner voice commended me just then. *Ladies and gentlemen, take notes, because my man Job McCants just spoke some truth.*

Thanks.

Bridges looked at my beaded necklace, which had a wooden cross that hung on my chest. He nodded his head. "My mamma still preaches Jesus to me too, and you know what Job," he said looking me in the face, "you're right."

"Yeah, well," I started to say, "I'm far from perfect and still have my weaknesses and struggles in life, but with a little work anything's possible."

*Amen J. What's got you in the positive today?*

Thinking about times with Naomi has put me in a good mood.

*Maybe you should think of those times more often.*

Yeah.

Jehu Bridges patted me on my shoulder just then. "You're a good guy, Job. I wish I had a friend like you growing up."

"I wouldn't say I'm good at all," I replied back. "Just changed."

And that was the truth. With some of the things I'd be doing soon, good seemed a world away from me.

I arose from the park bench. "I'll talk to you tomorrow, Bridges." I started walking away.

"All right Job. If you need anything, don't hesitate to call," the detective said arising as well and making his way in the opposite direction.

I took a few steps and stared at that couple on the blanket again. That used to be Naomi and me. I missed her so much.

Turning around, I said to Bridges, "Hey, Jehu."

He turned around. "Yeah."

I looked at the couple again before saying, "Be thankful that you have a wife." The emotion right before tears start to wet the eyes overtook me. "Because some of us don't."

Bridges' face saddened, and I'm pretty sure he wished he could've taken back the "hottie" comment as he dropped his head low.

I turned back around, making my way out of Foundation Park.

# 13

When I entered Mount Vernon the following day I had to admit, it felt good to be back home. Although the day was dark and overcast and showers looked imminent, not a drop of rain had fallen as I felt something old and familiar make its way back into me.

Passing the viaduct on South Main Street, I saw a rebuilding project was taking place at the historical Buckeye Candy and Tobacco Company brick building. Constructed in the early 1900s it still held its ground, like a long-time resident who still lived to tell of times past.

Many people didn't know, including myself for the longest time, but this old building actually survived two floods that took place in 1913 and 1959.

Many people also didn't know that this used to be a secret hangout for me and my friends back in high school after the place went out of business and closed down. After it closed, it was like a ruin that attracted young people.

The Tobacco part on the building had it just right, and that's what we used to do there: smoke cigars, play cards, and act like we were tough guys. It was all fun and games until the cops busted us one evening. I never smoked a cigar until that night at The Buckeye Candy and Tobacco Company building. After running and getting away from the cops, I turned a pale green color when I looked at myself in the mirror back at home, and then puked my guts up until it seemed I had no more left. When my mom and dad asked if I was all right, I told them I must've been coming down with something.

I never smoked cigars again.

Paragraphs Bookstore was on my left and I headed straight to the admirable Mount Vernon downtown square.

Old style brick buildings and mom and pops stores were to my right and left as I cruised through downtown. Early 1800s looking street lamps provided light for the city when darkness fell and most of the businesses and stores boasted their seasoned appearance. The town clock still chimed its tune every hour on the hour and Mount Vernon still looked absolutely good, I thought.

It was good to be back home.

Holding off on why I really visited, I decided to go to my roots; that is, to my old house on Heritage Lane where I grew up.

The drive turned greener and sunnier as I went from an urban setting to more of a rural setting. Heritage Lane wasn't out in the boondocks by any means, but it was more out in the quiet country than it was in the vibrant inner city.

Cyrus, my brother, lived out this way with his family, but I didn't tell him I was coming into town. Cyrus and I have a great brotherly relationship, but on this day I wanted to be left alone and kept to myself.

Pulling into Heritage Lane, the past came alive, like my brain's switch was flipped, taking me on a stroll through Memory Lane.

Heritage Lane had a cul-de-sac, similar to where I now lived. One way in and one way out. Some of the houses here were separated by numerous trees so that privacy was gained. Other large homes stood by themselves next to their neighbors, but one thing about Heritage Lane still remained: it was quiet and peace could still be breathed in its air.

One quick childhood memory.

Heritage Lane ran off of a busy road called Old Mansfield Road. The speed limit used to be 55 mph, but an agreement by the township bumped it down to 45 mph.

Anyway, my brother Cyrus, his knucklehead friends, and myself would walk to the top of Heritage Lane back during high school nights and would "moon" vehicles and throw eggs at cars that passed Heritage Lane on Old Mansfield Road.

I never did the egg throwing, but I gotta admit, I did have a cheek, or two, when it came to the "mooning."

To make a long story short, a Jeep that my brother and his friends egged stopped, then kept going over the small hill on Old Mansfield Road; and then, without us realizing it was the same vehicle, made its way back around, apparently turning around after some time, and made its way back toward us. When it got to Heritage Lane the driver turned on his brights, swerved into Heritage Lane like Dale Earnhardt Jr. while Cyrus and his friends still stood in the opening, nearly hitting Cyrus and John, one of Cyrus' friends, and sending all of us running in all sorts of directions.

I'm not bragging by any means, but I'm fast, so I was off like Usain Bolt ahead of everyone else. The driver of the Jeep never got out of his vehicle, but I could hear him hollering some not-so-friendly words from his driver's side window.

Meanwhile, I was sprinting in the dark not able to see much of anything ahead of me. We were out of the Jeep's sight and home sounded so good with every fast-paced step I was taking. That's when it happened: I ran head-on into something hard; so hard that I left my feet and the next thing I knew I was staring up at the majestic, star-filled night. I could hear Cyrus and his friends laughing as they were all witnesses of the scene. I never blacked out, but the pain I was feeling was nothing to laugh about. What was worse, I moved my mouth up and down and I was crunching on tiny pebbles that were hard. My fear: I just chipped all of my front teeth and my parents were going to kill me after they saw the dentist's bill!

But when my sight was able to adjust to the night, I saw a post and something was hanging on it by a thread; it swung back and forth because my running into it had broken its other end. When I was able to make out what it was, everything made sense and what I was chomping down on also made full sense.

I had ran right into a heavy bird feeder that hung on a metal post, breaking it, and what I thought was a mouth full of my teeth was really a mouth filled with bird feed!

In pain, we all finally made it back home and when I looked in the mirror, the sight was ugly. I inherited a large laceration to my upper lip and the cut was so deep that my mom had to take me to the hospital for stitches. The other minor lacerations and scrapes to my face made me look hideous. My friends, who saw me at school a couple days later, even thought it funny to start calling me Scarface.

My pops worked that night, but we told him later that we were playing basketball and I fell into the bushes that were planted behind our basketball court area.

Yes, I'm not perfect.

I shook my head and smiled as I thought of these childhood memories out here on Heritage Lane. There were a lot of great times. I thought I'd mention one to maybe make you laugh or put a smile on your face.

I didn't pull in, but when I slowly passed our old home, a good feeling penetrated my heart. The new owners put a copper standing-seam roof on the brick house and the landscaping had been given an update. Two children, a small boy and girl, looked to be playing a game of P.I.G. on the basketball court. I drove on down to the end of the cul-de-sac, turned around and made my way back, stopping across from my old home.

The front porch swing was still there. Naomi and I had many make out sessions on that Poly-Wood swing. The left side garage door had yet to be replaced; Cyrus' and my baseball throwing dents were written on it like graffiti, but the owners probably thought, "Why fix it?" when their children would probably also play sports. A lot of memories went into that place and it made me sad to think how fast time goes by, but it also made me happy because those memories were engraved into my heart, never to be forgotten.

Pointing her finger, the little girl saw me and her and her brother, a red-haired boy, paused and looked my way. I think sometimes way more into things than most people, but to me I didn't want to come off as a pedophile; so I got outta the vehicle the same time I saw the mother of the children walk out of the right-sided garage, acted like I was checking my front passenger side tire, looked up, knowing that it was fine, and to my surprise the woman actually smiled and waved.

She hollered, "Everything all right?"

"Yes ma'am," I replied. I kicked the tire, like I was checking the pressure, and then I walked back toward the driver's seat.

*Real slick J.*

I thought so too, thanks.

"Have a nice day," the mother of the children said.

"Thank you, you too." I stood in front of my driver's seat and took one last look at the house I grew up in. "Hey, ma'am?"

The woman who decided to start playing basketball with her children stopped for a few seconds. "Yes."

"You have a very beautiful home." I waved goodbye.

"Thank you." She also waved goodbye.

I sat back in my truck, put it into drive, and made my way to the top of Heritage Lane. My next stop wouldn't be filled with happiness or things to laugh at. I had stalled long enough and today was finally the day.

The day when I finally decided to visit my buried wife at Mound View Cemetery.

†     †     †

Mound View Cemetery sits just behind Dan Emmett Elementary School, my old stomping grounds. Established in 1833, the cemetery was named after an ancient Indian mound and dates on the gravestones go back before 1833. Several mausoleums, or those small buildings within a cemetery, had held up over the years and were well taken care of. Although cemeteries produce tears and heartbreak, Mound View Cemetery was scenic as trees with long branches stood on top of the large hill and many old-fashioned tombstones were scattered around this home for the dead.

Cemeteries give most people the creeps, like they're walking on contaminated ground; however, graveyards to me were places of solace that invited a comforting peace.

Let me say, I knew God was taking care of my wife in whatever Heaven-like environment she was in, and I didn't have any fear or worry that she wasn't being taken care of. We humans don't have all the answers to the afterlife; but, for the true believer, there shouldn't be any uncertainty about their final destination.

I once read something like this in the Bible; I believe it was in the book of *Ecclesiastes*: *After all, everyone dies - so the living should take this to heart. Sorrow is better than laughter, for sadness has a refining influence on us.* I thought about that hard just now.

To the first part, we all die and I believe the living should be appreciative and grateful for each and every day that God gives that individual person life. Now, to the second half, we as humans would much more rather partake in laughing than sorrow, right? But the more I thought about this, the more it made sense to me. Sorrow and sadness is by far better because it readjusts our heart's attitude and mindset, and it impacts our mood, thoughts, and actions more. It reaches into the deep chambers of our hearts and says, "This event, though sad, is going to help you grow and open your eyes, mind, and soul to the more important, meaningful things in life."

Maybe this only makes sense to me, I dunno, but maybe you can get something from it as well.

*I feel you, J.*

As I walked between countless gravestones, I searched the area where my wife was located thanks to my family telling me where it was. The names of the deceased written in stone were all about me, like generations upon generations of people I didn't even know were silently greeting me.

That's when I looked up and saw my wife's name staring at me, drawing me to her side. I stood before her gravestone and I quietly cried, tears gliding down my face. Recent flowers had been placed on top of her gravestone and the sun shining on them gave them a livelier, richer color.

I knelt down, wiped a few dead blades of grass off her stone, and looked at the writing on her gray, finely cut gravestone that had a cross on it:

Naomi L. McCants
August 25, 1983 – May 6, 2016

Though she was now buried, my wife still seemed so alive to me. It seemed not that long ago that we were going on runs together, eating popcorn and watching a movie by the other's side, making love as our hearts were one….there was so much I was thinking.

Now it was gone. All gone. Bitterness began making its way inside, like it was mixed in with the blood running through my veins.

"Baby," I started to say, but mumbling was the only language coming from my mouth. That's when I really started to cry, weeping like I never had before. After about five minutes, I was finally able to reclaim some sort of composure.

"Naomi," I wiped the remainder of my tears away, "I love you and miss you so much. My life is nothing and is dead without you." Two birds passed overhead, their shadows staining the ground momentarily. I stood up because my knees couldn't stand the strain of squatting any longer.

"Though you aren't here in person, my wife, I know that you see me. I'm not sure where to go from here or what the next page is to be turned in my life. But…." I paused turning around. An older couple driving a gold Buick made their way into the cemetery. I'm assuming to also visit a loved one.

I turned back toward my wife. "But I will make amends. Some way, some how, I will make right with what happened."

That right was the justice system putting away three of the four SSS members who'd been caught. If that didn't work, which I couldn't ever imagine not happening, at the time, then something else would have to be done.

But surely the justice system was going to be on my side and get these guys sent away for a long time.

Eventually, Rufus Booker's time would also come.

I closed my eyes. The breeze mixed in with the sun shining on my face felt refreshing. An abrupt sensation swept through me, like Naomi was standing by my side, holding my hand, and calming my troubled spirit.

I opened my eyes, a thought coming to me just then. Removing my wedding band, I made a divot in the ground with the back end of my shoe up against my wife's gravestone. I knelt back down.

Burying my wedding band and placing the small chunk of earth back to its original place, I said, "We are still one Naomi, my wife, in life," I paused looking up skyward, "and in death."

I kissed my hand and rested it on her name for a short time. I stood back up, sensing my wife saying that she loved me. Looking down upon her gravestone, I said, "Too me, Naomi."

I turned around, walking back toward my vehicle. What started as a stormy-looking day transformed into a day of brilliance with the sun shining high and the clouds forming their own pieces of art in the sky.

Naomi could do just that: light up whatever seemed to be in the darkness.

My inner being didn't say a word during this entire time. It knew Naomi and I needed our time together. Plus, in all honesty, what person wants to barge in on another when they're going through a difficult time?

I was just getting ready to close my driver's side door when my iPhone rang out. Digging it outta my pocket and recognizing the name displayed, I answered.

"Hey Jehu."

"Hey Job, got a minute?"

"Shoot."

"Talked to the lawyer today." We agreed on an attorney and Jehu took care of the arrangement when we spoke, which was later in the day after we decided to talk at Foundation Park.

Bridges went on. "We're meeting tomorrow afternoon for the pre-trial hearing. One o'clock good for you?" His voice sounded down, I thought, like he knew something that I didn't.

Yes, I thought inside my head. It was just a matter of time before the bad guys got put away, and for a long time.

"Sounds great Jehu." I then added, "Everything all right?"

"Yeah." Again, there was some sort of uncertainty in his voice.

Maybe he was just having a bad day, or maybe he was under the weather. People were always judging others when they had absolutely no idea what that person might be going through.

"Then I'll see you tomorrow," I said.

"Sounds good," detective Bridges returned. "Have a good day, Job."

"Thanks Jehu. You too." I ended the call.

After I closed my door, I turned to my right to see Naomi one last time. A beautiful, bright red cardinal bird stood on top of her gravestone. That was Naomi's favorite bird; this had to be some sort of sign.

I smiled, started my truck up, and hopped onto Wooster Road.

Making my way back to Columbus.

# 14

I sat in a small room at the county courthouse that consisted of four walls, two of which had tall seven-tiered shelves that held many legal books that lawyers know all about; they were books of confusion to me. The mahogany table stood in the middle and besides that the room was mostly empty. A stuffiness that felt like a small person wedged in between two large people on a plane seat also filled the room. Two windows to my right at least provided some light and life.

The courthouse gave me a queasy feeling. It reeked of crime and lawlessness, just as a landfill contains the nasty stench of human garbage. There was something sinister in the court of law that needed to be righted, and a gavel being struck when I first walked down a hallway made me tense a little.

Sitting at the table with me was detective Bridges and Spence Harper, the attorney defending me, who walked in with a briefcase and who Bridges and I had to wait on. Bridges told me to wear something nice as court would be following our hearing, so I wore one of two suits that I possessed; it was a dark blue one that I wore a tie with.

Spence Harper was clean-shaven and he had a standout chin to go along with his face. You could tell he was a lawyer just by the way he walked down the street. Dressed as a typical attorney, he had an air about him that meant business.

Harper skipped the pleasantries and got right to the point. He folded his hands in front of him, resting them on top of the table. "Today shouldn't be difficult, Mr. McCants." He looked me in the eye; his eyebrows were bushy and he smelled of Old Spice. "When the judge asks, you tell the judge exactly who you saw on the night of your wife's unspeakable death and identify Kevin Durgess, Tyrese Taylor, and Derek Westbrook as your wife's killers. Your testimony will cause the public defender of the three just mentioned to throw in the towel and bargain; that is, come to a deal shortly after that will get these guys sent to prison today."

Deal? What did Harper mean by that comment? Hopefully it was a deal that was going to get these guys sent to prison for life so they couldn't commit anymore barbarous acts ever again.

"Mr. Harper...." the attorney cut me short.

"Call me Spence, Mr. McCants."

"Spence," I said looking confusedly at him, "what do you mean by a deal?"

Spence Harper looked over at detective Bridges and then cast his eyes downward. I looked over at Bridges whose face was written with regret and he slowly shook his head at me, signaling to me that I wasn't going to like what I was about to hear.

My attorney then spoke, once again getting right to the point. "The deal is that I can get you two to four years for each of these guys, Mr. McCants. And by two to four years I mean a for sure guaranteed two to four years."

I leaned back in my chair and tossed my arms upward. "I want these guys to go away for life. I saw, I watched them kill my wife before my eyes." My temper was rising and I'm sure my face was turning a tomato color about now.

I looked back to Jehu Bridges who looked at me with sadness, but I knew that he knew about this deal by the look on his face after the mentioning of a deal came up.

"These are the facts, Mr. McCants," Harper started to say, "the murder weapon is gone, there is no blood or DNA other than that of you and your wife, there's not a household camera to back your claim, and unfortunately you're the only witness, which is good, but it isn't going to hold up solely in court. And, sorry to bring up, but you were in a coma for three months, Mr. McCants; so you can see how this may look in the court's eyes."

Bewildered, I looked up and stared at the ceiling as Harper went on. "The only other option is that we try for a life sentence, which I can tell you will end up getting these guys off and back on the streets after telling you the many flaws that the public defender will bring up and expose."

Sitting back in my chair, I was lost. How was this justice? So what about these flaws that Harper pointed out. One's word just wasn't good enough these days, and I understood with the world that we lived in, but still. A measly two to four years was nothing compared to what these guys did to my wife and I. But, on the other hand, attempting to get these guys for life seemed an option that the court may be partial toward, for their sakes, which would result in getting them back out in the world when they could've spent some time in prison.

What to do? It was like two doors with unknown conclusions were before me and I had to pick one that would set into motion a new string of events.

"I want to add," the attorney continued, "many of us lawyers don't even go after and make deals in cases where there is only one witness involved."

That made me feel great. Spence Harper was really starting to tick me off. I looked at him, thinking that his face would look better with a broken nose.

*Cool it Job. Keep your head.*

You're right, but I'm fuming as we speak.

Spence Harper leaned back in his chair, his hands resting on his legs. "Maybe karma catches up to these scumbags and they get killed in prison, or maybe they get their lives turned around; I don't care, but I'm telling you that this is a one-time deal. Sorry, Mr. McCants, but go with it or away from it. It's your choice."

This deal, detective Bridges knowing it and keeping it from me, Spence Harper and his mouth, a weak justice system that I felt was failing me....it was all too much. Inside of me a volcano was close to the point of erupting.

I'd had enough.

I looked at Spence Harper, gave him a dirty look, which caused him to look away from me, and then I stared long and hard at Jehu Bridges who met my eyes and didn't look away. He could've told me about the deal, but he knew me well enough to know how I'd respond.

Plus, this explained his mood on the phone yesterday when I was at the cemetery visiting my dead wife. He knew what my plans were that day when I had told him during our conversation about a lawyer. I couldn't really blame him for not telling me. Honestly, who'd upset someone with news like this when that person was already down enough?

Standing up disappointed, I marched to the closed door that led to a hallway. Stopping before the door, I turned around, looked at Spence Harper, and said, "Here's my choice." And then I punched a softball-sized hole through the wall closest to me. I had pretended that it was his face. The pain shot through my hand like an arrow wound but I didn't care.

*J, you gotta stop punching holes through walls. You're killing your right hand.*

I ignored my inner voice, opened the door, walked out, and slammed it shut. Two ladies in the same hallway jumped at the sound of the slamming of the door and walked away after they saw my rage-filled face.

Through the opening under the door, I heard Spence Harper say, "Who's going to pay for that?"

Jehu Bridges countered with, "The city's covering it. He's going through a hard time Spence. Cut him some slack, would you. How would you be if you went through what he did?" The detective paused and then said, "And now this is laid on him."

Spence Harper had nothing more to say. Finally, something his mouth didn't have a comment for.

Jehu Bridges really was my friend, I remember thinking.

I walked down the hallway, turned a corner, and made my way to the sunny outdoors. Fresh air is what I needed.

Fresh air to fill my hurt and dying soul.

☦    ☦    ☦

About a half hour later I was sitting in a courtroom with Spence Harper beside me. The judge was an older man with a white beard; he looked like he hung on the edge of retirement, but what had my attention more were the three people who sat across from me with their public defender: Kevin "K-Dogg" Durgess, Tyrese "TT" Taylor, and Derek Westbrook.

Derek looked scared and I almost felt bad for him, but then I remembered that he also had a part in the killing of my wife. He couldn't look over at me, but the other two smiled at me from where they sat and Durgess even had the nerve to wink at me at one point.

What kind of people were these? They harmed and killed my wife and almost me and yet they acted in this inhuman of a way. How many other people did they threaten, harm, or kill? I'd heard of it, but I had never seen such evil this up close and personal.

My palms sweated and my pulse heightened to a rapid pace. I wanted to stand up, walk over, specifically to Durgess and Taylor, and beat the life out of them.

*Don't do anything stupid J, especially in the court of law.*

I'm not, but it's hard not to.

Spence Harper stood up and approached the judge's bench with a file in his hand and said for the courtroom to hear, "Your Honor, I'd like to enter the statement of a witness who was present during the home invasion and homicide that took place on May sixth of this year. The witness is the husband of the victim, Job McCants."

87

"And why can't this just wait to be brought up in trial, Mr. Harper?" the judge said looking down from his bench. Judge Porter - that's what the gold nameplate in front of him read - wore his glasses so they sat midway on his nose and he was a little on the heavier side.

Harper looked toward the public defender and back to Judge Porter. "Because, Your Honor, I believe that if this information is entered today, the defense's plea will be changed to guilty, and a trial will not be needed."

The judge nodded his head. "I see, Mr. Harper."

I looked across from me to see the public defender whispering something to Kevin Durgess and Tyrese Taylor who had their bodies turned in his direction, heads leaning toward what he was telling them.

Inside, I started to think many things. Flashes like lightning filled my head with images of the night of the home invasion and when Naomi was killed right in front of me.

....awakening to her screams....the butt end of my shotgun sending me into unconsciousness....Naomi sitting before me with the seconds of her life ticking away....the shots that ended her earthly life....me going after Booker and being hit, sending me on the ground....the shot to my head that sent me into a coma for three months....

It was all coming back to me. This nightmare filled with many horrors was making its resurrection known within me. Hate mixed with anger and revenge was soaking into my heart.

*Job, be careful. This is what I was warning you about.*

Ignoring the voice, my thinking continued.

Instead of getting life, I was dealing with a puny two to four years. But I saw them kill Naomi right before my very eyes. If this went to trial, which would be made by my decision, then these bad guys might be right back on the streets if it didn't pan out how I'd hoped.

But nothing was panning out how I had hoped.

Then it hit me. It hit me hard, like Barry Bonds sending a homer out of San Francisco's ballpark. I wasn't sure about the thought at first, but the more I thought about it, the better it felt and sounded.

*Job, I'm telling you, this isn't the way to go. Get rid of that thinking.*

But something's gotta be done, and this path seems to be the way, to me.

*That's right. TO YOU. But what would Naomi want, or more importantly, what would God want?*

You have a point. I don't expect God to be on my side with this, but I know what Naomi would want.

*And it isn't that.*

You're right. But it's what I want, and I'm the one left here to deal with it.

*Don't do this Job. It's not the way.*

What hit me hard is that there was a third door available when I only thought two were before me. I could control a lot with this new door; there were still unknowns, but I could take matters into my own hands with this new way.

*You really think you have control over anything? Let alone the idea that you're flirting with right now?*

I was hopeful about the conclusion with what I was thinking. Of course, curveballs could be thrown, but when did life not throw those?

Looking back over to the small crowd across from me, I gave them a stone hard, stern stare. My eyes were as cold as ice and a fire that had commenced within my heart was now metastasizing to the rest of my body.

My mind was made up; I knew exactly what I was going to do. It was what I was wanting when I laid in the hospital after I awoke from my coma, and it was what I was wanting now.

Revenge.

I'd be partial. Partial toward my way.

*J....*

"Mr. McCants," the judge said more loudly the second time.

I snapped out of my thinking. "Yes sir," I said meeting the judge's eyes. I then arose out of my chair.

"Mr. McCants, you're claiming as evidence that Kevin Durgess, Tyrese Taylor, and Derek Westbrook who you see sitting there," Judge Porter pointed to my wife's killers, "invaded your home on the evening of May sixth of this year and attacked your wife which resulted in her death?"

I stood quietly, weighing the idea that was getting brighter in my head. Judge Porter went on. "You're saying, Mr. McCants, that you'll testify to these events in a trial?"

To me it felt like all eyes in the courtroom were watching me, and the anticipation of the moment was at its climax, like a crowd biting their fingernails waiting to see if the basketball player's final free throw shot would either tie or lose the game.

I wasn't sure if I'd be able to do and carry out what my head was creating, but one thing was certain: I was going to take matters into my own hands and seek justice myself.

"No I will not, Judge Porter." I heard some sighs of disbelief in the courtroom after I made the comment. Those sighs didn't belong to any of my family because I didn't tell them about today; I felt I needed to do this alone.

Turning around and looking at detective Bridges, it was as if he couldn't come to terms with the decision I just made. Harper look bemused, like his face said, "What are you doing?"

I then gave my reasoning. "Following my wife's murder, I was in a coma for three months. I can't be sure about the events of that evening anymore or," I said looking at the three SSS members, "the persons involved."

The judge's face turned sad. "I see, Mr. McCants."

Judge Porter then said something to Spence Harper and the two had a short back and forth conversation, but my ears weren't hearing any of it.

I was too focused on something else.

Revenge.

"I'm going to dismiss this case," said Judge Porter as my ears returned to the present. He then looked at the three of my wife's four killers. "Kevin Durgess, Tyrese Taylor, and Derek Westbrook," he said resting his glasses more on the top of his nose, "you're released from custody and you may collect your belongings."

I started to make my way toward the little gate that would take me to the middle of the courtroom and then down the path that led to the double doors that would take me outta here.

Before going through the little gate, I stopped and took one last look at the three SSS members. For the first time Kevin Durgess and Tyrese Taylor didn't have a smile to beam my way; instead, their faces looked unsure and Derek Westbrook finally looked up at me, but to my surprise his eyes were glassy, tears filling them.

Something inside of me was telling me that I couldn't carry out with what I was thinking to Derek Westbrook. He was too young. But he had a part in my wife's murder too.

Turning away from them, I made my way down the middle of the courtroom. Catching Jehu Bridges' face, his concerned look had pity combined in it.

Continuing down the courtroom, I thought hard into what my mind was contriving. Could I really do what I thought I might do?

*Job, you can't do this. It's not right.*

I've already started on this path. I can't change what I just said to the judge.

*But you can change your thinking and not do what you think you wanna do.*

That's true, but something's gotta be done. Naomi's death will not end with me doing nothing.

*Get your head right J. Think about God. Don't turn away from Him. Remember, even you know Naomi is being taken care of right now.*

My I-got-your-back-bro kinda being was absolutely right. But I was a man torn apart, and one important question remained in my head as I pushed open the double doors of that courtroom.

Could I really kill the SSS members who had killed my wife?

# 15

Revenge.

By definition revenge is to exact punishment or expiation for a wrong on behalf of, especially in a resentful or vindictive spirit.

I breathed it into my lungs in that courtroom. Like oxygen being administered to a patient through a non-rebreather mask, so revenge filled my being with a new kind of air.

Outside the county courthouse, I walked to my vehicle with anger-filled steps. The day may have been shining like a diamond ring, but to me it was an afternoon of gloom and darkness. I passed some people walking down the courthouse's steps and others moved outta my way when they saw the look on my face, like they knew I was a man who had just received unfavorable news.

But what kind of revenge was I really going to dish out? Killing them had certainly crossed my mind, but was their blood on my hands going to bring Naomi back?

*No Job.*

I know.

Was there a way I could place them in some type of uncomfortable, torturing atmosphere and have them confess to their deadly sin?

*Still not the way to go Job.*

You know everything, don't you.

*I know this isn't the way to go about this.*

Where was I to go from here, I thought? I knew right from wrong, but justice I was going to make mine and avenge the death of my wife regardless of which way I should go about it.

Was this Christian of me? Without question, no. Had I been falling away from my faith since I awoke from my coma? Right on the money, yes. Did temptations and what looked to be right try and deceive me? No doubt, yes. Was there still faith kindling in my heart that was shouting at me, "Leave this be. Nothing you can do will bring Naomi back. It was senseless and inhuman what happened to her, but life does go on, and you know she wouldn't agree to you carrying out these thoughts that you've devised inside that head of yours!?"

*No doubt, yes!*

I arrived at my vehicle with all these thoughts crammed into my head. Anger, rage, and fury was built up within me, but also in the mix was sorrow, heartache, and a sense of being lost. That's when the voice behind me spoke.

"McCants!" The voice roared loudly. "What was that just then in the courtroom!?"

I didn't need to turn around to know who the recognizable voice belonged to; I was getting to know Jehu Bridges pretty well.

Standing still for a few moments looking at the reflection of myself in my driver's side window, I finally turned around to see the heated face of the detective.

"What'd it look like? Come on Bridges, you saw for yourself."

Bridges closed in, getting closer to me and lowering his voice. "To me, Job, it looked like a man who made a foolish decision and thinks he can take matters into his own hands." He removed the toothpick from his mouth with his right hand and tossed it across his body onto the parking lot. "I saw the look in your eyes when you looked at me in the courtroom. Trust me, man, this isn't the way to go about this."

*At least detective Bridges sees my point.*

Shut up.

*Okay, sorry.*

So my face was telltale to Jehu Bridges of my true intentions. I didn't care, but I wouldn't confess to anything. This probably wasn't the first time he'd seen things like this.

"So is that what you plan on doing," Bridges carried on, "be a big bad man who takes on members of the notorious gang SSS, not to mention Booker, the head honcho, and try and get yourself killed while doing so?"

I finally spoke after about a half minute of silence. "Maybe....I don't know....I'm lost....I...." but I really didn't have the words.

Jehu Bridges could sense I was like a stranded puppy out on the streets with my tail tucked in between my legs.

"Job, I've seen people act like this in the past with similar cases. Emotions run wild and we all grieve in different ways but," he stopped short to find the words to say next, "don't do something stupid that you're gonna regret the rest of your life."

I knew Jehu was only looking out for me and that he really cared, but when he said the word "stupid," it just hit me the wrong way.

93

My temper started to speak for me. "What do you know? They killed your brother and you're still no closer to busting these guys. Me," I said slapping backwards with my hand my driver's side door, "I'm gonna do something about this. I'm not sure exactly what yet but…." I slowly said lastly, "but I'm going to do something!"

Detective Bridges stood quietly, his face turning sad at the mentioning of his brother. I shouldn't have brought it up, but it's unfortunate what is said when tempers flare. He shook his head and then held it down.

"I too have thought things that I wanted to do to Booker and his punk posse since Jerome's death but," Bridges then looked me in the eye, "but it wasn't going to bring him back to life, and who would I have been turning into?"

I just looked at him, but I knew what he was getting at.

"That's right, no better than the scum who did him in." Bridges fingered at his goatee. "So don't act like you're the only one who's been in your own shoes Job."

Another temptation that looked like light designed another option in my head just then. I'd bait Bridges and see if he'd go with it or, worst case, he'd rebuke me for it.

"Bridges." The detective made his way over to me and leaned up against my truck.

"Yeah."

As we stood there, I noticed the sharp color of red sunset maple trees in front of the courthouse as their branches swung from side to side from the pleasant breeze. To my right a school bus loaded with children made its way down Main Street, their laughs and chatter filled the Columbus air. An elderly couple walked hand in hand down the sidewalk, their smiles bringing some warmth to my icy heart.

That should've been Naomi and I years from now.

"Booker and SSS killed your brother." I looked up to the sky. "They killed my wife." Looking over at the detective, I said, "Why don't we both work together and do them in ourselves?"

*I know you told me to shut up, but he's an officer of the law. What are you thinking?*

Bridges didn't speak, at first. By looking at him, I could tell the option was weighing heavily on his mind, like inside his head was a two-pan balance wavering between what side to take.

"Job," the detective finally said.

"Yeah."

"You're losing it." Not the words I was hoping to hear, but then again what should have I expected?

Bridges went on. "I warn you, again, if you travel down this path too far, Job, you're gonna end up getting yourself killed." He looked over at me. "Even if you would be successful, what would you be accomplishing?"

The truth of that statement stung me like a bee to the heart.

"I'm gonna pretend I didn't hear that statement about you and I going after SSS, Job," Bridges said looking at the ground, "and I'm going to attribute it to the emotional torment you've suffered."

Jehu Bridges was doing and saying the right thing, but the option of this new, third door was winning me over, like the Dark Side taking over Anakin Skywalker in Star Wars.

"Figures," I angrily said. "If you wanna get something done these days, then you're better off doing it yourself." I opened my driver's side door and was making my way in.

"Let us do our job Job!" Bridges said, anger also rising in his voice as he grabbed my driver's side door with a sure grip. "You're a good man," he said looking at me, "don't let what happened ruin you."

I grabbed my door and was getting ready to pull it in. "It already is." Pulling the door toward me, the detective's strength kept it ajar.

"Job," he said, sadness tattooed on his face, "if you need anything, you know I'll be there." And with that I slammed my truck door shut.

Starting my truck up, I peeled out and made my way toward Main Street.

Why had I been so difficult with Jehu Bridges? He was only trying to help. How could I have treated him in the way I did? He seemed to be the only person besides my family who cared to keep me on a level path. Why did I push his advice back in his face as if it were useless information? He had seen these things a lot and I'd acted like I had seen them longer than he had.

*He's your friend J. Good friends are hard to find these days.*

Yeah I know.

I looked in my rearview mirror to see Jehu Bridges standing there alone, like he signified goodbye to a friend who was taking a dangerous and possibly deadly route.

*You know what's right. Don't let the darkness blind you to the truth.*

I know, but....

That's when that third door option came back alive and the right, which was actually wrong, dug its way back into my being.

The sight to my left brought it all back again.

Making their way down the same steps from the courthouse I had were Kevin Durgess, Tyrese Taylor, and Derek Westbrook. I stopped

95

toward the bottom of the steps in the parking lot, rolled down my window, and gave them each a death stare.

Stopping midway down the steps, only the two older ones, Durgess and Taylor, looked at me. Westbrook looked down at the ground, ashamed to look at me.

It was like a scene taken right out of a movie. You know, the part where the good guy encounters his enemy and they have that long-drawn-out moment where nothing exists except for that awkward meeting.

Like they did in the courtroom, "K-Dogg" Durgess and "TT" Taylor actually had the nerve to smile at me.

It was in that heated moment that I knew exactly what I was going to do. Wrong as it was, I knew what I was going to do, and I knew what I wanted.

Revenge.

Peeling out again, I sped out of the parking lot onto Main Street. Darkness, hate, and revenge consumed my heart and destroyed any kind of goodness within it.

*J don't....*

Don't bother. My mind is made up.

*Very well. I'm still here and will get at you at times, but this path you're walking alone.*

Alone.

The word struck deep, like a knife cuts into flesh. Alone I would walk, and alone I would carry out whatever madness I would store up for those who had killed Naomi.

I had a lot of planning, devising, and work that had to be done before I could go through with what I would personally deliver.

It would take a couple of months of paying people off for information, guns being illegally purchased so nothing came back to me, walking dark inner city streets to get a layout of my new turf, and visiting places where my enemies were known to hangout.

And many other things that you will come to find out. Some expected, some unexpected.

Not to mention keeping two eyes on my own back for Booker and SSS, knowing that they probably still wanted me as dead as a doornail.

It would be the end of summer, but then the time would finally arrive to hand deliver what I had been storing up for Rufus "D-Locks" Booker, Kevin "K-Dogg" Durgess, Tyrese "TT" Taylor, and Derek Westbrook, though, I still had my doubts with the last member.

Revenge.

I wanted it in the hospital, I wanted it in the courtroom, and I now knew for sure it was what I was wanting more than anything now.

It would be mine.

Revenge.

# PART 3

Dear friends, never take revenge. Leave that to the righteous anger of God. For the Scriptures say,

"I will take revenge;
I will pay them back,"
says the Lord.

*Romans 12:19*

# 16

## TWO MONTHS LATER

It took two months to pass before I had everything in order. It took two months to pass before I hoped that all my effort would go as I had planned. And it took two months to pass before I actually took my first steps in the direction of executing justice on my own.

Trust me, I had been a busy man, and in no particular order did I go through the following.

I went back to work about a week after the pre-trial hearing, but after a couple of weeks it was too hard to focus my attention on others when I had too much on my own mind. My EMS chief told me to take a week off because he knew I just wasn't myself. Between that, personal time, vacation, and a few sick days, I managed to get all the time I needed off, plus more, to get everything prepared and ready to go after Rufus Booker and SSS.

Also, in hopes that no one would ever find out, I had removed IV supplies, syringes and needles, and some vials of medication, one being a paralytic, from our supplies room and drug storage. I thought of Tyrese "TT" Taylor with the Vecuronium, or the paralytic that I had stolen from the station.

One day I visited my bank and took all the money I had out of my savings account. I still had some money in my checking account, but it was worth depleting my savings; I knew what I was wanting was going to cost money, and I knew it wouldn't be cheap. The clerk counting my money made a joke afterwards, with a smile, about me "getting the heck outta dodge" and never coming back. Grabbing my money and stuffing it into a book bag Naomi had bought me, I had ignored the comment with a serious face. The clerk's smile disappeared pretty fast.

Without a haircut, I had let my thick brown hair grow out for a while now. Nothing like Duck Dynasty, I kept my beard trimmed but long enough so that I looked different. As with my outward appearance, so my inside was transformed as well. My heart was black, my attitude was all-serious, and I hadn't smiled in a long time. I was becoming a person who I thought I could never be.

But I was becoming that person.

Throughout this time my family visited and I had put on a pretend me who seemed to be doing all right, but really it was just like make-up over a woman's face; I was only hiding what I was truly feeling deep down inside. Cyrus could tell I wasn't myself, but he wasn't going to bring it up in front of our parents.

I had ADT install a good security system in my house as well as place several cameras in key areas on the outside and inside of my home.

Detective Bridges stopped by several times and tried calling multiple times, but each phone call I didn't return and every time he tried to confront me I ignored or turned away from him. I didn't answer my door on two occasions that I know of for sure, and one time I actually turned around after making my way onto my drive when I saw his vehicle parked outside my house.

Was Jehu Bridges my friend? Yes. Did I want to talk to or see him now or anytime soon? No.

I wasn't even sure if I could go through the beginning stages of my plan until one night all the pain came back and I found myself starting up my truck and driving into downtown Columbus.

Where should I even start, I remember thinking? Columbus was big, but I knew SSS had spread like a cancer to many neighborhoods - not to mention my own - in the city and had even reached into the rougher parts of Columbus's downtown.

But who was I? A paramedic living in a comfortable part of the city getting ready to walk dark and hard streets in sections of the city that could possibly get me hurt or even killed. And who was I armed only as myself taking chances of maybe running into people who I had heard about on television.

Totally unprepared, I decided to park downtown in a nicer end and slowly make my way to the outer edge of the rougher side.

For the first week, I decided to just walk around and get acquainted. I didn't ask questions about SSS or the ones I was looking for because I didn't want word getting around that someone was putting his nose in places where it didn't belong.

I knew walking these streets and going into some of the places I did could get dangerous, so I decided it was time to start asking about something that I needed.

Guns.

One day, in the afternoon, I entered a bar on the east end of a rough section of the city. A white lady wearing a mini-skirt asked me before going into the bar if I wanted to "have a good time." Standing to the side of the bar's door like a beggar pleading for some money, I looked at her, shook my head, and opened the door to enter the bar. I heard, "You couldn't handle me anyway baby," as the door closed behind me.

I'm not going to explain or go into every detail of what I went through during those two months, otherwise I'd only bore you and take up too much time; but through a conversation I had with a guy one night on the streets, I was told that guns could be illegally purchased from a guy named "Rex" who owned a bar on the east side of the city.

So with my book bag strapped tightly to my back, I stood still, looking over Lucky 7's bar. A jukebox to my left blared *Paradise City* by Guns N' Roses and some woman smashed a beer bottle over some guy's head.

*Great time to show up.*
Yeah, no doubt.
*What are you getting yourself into J?*
Just bear with me.
I didn't get a reply.

Just then the bartender came out from behind the bar area and a huge man, highly tatted and hairy, arose from a booth nearby and both men made their way to the man lying on the ground who just got hit with the beer bottle. The big man said something to the bartender and then they both picked the man up and headed toward my direction. The big man who reminded me of a motorcyclist from a bike gang was just the man I was looking for.

Wearing a shirt that had a large V ripped in the upper middle section, I could see underneath his hairy chest was tattooed in black ink REX. Stepping out of their way, Rex kicked open the bar's door and with a count of "1....2....3...." they heaved the man who was hit in the head with the beer bottle outside. Rubbing his hands together like he was shaking off dirt, Rex made his way back to the booth and the bartender took his place back behind the bar.

What was I doing?
*I tried telling you.*
Contemplating, I stood there weighing what I should do. In the end, I knew I had to be hard and not soft, like some Barbie in front of these hardcore folk.

I headed in the direction of Rex sitting in the booth.

Keeping a stern look on my face, I walked slowly like I'd been in the place a hundred times instead of just once. A couple faces looked my way from the bar, but then they turned around and went back to their drinking. Bottles galore of liquor bathed the back shelving of the bar and

101

many stools were filled with who I assumed were the "regulars." A small section of one wall had a dartboard with many darts stuck in the wall next to it, and two pole tables were in the process of being played on by two men and women who stared me down like I was a foreigner who just made his way into the bar from some other country.

Walking the last stretch, I came to stand in front of Rex as he counted money that was sprawled out all over the booth's table. My figure cast a shadow over Rex's money. Sighing deeply, he stopped and looked up at me.

"What do you want?" His long beard and large frame made him look more ferocious.

Playing stupid, I said, "I'm looking for Rex."

Looking back down and counting his money, Rex said, "I'm him."

Removing my book bag from my back, I sat down in the booth across from Rex. "I was wanting to…." but Rex cut me short.

"Did I say you could sit, newbie?" Rex looked me right in the eye.

Two can play this game, I thought.

"No," I started to say, my foot shaking so Rex couldn't see, "but I did anyway."

*Wow, someone grew some guts.*

Rex again sighed deeply. "A smart mouth huh," he said sitting frozen still, "I used to break people like you just for fun." Starting to stand up, he said, "So here's what I'm gonna…." but then I cut Rex short.

"I'm looking to buy some guns and I hear you're the man to talk to." Rex was about halfway up when he decided to stop, resting his hands on the table. "I got three grand" - I really had four - "so you willing to work with me or not?" Instead of swallowing hard and looking nervous, I tried to sound smooth and look as tough as nails.

Rex then stood up, looked down at me with a smile, and said, "Well then, why didn't you just say so? Let's work."

And with that I had stood up, letting Rex lead me to some secret room in the back of his bar.

† † †

"You name it," Rex said when it was just him and I in a back office-like room with a plethora of guns in front of us, "I got it kid."

Standing, I looked over the many guns: handguns, automatic guns, semi-automatic guns, shotguns, and some other things in addition to guns, which included grenades, bulletproof vests, and other things I didn't want to ask Rex how he got his hands on. I'd never been much of a shooter in my life but I acted like I had in front of Rex. The room was like a small guns and ammo store, only these weapons were on the illegal list.

With my left arm across my abdomen and two fingers of my right hand on my chin, I scanned each gun wanting to make sure I got exactly what I would need.

*Hello! Job, it's me. Do you even see what you're getting yourself into?*

I know what I'm doing.

*You're fortunate T-Rex hasn't already made lunch meat out of you.*

Again, I know what I'm doing.

*Whatever you say J. It's not too late to back out.*

Picking up some guns and trying them out, Rex sat behind a desk that had assorted ammunition and gun manuals scattered on top of it. He could probably tell just by watching me that I was new to all of this.

"So how'd you hear about me?" Rex said leaning back on his chair.

"Word gets around." I said as few words as I could with a keep-things-to-myself demeanor about me.

Replacing a gun back on a table, I tried out at least a dozen more before making my decision. One in particular had Rufus Booker's name written all over it; that is, if I was ever able to track him down and meet him face to face. A shiny silver handgun also caught my attention; it made me think of Kevin Durgess' mocking grin in the courtroom. This would be just the one to make his smile go away.

I hadn't given any thought to Derek Westbrook just yet.

"I'll take these ones," I said to Rex, resting my hand on each of the three I had chosen. The shiny silver handgun, a shotgun to substitute for my old stolen one that was used to knock me out, and the one I had in mind for Booker.

"Nice taste," said Rex. "That silver .357 Magnum model 686 Plus and pump action shotgun are two of my favorites." He stood up and said, "The Sig Sauer is a nice choice too." I didn't know if he was serious about the comment or was just flattering me; after all, this was business, and he was, I'm sure, excited to be making another profit off another Joe Schmo.

"Three grand is enough to cover those," Rex went on to say.

I opened up my book bag and removed a wad of cash that was rubber-banded together. Tossing it on Rex's desk, he grabbed a large rugged duffle bag to put my guns in.

*Congratulations. You just made a deal with an illegal arms dealer.*

Not the wisest move, I know. At least nothing will come back on me.

"I'll tell you what kid," Rex started to say, "I like your style and quietness; I'm gonna throw in this bag, along with your guns, the manuals and enough ammo to last you a little while.

"And you know what," Rex went on, looking me up and down, "I'm gonna give you a couple grenades on the house."

My confused look told Rex I had no clue how to use a grenade. That's when Rex grabbed one and taught me grenade tactics 101.

"These are standard issue M26 grenades." He explained every part of the grenade and then told me what to do if I was to use it. "First, pull the safety pin," he started out, "and hold it correctly like this," he showed me, "making sure you don't release the safety lever, otherwise you better get rid of it in a hurry. Next, throw it, which will loosen the lever, which will engage the fuse, and then after three to four seconds...." Rex stopped. With his right hand he made a fist, and then he opened it up quickly and said, "Boom."

I didn't say a word; I only nodded my head. I had no idea what I would do with grenades, if anything, but I accepted the free additions gladly.

After packing my new purchases, Rex placed the duffle bag on a table in front of me. He then removed the rubber band and began counting the money I had tossed on his desk.

About halfway through counting, he said, "What's the guns for anyway, kid?"

With my book bag that Naomi had bought me strapped back onto my back, I lifted the duffle bag and rested the straps on my right shoulder.

"Personal business."

I then turned around, making my way toward the back entrance that Rex said I could take after we made the transaction.

Opening the door, Rex said behind me, "Kid, wait." I stopped, turning back around toward him. "There's four grand here."

"Yeah," I said, looking at him, "I know."

It hit Rex just then. "Appreciate it. You're always welcome here kid."

*Nice. If things go south at home, you can always move in with T-Rex.*

Not listening to you right now.

And with that I made my way out the back entrance, figuring I probably wouldn't ever see Rex again.

# 17

It got to the point where I was walking armed around Columbus, Ohio, looking for and asking about SSS, specifically the four who I wanted revenge on.

I went out mostly during nighttime and found myself talking to druggies, prostitutes, basically anybody who knew something about those who I was looking for. One night, I even found myself talking to some members of NEB, or the North End Boyz, the gang who opposed SSS. They didn't mind talking to me and were even glad to after I'd told them I had a vendetta out for SSS, specifically Booker, too.

How I walked around the cold, hard streets of Columbus and didn't get hurt or killed still shocks me. Maybe it was the look in my eyes, maybe it was my face that signified a fierce authority, I don't know, but nobody messed with me except on two occasions.

The first one a druggie thought he could just attack and get whatever he could off of me. It happened when I was walking down a side alley that had large dumpsters on either side of it. It had just finished raining minutes earlier and water was still dripping off the fire escapes of the old buildings. Bright lights from a downtown club reflected off puddles in the alley, and then that's when I heard the druggie's voice.

"Got any money man?" Looking down and to my side, the white guy sitting, leaning his back against one of the dumpsters looked like he hadn't showered for days and his face was so sunken in with spots of red on his cheeks that I was sure he was a user of methamphetamine.

Had he asked for food, I probably would've given him some money. But I knew what he really wanted money for. I acted like I didn't hear him and kept walking.

Without warning and with speed I didn't know the man possessed, he tackled me from behind, sending us both on the alley's hard surface. Turning onto my back, the night sky was deep dark, but the downtown club's lights lit some of it up like a pink and green rainbow.

Standing over me with a knife, the druggie said, "Give me whatever money you got, or else." He then took his knife and moved it across his throat, letting me know what the "or else" meant.

Adrenaline boosting within me, I kicked up at the open spot: the man's groin. He let out a loud yell and bent forward from the pain. Standing up and like a field goal kicker, I delivered a heavy kick to the man's face, and then he dropped to his side on the ground.

Removing the Sig Sauer from my waist, I pointed it at the man.

*J!!! What are you doing?*

I....don't....know.

My hands shook as I pointed the gun at the man. I knew I couldn't pull the trigger even if I wanted to. With tears filling my eyes, I looked in front and behind me. When I didn't see anyone, I sprinted to my truck and made my way back home.

That night I cried and actually prayed to God. I knew I'd been wrong to even place myself in that kind of environment in the first place, and I knew I had nobody else to blame except for myself. But I had already been drawn into this black abyss. Though I couldn't see every obstacle that I was causing to be placed in my way, revenge always hung on my heart like a Christmas ornament hangs from a tree.

My I-got-your-back-bro kinda being reminded me that night to turn to God and leave this matter behind me before things got worse.

God.

He was someone who many people said they believed in, but their lives showed they actually didn't care about Him as shown by how they were living their lives.

God.

He was someone people liked as long as they got to pick and choose what commands of His they wanted to follow.

God.

He was someone who I still believed in, but I also knew that He didn't agree with what I was doing. I didn't expect Him to permit me to live with what I was carrying out. Matter of fact, I expected He had death laid out somewhere on this dark road that I was traveling.

And you know what, I totally deserved it.

Death.

The second occasion when I was messed with was when I was at a nightclub asking certain questions about SSS. Specifically, I asked where Kevin "K-Dogg" Durgess and Tyrese "TT" Taylor hung out.

The club jammed some kind of techno/R&B music and younger people in their twenties were grinding on the dance floor. Sitting and drinking a glass of water at the bar, I happened to overhear a conversation next to me between a girl and guy who were drunk.

"Ty....Tyrese better wa....watch his back," said the guy who looked like he was in his mid-twenties. "My sister isn't some....some kinda toy, you know."

The girl wasn't as drunk. "You mean," she said looking at the guy, "your sister is one of many of Tyrese 'TT' Taylor's girlfriends?"

They had my full attention, especially when I heard the name "TT" Taylor being brought up.

"Un....unfortunately."

"You better talk to her and," she said taking another drink of whatever she was having, "you better not get too involved, otherwise you might end up dead."

I knew just what to do.

Acting intoxicated, I said, "Man bro, I hear you." They both looked over at me with annoyed looks. "I got a sister too who used to date 'TT' and," I took another drink of my water, which they were thinking was something else, "he got her knocked up and I wanna get even with him."

That seemed to spark their attentions, more so the guy.

*You're turning into a good liar. That's not good.*

I'm going to do whatever will get me face to face with these guys.

I went on. "If only I knew where he hung out." I took another drink and fake burped.

The girl looked at the guy she was with and nodded her head in my direction, like she was saying to him, "Go on, tell him. Better this guy deals with him than you."

He told me where Taylor hung out. I'm sure he wanted me to deal with him before he thought that his sister would be the next one "knocked up."

"He....he hangs out at Ricky's, you know, the arcade downtown on this end." I hadn't heard of the place, but I'd find out where it was. "That's where....where he sells drugs to the teens and does some of his dirty business for SSS."

I sat up straighter in my chair. "Is 'TT' there all the time?"

"Most of the time," the guy returned, "when he's not out causing all kinds of....of other trouble."

I didn't realize it until that moment, but the other guy in his low twenties sitting on the other side of me hung on every word I was saying. Getting a quick look at him, he left, so I figured that was the end of whatever that was.

The loud music changed to a different song just then. "Come on," said the girl who was with the drunk guy, grabbing him by his arm, "this is my song!" And with that, the girl hurried the guy out onto the dance floor.

At least I had found out that night where one of the members could be found. I hoped that my chances would follow suit for the rest. Finishing off my glass of water, I stood up and was going to make my way out of the club; but, when I turned around, I was denied that.

A black mid-twenties male stood in my way, a serious look on his face. I went to one of the sides of him to make my way past him, but when I did, again he stood in my way.

It didn't hit me until just then, but I was on the south side of town: SSS territory.

The young man spoke. "Why you asking about 'TT'?"

I attempted to make my way to the other side of him, but again he stood in my way and this time he placed a hand on my chest and pushed me back.

Who was this guy? Then I remembered the guy who sat next to me at the bar and left real quickly after I said the name "TT" a couple of times. To confirm my suspicion, I looked around and saw him eyeing me from the other end of the club.

"I said," the man in front of my face was saying, "why you asking about 'TT'?" He had a bandana wrapped around his head and a large chain around his neck. "If you're looking for trouble, you found it partner."

I didn't have time for this. The club was loud, people were standing all around shoulder to shoulder, and I did what would get me outta here quick.

*That's not a good idea J.*

Any better idea to get outta this?

Nothing in return. I was on my own.

Pulling the Sig out from my waist, I pressed the muzzle deep into this man's stomach. Nobody noticed. Then I thought quickly, why not add a bonus tonight.

The man's face fell and I could tell he didn't know what to do with my move. I acted like we were friends, got closer to him, checked his waist for a gun, and when I felt a small handgun, I removed it and stuck it into my pocket.

"You don't know what you're doing man. If I find you, I'm gonna...."

"Yeah yeah, you SSS members all talk the same. Do me a favor and shut up and listen, otherwise my gun's gonna go *pop pop*." I sounded smooth and acted tough, but just like I'd been in the alley with the druggie, I was all shakes inside.

108

"You get only one chance," I said before delivering the bonus round. "Kevin 'K-Dogg' Durgess. Where's he hang out?"

He didn't answer me. I then provided some persuasion. Keeping the muzzle dug in, I slid back the slide and let it go. That did this gangster in.

"Come on man, everybody knows where he hangs out."

Tilting my head back with my chin sticking out and my eyebrows going up to my forehead, I nonverbally told this man that I didn't know.

"He runs Bottoms Up, the strip club on 31st and Lewis!" he yelled over the music.

Two birds with one stone this night, I thought.

"Now what you gonna do?" said the man looking at me.

Another idea came to me. I got close to his ear, the music vibrating the floor below us. "This." I swung the gun hastily behind me and hammered it right into his stomach, sending him on his knees praying for air to fill his lungs.

*Who are you anymore?*

Like a running back juking defenders, I made my way through the club's maze, making it outside with no one behind me.

I took the gangster's gun out of my pocket and threw it into a trashcan outside the nightclub.

Running to the security of my truck, I sped back home.

† † †

Before the end of these two months, there were definitely things I would've done over again. For instance, I would've asked the gangster in the nightclub where Rufus Booker hung out, but unfortunately I was put on the spot and didn't think about it. Although, at the nightclub, I had asked about Kevin Durgess instead of Rufus Booker. Doesn't make sense, right?

But it didn't seem to matter because whoever I had talked to on the streets, or in clubs, or in bars didn't seem to know where Booker was, like he was some secret agent who only a few knew about. With this, I figured even the gangster in the nightclub didn't know where the kingpin of SSS was at. Plus, I wanted Booker to be the last one I dealt with; I had something very special planned for him, and I figured I'd have enough time to find out where he spent most of his time at.

Hopefully.

109

Like the board game chess, I wanted to eliminate Booker's lower ranks before I dealt with the king. Like the grand finale of a fourth of July fireworks display, I wanted to make for an explosive ending. I also figured my method of getting rid of and making disappear his "soldiers" below him would make him more vulnerable and more likely to make a mistake that would get him to come out of his hole like a snake. That's when I'd come in and remove the head from the serpent.

Removing Kevin Durgess and Tyrese Taylor from the picture would most definitely get Booker's attention; Derek Westbrook was probably someone he could care less about.

But how would I find out where he was even with going through all this? Would he come for me instead? Was it possible Rufus Booker would know that it was me all along causing this trouble?

Questions like these and many others were still all in the mix, but I was hoping that some of them - I prayed all of them - would be answered while delivering justice to those who had wronged me.

Like a teeter-totter going from one side to the next in my head, I still had my doubts that I could even go through with all this. Yes I had already purchased guns. Yes I had already partook in some violence with the druggie in the alley. Yes I had lied many times, even saying I had a sister who got "knocked up" just so I could find out where Tyrese "TT" Taylor hung out.

*And yes you even pulled a gun on a gangster and left him breathless on his knees at a nightclub.*

Thanks for mentioning.

Thinking about my faith that hung like a hangnail, I'd avoided prayer and God for a while now. I felt too guilty to talk to God when I had revenge and hatred in my heart. Knowing He wouldn't agree with my actions, I didn't expect Him to want to have anything to do with me.

The concoction between what started out at my home the night I killed DJ Booker, to finding Manhattan's head in a cardboard box, to the murder of my wife, to the "deal" that my attorney Spence Harper had planned, to the injustice in the courtroom....

Basically what I'm getting at is that it transformed me into a totally different person. The old me was deceased and the new had been given birth to. This once devout man of God was now a wandering sheep who lost his way. I had become a person who looked at right as wrong and wrong as right. Doing what was good was now dead to me and was replaced with revenge and getting even.

I had become a lost soul who turned his back on God.

110

One night, I did what many sinners did when they became aware of their sins and when they knew they had fallen short of God's standard: I prayed.

"God," I prayed on my knees with my elbows resting on my bed, "I don't know who I am anymore. I've done things I never thought I would ever do. I know I've been wrong and that turning my back on You isn't the way. But...." I opened my eyes to see the sparkling stars winking at me and the pale moon shining bright through my bedroom windows.

"But," I fumbled for words, "I know what's right, but the right seems weak and just giving up. God, I don't expect You to back me on this and I know I'm taking matters into my own hands." I closed my eyes, bowed my head, and went on, "I'm to leave revenge to You, I know, but," I sniffed, clearing my nose, "but this is just how it's going to be."

It didn't seem right praying to God when I already knew what I was going to do, like I really wasn't praying for His direction or decision. Just basically, well, I don't know what for certain.

"If I get through this, God, then I believe the hatred will be wiped away and my heart will be free of this burden. I'm not really sure what I'm asking for or getting at, but I do believe God, it's just...."

And that's when I stopped praying. The words I most certainly didn't have, like I was somewhat expecting God to understand my side of things and go along with it when He was sovereign, righteous, and holy. I wanted God to get me through this and I wanted to be the man I used to be, but I knew I could never be that man again until everything that I wanted to do was done.

I couldn't fall asleep that night as I thought about nothing but God.

Walking the mean streets of Columbus had made me tough, and the encounters with various people of different backgrounds had certainly made me "street smart" and more aware of my surroundings and the people in them. I'd seen some rough parts of Columbus with the areas our station covered on the medic, but the parts I'd seen lately were like different zones I didn't even know existed.

I had scoped out Ricky's arcade where Tyrese Taylor hung out and supposedly ran some sort of drug business. I'd stood outside Kevin Durgess' Bottoms Up without going in - I'd never been in a strip club in my life and didn't want to start - but I knew it was going to have to be in my plan to go in if I wanted the man.

Derek Westbrook I didn't even bother asking about. I didn't have the heart to mess with a kid, even if he had been in the wrong. It took me a while, but I finally came to grips with it; however, if he tried getting in my way, then that was another thing.

111

Paying people off for information had made much of my planning easy. I now knew layouts of the places I would soon be entering. The visiting of these places gave me something visual to keep in my head, like the snapshot with my eyes would store it permanently in my brain.

Like I said earlier, there's a lot of details and things that happened that I won't bore you with mentioning. But finally, the time had almost arrived to put my lengthy and painstaking work into action. Besides some minor details here and there, there was one large hole that still needed filled in to finalize my plan.

That's when the city of Mount Vernon came in handy.

# 18

Back in my hometown of Mount Vernon during one of the days of those two months, I found myself driving around looking at old buildings that had either been condemned, abandoned, or were structurally unsafe.

Even though buildings like these weren't supposed to be entered, the Mount Vernon Fire Department, as my brother told me, posted red placards with a white X on them to warn that no one under any circumstance was permitted to pass into such structures. Fines were said to have been handed out in such matters if the trespasser had been caught.

Condemned, abandoned, or structurally unstable buildings are great places to store something or to even stay at - if you're willing to take the risk - because they're vacant and people know that they're dangerous and that something bad could happen in them at any time.

A place like this is just what I was looking for.

I remembered the old PPG (Pittsburgh Plate Glass) building and made my way out toward it. Years ago, some local arsonists tried burning the place down, but the building was so sound and made of excellent materials that it withstood the damage. Sitting in my truck scanning the area, this definitely would be a great place for my business if it weren't for some new Ariel Park that was being planned for.

I continued my search.

I thought of another building that was just outside Mount Vernon in a little city called Centerburg. The only reason I thought of it was because it used to be a haunted house where I had gone to as a kid. One night, when we were younger, I took Naomi on a cool autumn night and she couldn't keep her hands off me as people dressed in all sorts of monster-like costumes jumped out at us. Before it was a haunted house the old brick, multi-storied building had been a Bible college.

*Bible....God....you getting the quiet message of maybe turning away from this now?*

Nice try.

113

Pulling into a small drive to the side of the ancient building, it still towered like a castle and heavy, thick green ivy covered most of it. Bricks had fallen off from age and it still had that haunted look all over it. Unfortunately, this building wouldn't do either.

A golf course butted right up against this old building. Too much attention was already drawn here and I definitely couldn't risk getting caught. Golf, I hated golf.

*Golf requires goofy pants anyway.*

HaHa! Thanks for the laugh.

Again, I continued my search.

After about another hour or so, I was driving on the brick street of North Mulberry, and then that's when I was finally hopeful about what I was looking for.

The abandoned Mount Vernon High School building that was built in 1939.

The old MVHS took up an entire block and used to be quite a sight to see, or so I'm told. It still stood tall and somewhat proud, but it had definitely aged over the years and looked nothing like what people used to say about it.

However, adding to my hopes, it had no trespassing signs around the entire perimeter and those red fire department placards were on every side of the building I found out after driving around the antique-looking high school. The brick building, like the old Bible college, had ivy growing on it, holes were in many of the windows from kids throwing rocks through them, and nailed plywood had substituted many of the other windows.

The front and sides of the building would be too risky for my business, but the back of the building was made just for what I would be carrying out.

In the back of the abandoned MVHS, an abundance of pine trees and other trees provided absolute privacy. It was like a boxed-in forest in the back that had an old basketball court that was now clothed in grass from over the years. No houses could be seen as the trees touched the building on both sides, and the faded limestone drive led up to the back of the building. A rusted gate blocked off the back entrance, but that was easy to open and re-close; and as long as I turned my headlights off before approaching this back way, there was no way anyone would know I was even here.

This was the perfect place.

*It's also perfect for getting caught and getting busted.*

It's perfect.

But just to make sure, I made a phone call to my brother.

Cyrus worked for the city of Mount Vernon, and he knew things about the guts of the city that most people didn't know about. If I wanted something answered about something in this city, Cyrus was just the man to talk to.

After entering the password on my iPhone, I clicked on my Favorites and pressed Cyrus.

"Hello," came my brother's voice.

"Hey bro, how you doing?" I tried to sound like I was in a good mood.

"Hey bro. Doing great. How you holding up?"

"All right. Hey, got a question." I wanted to make this fast.

"Ask it."

"I'm in MV today...." but Cyrus cut me off.

"You're home? You shoulda gave me a heads up. Stop on out."

"Maybe I will if I have time."

Cyrus paused and then said, "Sorry, back to your question."

"What's up with the old high school on Mulberry?" I wanted every detail explained, so I then said, "The red placards, the no trespassing signs, you know, the works?"

Cyrus went on to explain. "The red placards with the white X the Mount Vernon Fire Department put up to let everyone know that the building's unstable and is hazardous to life. Basically, keep out and away. The no trespassing signs have been placed everywhere to keep people out who'd lived in there and for the kids who have broken most of the windows." Cyrus then stopped to sneeze.

"Bless you."

"Thanks bro," said Cyrus.

*Bless you? See, J, there's still good in you.*

Cyrus carried on where he left off. "There's also neighborhood watch signs posted to add to the red placards and no trespassing signs. So far," Cyrus continued, "nobody has been found inside for the past few months and the place has been totally left alone."

I jumped in to find out more from Cyrus. "My gish, that place got cameras too and people watching over it?" I laughed to make the conversation smooth.

Cyrus laughed and then said, "No, nothing like that Job. No cameras or people watching over it." My joke hid my true intention and worked.

*You're getting good, but in a bad way.*

"Some guy who works for the city had checked the place once a month, usually the first, and he'd told us city guys that all's clear. So," I heard a door close in the background, "they had him stop checking since the past few months have shown nada going on in the place."

More information that I didn't even need to ask for. I hated using my own brother like this, but I needed to make sure before I delved into my business.

"I shouldn't be telling you what I'm about to say next Job," Cyrus went on, "but you're my brother and I know my words are safe with you." Cyrus paused again before saying, "The red placards the fire department posted are real, but the message they're sending is bogus."

"How so bro?"

"That building's not really unstable." Cyrus explained. "The city basically made MVFD put those signs up to instill scare and fear into anybody thinking about passing through that old high school's doors. And guess what," Cyrus said, "it worked. Nobody seems to have entered since."

"Interesting." This was all sweet music to my ears.

"Now the city is hoping someone comes in, buys it, and does something with the place."

"Say," Cyrus inquired after a short moment later, "why you asking about the old 1939 high school?"

I had to scramble to come up with something. "I was driving around and happened to pass the old high school. Was just wondering what was up with it."

*Real smooth.*

"Got ya."

"Well, all right bro," I said to Cyrus, "I'm gonna get off here. I have another stop before I head home."

"I hope you have two, which includes my house."

"I'll try." I never did make it out to Cyrus' house.

"All right Job. Love ya man."

"Love you too Cyrus." I ended the call.

This was the perfect place.

A few days later, during the middle of the month, I'd made my way into the old MVHS building one night getting through a door I had did some research on.

Thank you YouTube.

After walking around all the floors of the entire building and studying it, there were no blankets or sign that this was anybody's home, and there was no sign that the place had even been broken into recently. There was ample space, many rooms, and the lower floors of the building, especially the dark, dungeon-like basement, would serve just fine.

The inside of the old school resembled a warzone. Broken tiles, fractured bricks, and other materials served as the floor. Holes, some large, could be accidentally stepped into on the upper floors, causing one to fall to either their death or a terrible injury down below. Retired and rusted bathroom sinks and toilets were scattered in several rooms, and old student desks and auditorium chairs were in others. Two ancient basketball hoops barely held in the old gymnasium, and graffiti was written on its walls. Corroded pipes ran throughout the abandoned school, the staircases to get from one floor to the next creaked, and the old MVHS was nothing like it used to be. There was so much more I could say about this place, but at least you now have some kinda idea.

I wanted my victims to be far from home. This place suited me well.

This was just the place I needed. The only other thing was to start setting up everything inside. That final large hole in my plan had just been filled.

Everything would soon be ready.

&#8225;     &#8225;     &#8225;

At the end of these two months, the finishing touches had been applied and I had everything ready as best as I could. Many hours and labor went into all of it, but I believe that I was finally ready.

For some reason unknown to me, Rufus Booker and SSS kept away from me. Even after looking over the security camera footage every day and night at my house, still there was no sign of those who had killed my wife.

Why hadn't they come back for me? I was always ready and prepared for them, day and night, when I wasn't out perfecting my plan. Did Booker know I was just now a suffering and broken man without my wife and that's what he wanted to leave me as? Knowledge of me being alive was certainly told to him after the courtroom showdown with his cronies. Was I just now someone worthless to them who they didn't care about messing with anymore? Still so many questions lingered, but I didn't care anymore because one thing was set in stone.

I was ready and going after them whether they'd forgotten about me or not.

But for the moment I let all these questions and thoughts and concerns sweep away with the breeze, because I had just pulled into Mound View Cemetery. I felt compelled to see my wife one last time before I avenged her murder.

I'd thought about Naomi a lot over the past two months and I'm sure she was rolling in her grave from my behavior, my attitude, and my new way of life. I knew she wouldn't have agreed with me taking revenge and doing the things I would soon be doing, as well as the things that I had done already.

I had always heard people say, "I would've...." or, "This is what I would have done...." or, "If I were in that person's shoes, let me tell you, I would've...." but talk is cheap, and most people wouldn't even do a quarter of the things that spewed forth from their mouth. Currently, I was in one of those situations, but I was actually going to let my actions speak for themselves.

People always thought they knew what they would do in certain situations; however, when placed in that position, did any of us actually really know what we would do? I, for one, never saw myself being in the position I was in, let alone even thinking about the things that I thought I might do; but now here I was, just about ready to put my thoughts, desires, and images into action.

Closing my truck door, I made my way to Naomi. God created a beautiful day with the sun shining bright yellow and puffs of clouds that resembled extra large pillows hovered overhead. Blowing my hair with a moderate force, the wind felt good. The green grass made that soft crunch sound with every step I took. Most people never thanked God for giving them another day to live and enjoy, but here I was thanking Him when my heart was in the wrong.

I stood before Naomi's gravesite and looked down at her name. The groundsmen had done a good job because I didn't have to remove any grass clippings or tidy up the flowers that had recently been placed on top of her stone. The sun swept over my wife's name, making it shine like a gem.

Kneeling down on one knee, I looked over the cemetery; I was the only one here. That's when I had my last conversation with my wife before I went through with what I was about to do.

"Hey babe, I...." I started to choke up, but I fought the urge to cry back. "I have no more tears, no more sense, and lately, I feel like no more heart." I paused to look up to the sky and then back to her name, like her face was before me having a conversation. "I know what I'm about to do isn't right but," I paused again. This was so hard. "But it's the only thing I know to do. I need justice, I need to make things right, I need....I need....you." That's when a wave of emotion came crashing into me, but tears I had none for.

I carried on. "I'm not gonna say I'm doing this for you, because you wouldn't want this and I know you don't want me to put myself

118

through it because it's wrong. But," the wind blew stronger in my face, "but just know that I love you so much and I did the best I could to be a good husband and make you happy in life. You brought meaning, hope, love, and joy to my life and heart." Something spiritual came outta me next.

"You lived how Jesus, our Savior, wanted you to, and it's because of you that He's still alive in my heart with the smallest bit of faith I have left. I still believe and trust in Him, but I'm slipping and," I had a hard time finding words, "well, you know what I'm getting at. I know I'm not doing as He would want me to, and I can only pray that He will forgive me for what I'm about to do if I get through it alive."

I concluded. "Know Naomi, my lovely and beautiful wife, that your husband loves you and that this love we still share lives on even though you aren't here with me." I arose from my kneeling position, the sun warming my face. "Too me, baby."

I turned around, put my black sunglasses on, and made my way back the way I came. But when I turned around and put those sunglasses on, something old fell off me and was replaced with newness, like I was some kind of animal that shed its skin and was transformed into something totally different.

I can't quite put the feeling into words, but it was similar to a Dr. Jekyll/Mr. Hyde sort of sensation. I was the same person, but something had changed. One heart I still beat with, but there was a quiver that gave it new blood. Like a young irresponsible punk who had grown to become disciplined and mature after going through basic training in the military, I was made of something the same but also different.

Turning back around before coming to my truck, a cardinal bird stood on top of Naomi's gravesite. Maybe it was a different one than the one I saw the first time I visited my wife, but a feeling inside told me it was the same one.

I smiled.

I'm pretty sure it was the only smile I had shown over the past two months. I wanted to cry, but there was no more room for tears.

Revenge had to be delivered with a two-edged sword. I'd go over the details one last time although I'd gone over them a hundred times.

One day I would let pass, and then the next day was Saturday. A Saturday night when Ricky's arcade would be hopping and full of people, and a night when Tyrese "TT" Taylor would meet the new Job McCants.

The time had come.

# 19

Rogue.

There are many different definitions of the word in the dictionary, but one in particular seemed to fit me perfectly: no longer obedient, belonging, or accepted and hence not controllable or answerable.

I no longer obeyed many laws, both moral and civil.

The society I lived in I felt I didn't belong to anymore.

Accepted? My behavior and actions most definitely wouldn't be that.

Like a wild fire, I would be beyond the control of many.

That left answerable. God was the only One who I would have to answer to in the end.

Standing outside Ricky's arcade, this is who I had become.

Across the street, I looked at Ricky's where many youngsters of all ages stood in front of the popular arcade on the sidewalk. Some were black, some were white, and some were even Mexican. A small group stood in a circle smoking cigarettes, others were making conversation with the opposite gender, and some checked their pockets making sure they had enough money to play games.

Or to buy drugs.

How could someone like Tyrese "TT" Taylor sell drugs to kids and think that was an honest living? But he wasn't an honest person, I thought, and drugs was a way of life for him.

The sign for RICKY'S shined bright red above the sidewalk and a bird had made a nest in the R where it formed a circle. Flickering on and off was the apostrophe that separated the Y from the S.

Everything to the side of the building was laid out and ready in front of the arcade's large bathroom window. The car I rented was parked in the alley in front of the heap of black trash bags that stood next to a dumpster.

I paid some guy on the streets off a week ago in advance to keep a watch on my rented car. The other half, I told him, would be paid when I was finished - to make sure he wouldn't snub me.

Looking quickly down the alley, there Al stood with his back up against the rented car acting like it was his.

All was going as planned.

Taking a deep breath, I started to make my way across the street to the arcade dressed as I was with a briefcase in my hand. This was actually it; I was beginning what I had planned.

I was commencing my revenge.

Arcade anthems and video game tunes screamed loudly out on the street from within Ricky's from double doors that were wide open to the public. Teens and young adults probably ranging from fourteen to twenty-some years of age looked me over wondering what a well-dressed man like me was doing walking into a place like this.

When I made it to the double doors, I turned around, rested my briefcase on the ground, and dug each of my hands into the pockets on my side. A couple young men in their twenties gave me a weird look, and one even grabbed for his waist, I'm assuming getting ready to place a hand on his firearm.

Before he could though, I shouted, "Kids," that's when I had all their attentions as their eyes affixed on me, "have fun!" That's when I removed from my pants pockets two large handfuls of one-dollar bills and tossed them in the air. Instead of white snow, it was green paper falling from the sky.

Looking at the young man who thought about grabbing his gun, he decided to rest his arm down to his side after he saw what I had done. The kids went crazy catching George Washington's in the air and picking them up off the sidewalk.

This was all part of the plan. Get everybody happy and keep them busy, which would keep them away from what I was really doing here.

Picking up my briefcase and turning around, I made my way into Ricky's.

Childhood hit me like a slap to the face as I recognized games I'd played as a kid. A Mario Brothers game was being played by a little kid who appeared to be with his older brother, NFL Blitz was being played by two older kids who looked pretty competitive playing against each other, and a huge X-Men game that could hold up to six players at one time was swamped with teens of several ages.

To my right were older boys competing against each other in Super Shot Basketball, you know, the game where you have so much time to make as many baskets as you can before time runs out. Lined up on my left was Skee-Ball where a group of older girls looked across the room smiling at the boys playing Super Shot Basketball.

The place reeked of cigarette smoke and sweat, but overall it was a pretty cool hangout for kids.

That is, except for the drugs.

I looked toward the back of the arcade where the twenty-some-year-olds hung out, some sitting and some standing around tables that were polluted with ashtrays, cigarettes, and beer bottles. But what had my attention more were the white packages and grocery-looking plastic bags that also covered the tops of these tables.

Drugs. I just couldn't tell exactly what.

And sitting in the middle of them all was just the man who I had come for.

Tyrese "TT" Taylor.

He wore a backwards hat with a large chain sporting on his chest. Tattoos on his neck with a gold watch wrapped around his right wrist, he sure did act like he was something big. I happened to see a couple teens make their way up to him, but Taylor let some other guys sitting next to him handle the business as there was a trade-off between money from the teens and whatever drug was being removed from a plastic bag by Taylor's guys.

Mary Jane (Marijuana), X (Ecstasy), and Heroine were huge these days, so maybe that's what was in the plastic bags. I figured cocaine was probably what was in the white packages that had duct tape wrapped around them.

The teens walked away and I shook my head in disgust. What was this world coming to? Dealing with "TT" Taylor was going to be my pleasure.

Just then, with what I was hoping for, one of Taylor's men got up from sitting down and made his way toward me. Passing me as if I was invisible, he walked over to a couple kids playing Street Fighter and got close to the ear of one of them and whispered something into it.

Taylor's guy turned around and was heading back to the table.

*This is your last chance to turn around before maybe getting yourself killed.*

Nah, this is it.

*So be it.*

Before Taylor's guy walked past me, I said, "When you and 'TT' wanna stop playing kids games and step up to the big leagues like real men, let me know."

The man, dressed similar to Taylor, looked at me like I just embarrassed him in front of a crowd and said, "What'd you just say?"

122

With a cold hard look, I said, "You heard me."

My attire as well as my comment about the "big leagues" must've gotten this gangster's attention, because he didn't reply negatively or wanna start something. The briefcase helped the cause out too.

"My associates," I went on, "are interested in Mr. Taylor's work and would like to do business; that is," I said somewhat condescendingly, "if he's willing to man-up and leave children's games behind."

I spoke professionally with a hint of exaltation so that this guy would know that I meant business and was for real.

Looking toward Tyrese Taylor sitting down, he saw that one of his friends was talking to some stranger who he didn't recognize. He stared at us for a long moment, like there was something important being discussed that he wanted to be a part of.

I also noticed that the young man who grabbed for his gun before I made my way into Ricky's was now standing behind Tyrese. They both looked at me, the young man whispering something into "TT's" ear. Tyrese nodded his head and stared at me.

He didn't recognize who the man was wearing the nice suit who had his hair grown out along with a nicely trimmed beard. He didn't notice it was me, Job McCants, whose wife he helped kill along with the other three members of SSS.

Probably seeing dollar signs spinning in his head for himself, Taylor's guy who stood by me said, "I'll have to talk to 'TT.' What exactly are you offering?"

I wasn't going to give this guy any details because there were none. Inside, I knew what I was offering: revenge.

"You tell Mr. Taylor if he's interested," I started to say, "to meet me in the back bathroom," and then I stressed the last word, "alone."

"So it's gonna be like that, huh?" I'm sure Taylor's guy was wanting to know more so he could have some idea what this was all about.

Giving a dirty look, I said, "It's gonna be just like that." Taylor's guy didn't know what to say. "If these simple orders can't be followed, then we know there's no business to be done here."

Exhaling forcefully through his nostrils, like someone had just talked down to him, Taylor's guy walked away and went in the direction of "TT."

That's when I gave "TT" and his table a long, solid stare, and then I made my way to the back bathroom of Ricky's arcade.

† † †

The back bathroom of Ricky's was actually not as bad as I thought it might be. Many autographs and messages were written on the doors of the bathroom stalls, paper towels were scattered on the ground next to the wastebaskets and sinks, and the off-white tiled walls had cracks like an earthquake occurred within them years ago.

Besides that the room was somewhat kempt.

When I entered the bathroom and after I placed my briefcase on a bench next to one of the sinks, I thought about what I was actually getting ready to do. The months of planning, the days spent making sure everything was just right, and the work that I spent countless hours on to make this vision an actual reality was finally ready to be unleashed.

Would Tyrese Taylor really enter this room, or was I going to wait around until he never showed and then leave? Was he going to take the bait I laid out for him and bite it with thinking that I had something great to offer him, or would he ignore who he thought was a stranger who basically said he played children's games and hadn't made it big time yet? And was I really able to go through with what I had planned for so long, or would I get cold feet at the last moment and not be able to do any of it?

*Cold feet are better than dead, buried feet.*

Nice. Appreciate that.

*Just trying to get you to turn that other way J.*

Really? I hadn't thought so.

Obviously, I was being sarcastic as I stood toward the back of the bathroom facing the entrance.

*Nice. Appreciate that.*

I thought you....

That's when the door to the bathroom opened and making his way in and closing the door behind him, and locking it, was Tyrese "TT" Taylor. Number one of three enemies who I had marked for judgment.

*Your show now. I'm out.*

He looked at my briefcase, smiled, and then looked back my way. "You armed?"

I shook my head.

"Take off your jacket and then do a three-sixty," he raised his chin up at me, "just to make sure." I did as he asked and after I was done, he was satisfied.

"You next," I said impassively. "And go ahead and show me the insides of your pockets and lift up the bottoms of your pants while you're at it," I said raising my chin, "just to make sure." I wanted to make sure I was hardcore and that he knew I was the one in the room who had the upper hand.

Control meant a lot here.

After doing a circle while lifting up his shirt so I could see his waist, and then raising the bottoms of his pants, Taylor had no weapon.

He thought he could trick me, but I'm thorough. "Pockets. Now."

Sighing deeply, Taylor lifted all his pockets, but the last one happened to have a small handgun in it. His face changed, like he'd just been caught stealing a cookie from the cookie jar as a child.

"That's not a good start, Mr. Taylor."

He looked at me, waiting for some kind of order.

"Toss it in the toilet." Taylor walked to the first stall. "No," I said, "the second one." From nervousness, I peed in that one while waiting on him to show up. It had been bright yellow and I didn't flush.

"Man, somebody peed in this one," Taylor said standing outside the stall. I almost laughed, but I held it in.

"Mr. Taylor," I said in a serious tone.

But then something unexpected happened, something I hadn't planned for. Walking away from the second stall and pointing the gun at me, Taylor said, "Why not just end you now?"

My heart racing almost outta my chest, I remained calm.

*I'm back in. Now what? J, you shoulda listened to….*

Shut up! Let me think.

"I said," Taylor said again, "why not just end you now?"

Trying to find words like in a word search, I said with authority, "You do that, Mr. Taylor, and you won't make it out of Ricky's alive." A total bluff, but I had nothing else. I added, "And you can go ahead and kiss hundreds of thousands, possibly even millions someday goodbye in the process as well." Again a bluff, but money made people think differently.

Taylor weighed the option; it was like I could see what he was thinking through his forehead. In the end, he lowered the gun and tossed it from where he stood into the toilet of the second stall. The splash confirmed it.

*Phew, that was close pal.*

You're telling me.

"Why me?" asked Taylor.

"Because when we see a winner, we know we gotta have him on our team." I totally lied.

"Who's we?"

"You'll find out soon enough." I had him just where I wanted him.

"Do I know you?"

Anger arose within me, but I held it in check. "Kind of."

Taylor then blabbed for a while. "I knew you were the real deal man." He was probably sucking up after contemplating about killing me, or, on second thought, he looked like he was serious about the comment.

125

"My boy told me you were making money rain outside, and when I see this fancy dressed guy come into my place looking all serious and business-like, I knew there was something big about him."

I barely listened to him; I actually couldn't believe Tyrese didn't recognize me. Guess my new look really hid the old me.

"And," Taylor blabbed on, "you're saying I'm gonna make thousands, possibly millions?" He was getting overly excited and dreaming about what this could mean for him. "What's the details and when do we start?"

I said with a smile on my face, "Now."

"Really?" Taylor smiled back, teeth full of gold.

"Let me show you some figures that are in my briefcase, but first," I said walking toward the bench where my briefcase was, "you want to see your new car as a token of our appreciation?"

Taylor's eyes widened. "What?"

Making it to my briefcase, I didn't open it just yet. "Stand on top of that bench over there and look out the bathroom window into the alley." The large window of the arcade's bathroom I had already opened before Taylor made his way in. A bench stood below the window although it wasn't too high up.

He laughed happily and said, "No way."

Making his way over, passing me, and standing on top of the bench, Taylor looked out. That's when I opened my briefcase and took hold of what was inside.

"What," Taylor started to say, "that's the car?" He was dissatisfied. "That things a piece of...." he then cursed.

He turned to look at me, but when he did, he had the muzzle of my .357 Magnum staring him right between the eyes. He was totally caught off guard and didn't know what to do except look petrified.

"Do you recognize me?" I said.

"I'm gonna kill...."

I hit him lightly on the side of his face with the .357; however, the laceration from my hit made his face start to bleed.

"Shut up. Listen." I was meaner than a snake now. "Look at me. Do you recognize me now?" It was like I was pleading for him to see the old, real me.

With blood streaming down the side of his face, Tyrese Taylor looked long and hard at me. I hoped he would see past the beard and could picture me without long hair. His eyes narrowed, like he was studying my face hard, and then that's when his eyes widened like he had just seen a ghost.

"You."

I didn't say a word, at first. I just let the moment stay frozen with him now knowing who I was. Finally, I spoke.

"Look back outside."

He wasn't sure about what I asked of him. Scared, he paused, and then said, "Man don't kill me here. Not like this." Begging, his eyes started to get watery.

"I'm only saying this one more time," I said touching the muzzle of the gun to his forehead, "look back outside!"

*Job, look at what you're....*

Butt out.

Trembling, Taylor slowly turned toward the window standing on the bench and looked outside. He wasn't very heavy and I knew I could handle his weight. Anticipating like I was going to kill him, he put both hands on his head and tensed his body like a taut rope.

The night they killed Naomi came back to me like a memory I would never be able to forget. I remembered Tyrese Taylor's laughter that night, I remembered him slapping hands with Kevin "K-Dogg" Durgess after Durgess knocked me to the ground, I remembered he too shot Naomi, I remembered....

And with that, I hit Taylor hard on the back of his head with the .357. His body instantly went limp, but I jumped on the bench, dropped the .357, and held him up; and with an anger-filled strength, I lifted him up and pushed his body out the window. A loud sound was heard next, but I knew what it was: the body of Tyrese "TT" Taylor coming down hard on top of a dumpster's impact lid. Looking out the window, I saw his body roll until it fell on top of some black trash bags below.

Tucking the gun between my waist and belt, I hurled the briefcase outside, grabbed my jacket off the ground and put it back on - I didn't want anything left behind - jumped out the window, landed on top of the dumpster's lid, and then jumped down onto the alley's hard surface.

Al stood and watched the whole thing outside. I didn't have time to look at his face to see what he thought.

Opening the back door closest to me, I threw the briefcase inside, took my jacket off and tossed it inside as well, and ran to Taylor's body.

"Al, help me get him in the trunk." Without hesitating, Al opened the trunk and helped me lift "TT's" body. Putting his body in, I slammed the trunk down. Closing the side door, I looked at Al as I breathed heavily with beads of sweat starting to roll down my head and face.

Al was overweight, black, and had a scruffy beard. His face was kind and I came to find out he lived on the streets. I paid him well for his service.

Digging into my pocket, I pulled out the remainder of what I owed him. "Al," I said looking at him, "I'm a man of my word. Two hundred then and two hundred now." I put ten twenty-dollar bills into his hand.

"Thanks sir," said Al.

"No," I said, "thank you Al."

I ran to the driver's seat, started up the rent-a-car, but I didn't put it into drive. Instead, I rolled down my window and had one last thing to say to Al.

"Hey Al."

"Yes sir," he said approaching my driver's side door.

"Is that where you live, outside the apartment complex on Jefferson?"

"Yes sir. That's where I can be found."

"All right, thanks. Your service might be needed again."

Al smiled. "With pay like this, you got it."

I put the rent-a-car into drive and made my way to Mount Vernon.

# 20

Tyrese "TT" Taylor sat tied to a chair in the old Mount Vernon High School with an IV in his left arm. Duct tape adhered to his mouth and his face was filled with horror. Looking around the dark, damp, and old smelling basement of the MVHS, Taylor wondered where on earth he was.

After I left Ricky's with him stashed in the trunk of my rent-a-car, I drove to Mount Vernon. With headlights off and slowly going up the faded limestone driveway of the old high school, I stealthfully parked up against the back door. From there, I transported the unconscious Taylor over my shoulder inside to the dungeon-like basement. I must've hit him harder on the back of his head with the .357 than I thought I had, because it took a splash of water in his face to awaken him.

I lived and learned from this for the next time. By next time I meant for Kevin "K-Dogg" Durgess.

It had been very early in the morning when I got him tied up and situated just how I wanted him; so before dawn arose, I left the school and stayed at a cheap motel in Mount Vernon so I could stay close instead of being further away in Columbus. I didn't say anything to him while getting him tied up and secured to the chair, though he had much to say to me. When I was finished, I just gave him a long stare in his eyes, hit the lights off as I made my way out, and left him in the darkness.

Now here I was one night later looking into the eyes of one of the men who killed my wife. I wondered that night in the motel what he was thinking.

What did he think with knowing it was me who did this to him? What did he think I would do to him? What would he try to say or do in his present condition?

I had a hard time sleeping in the motel last evening, but things would get easier after dealing with "TT" Taylor. Doing many things the first time was difficult, but with practice, one eventually became well versed in those same things. After dealing with Taylor, dealing with Kevin Durgess and Rufus Booker would be like a walk in the park.

129

Surprisingly, finding out during my planning stage, electricity still ran throughout some of the building, particularly the lower section. Maybe it had been left on from when the guy who worked for the city checked on the place during the previous months like Cyrus told me about and they forgot to turn it off. I didn't know and I didn't care, but I was glad I was able to use it instead of having to run generators or do what I wanted to do by some other means.

The basement of the old high school was in desperate need of dehumidifiers, an old pipe dripped water that echoed throughout the room, and one of the tubular fluorescent lights overhead kept flickering off and back on. This room with all its contents was like something taken out of a *Saw* movie.

I removed the duct tape from Tyrese Taylor's mouth slowly so he would feel some discomfort.

Testing and making him feel like he was some sorta lab experiment, I started things off.

"State your name," I said to Taylor.

"Wha....what?"

I rolled my eyes. "Who are you?"

"I'm....I'm Tyrese Taylor." He gave me an odd look. "But you already know that."

I went on. "And you're the member of what gang?"

He didn't answer.

"What gang do you belong to, Tyrese 'TT' Taylor?"

"S....SSS."

"Thank you, Tyrese 'TT' Taylor of SSS, now, tell me all you know, from the time you first came to my house with DJ Booker till the time you killed my wife." I got right to the point.

With his arms tied behind him and his legs tied to the bottom of the chair, Taylor looked at me scared, like he couldn't believe the position he was currently in. "How'd....how'd you...." but I cut him off.

"How'd....how'd" I mocked him, "how'd we come to this position? Short and sweet, I've been walking, talking, and getting to know the streets, SSS, and, of course, the men who killed my wife."

It was like his face dropped even more after I mentioned him being a part of killing Naomi. "But that's not why you're here. You're here to answer my questions, or else."

"Or....or else what?" Taylor said with both fear and wonder in his voice.

I paced back and forth and then looked at Taylor right in the eye. "Do you know what happens," I started to say to Taylor, "when the human body is withheld a sedative and given only a paralytic agent instead?"

I knew what would happen, but I'm sure Taylor didn't.

He was lost by the look on his face. "What....what do you mean?"

I walked over to a workbench near Taylor and grabbed a vial of Vecuronium along with a needle and syringe.

"This," I said holding up the Vecuronium and showing Taylor, "is a medication that will paralyze your body, and that," I said pointing to his left arm, "is an IV that's connected to that sodium chloride bag you see hanging beside you." I used some rope that I tied around an overhead pipe with a coat hanger hanging upside down connected to it to use as a hook to hang the sodium chloride bag from.

Sodium chloride was basically salt water. Every patient that I'd started an IV on in the back of the squad received fluid from a bag of sodium chloride.

Turning the vial of Vecuronium upside down and inserting the needle through it, I drew the medication out of the vial into the syringe, all while holding it up and out in front for Taylor to witness.

Though the room was cool, I saw small drops of sweat starting to form on Taylor's forehead. His knees shook a little, and it even seemed that his face grew a little pale in color.

"If you don't tell me what I wanna know," I said taking a step toward the IV bag, "then I'm going to administer this paralyzing medication through your IV line. And if I do that, well, I'm sure you're smart enough to figure out what happens next."

Taylor shook in his chair, but even with what strength he could muster, he only moved the chair maybe half of an inch.

"Relax 'TT'," I said. "Just answer my questions and all will be well for you."

Although I had him peeing in his pants and I could tell he knew what would happen if I pushed this medication into his IV line, I said anyway, "Many real life people have been paralyzed for surgery, Taylor," I said taking a step backwards, "but many of those same people came out of unconsciousness during the surgery to feel the pain and later recalled certain events." I said to make him cringe even more with a smile on my face, "The term's called 'anesthesia awareness' and many have suffered psychiatric/psychological damage as a result." I wanted him to think I was a complete psycho and someone who was off his meds.

I concluded, "The things I could do to you while you're paralyzed are many, but I wanted to forewarn you what can happen if you don't answer my questions." Raising my eyebrows and tilting my head back, I said, "Do I make myself clear?"

Taylor nodded his head quickly several times and said, "Ye....yes."

131

I then began my interrogation.

"Whose call was it to make the hit on my house in the first place?"

Swallowing hard, Taylor responded, "Rufus's."

"Why?"

Looking down, Taylor said, "Part of our initiation process."

"Why my house?"

"No reason. It was just the one Rufus said stop at."

"And let me guess," I started to say, "Rufus came back to avenge his brother's death?"

Taylor nodded without saying a word.

"You'll have to forgive me because I was in a coma, but it was you, Rufus, and who was the other big-named SSS member who was at my house the night you all killed my wife?"

"Ke...." I could tell Taylor didn't wanna tell, but finally he said, "Kevin Durgess."

I tried to think of other questions, but right now my mind was drawing a blank for some reason.

Taylor asked a question instead. "How'd you find me?"

I looked at him with an all-serious face. "Don't worry about that. Just shut up and sit there." I raised the syringe in my hand to instill some fear into him.

He shut up pretty quick.

Not that I was going after him, but I had a question about someone who had crossed my mind a couple of times. "Derek Westbrook," I said lowering the syringe, "where's he been at?"

Shaking his head, Taylor said, "Derek left the gang after we saw you in the court room. He never did act the same after your...." but he stopped mid sentence.

"Go ahead and say it you punk." I knew what Taylor was going to say. "He never acted the same after what happened at my house the night you all killed my wife."

The room went dead silent. Taylor's head hung so low that I thought he might lose it.

"Let me guess," I went on, "the kid's first real experience?"

Again Taylor nodded.

"Tell me all you can about SSS."

At length, Taylor filled me in on his gang, their birth, their spread, and what they did. I already knew a lot of what he told me, and it still made me sick with how human beings could act in such evil ways.

From drugs, to guns, to home invasions, to murders, to money, SSS ranked number one on Ohio's most notorious list.

"We're spread out through a lot of the city and are getting bigger," he said at one point. "Black, white, Mexican, you name it, they're all in the mix with SSS," he said like he was proud of this fact.

That made me think of something. If they met and did things together, then that meant meeting places.

"Where do you all meet up at, and is there a main base of operation?"

Taylor was reluctant at first, but then answered, "You found one already, Ricky's arcade, which is where I do my business. There's a strip club...." but I cut Taylor off.

"Bottom's Up, I know."

"How do you...." but I cut Taylor off again.

"We'll get to that later. Go on."

Going on, Taylor said, "The only other places we meet up are at a few nightclubs and the occasional member's house." I could sense he was leaving something out, and the shaking of his foot gave it away.

"Where else Tyrese?"

Shaking his foot more, Taylor got nervous.

Raising the syringe again, I said, "Taylor, need I remind you of what...." but Taylor interrupted.

"It's called The Kingdom." I looked at him confusedly. Taylor went on to explain. "It's where we deal business, cook (meaning make their drugs), and make things happen."

"Where's it located?"

Not wanting to tell me but, more importantly, not wanting to become paralyzed, Taylor told me. "The Kingdom's an abandoned building that's on the outer edge but still within the city. It used to be some kinda toy business until it went outta business. Been there for years. Chain link fencing surrounds the entire building and that yellow police tape is wrapped around the fencing. There's a bridge nearby The Kingdom as you come into the city."

"What's the name of the street it sits on?"

"Commerce Drive. You can see the building from the bridge."

I had one final, important question. "Where's Booker?"

Taylor didn't speak. I didn't even bother with the syringe anymore. I said more sharply, "Where's he at Taylor?"

"I don't know."

"He at The Kingdom?"

"I don't know."

My temper was coming alive. "Taylor! Tell me!"

133

"Man I don't know!" He looked me right in the face. "Nobody's seen him lately, not even myself. He stays low-key if you know what I mean. He could be anywhere."

I stood firm and quiet, staring Taylor in the eyes and wondering if he was really telling the truth. With the syringe in my hand, I was going to find out.

Walking over to the sodium chloride bag, I held the IV line in my hand with the needle of the syringe a fingernail away from the medication port.

"NO! PLEASE! MAN I'M TELLING YOU THE TRUTH!"

"Where's he at 'TT'!"

"I DON'T KNOW! PLEASE!"

I jammed the needle into the port and pushed the fluid of the syringe into the IV's line. With horror on his face, I watched the fluid enter into Taylor's vein. He started shaking and crying, like he was just getting ready to be executed electric chair style.

"I WAS TELLING YOU THE TRUTH!" Taylor screamed at the top of his lungs. "I….I think I feel my body going numb." Taylor started to panic.

I wanted to laugh, but I held it in for the time being. Instead, I moved in front of him with about twelve feet separating us.

Taylor started to speak rapidly with terror in his voice. "What's going to happen to me? How fast does this stuff work? What are you going to do to me? I was telling you the truth…." Taylor cursed at me.

Enough was enough. I put Taylor to the test and he came out telling the truth after all.

"Relax you big baby," I said to Taylor. "There was nothing but water filling your vein just then." Quizzically, he looked at me with tears in his eyes.

Unknown to Taylor was my plan. I wasn't a monster, and I never intended to make him suffer by paralyzation. By removing the Vecuronium from the vial, I sterilized the inside of the vial and replaced it with water, but I wanted to leave the sticker on so Taylor knew I was for real. And I knew that by threatening him with it I would get answers; and I knew by actually threatening to push it would give me the fullest truth.

I got the truth.

"So….so there was never anything that was going to paralyze me?" Taylor said with a shaky voice.

"Nope, but thanks for telling the truth," I replied.

With the realization of what just happened, Taylor bowed his head and began sobbing. I gave him a couple minutes until he could get his bearings.

"Who....who are you?" Taylor finally said after the tears ceased.

Fire filled my being just then. "I was a paramedic who lived in Columbus who had his wife taken away from him by ruthless boys who think they're men. And now," I said moving my hand behind me, "I'm just a man dead inside who's going to have his revenge against those who killed her."

Removing the .357 from behind me, I pointed it at Taylor. "And you're lucky number one," I said impassively. "Your boy, Kevin 'K-Dogg' Durgess from Bottom's Up, is next. And after him, that leaves only Booker."

*J, think about this.*

It's already been thought.

*You proved your point and got what you wanted. Now enough is enough.*

I say when enough is enough.

*You're gonna regret this the rest of your life.*

I lowered the gun to my side and thought hard. Was I really going to do this? Was it worth it?

Taylor let out a soft laugh. The terror and panic passed from him, and now he thought he had the upper hand for the time being. "You can't do it, can you?" He smiled, and the fire within me reached its maximum temperature.

I gave him a look. I'm not sure what it looked like, but it was enough to make his smile disappear. The terror and panic reclaimed their positions within Taylor.

"You killed my wife...." and that's when something else came to my mind just then. I'd been so focused on Naomi only that I had totally forgotten about Manhattan. "And you killed my dog."

I raised the .357 and pulled the trigger.

*Job....*

# 21

A little over a week would go by before I unleashed phase two of my plan - going after Kevin "K-Dogg" Durgess - and, although different emotions swept through me at the time, I didn't regret what I had done to Tyrese "TT" Taylor.

A new look I would need for Bottom's Up just in case any SSS members would be present who had been at Ricky's arcade the night I went after Tyrese Taylor. I couldn't go as the fancy-dressed businessman as I had. Like a chameleon, I would need to look different.

Stopping by the station where I worked, I grabbed some more supplies from our EMS room. I loaded my book bag with some of the following: a saline bottle, bandages, dressings, IV materials, and a few other essentials. Zipping my book bag, I mainly grabbed the trauma related supplies as a last resort if Kevin Durgess wouldn't talk to me or give me what I wanted.

I happened to make my way into the station without being spotted. Opening a door that led to a small hallway with two flights of stairs on the left, only another door stood in my way to leaving; but my hopes of leaving without company were shattered when that door opened and making his way in was my EMS chief and coordinator, Leo Watson.

Looking up, flinching with not expecting me nor recognizing who I was for a few seconds with my hair grown out, Leo said, "Man, Job, you scared me."

EMS chief and coordinator Leo Watson was an average height, short brown haired man who had a stocky build. He was definitely a man who knew EMS like the back of his hand, and running with him in the back of the squad proved it. We had a good relationship and he'd been very supportive and offering to lend a hand in any way since Naomi's passing and my time of trial.

"Sorry chief," I said standing there, "didn't mean to."

"Everything all right? What are you doing here?" The door closed shut behind Leo.

"Was just," I searched my brain for some excuse, "checking up on my time off and wanted to grab a few things."

Mostly the truth.

*Yeah, mostly.*

Leo looked at me curiously, but then changed the subject. "How you been Job?"

"Hanging in there."

"Why don't you come upstairs and say hey to the guys. They've been asking about you."

"Nah, I just...." but Leo put his arm around my shoulder and headed me toward the stairs. I reluctantly started making my way up the first flight of stairs.

"Come on, it'll do both you and the guys good."

At the kitchen table, I was greeted by some of the guys I worked with. Chad and J.D. gave me a hug, while Brad and Josh shook my hand and patted me on the shoulder. The rest of the guys I worked with were on a special detail run of a supposed drug raid, according to Leo.

Sitting between Leo and Josh, I was asked how I'd been getting along and if I needed anything. One of the guys called me "caveman" because of my short beard and long hair. We made small talk about life and work, but I had other matters on my mind that I wanted to deal with.

Our station stayed extremely busy with the area we covered for the city of Columbus. We basically had a two-part station - one half being the EMS side and the other being the fire side - that averaged anywhere between 15 to 25 runs a day. Like most stations, we also remained busy doing station chores - a different one for each day of the week - and the station was basically our second home as we worked 24-on/48-off hour shifts. Unlike what many people think and say about fire/EMS guys sitting all day on recliners, watching TV, and waiting for the next run to be toned out, it seemed we rarely got to have any downtime during the course of a single shift.

Although my passion was to be dual-certified as a firefighter/paramedic like some of the guys, I had to accept being a paramedic only, for now, because they had enough personnel already on the fire side.

Sometimes you'll hear people in this profession say, "We love fire, but hate the EMS side." However, with this job, and, percentage speaking, EMS won by a landslide given the way the people of this world were and also because fire prevention had been doing its job.

Also like most stations, egos and personalities can be barriers to getting along. There were some who thought themselves more distinguished than others, there were those who thought they knew it all,

137

and there were others who thought they were God's gift to the world; but, with great thanks, the guys on my crew came to work to get along - with ourselves and others - do our job, and go home safe, all while having some fun, knowing one another personally, and doing things together outside of work.

Facing one of the windows, the day outside was gray and rainy. At times the rain came down in torrents, and people with umbrellas on the sidewalk struggled against the wind that had started to pick up by the way they had to force themselves onward. Stop and go lights flashed their glow as they swung from side to side, and drivers in a hurry honked their horns as traffic got backed up.

Just then, without warning, I heard loudly coming from the day room into the kitchen, "TURTLE POWER!" Looking to my right, it was quite a sight to see.

Some guy I hadn't seen before, good build with brown, puffy hair, had no shirt on and he was dressed only in his underwear with high white socks and sandals on; but what had me laughing inside so hard was that he had a Teenage Mutant Ninja Turtles book bag strapped to his back with a red eye mask wrapped around his head, like he was Raphael, the Teenage Mutant Ninja Turtle who had the attitude.

Running into the kitchen, he jumped in the air, spun doing a 360, landed on his feet, and sprinted out of the kitchen.

I looked around the table at my fellow crewmembers wondering what on earth had just happened. Silence filled the kitchen for a very short time, but then laughter exploded in it, which also included coming from me. It was the first time I'd laughed this hard since Naomi's death.

A few guys banged their hands against the kitchen table with their heads down laughing, Leo shook his head with a smile on his face, and Josh and I had tears in our eyes.

Finally getting calmed down, I asked, "Who was that?"

Leo turned toward me and said, "That's our new guy. He was supposed to be cleaning bathrooms and going over medication protocol, but I guess humoring us instead was more important," he ended with another smile and a short laugh.

"He's gonna work out just fine. Fits right in and does a good job," Leo went on. "Actually," he said looking me right in the eye, "he reminds us of you when you first started. Full of energy, a hard worker, and wild, but in a good way." The guys laughed at the last comment.

I nodded my head. "I'll be looking forward to meeting him. He already makes me laugh." Inside I was sad for a minute. I loved this job, but I also knew that what I had been doing recently might render me

138

jobless if I got caught. But what I had been doing was more important than this job, or so I thought.

Getting caught was already a chance I knew I was taking. Actually, in all honesty, I was planning on getting caught.

Over our heads, the long loud tone, which was followed with multiple fast-paced tones, went off signaling a squad run. The female dispatcher's voice called out, "Medic 491, Medic 491, you have a squad run to 316 Park Street, 316 Park Street for a cardiac arrest. Caller advises this was a witnessed arrest and CPR is currently in progress. This will be a 42EMS assignment. Dispatch out at 14:22."

Chad and J.D. arose to take the squad run. Leo then said, "Brad, Josh, you two head that way emergency status as well since it's an arrest. The new guy stays back with me in case we get anything else. Tell him on your way out." The two others got up to help the first-out medic. That left the kitchen quiet with only Leo and I remaining.

We watched both of the ambulances make their way out of the bay into the busy downtown street with their lights flashing red and white. Their loud sirens echoed off the nearby buildings as they sped to hopefully save a life.

I loved this job.

"You doing okay, Job?" said Leo making his way to the coffee maker for a hot cup of joe.

"Given with what's happened, I'd say I'm doing all right."

"Coffee?"

"Nah, no thanks."

"You know," Leo said with his coffee in hand, retaking his seat next to me, "if you need anything, you know we're all here for you."

"I know," I started to say, "and I appreciate it chief."

"What have you been up to?" Leo took a cautious first drink and then said, "You know, to try and take your mind off things?"

*Yeah, why don't you tell him what you've been up to, J.*

"You know," I tried to find something, "going for runs, visiting my hometown, this and that."

Leo's face was earnest and his voice sincere. "Can I be honest with you about something Job?"

"Shoot."

"I don't know what I would do if I were in your shoes. Part of me would want to try and move on and live my life, but," he said looking down, "another part would want to get even somehow with those who did what they did."

It was like something sharp, a knife or a sword just pierced me to the core just then.

139

I didn't say anything, which caused Leo to carry on. "But I don't think revenge would be the way to go. Just wouldn't be right, you know? It's like you'd be no better than those who committed the misdeed."

*He's really twisting the knife in the heart now, but he's right J.*

I didn't reply back to my counselor, but it was right.

"Yeah, I've had my thoughts," I said to Leo. "I've heavily struggled through it all."

*Thoughts? You've had more than thoughts. You're putting into action.*

Zip it for a minute, would you.

*Yes sir.*

"I just…." but Leo stopped, shaking his head. "I'm blabbing. I'm sorry Job."

"It's all right. I know you mean well." I started to arise from my chair, not being able to handle a conversation like this right now. "I gotta get going anyway. I have some things to do."

Leo and I shook hands and he told me, again, that if I needed anything to not hesitate to ask. Grabbing my book bag, I started making my way out of the kitchen.

"Job," Leo's voice spoke behind me.

I turned around. "Yeah."

"You're sure you're all right?" He let the question sink in for a few seconds and then said, "Something seems different about you."

I looked Leo in the eye, looked down, and then back into his eye. "I'm all right," I said with uncertainty in my voice. Turning back around, I made my way out of the kitchen.

"Take care brother," said Leo behind me.

Making my way outside, I stood with the rain pelting down on me. The wind swept over my face, blowing my hair, and soon I would look like a drowned rat; but I just stood there, like I was dazed in some other world in my mind.

Leo was right. There was something different about me.

I wasn't that guy who used to work as a paramedic, caring for everyone and wanting to save the world. I was no longer that guy who I used to be, satisfied and content with what I had. And I wasn't that guy who used to have a profound, steady faith in God.

Now I was a rogue, wanting to get even. I was a person reborn, bent on getting revenge. And I was a wavering sheep, my faith barely holding on.

Standing outside the station soaking wet, the new in me wanted to go back to the old; but until I carried out and finished what I had started, the new would remain alive.

I was just that.
Different.

# 22

Pulling into my driveway, I put my truck into park. The rain had stopped for the time being, but dark gray clouds off in the distance were heading in my direction as I made my way to the front door. A pair of headlights moved over my house, and when I looked at the vehicle that had just pulled into my drive, I knew there would be no avoiding him this time.

Jehu Bridges pulled into my driveway, turned off his lights, killed the engine, and got out of his vehicle. I stood halfway between my front door and his vehicle.

"You're a tough man to track down Job," said the detective.

I didn't say a word.

"Mind if we talk for a few?" Bridges shut his car door.

Sighing deeply, I started walking toward my front door. "Come on in before it rains again."

In my kitchen, Bridges took a seat while I stood on the opposite end of the kitchen island. Offering him a drink, he asked for a bottled water while I poured myself a glass of chocolate milk. Bridges removed the toothpick from his mouth, swallowed a couple small mouthfuls of water, and put the toothpick back in his mouth.

Emptying my pockets, I placed my cell phone, wallet, and keys on the kitchen countertop next to me.

Detective Bridges got right to the point. "I know you've been ignoring my calls as well as my visits, Job. I can't say I blame you, but pushing me away isn't helping either."

I downed my glass of chocolate milk pretty quickly. Walking over to the sink, I had my back to the detective as I rinsed out my glass and put it in the dishwasher.

Turning back around, I said, "Yeah, so."

Bridges' face looked angry for a second, but then changed, like he didn't want an argument to commence. "Job, I'm your friend. Why are you treating me like this?"

142

*You're acting like a jerk Job. Here you have a friend who goes out of his way for you, and you have the audacity to treat him like this. What's wrong with you?*

"When I first started getting to know you," Jehu went on, "you were someone different. A man who was faithful to his wife, treated people the way they'd wanna be treated, a man who I respected and who had morals that any good person would appreciate."

*Ahem, he's speaking about that old you who we all miss.*

"Now," carried on Bridges, "I don't even know who you are anymore. You look like you haven't shaved for days, your attitude sucks, and I don't hear from you though I've tried multiple times trying to contact you."

Bridges waited for me to respond. After a short time, I finally did. "What do you expect, Jehu? That wife who I was always faithful to is dead, and people? I don't care much for many people these days with the way this world is; and, in all honesty, I could care less about who respects me and my morals.

"With what has happened," I went on, "it's changed me inside and out. What would you do?"

The detective didn't say a word; he just sat there trying to find something. He finally did. "I know one thing. I wouldn't shut those people out who made themselves available and who cared about me."

*A comeback?*

Nope. He's right.

I sighed deeply again, nodding my head. "You're right Jehu."

"I know, I always am," he said with a smile on his face, obviously joking.

It made me smile.

"Changing the subject," Bridges said, "I wanted to bring something else to your attention." He sat up straighter with a more serious look on his face. "I've been asking around and one of the SSS members who was involved in your wife's murder has gone missing."

Saying nothing, I stood quietly. But Bridges looked at me for a long moment, wondering if my face would give something away.

"Okay, and…." I said, giving him a puzzled look.

"The member is Tyrese 'TT' Taylor. He's been missing for about a week now."

Trying to find a legitimate reason to give Bridges, I said, "Maybe he jumped ship and left town, or maybe he's found a new home somewhere else in Columbus. I don't know and I don't care."

Jehu stared at me. "Nah, not a guy like Taylor. He had too much going for him here in this city." He took another drink from his bottled water and carried on. "Tension is heating up between SSS and NEB, our two rival gangs in Columbus, but Taylor stays true to Rufus Booker and SSS."

I shrugged my shoulders, not sure what to say to that.

"I was also told from a source at Ricky's arcade, which is supposedly where Taylor does his business, that the night Tyrese Taylor went missing," Bridges said squinting his eyes at me, "a business-like white man with long hair happened to be at Ricky's moments before Taylor went missing."

Inside I was talking to myself. "Act normal. Don't look guilty. Keep your eyes on Bridges and don't look away, otherwise he'll know. Look like you have absolutely no idea what he's talking about."

Shrugging my shoulders again, I said, "Yeah, and...." shaking my head and giving him a confused look.

Jehu Bridges let things sink in for a short time before saying, "So you had no idea before my showing up tonight about Tyrese Taylor and his disappearance?"

Shaking my head, I said, "Nope."

*Liar liar....*

"Job," the detective gave me that tell-me-the-truth look.

"Seriously Bridges, I had no idea."

*Pants on fire.*

Bridges nodded his head. I wasn't convinced that he believed me.

"Off the record," Bridges removed the toothpick from his mouth, holding it with two fingers, "is there anything you wanna tell me, Job? This may be one of those very few times where I can help before something gets worse."

I came right out and said it, anger making its way out of me to dramatize the scene more. "You might as well just say it Bridges. You think it was me at this Nicky's," I purposefully looked confused, "what was the arcade's name?" I acted stupid, like I couldn't remember.

"Ricky's," said the detective.

"So," I slowly played it out, "you think I have it in me to find out specifically where Taylor was, get to him, and somehow magically make him disappear?" I raised my arms with my palms up to chest level, like I was saying, "Are you serious?" For a bonus, I added, "And all while in an environment that is dangerous?"

*Like I said before, you're getting good, but in a very bad way.*

Bridges was weighing what I had just said. It was like a ping-pong game was going on in his head, deciding which side to take.

"You're right," the detective finally said. "I can't say that I can see you doing all that. It's just, since the last time I saw you at the courthouse,

144

you just weren't yourself and looked like you were a man capable of anything. Sorry to jump to conclusions."

"No hard feelings," I said. But something in Bridges' voice made me feel like he still didn't fully believe me.

*And why should he? It's not the truth.*

Needing to clear my head a little, I said, "I need to use the bathroom. I'll be right back."

Jehu nodded his head.

Closing the door behind me, I looked at myself in the guest bathroom mirror. Who was I? Who had I turned into? Bridges was a good guy on my side and still I continued to shut him out. He really was my friend, but I stubbornly resisted him, like he was something bad for my health.

Turning the cold dial on, water started running down the bathroom sink. Bending down, I filled both of my hands with cold water several times and splashed it on my face. Shutting the water off, I grabbed a hand towel and patted my face dry. The cold water felt refreshing and I felt like I could breathe again. Looking at myself one last time in the mirror trying to figure out who I was, I opened the door and made my way back into the kitchen.

Standing this time by the kitchen island instead of sitting, Jehu Bridges held his phone up in his hand. "Gotta go Job. Work calls."

Since I hadn't treated him the greatest, I offered some kindness. Holding out my hand, the detective shook it. I said, "Thanks for checking in on me, Jehu. I'm sorry how I've been acting. You," I paused, "you really are a friend."

"If you need anything," he repeated again, "anything," squeezing my hand tighter, "then you get a hold of me. I'm serious Job."

"Thanks Jehu."

Letting go of my hand, I led Bridges to the front door, opened it, and watched him start up his car and leave. He stayed parked at the entrance of my drive for a long minute, and then made his way back into the city of Columbus.

Making my way back to the kitchen, I looked at the kitchen countertop quizzically. "That's weird," I said to myself, "I could've sworn I put you over there." I couldn't really remember, so I didn't think much into it.

My cell phone sat in the middle of the kitchen island, though I was pretty sure I had placed it with my keys and wallet closer to where I had stood. Maybe I had picked it up during the conversation with Bridges to look at the time and placed it there instead.

145

Or, would Bridges really look through my phone, trying to find something? Something was telling me Jehu Bridges wasn't buying what I had been trying to sell him.

Like he didn't believe me.

# 23

After giving myself a crew cut, getting rid of the beard so my face was as smooth as a baby's bottom, and dressing more appropriately for the environment, I was ready for Kevin "K-Dogg" Durgess and Bottom's Up.

Oh, how could I forget, and a little visit to Al with a new change of plan - I'll tell you about that later - had me hopefully smooth sailing.

Like I had with Tyrese Taylor, I wasn't at first sure if I could go through with this as I stood outside Bottom's Up. That lasted only about ten seconds though. Kevin Durgess was the one, I thought, who mocked me more than the others with his flashy smile, he was the one who sent me onto my side when I was about a foot away from getting to Booker moments after Naomi was shot, and he was now the second of three who I had come for.

This time the decision was much easier for me.

I can't say that I was thrilled about going into a strip club for the very first time; but, if I wanted Durgess, then that meant going in.

I'm going in.

*Although I don't agree with you on this, I'm going in with you.*

Thanks buddy.

The block on this side of the city was loud and bright. Women with too short of mini-skirts on were flaunting their bodies while immature men drooled over them in hopes of "getting a piece." Several times I saw drug trade-offs happen right in front of my eyes with a quick motion of the hands. I was even asked one time by some white lady dressed in tight clothes if I wanted some "blow." Two large men, one white and one black, stood outside Bottom's Up patting down each and every person who entered into the strip club. They were dressed nicely, and with their sunglasses on, they kinda reminded me of the Blues Brothers.

I felt like a high school student who accidentally walked into the wrong classroom. A different world I wasn't accustomed to was about to be entered.

*You can always turn back.*

I'm already here.

*Just thought I'd try. Maybe one of these times I'll get you to turn around.*

Doubt it, but keep trying.

*Always will.*

Lights shined so brightly around me that I thought I was at Times Square for New Years awaiting the ball to drop instead of standing outside a place where topless women danced. Like dominoes, lights took their turn lighting up all around the outside of Bottom's Up. A large vertical sign above the building read Bottom's Up that had a woman leaning up against a pole that kept flashing on and off quickly, like when the electricity in your house flickers on and off.

Also on this block were a couple bars, a small diner called All-Nighters, a convenience store, and, like Ricky's arcade, back alleys. Groups of people stood around the entire block, and it was like this section of the city had no time to sleep.

With knowing beforehand that I couldn't enter Bottom's Up armed, I could only hope that Wendy put the gun in the men's bathroom exactly where her, Al, and I had discussed.

Taking a deep breath, I made my way toward the two bouncers dressed as I was. I knew I needed to try and fit in more with my attire compared to standing out last time at Ricky's arcade.

There I stood before the two bouncers: hat on backwards, a silver cross necklace sporting around my neck, a t-shirt from St. John where Naomi and I had vacationed a couple years ago, jeans, and running shoes.

The black one patted my body down while the other bouncer removed my hat to make sure I wasn't hiding anything underneath it. When they finally concluded, the one who patted me down said, "Go ahead."

I then slowly made my way into Bottom's Up.

The entrance into the strip club reminded me of a football stadium's tunnel, like when the amped up players run through it before making their way onto the field being cheered on by thousands of fans. Walking further inside the dark hallway, laser-like rays of colorful light danced on the floor, walls, and ceiling; and the further I walked, the brighter they got.

Running into my shoulder, some guy who could barely walk in the direction opposite me, obviously intoxicated, got up in my face like I was the one to blame and said, "Hey man," he slurred his words, "watch where you're walking. Unless," he kept slurring, "unless you wanna go out back and get messed up." His buddy next to him just stood there.

148

I wasn't in the mood and I already walked into this place with a bad attitude, as well as my temper on my shoulder.

Getting closer to him, our noses almost touching, I said with the meanest look I could give, "Don't sing it. Bring it." I added, "As far as I'm concerned, there's gonna be two hits. Me hitting you," my face turning red, "and you hitting the ground." I stood firm like a statue and held my ground.

*Easy J. You haven't even made it twenty feet in and you're already making enemies.*

Nah, forget him.

"Matter of fact," I went on, "why don't you go outside, practice falling down, and I'll be out in a minute."

*HaHa! All right J, I'll admit, that was a good one.*

Even a blind squirrel finds a nut here and there.

Not knowing what to do, the guy stood there and took a couple steps back. "Geeze man," he said holding his hands up, palms out toward me, "I was only messing." He and his buddy started walking toward the exit.

I heard his friend say as they walked away, "That guy woulda rung your bell." Inside, I gave a little laugh. Turning my attention further inside the club, I walked the last little stretch until I finally made my way into Bottom's Up.

I stood there, slowly scanning the place over.

Lights shined brightly in addition to the colorful, laser-like lights. It was jammed pack with men ranging anywhere from twenty to fifty-some years of age. 2pac's *California Love* filled the place with music and many men were either taking shots of liquor, downing bottles of beer, or holding out money toward the topless women who were performing on stages that were higher than the tables and chairs where the men sat.

*Well, still glad you decided to come here?*

I was never glad in the first place, but the reason I'm here far outweighs what I see before me.

Trying not to judge others, I thought about places like these. Here were men being entertained by almost fully naked women who they didn't even know. Money was being spent to see a gender and body part that you would think many of these men would have grown mature toward since long ago. And also adding in the money being spent on alcohol which would invite enticing fantasies into the minds of these men with the same women they were throwing money at.

How many of these men were married? I had seen wedding bands on a few. What kind of relationship did they expect to have with these women? A temporary, short-lived one filled with lust that would be forgotten by tomorrow morning. And what would growing up kids think with the example we were setting here? That it's okay to get drunk and toss money at topless women when God gave relationship a different, more defining meaning.

I guess I just didn't see the point. But this was also coming from me, a man who didn't conform to this pattern but who believed in being with a woman like this in front of me in this club only in a dedicated and committed marriage. I'd had my days of youthful lust, but nothing was more purer in a relationship for a man than to be wholeheartedly devoted to his wife and only her.

A DJ who stood on top of a second story platform with large headphones on his ears said into a microphone, "Now, gentlemen, here's the lady you've all been waiting to see." He then changed the song being played and shouted into the mic, "The one, the only, and the beautiful," he paused to really drag it out, "MISS TONYA!"

Making her way onto the main stage was just the woman who I was waiting for: Miss Tonya. Her real name was Wendy Collins but she went by Miss Tonya for her stage name. She was dressed with little on, and I knew the top part would be coming off any minute. Guys in the club hollered her name and others woofed like dogs. Money had already been thrown onto the stage where she was about to perform.

I made my way further into Bottom's Up, blending in with the crowd.

*Be careful J.*

Standing between two men on the outer edge of the crowd, Wendy began her performance, but I refused to look below her neck. I had respect for women, and I didn't want to dive into this tempting ocean that all these men around me had already been swimming in.

Making her way toward me, a topless waitress carrying a tray for drinks stood before me and said, "Hey baby," she looked me up and down, "can I get you anything?" She puffed her chest upward, wanting to make a show with what she had.

*Try not to look down buddy.*

Trust me, I'm not.

Shaking my head, I brushed her off and dug deeper into the crowd of men.

"Jerk," I heard her say behind me.

*Well done.*

Thanks buddy.

In the middle of the crowd, I looked more around the club. A large horizontal bar area took up a quarter of Bottom's Up. Men sat on bar stools and some stood with money in hand to pay for the next round. Several stages were set up on the opposite side of the bar; two smaller ones to the right and left, and a larger one in the middle where Wendy was dancing.

Meeting with her last week, Wendy was actually a nice woman who was struggling to make ends meet. This, what she was doing now, she told me, was just temporary until she could make a better life for her and her son.

The remainder of the first floor had tables, booths, and places to stand. There were a few hallways to the left side of me that I was told led into multiple rooms for private one-on-one dances for men who were willing to pay bigger bucks.

This is where I would be heading soon.

Other than that, restrooms were on my right side.

Looking upward, a second story allowed men to stand or sit and watch the entertainment unfolding below them. The DJ who wore his hat sideways spun records and danced along to the music right above where Wendy was dancing. I looked up and behind me, and then that's when I saw the man who I had come for: Kevin "K-Dogg" Durgess.

He sat, leaning back, in the middle of two men with two decent sized bouncers behind him. They reminded me of the Blues Brothers outside Bottom's Up, but they were different ones.

Picking up a small, mixed drink glass filled with ice, Durgess took a long gulp and smiled toward Wendy. He nodded his head and raised the glass in what looked like a show of honor toward her.

It was that same smile I saw in the courtroom and the same one he had flashed me while making his way down the courthouse's steps.

Tonight it would be wiped off.

As Wendy had told me, when her performance was finished, Durgess would make his way down and she'd perform for him one-on-one in one of those rooms that was down on my level.

That's when the part in the plan called for me to intervene and take Durgess just as I had taken Tyrese Taylor.

There would be only one problem, she had told me: the bouncer who'd be outside the closed door waiting on Durgess.

I kinda had this planned for, but I took one step at a time.

Making my way closer to the stage, I waited for Wendy to see me. Knowing to look for me, she scanned the crowd of men as she danced. Finally, her eyes met mine, and she paused slightly. Nodding my head, she smiled, nodded her head in return, and continued her performance.

That was the signal that all was a "go."

I turned to my right and headed in the direction of the restrooms. As I swam through the crowd of men, I heard the DJ shout, "Gentlemen, give it up for the lovely and beautiful Miss Tonya!"

151

Shouting, whistling, and clapping, men gave Wendy a loud and standing ovation as she made her way off the stage. I still heard the loudness as I made my way into the restrooms on the right hand side; the side where she told me she'd hide the Sig Sauer in the third stall, underneath the toilet's tank cover.

I chose the Sig because it was black and wouldn't be as easy to spot compared to the shiny .357 Magnum.

Walking into the third stall that was vacant, I closed the door, locking it in place. For a strip club bathroom, it was fairly clean. Standing in front of the commode, I lifted the tank cover and sat it on the toilet seat. Looking inside, there was a towel neatly folded with something inside of it. Picking up the towel that had a little bit of weight to it, I kept unwrapping until I gripped what Wendy had placed in the exact spot we had talked about.

My Sig Sauer.

*You sure you still wanna go through with this J?*

Without a doubt.

The decision was actually easier to make after dealing with Tyrese Taylor, as I thought it would be.

Tucking the gun between my waist and jeans in the front side, I pulled my shirt down to hide it from anyone's view. Opening the stall door, I walked to one of the sinks and washed my hands, more so because I wanted cold water to cool me down some.

Alone in one of the bathrooms at Bottom's Up, I stared at myself in the mirror. Wiping my hand across my face, I then placed my hands on either side of the sink, bended forward, and looked at my face real hard.

I thought some things to myself just then. Will I be as successful pulling this off as I had been with Tyrese Taylor? Time would soon tell. Was I going to be able to keep all eyes off me except for those of Wendy and Kevin Durgess? I hoped so. Would Al be ready? I'm sure he would; I was, once again, paying him well for his service.

It seemed very backwards of me at a time like this, but I said a little prayer anyway as I stood in front of the mirror. "God, help me get through this. You know my true intentions. I know not all is right with what I'm doing; but, in the end, it will make sense to everyone else." I stumbled to get my last words out. "As before, I don't expect You to help me with this, because it's wrong but," I said trying to find words, though praying for something like this just didn't seem right, "please watch over me God."

And with that, I opened my eyes, stood straight up, and stared at the new me who had been birthed some time ago.

152

With a grave look on my face, I headed toward the bathroom door. Opening the door back into the atmosphere of Bottom's Up, the music seemed louder and the crowd of men more wild.

Scanning the area across from me, there stood Wendy - clothed - waiting outside the middle hallway that led to private one-on-one dance rooms. Standing beside her was one of the bouncers who I saw standing behind Durgess on the second story. Looking to my left, Durgess was making his way down the second flight of stairs that led to the first floor.

Soon he would be taking Wendy into one of those private dance rooms. Soon he would get his final show before his world came crashing in. And soon he would be the second member of SSS who faced my wrath for taking part in killing my wife.

Wendy said he always paid her well for the private dances she would give him on a weekly basis. Tonight would be the richest of them all.

Seeing me from across the club, Wendy nodded her head, and I was pretty sure she winked over at me as well. Durgess approached her as she took her eyes off of me and smiled toward "K-Dogg." Offering his arm like a gentleman, Wendy took it, and there they went.

Wendy, Durgess, and the bouncer made their way deeper into the middle hallway that would lead to the last private dance room on the right. The room where she told me she always performed for Durgess.

Feeling the gun on me, I took a deep breath, and then I made my way across the strip club toward that same hallway.

# 24

Walking down that hallway, it was dark with torch-like lights being the only light provided. They were installed on either side of the hallway on the wall and flickered their glow. There were four doors on each side of me that lined the hallway further in, and a small tunnel had to be walked through before coming to each door of a private dance room.

This hallway was also convenient because it had an exit door at the end that led to a back alley. The red light that read EXIT was straight ahead.

The hallway was empty except for the bouncer I'd seen with Wendy and Durgess who was sitting on a chair outside the small tunnel of the last room on the right.

That's when I started putting on my show. Acting drunk myself, I stumbled right and left and sang small parts of *California Love* that I had just heard and could remember. "In the ciiii....tttyyy....city of Compton," I paused, "we keep it rockin', we keep it rockin'." That's when the bouncer looked my way, but I kept on. "Shake it, shake it baby," I continued, "shake it, shake it....shake it baby." I tried to sound just like the song had.

*Nice act. You should try out for a play sometime.*

Approaching the bouncer, he arose from his chair and stood tall like the Great Wall of China. He didn't find me amusing but I stopped in front of him, looked up, and said, "Hey....hey bro, I gotta pee." He sighed deeply, obviously annoyed with me. "Can....can I use that bathroom behind you?"

"Get lost you wannabe Eminem," the bouncer said condescendingly, "before I get you lost." He shoved me on my shoulder.

*Be careful with Gigantor, Job, he looks like he eats people like you.*

I staggered backwards, like he pushed me harder. Holding my arms up, palms out, I said, "Hey bro, no....no need to be so rough." Wrapping up this show, I then looked behind him as if someone was there and said excitedly, "Miss Tonya, Miss Tonya, is that you?"

154

The bouncer went to look behind him, but when he did, that's when I grabbed the Sig and waited for him to turn back my way.

Looking behind him and seeing no one there, the bouncer sighed deeply, his body tensed like he was going to pummel me when he turned around, and he started to say, "I'm gonna tell you one last time...." but when he had his head halfway turned toward me, it was too late.

Lifting the Sig in the air, I swung it toward the bouncer's head until it made contact. When it did, he let out a soft exhale and hit the ground like a sack of potatoes.

He was out cold. I figured he wouldn't awake for a while.

Turning to my right, nobody else was in the hallway, so I moved the bouncer's body, with great effort, further into the small tunnel leading to the last door on the right so nobody would see him from the hallway.

Wiping the sweat away from my face, I kept the gun in my hand and made my way to the closed door that led into the private dance room where Kevin "K-Dogg" Durgess was.

I could hear music within the room as I glued my ear to the door. Durgess said aloud, "That's why you're the best baby."

Turning the doorknob ever so slowly, I peeked in and Durgess didn't hear a thing with the help of the music. He sat on a small sofa with his head and back to me with Wendy dancing for him in front. Pushing the door lightly, it swung most of the way open. The small tunnel was dark, so no external light had made its way in.

Wendy didn't look my way because she was expecting this; it was all part of the plan. Making my way behind Durgess, that's when Wendy looked at me and I gave her the go-ahead nod, always keeping my sight above her neck. She put her hands over her nose and mouth, as if something was wrong, and her face looked frightened.

Seeing this, Durgess said, "Baby, baby what's wrong?"

That's when I sank the muzzle of the gun deep into the back of "K-Dogg's" head.

"This is what's wrong," I said.

Sitting frozen like an ice cube, Durgess didn't know what to do. At last, he spoke. "I got money, women, jewelry, whatever you want, just don't go pulling that trigger."

Looking at Wendy, I said, "You scream Miss Tonya, you're dead." She just stood there looking scared and kept quiet. Again, part of the plan. I didn't want anything coming back on her. She needed to look like another victim.

Focusing my attention back on Durgess, I said, "You can keep your material possessions, 'K-Dogg.' I just want you," I said digging the muzzle deeper, making Durgess grunt.

Raising his voice, Durgess said, "Brutus, Brutus come in here and take care of this guy!"

Digging the muzzle as far as it would go, my temper was on fire. "Brutus can't help you. How do you think I got past him?"

Durgess had no response.

"Hey man," Durgess said, "who the," he cursed, "are you?"

"You'll find out soon enough," I replied.

I added, "If you don't wanna die in this filthy club of yours, then stand up, slowly, and start making your way to the exit just outside here."

Durgess hesitated, as if he was testing me. He finally said, "No way man."

Pushing the hammer part of the gun down with my right thumb, the small *clicking* sound was heard, more so for Durgess' ears. I said, "Yes way man."

Shaking a bit, Durgess reluctantly said, "All right, all right, just don't shoot."

Standing up, Durgess made his way to the open door and I jammed the muzzle of the gun into his back, at the level and side where his heart was located.

Looking back quickly, I winked at Wendy. Removing her hands from her face, she smiled and winked back. I was hoping this would be her cue onto bigger and better things for her and her son.

I knew it would be. She was wanting out of this life.

Making our way to the edge of the small tunnel, the bouncer whose name I found out was Brutus still was out cold. Peeking down the hallway with Durgess' body barely sticking out, it was empty.

"Go on," I said, "push that exit door open."

Durgess stood still and paused. "You don't know what you're doing or who you're messing with."

Quietly letting that sink in, I said, "Yes, I do." I gave Durgess an answer. "Revenge is the name of this game of what I am doing, and," I continued pushing him onward, "I'm messing with Kevin 'K-Dogg' Durgess of SSS, or better known as the South Side Soldiers."

I ended with, "You satisfied?"

Durgess had no reply.

Pushing the exit door open, we made our way outside, the exit door shutting behind us. Al wasn't here, and I wondered where he was. "Stop and don't move," I said to Durgess.

He could sense something wasn't right. "What's wrong, part of your plan not going as you had hoped?" he said mockingly.

Seeing my rent-a-car - this was a different one - pull up with Al behind the wheel, I smiled, glad to see him. Pushing Durgess toward the back end of the car, I said, "I'm sorry, 'K-Dogg', you were saying?"

Once again, Durgess didn't have a reply.

Al and I had already talked about not using our names in front of Durgess, especially me just yet.

Getting out of the vehicle and walking toward the trunk, Al said looking at me, "Sorry I was a little late. This is a busy street." Al then opened the trunk and waited for us.

"It's all good," I started to say, "I'm just glad to see you." Durgess stood in front of the trunk with me standing behind him.

"So," Al said, "'K-Dogg' was one of them, huh?" He was referring to "one of them" as in who took part in killing Naomi. I had filled Al in on a little of what I had went through and why his service was needed.

But just enough.

The little, the better, I thought. I didn't want anybody else getting in trouble or their life being threatened like mine had been.

"Well," I said nudging Durgess, "this is about the time when you get into that trunk." I made sure to leave nothing in the trunk so Durgess couldn't use it as a weapon once I got him to Mount Vernon.

Resisting, at first, Al and I ended up having to basically throw him in. Sitting up in the trunk, Durgess started to curse at me and utter all kinds of threats. That's when he stopped abruptly and his face changed.

He studied my face with squinted eyes, like I was some sort of rare breed animal that needed a closer look, and then that's when it hit him. A mask of pure fear adhered to his face just then.

"You?"

I stared down at him, intensity written on my face. "Yeah," I let the fact that he had just figured out who I was settle in, "me."

Having enough, I finally grasped the trunk's door with both hands and slammed it down hard; it came slamming down on top of Durgess' head, not closing the trunk.

I slammed the trunk door down again, and this time the trunk was securely closed.

I didn't hear him say anything else. The impact must've rendered him unconscious just as my swing with the Sig had done to Brutus.

"What are you going to do to him?" asked Al.

Shaking my head, I said, "Not sure yet. Time will tell."

Shaking hands with Al, I then reached into my pocket. "Five hundred then and five hundred now," I said giving Al the second half of the money that I owed him.

Accepting the money, Al slapped the small pile against his hand. "You need me, you know where to find me."

I nodded my head. "You want a ride home?"

"Nah," said Al, "I'm hungry. I'm gonna get something to eat at All-Nighters." That was the diner I saw back on the street before I made my way into Bottom's Up.

"In that case," I said digging back into my pocket, "here's another twenty. Dinner's on me." Al took the money with appreciation.

*That was nice of you. See, there's still good in you Job.*

Walking toward the driver's seat, I heard Al say behind me, "You seem too good of a man to do what you're doing."

Stopping, without turning around, I had to think for a few seconds. "Good men can be pushed over the limit, making them do things that they thought they would never do."

"Mmm," said Al. "Well, I hope you find what you're looking for in the end."

"Too me," I accidentally said, thinking of Naomi.

"What?"

I cleared my throat. "Me too," I corrected myself for Al.

"Take care, you hear," said Al walking away.

"You too." I ended with, for some reason, "God bless you."

I heard Al say as he walked down the alley, talking to himself, "First the guy at Ricky's, then 'K-Dogg', and then twenty extra dollars and 'God bless you?'" He paused and then said, "This man doesn't make any sense, but he's nice and pays good. I like'em."

Laughing, I sat in the driver's seat. My mood changed when I thought back to what I had just done and would soon be doing.

Putting the car into drive, I started making my way to the old Mount Vernon High School.

# 25

Rewind back with me to last week.

I happened to be in Al's neck of the woods, so I figured I'd stop by and pay him a visit. Plus, with knowing he lived on the streets, I bought him something to eat.

Seeing him sitting on a bench near some basketball courts, I parked my truck, got out with a bag from McDonald's in my hand, and made my way to the man.

The sun had just set, painting the sky with a vivid blood orange and yellow. A younger group of kids played on one half of a basketball court while teens played on the other end. The second court was being played on by adult men of varying races: black, white, Mexican, and I even saw a couple Asians.

It was nice seeing people of different ethnic groups being able to play together as one. Too bad the world didn't look more like this.

*Amen brother.*

Taking a seat next to Al on the bench, he looked my way. "Well hey there stranger," he said as I handed him the McDonald's bag.

"Hey Al," I started to say, "thought you could use something to eat."

"That was very kind of you," Al returned opening the bag and removing a sandwich. "Thank you."

"No worries."

I let Al eat his burgers and large fry while I watched the action on the basketball courts. When Al finished eating, he washed it all down with the bottled water I'd bought him.

"So, stranger," Al said, "what's your name?"

"Job." I didn't give him my name when I needed help with Tyrese Taylor. I just told him I had a small job that I'd pay him well for. Names didn't matter at the time, but I felt the need to give it to him now, especially with getting ready to ask him again for his help.

"Well, Job, I know you didn't come here just to feed me." Al was a pretty smart guy, I thought. "I'm figuring you're needing my service again."

I was taking a bigger chance this time around, but I had already proved myself to Al by being a good paying employer.

"You don't beat around the bush, do you Al?"

"Ain't no sense to."

"Okay, here it is." I leaned forward on the bench, rested my arms on my legs, and folded my hands together. "I need a driver to meet me in a side alley at Bottom's Up, the strip club on...." but Al interrupted.

"I know the place." With a few fingers of his right hand, he began toying with his beard. "What's the pay?"

Keeping our business out of the public's view, I reached into my pocket and pulled out five hundred dollars. "Five hundred now, and another five hundred when the job's finished."

Al wasted no time. "Count me in," he said taking the five hundred dollars from my hand. "You treat me well, plus you pay good. I'm your driver."

*Al's no fool. With pay like that I'd work for you too, only for different reasons of course.*

"That was easy."

"Like I said, you treat me well, plus you pay good."

Al then added, "Who we packing in the trunk this time?" I didn't want to give out the name and Al could tell. "Come on," Al started to say, "if I'm your driver, then I'd say I'm entitled to know."

Clearing my throat, I said, "Kevin Durgess. He also goes by the name...." again, Al cut me short.

"'K-Dogg.'" Al's face looked somewhat mad.

Puzzled, I asked, "How'd you know?"

"Most people around here know that punk." There was distaste in Al's voice. "I have a friend, Wendy, who dances at his club."

"And...." I said.

"And, he's a scumbag. He's given Wendy one too many black eyes." Al went on to fill me in on some more information. "He's a higher up member for this SSS gang" - which I already knew - "and he thinks he's big stuff because he owns a strip club which brings in business for his gang. He thinks he can just treat women in any way he wants to treat them.

"Wendy, my friend, is one of those women. Real beautiful and good at heart. She's only dancing for a short time till she can get back on her feet, but she's his number one girl and he has her dance for him privately at his place. But when he gets to drinking," Al continued, "he's been known to get a little rough with Wendy." Al started shaking his head and then held it down. "If I could, I'd get her outta there myself."

I could tell that Al cared for this woman and that there was some sorta parenthood-like relationship here. "How do you know her?"

Al lifted his head and looked at the sky. "I met her one night outside Bottom's Up while I was walking, probably through that same alley where you're wanting me to drive." Al leaned back on the bench and went on. "She saw that I lived on the streets, so she decided to buy me some food. She then told me 'meet me here every night except for Sundays and I'll make sure you have something to eat.'

"So, basically, she feeds me out back at Bottom's Up and we've gotten to know each other pretty well through conversation. She even lets me shower at her place sometimes and stay the night, but I don't like being a nuisance, so I don't stay but maybe a couple times a month." I could tell Al was very appreciative for her. "She's a single mom and her boy is a good kid."

Now I had a plan somewhat already drawn up for Kevin "K-Dogg" Durgess, but a bright light turned on in my head just then.

Maybe my plan would be re-drawn to the point where getting to Durgess could be made easier.

"If you're going after 'K-Dogg', then I'm all in for this," said Al.

I thought about that. "Al."

"Yeah."

"You said Durgess sometimes beats Wendy, right?"

Al slowly nodded his head.

"You also said she's only dancing for a short time until she can get back on her feet, right?"

"Yeah."

"And you said if you could get her outta Bottom's Up you would, right?"

"Yeah Job. What are you getting at?"

I smiled. It was then that Al knew where I was heading with this. He smiled back.

"Take me to her," I said.

"With pleasure," returned Al.

# 26

Al knocked on Wendy's door.

On the drive over, we talked and he knew exactly where I was heading with my thinking. Wendy was being beaten, was wanting soon to be done dancing, and she now had two men who would help her out of Bottom's Up.

What better way than to remove the biggest threat: Kevin "K-Dogg" Durgess.

Opening her apartment door, she smiled when she saw Al. "Hey Al!"

"Wendy," said Al, "good to see you sweet heart."

"You too." She looked over at me. "Who's your friend?"

Al looked at me and back to Wendy. "He's someone who's about to become your friend too." Wendy wasn't sure what to make of that. "Wendy, this is my friend Job," Al went on, "Job, this is Wendy."

I held out my hand; Wendy took it and we shook. "Nice to meet you," I said.

"Likewise." Wendy opened the door wider. "Please, come in."

*She's easy on the eyes.*

I'm not here to marry the woman.

*I wasn't implying that, just stating the obvious.*

Making our way in, Wendy's apartment was kempt and clean. It had a homey feeling about it, and the picture of Jesus Christ on one of the walls made me stop and look for a long moment.

There was my Lord and Savior looking right at me and I felt dirty and guilty looking back at Him with what I had been doing. In a way, it was like I was looking at Him and saying, "I know Your way is the only true and right way, but I'm sidestepping for a little while until I can make things right in my own way."

Looking away, I followed Wendy and Al into the living room. An entertainment center with a decent sized TV, along with a Super Nintendo console sitting on the ground below it, stood in front of a large sofa and recliner. Wendy must've had a scent plug-in somewhere in the room because it smelled good as I took my seat on the sofa. Wendy also sat on the sofa while Al plopped down on the recliner.

I placed my book bag on the ground.

"Where's Stephen?" asked Al.

"In his room playing," returned Wendy.

I looked over at Wendy as her and Al made small talk. She was by far a beautiful woman who looked a few years younger than me, but the way she dressed and acted made me think she was far from a strip club dancer. Modestly attired, her white skin had a tinge of self-tanner, which looked natural, and her brown hair hung below her shoulders. Sporting a gold cross necklace around her neck, she was polite and made me feel right at home.

Al's voice then caught my attention. "This guy can get you out. We have a plan that we think will work. You just need to give us some details and plant something for us."

Wendy looked to me. "Why do you wanna help me?" Her face looked concerned, but curious at the same time. "I don't even know you. Have you been to the club?"

Smiling, I said, "No, I've never stepped foot inside a strip club in my entire life," to answer her last question. "I'll be honest with you, Wendy," I carried on, "my initial intention wasn't to help you but to go after Kevin Durgess; however, when Al told me about you, I saw both a woman who wanted out and a way that would make my job easier."

Wendy thought on that. "So, you're using me?" she said with a somewhat mean look.

I assumed she would think this, but I was prepared to answer her truthfully. "Absolutely not," I replied, my face earnest. "I look down on men who abuse women, and I'm sorry with what you've had to go through." Her face softened, like she was taken aback with my words. "Al told me of your situation and you wanting out. If you want the beatings to stop and if you want out of this current lifestyle, I believe I can make that happen for you; that is," I said looking into her eyes, "if you're willing to help.

"Plus," I added, "I hear you have a little son and you're wanting better things for both you and him." I opened my hands for understanding. "With that said, he needs his mother. Not one who is treated like trash, coming home with bruises, and who's doing something she's not proud of.

"You seem like a nice woman. I'm going after Kevin Durgess anyway, but if I can help out someone in desperate need like you in the process, then that's a bonus." I also thought it would make me feel a little bit better about what I would be doing, like I was mixing good in with the badness.

*If you're trying to justify what you're going to do to Durgess as right by helping Wendy, then you've lost it pal. Then again, you kinda have.*

I'm still sane. Zip it.

With tearful eyes, Wendy wasn't sure what to say. "I don't know who you are, Job, but what you just said," she wiped a tear away from her right eye, "is probably the nicest thing anyone has ever said to me."

I felt bad for her. Compliments and a helping hand seemed unknown to this woman.

Al cleared his throat. "So, Wendy, are you in or out?" To help make her decision easier, Al went on. "He beats you Wendy, he treats you terribly, and," Al said with a fatherly tone, "you've been telling me you're wanting out. This....this is your chance."

Wendy thought on it for about a half a minute before I spoke.

"Nothing will come back on you. I give you my word. All you need to do is tell me how a typical night in the club goes with him, the location of certain things, and," I said leaning forward, "and I need you to plant a gun."

Her face looked unsure after I mentioned planting a gun. "Don't worry," I told her, "I'm not killing anybody; it's only to scare Durgess and to get him to go with me." I then added, "You wanted out, so here's the way. This opportunity may not ever present itself again."

Thinking again, Wendy leaned back on the sofa and put her hands together. Clutching her cross necklace with her right hand, she said, "I really want out, but I don't know if this is the way. But," she then said with conviction in her voice, "you and Al are the only people who have cared about my situation and who are willing to help; so," she paused, "if Al trusts you, then I also trust you.

"Thank God Durgess only uses me for dancing and not sex. He's a pig who may pay me well for private dances, but yes, I'm wanting out, desperately." She started to get emotional. "I got my GED a couple years ago and now I'm taking on-line classes to hopefully become a nurse and make a better life for Stephen and I. I'm a single mom, I've never tried drugs or sold my body for money, and I'm trying to make ends meet. I hate what I do, but I also do it to put food on the table, keep a roof over our head, clothes on our back, and pay bills."

*Wendy's actually a good-hearted, genuine woman.*

I'm thinking so too. I wonder what happened in her life for her to get to this point?

*Dunno. All make mistakes; unfortunately, not all learn from them. Looks like she has.*

I sat a little closer to her to let her know that I cared.

"What I do is only temporary," Wendy continued, "and I've been waiting to get out for sometime. If you say you can get Durgess outta the picture without anything coming back on me...." I interrupted Wendy.

"I can, and," I paused, "I will."

She seemed satisfied. "Then....then I'm in."

We sat quietly for about a minute looking from one to the other at times.

"Wendy," Al broke the silence, "I've seen this man here work." He pointed his finger at me. "Trust me, he'll get done what he says."

Wendy smiled, a brighter and safer future in her sight. "Tell me what you need."

"I need to know...." but a door in the apartment suddenly opened and making his way into the living room was Stephen, Wendy's son.

He looked just like her and, although I didn't know his age, he was small and could talk pretty well. "Mommy, mommy," he dove into Wendy's arms. Looking toward the recliner, he said, "Hey Al!"

"Stephen, my man!" said Al.

Al and I smiled while Wendy kissed Stephen on the top of his head. "Honey, mommy's gotta talk to Al and this other nice man. Can you go back in your room and play for a little while longer?"

"Who's that?" Stephen pointed at me.

"His name's Job," replied Wendy.

"Hi Job. That's a cool name."

I waved. "Hi buddy. And thank you. Stephen's a cool name too."

Planting his feet on the carpeted floor, Stephen started walking back to his bedroom; but before passing me, he held up his hand. "High-five Job."

Slapping him a high-five, Stephen shut the door behind him when he reached his room.

*Good kid.*

Yeah.

"He usually doesn't take to strangers," said Wendy. "There must be something about you, Job." She seemed to light up after saying this.

*I think Wendy kinda likes you J.*

That'll be enough of that.

*Just saying.*

"He seems like a good kid," I said.

Al then said, "All right, back to business."

165

"I need to know how things go with you, you and Durgess, and the location of where things take place, Wendy. Are certain nights different? Al tells me you dance for him. Where does this take place? Just tell me the works."

"It's all the same with Durgess," said Wendy, "nothing ever changes." She went on to tell me about how a regular night was inside of Bottom's Up and what Durgess expected from her.

Wendy didn't perform until later because Durgess wanted to keep the men inside the club waiting for the best and to keep the place "hopping" in the meantime - Durgess' words Wendy told me. After her stage performance, she told me, Durgess would come down from where he watched on the second story, have one of his bouncers meet her, and then he, Durgess, would escort her into a private dance room where she would dance to music for him.

"When do you perform?" I had asked her.

"Around 11:30."

"When will I know you're about up?"

"Trust me, you'll know. Though I hate it, they always make a big deal out of it."

"After you perform, where do you meet Durgess?"

"There are three hallways on the left side of the club, and each of them lead into smaller hallways that then lead into private dance rooms. Durgess always meets and escorts me down the middle hallway, and he always takes me to the last room on the right."

"Where does his bouncer go?"

"He follows us from behind and waits outside in the hallway until I'm done."

"Okay, go on."

Wendy then told me that she performs a couple of dances for him. When she's done, she gets dressed, collects her earnings, and goes home.

She also told me that there's an exit door in the back of the middle hallway that leads to a side alley.

Very useful information.

"My problem is," I told Wendy at one point, "I've scoped out the outside of the club before and there's two bouncers who check every person before they're allowed to enter." Al sat up and leaned forward in the recliner, hanging on every word. "I'm not sure how to get a gun in except through you."

Wendy smiled. "Leave it to me. They don't check us girls." She explained. "I'll show up in the morning, say I forgot something, and plant it...." she thought for a long moment, and then a light bulb went off in her head, "in one of the bathrooms. I saw it in a movie once."

166

Genius, I thought.

"On the right side of the club," Wendy said, "there's three sets of bathrooms. I'll plant the gun in the bathrooms on the right hand side in the third stall under the toilet's tank cover. I've been in those bathrooms before. That work for you?"

"Works perfect, Wendy." She was pretty smart too, I thought.

With the mentioning of the exit door, I said looking at Al, "That's where I'll have you meet me. Outside that exit door in the side alley."

Al nodded his head.

"Okay," I said resting my head in my hands and looking down, "let me try to piece this thing together."

# 27

It was mostly quiet for about twenty minutes. During that time, Al rested his eyes and Wendy filled several glasses full of water and brought them out for all of us; she then made something to eat for Stephen in the meantime. The pieces of the puzzle in my head were coming together quicker than I'd thought. It was amazing and I couldn't believe it. Picturing the club and what Wendy had just mentioned inside my head, it was like it was all meant to be. Finally, I opened my eyes, lifted my head, took a few long gulps of water, and told them what the plan was.

"Here's how it's gonna go down," I said, having Al and Wendy's full attention.

"Next Friday's the night. Wendy," I said looking at her, "have that gun planted by then. Al," I then turned his way, "since Wendy doesn't perform until 11:30, go ahead and park in the side alley around midnight" - I tried to base that time span on Wendy's performance, getting the gun, her private dance with Durgess, and me getting Durgess out.

Continuing on, I said turning to Wendy, "When it's your turn to take the stage and dance, be on the lookout for me in the crowd. If for some reason there's a problem, I'll shake my head, which means the plan's off; but if I nod my head, that's the signal that all is a go." Wendy nodded her head, acknowledging that she understood.

"From there," I went on, "I'll head to the bathroom to get the gun, which will be in the bathrooms on the right hand side in the third stall under the toilet's tank cover, correct Wendy?"

"Correct Job."

"After I get the gun and walk outta the bathroom, I'll stand outside the bathrooms and wait for Durgess to make his way down and take you to the private dance room." I tried to remember what was to take place next. Remembering, I said, "I'll wait a little for Durgess to get comfortable before making my way in. Then...." but Wendy cut me short.

"Don't forget about the bouncer who'll be outside in the hallway waiting for Durgess." Wendy paused and then said, "What are you going to do about him? All of the bouncers are pretty good size."

"Let me worry about that." I totally forgot about the bouncer. "I'll make sure he won't be a problem."

I needed more information from Wendy. "What's the layout of the private dance room like? Door location? Seating location? Is there anything major to prepare for?"

Wendy moved her body on the sofa to face me more. "You shouldn't have any problems. Where I'll be dancing is out in front and he, Durgess, has a small sofa, which he'll be sitting on and his back will be facing you when you come in. Him hearing you come in shouldn't be a concern either because he likes music being played while I'm in there."

Perfect. Coming up behind "K-Dogg" sounds like it wouldn't pose any threat to me being seen or heard. "Thanks Wendy."

"You're welcome."

I also asked, "Will the door be locked to this private dance room?"

"Nope."

Perfect.

"Now, when I come in," I started to say to Wendy, "act like you don't see me until I get right behind Durgess and I give you a nod. Then act like something bad is about to take place or something. And when I threaten you, just go along with it." I then explained my reasoning. "You need to look like a victim, because I don't want anything coming back on you or for Durgess or anyone else to think that you had something to do with this."

Touched by this, as written on Wendy's face, she said, "Thanks Job, I really appreciate that."

"It's the right thing to do," is all I said.

"I'll take Durgess from there, and then, Al," I said focusing my attention back to him, "that's when I'll plan on meeting with you in the side alley."

Al nodded and said, "I'll be waiting." He then added, "I'll even help you throw that scumbag in the trunk."

That was the plan, I think. At least I thought that was the whole of it.

"Job," said Wendy.

"Yeah."

"Just so you know, I'll be called by my stage name that night, not Wendy."

"And that is?"

"Miss Tonya." She paused and then said, "I hate it, but it's the one they gave me."

"All right, thanks for letting me know."

"Al, Wendy," I said looking at them, "I believe that's the plan. Any questions?"

Wendy shook her head.

Al's face looked confused. He said, "Job?"

"Yeah Al."

"You came up with all that in that short of a time?"

I thought about that and even answered him confusedly, "Yeah," I said, "I guess I did."

"That's impressive man."

*That's scary if you ask me.*

I unzipped my book bag and reached my hand into it. Pulling out the Sig Sauer, I said, "Here's the gun, Wendy." Placing the gun in her open hands, Wendy's hands shook. "Sorry," she said, "I've never held a gun before."

"Just don't pull the trigger and you'll have nothing to be afraid of," said Al.

"I can wait and give this to you next week if that'd make you feel more comfortable?" I told her. I felt bad about giving it to her now anyway.

"No," Wendy said. "With what you're going to do for me, this is the least I can do."

Going into her bedroom that was by the living room, Wendy came back out shortly after and said, "I put it someplace safe that even Stephen won't find."

Sitting back on the sofa, Wendy took a drink of water. Al leaned forward in the recliner and yawned. Wrapping things up, I said, "How about we meet back here sometime next week to go over the plan one last time just to make sure we're all good?"

"Sounds good," said Al.

"That's fine with me," Wendy started to say, "I'll make something for all of us to eat. Spaghetti with meat sauce and garlic bread sound good?"

"You made me that a few weeks ago and I'm begging for more," said Al. "That sounds great."

That did sound amazing, I thought. Wendy looked at me. "Count me in," I said with a smile.

Arising from the sofa, I said to Al, "Let's get going. It's getting late and I still gotta drop you off." Al rose up from the recliner. We began to make our way out of the living room, but Wendy's voice stopped us.

"Job."

Turning around, I said, "Yeah."

"Why are you doing this?"

"I already told you, Al told me of your situation and I thought...." but Wendy interrupted me.

"No, I mean," she started to say, "why are you going after Kevin Durgess? What did he do to you?"

My face growing sad, I hung my head down. I hadn't talked about Naomi to anyone outside of family and Jehu Bridges; however, strangers can oftentimes be closer companions than what people think.

Looking up with hurt and pain written on my face, Wendy and Al could sense something wasn't right. I hadn't even told Al my reasoning for what I had been doing, even after what happened at Ricky's arcade; but maybe he knew it was something so bad that even he didn't want to bring it up.

To answer Wendy's question and welcome them into my fractured world, I said, "He killed my wife, along with three other members of SSS. They killed her in our home right in front of my eyes, and for some reason God allowed me to live. Now, I have a revenge sentence out on all of them."

The two of them didn't know what to say. Looking at Al, his face looked like someone had just told him that he had terminal, inoperable cancer; and Wendy's was starting to turn wet from tears streaming down hers.

Saying nothing and just being there is sometimes the best thing we humans can do for one another. It certainly was at this time.

Breaking the awkward silence, I said, "Al, let's get going." I let Al go in front of me and Wendy led us to the front door.

Al gave Wendy a hug and said, "Good seeing you kid."

"Likewise," returned Wendy. "Thank you so much."

Al made his way out into the hallway and said, "Don't thank me. Thank that guy right there," he said pointing at me, "he's the one who's making it happen."

I looked at Wendy, nodded, and was making my way through the front door, but she stopped me by placing a hand on my shoulder. "Job, I...." but she didn't have the words. Tears started to wet her eyes again. "Thank....thank you." Emotion drove her to wrap her arms around me and give me a tight hug. It was the first time I'd been hugged like this since Naomi, and I wasn't sure what to make of it.

I ended up returning her hug and she held me for a long moment. I wanted to say something, but I also didn't have the words.

Letting go, I walked into the hallway with Al and we started making our way. Wendy's door closed behind us. When we got to the apartment complex's main entrance, I said to Al, "Hey, I'll be right back. I forgot something. Here's the keys." Handing the keys to Al, I made my way back to Wendy's apartment.

Knocking on her door, she opened up, smiled when she saw it was me, and I could tell she had been crying because her face was wet again.

"Hey," she said.

"Hey."

Unzipping my book bag again, I grabbed something else to give to her. I wasn't a rich man by any means, but I still had plenty to spare, and I figured she needed this more than I did at this time.

Placed in a small plastic bag, I pulled out five thousand dollars and handed it toward Wendy. "It takes a lot for someone to want to turn their life around. You got your GED, you're taking on-line classes, and next week you'll finally be done with that lifestyle you hate." I couldn't describe her face just then; it was a mix of joy and unbelief at the same time. "I want you to have this." Putting the money in her hand, I said, "This should help out in some way."

Tears again filling her eyes, Wendy said, "Thank....thank you so much Job. How much is it? I'll repay you at some point." She went to wipe the tears away from her eyes.

"You won't repay me one cent." The Bible says when you give, give with a cheerful heart, so I took a few words from that. "Don't worry about how much, just know that I give it with a cheerful heart."

*Well done Job, seriously.*

Turning to my left, I started making my way down the hallway again.

"Job, wait," said Wendy behind me. I turned around.

Running to me, she threw her arms around me, but this time I didn't return the embrace. "Where has a guy like you been all my life." She paused and then said, "Your wife must've been very special and lucky."

Letting go of me, we faced each other. "My wife was the greatest as they come, and," I paused before saying, "it was me who was the lucky one."

We stood there quiet for a moment. Wendy then said, "I mean this only in a friendly way." She then drew closer to me and kissed me on the cheek. "See you next week."

Saying nothing, I turned around and made my way to my truck.

On the ride home, Al said, "Job, I think Wendy likes you. I've never seen her light up as much as I saw her tonight.

"If you ever plan on getting serious with someone ever again," Al went on, "I think you two would be all right together. Plus that little man of hers warmed up to you pretty good."

I thought about that. Wendy wasn't some broad sleeping with all kinds of men; she was exposing herself a little to support her and her child, and she wasn't even happy about doing it. She had even wanted to pay me back at some point for the five thousand I'd given her. And here she was turning her life around when so many people continued to sink down further into the world's deceptive and sinful drain.

Her cross necklace, the picture of Jesus Christ in her apartment, her politeness and thankfulness, her willingness to turn her life around and decide to live with a new perspective, and the way she acted. There were definitely some fine qualities there.

But I didn't look at Wendy in a relationship way. I loved my wife and still did, and she was still alive in me as one. My love for her was deep, and it still carried on in me. I was only thirty-three-years old, but I didn't think I'd ever marry again after what happened to Naomi.

Or would I?

God knew the course of my life, and if I was destined to marry someone else, then He already knew. But right now relationships and marriage was one of the furthest things from my mind.

Plus, I thought, many of these things would never matter if I got caught: work, marriage, hobbies, you name it.

I never replied back to Al's comment. Instead, we drove the rest of the way in silence until I dropped him back off in his neck of the woods.

The following week, we all got back together to go over the plan one last time before putting it into action. Wendy prayed over the meal, flashed quite a few smiles my way at the table, and hugged me tightly before Al and I left that night.

I didn't know what to make of it all. She never crossed the line once, but I could sense she was fond of me. For being a dancer, she was very respectful and didn't just throw herself on me, unlike many women this day in age.

Oh, and Wendy kept her word about the meal. She made spaghetti with meat sauce and garlic bread to go along with it.

It was delicious.

# 28

Another section of the old Mount Vernon High School basement was similar to where I'd dealt with Tyrese Taylor, only this section was darker and had a bone-chilling feeling about it.

As I had with Taylor, I tied Durgess' arms and legs securely to a chair with duct tape over his mouth. Unlike Taylor, he'd been conscious, but it was easy getting him down into the basement with a gun digging into his back. I didn't say a word to Durgess the entire time and he didn't say anything either. I figured he was still in shock after discovering it was me who was doing this to him, like I was someone who'd been miraculously raised from the grave to dish out one thing and one thing only.

Revenge.

Leaving him in total blackness, I stayed at the same cheap motel that I had before after I'd taken Tyrese Taylor. Actually, I left him with some friends who happened to inhabit this part of the basement: rats. I initially felt bad about leaving him in there with them, but then I thought about what he had taken part in - killing Naomi - and then I ended up not feeling bad.

The next morning, I got around, showered, and started off my day by having breakfast at Bob Evans, which was located on a busy Coshocton Avenue. Running into some people I knew, they had asked what I was doing home and I'd told them I just got into town, was having breakfast, and was back home visiting family.

A lie, I know. I'm not perfect.

*Amen to that!* My counselor had told me.

Be quiet is all I replied back.

I didn't have the heart to visit Naomi. Instead, knowing I'd have time to kill, I went for a run on the Kokosing Gap Trail.

The scenery was thickly wooded with a green vastness of vegetation that spanned far and wide. Echoing a song of its own, the Kokosing River flowed near the trail. The rays of the sun tried to squeeze through the openings between the trees and animals such as birds, squirrels, and deer to name a few went about their ordinary, everyday business. With it being a weekend Saturday, the trail was busier than I thought it would be; so to keep others from noticing who I was - just in case - I wore a headband on top of my head, which was actually the sleeve of a t-shirt I had cut off, and sunglasses to go along with it.

I'd seen folks who I had graduated with and others who I knew from growing up in Mount Vernon. They hadn't recognized me, and I ran past them without giving conversation a second thought.

Soon this popular and well-visited trail would give birth to colorful leaves and a cool down when the fall would arrive. By far my favorite season, I could remember going on runs on this same trail during the days of my youth. Many of those days were spent with Naomi; days I would do just about anything right now to relive.

Passing the new Mount Vernon High School after my run, where Naomi and I had graduated, I spent the rest of the day visiting stores, reading, dozing off in my truck - you get the point - basically anything to count down to nighttime.

Counting down to confront and deal with Kevin "K-Dogg" Durgess.

I figured my time with Durgess would be shorter than it had been with Taylor because there wasn't much I had to ask him, and Taylor had filled me in on most of what I needed to know.

But I still had questions.

Finally, darkness had fallen, so I made my way to the old MVHS.

Opening the door to where I put Durgess, I didn't turn the lights on just then. Hearing the squeaky sound of rats, it even sent a chill down my spine. Finally flicking the dim lights on, there Durgess sat sweating with a horror-filled look on his face. A couple of rats looked like they were gnawing on his shoes, but he kicked them away as best he could, sending them scurrying to a corner of the concrete floor.

Grabbing a small towel from a workbench, I wiped the sweat from Durgess' brow. Patting his face to remove sweat beads, I tossed the towel back on the workbench and stared him down for a long minute. I wanted to start out with him thinking that I was unexpectedly caring.

But inside I had other things planned.

Breathing heavily as I walked in front of him, Durgess' eyes were wide and white, and I could even see the small red veins within the whiteness of his eyes.

Removing the duct tape from his mouth, his terrified look and fear struck eyes were only a masquerade.

"You mother…." sorry, he cursed, "I'm gonna bury you alive! You're gonna wish you were already dead!" He then tried to spit on my

175

face, but his saliva found my shirt instead. "I'm Kevin 'K-Dogg' Durgess of SSS!" he said boastfully. "You won't get away with this!"

Having enough, I aggressively placed the duct tape back over his mouth. Trying to move back and forth, and with muffled profanities, Durgess looked like someone from a psych ward.

Taking a few steps back, I stood there for what seemed like five minutes, which was probably only one, in silence, and then I pulled the .357 from behind my waist and let my arm hang down with the muzzle pointing toward the ground.

Durgess calmed down pretty quick. It's amazing how the quiet presence of a gun can turn a situation around.

"I'm gonna remove that tape from your mouth only one more time." I started to shake the gun in my hand. "Did you hear me? Only one more time." I settled my hand down. "I'm gonna ask you some questions, and," I said giving him a hard stare in his eyes, "if you start acting like you just did, then," and that's when I pointed the gun at my own head so Durgess would get my point.

*Wow, J, I think you're really losing it. Pointing a gun at your own head. Really?*

It's only for effect.

*Still. Haven't you ever heard of accidental shootings?*

Point taken. It won't happen again.

*Thank you.*

Approaching "K-Dogg" again, I removed the duct tape from his mouth and this time he was as silent as the grave.

"Thank you for making yourself known," I reminded him from yelling out his name just moments earlier, "now that that's done, let us get to why you're here." Durgess kept quiet.

"I take it you remember who I am?" I said. The memory flashed in my head just then from when he finally figured out who I was and said, "You?" before I slammed the trunk's door down on his head at Bottom's Up.

Without saying a word, Durgess slowly nodded his head, like he was scared to confess.

"And do you know why you're here now?" I said, my face turning red from the anger building inside of me.

With no emotion, Durgess again slowly nodded his head, like murdering Naomi had no impact on him whatsoever.

After reminding him of his severe transgression - I wanted that fresh in his mind - I continued on.

"And to add to that," I said taking a step back, "you live a crooked lifestyle and profit from a twisted way of life." I wanted to say, "And you like to beat women also," but I didn't want him thinking I knew Wendy on a personal basis; thus, leading him to believe that she had something to do with his abduction.

"Man you don't...." Durgess tried to say, but I broke him off.

"SHUT UP!" I roared. Durgess did just that.

*I would've too after the way you just looked.*

With anger and honesty mixed, I said, "You're an epitome of what's wrong in this world today." He didn't know what to think of that by the look on his face. "What purpose do you even serve being here?" Again, Durgess didn't know what to think.

With only one more important question left for me to ask, I stalled for a little. "With two of you outta the picture, there's only one left." Durgess' face changed, like he was puzzled at first, but then he just realized something.

"You were the one at Ricky's arcade?" News spread fast and wide in Columbus. "It was you who took Tyrese? What'd you do to him?"

Holding my head down for a few seconds and then lifting it back up, I said, "It was me," to answer his first couple of questions, "and his body's down here," to answer his last.

Durgess' shoulders involuntarily shook after I said this last part.

Kicking a few rats away who had made their way in my direction, I went on, "One by one I'm taking out all those who killed," I paused, "who killed my wife. Taylor's outta the picture, you're about to be, and all that's left is Booker." Like I had told you earlier, I resolved to leave Derek Westbrook outta this picture, as long as he intended me no ill will.

"For months I became well educated in the streets, your gang's ways, where you do business, and, of course," I paused, "how to go about getting rid of you."

"You're so dead you...." Durgess threatened me, but I pointed the gun at him to shut him up. Unfortunately, that didn't stop him.

He thought his fate was sealed, so I listened to his outbursts and empty curses until he was finally tired of talking.

Talking was something that Durgess liked to do.

Walking nearer to him, I sat the muzzle of the gun on top of Durgess' right kneecap. "Now that you're finally done, I have one last question for you."

*Job, I know you're thinking it, but don't do it.*

Like a light switch, Durgess changed from one emotion to the next pretty quickly. "What....what's your name again?" his voice started to crack.

With no emotion in my voice, I said, "Job."

177

"Job," Durgess paused, "Job, please, I'm sorry. I don't wanna die." His eyes appeared watery. "I'm sorry about killing your wife along with Rufus and Tyrese....I'm....I'm sorry!"

For some reason Durgess left out Derek Westbrook, probably because he too knew that the kid wanted nothing to do with killing my wife.

With no sympathy for the man, I said, "You ready for your last question?" The gun I kept glued to his kneecap.

With no reply, I asked Durgess anyway, "Where's Rufus Booker?"

Hanging his head down and shaking it, Durgess then lifted his head up with a serious look and said, "Your guess is as good as mine. I haven't seen him for a while."

Okay, I thought. I moved the gun to the left side of Durgess' kneecap. *Pop* came from the .357, which was then followed by continuous screams from Durgess.

If he wanted to play tough, so could I.

*JOB!*

"YOU, YOU SHOT ME! YOU CRAZY SON OF A...." Durgess cursed. Like Taylor had said after he thought I'd pushed the paralytic, Durgess screamed, "I WAS TELLING YOU THE TRUTH!"

Relaxing the gun off to my side, I said, "Stop your crying, it's only a flesh wound." The bullet passed through his skin, avoiding any bone.

Or so I had hoped.

And, like Taylor before him, it appeared Durgess really did tell the truth. The gun was initially only meant for intimidation, but it was in the back of my mind to use it to push Durgess further.

Guess he really did tell the truth.

Pleading his case further, Durgess screamed, "I DON'T KNOW WHERE HE IS! LIKE I SAID, I HAVEN'T SEEN HIM!"

"But you've talked to him, I'm sure."

"Yeah," Durgess began to say, finally calming down, "but that doesn't mean I know where he is!"

"He at The Kingdom?"

If you remember, that's SSS's main hangout where they cook and do business.

"That's my best guess. He practically lives there."

Useful information.

It was amazing how close partners ratted themselves out when in the company of someone who appeared to be a madman and when their life was on the line. Taylor had first fallen a victim to it, and now Durgess.

"I can't believe you shot me," Durgess whined. "We shoulda killed you...." but then he cut himself off.

178

But I knew what he was getting at. It's ironic what we humans start to say, and then how we wish we would've kept our mouths shut in the first place.

He was probably gonna say how they shoulda killed me after that day in court. Or maybe he was gonna say how they shoulda killed me because I was still a potential threat, though they probably thought not to this degree. With whatever he was about to say, he was gonna say how I shoulda been dead instead of alive.

Like I had said, talking was something that Durgess liked to do. I had just the thing for his talking mouth.

*J, this is enough!*

"Open your mouth," I said to Durgess.

He didn't do it.

"OPEN YOUR MOUTH!"

*J!*

This time, scared, Durgess slowly opened his mouth.

Putting the barrel of the .357 into "K-Dogg's" mouth, I said, "You talk too much." Pushing the hammer down on the gun until it made the *clicking* sound, I added, "You got anything else you wanna say?"

*I'm out. I don't wanna see how this ends.*

See ya.

Trembling from fear, Durgess tried saying something, but I couldn't make out what he said. Giving him a "What?" look, he said it again, and this time a fragment of what he said rang in my ears.

"What'd you just say?" I said, interest taking root in me. I removed the barrel of the gun from his mouth so he could talk clearly.

Swallowing hard, Durgess said the two words for a third time.

It was a name.

"So?" I started to say, "what's he got to do with anything?"

"He and Rufus Booker," said Durgess, "think about it."

I did, and after about ten seconds it finally hit home. Like a frozen sword piercing my heart, I stood stone cold still.

Lowering the gun to my side, I was shocked, like I couldn't believe what my ears had just heard and what my mind was thinking. I'd heard of the name that Kevin Durgess just spoke of before.

I knew that name.

"Why'd you tell me this just now?" I inquired, anger again rising in me.

With tears in his eyes, Durgess said, "Because it just came to my mind." Carrying on, he said, "Now do you understand why Booker never gets caught?"

Oh my Lord, I thought just then. A lot of nothing had just been put together, like a little child connecting each Lego piece, one by one.

This curveball would up my planning, and I'd have to figure something out with how to get to him as well. How? I thought. How could somebody like who Kevin Durgess just mentioned do this? I was still stunned, like the wind had just been knocked out of me, putting me on my back and leaving me looking up into a mysterious sky filled with lots of questions.

"What are you going to do now?" said Durgess.

While standing, I thought hard inside of my spinning head. Finally, I looked at Durgess and said, "This."

I raised the .357 to head level, and like I had done to Tyrese "TT" Taylor, I now did to Kevin "K-Dogg" Durgess.

I pulled the trigger.

# 29

Sitting outside on my front door steps, I watched the world revolve around me. At the same time, the inside of my head was whirling like a merry-go-round, only faster. So much bad I'd done, but I couldn't stop now.

*Yes you can.*

Especially after finding out - thanks to Kevin Durgess - who else was involved.

Booker still had to be dealt with too, and I wasn't even sure how I was to go about getting him. I couldn't just drive to The Kingdom, hope he was there, and kick down the door with guns blazing and take him like I had Taylor and Durgess.

What was I to do?

My mind quickly returned to the other individual who was abetting Rufus Booker. How? I couldn't stop thinking. How could someone in this man's position do this? What would drive a man who most people probably respected to lower his stance to that of a drug kingpin? Then again, what drives the heart of a man to allow darkness, evil, and eventually death to overtake him?

I thought of some examples: greed, wealth, power, influence, pride; and those are just to name some of the many things that can turn a man's once good heart into that of blackness.

To think that this man and Rufus Booker were working together was beyond me. It was like someone finding out that the child they were raising was actually someone else's seed who had been conceived through their spouse's affair: it was all too much to take in.

It was too hard to believe.

I felt like I was one of only a few who knew about a nation's deep dark secret.

But then a bright light lit up in my head. If I could get Rufus Booker, then I was sure I'd be able to get dirt on this other person through him, or at least I hoped. Then the secret I would make known to all.

I thought of a Bible passage just then: *For the time is coming when everything that is covered will be revealed, and all that is secret will be made known to all.*

Thinking on that for a few minutes, many things came into perspective. This man abetted a known criminal, whether he had an actual hand in it or not. He helped spread drugs and poison around the city of Columbus, even if he didn't measure and cook it. This unthinkable spawn of evil had caused tears and heartbreak, the loss of loved ones, closed caskets, and many other sufferings, whether or not his hand was on the murder weapon.

That's when it hit me to the fullest, like an uppercut right to the jaw: in someway, somehow, this man had aided in the death of my wife.

Clenching my left fist with anger eating away at my heart, I thought, "Yes." This man is certainly going to pay for his evil and sinful ways.

Taylor and Durgess were outta this original bloodstained picture that was painted on that murderous night when Naomi was killed. Booker was the only one left, and soon I'd take him down too.

In someway, somehow, I was going to get to him too.

*With the way you think and what you've been doing, I have no doubts.*

Yes there were many questions that still needed to be answered, and yes I had preparations and some planning to come up with; but I'd come this far, and I wasn't turning back now.

Like Jesus' disciple brothers, James and John, I wanted to call down fire from Heaven, though for a very different reason. And like Samson, the very strong and longhaired judge of God from The Old Testament, I wanted to pay back my enemies just one last time.

Of course, my selfish ambition - revenge - was what I was really harboring inside of me. It was wrong, I know, but my soul wouldn't rest until it was accomplished.

We as people were to treat others the same way we ourselves would want to be treated. Taylor, Durgess, and Booker hadn't done that. But I also knew I had wavered to the point where I was on their level, because it wasn't right with what I had been doing to them.

*At least you're willing to admit that. Most people are either scared or too proud or embarrassed to admit their mistakes. But growth starts with confession.*

Valid point.

You ever have those days where you feel like nobody cares about you, you feel so alone, or you feel like you're a terrible person, far from God's forgiveness and grace?

182

Today I was having one of those days.

Like a battle raging in my soul, good and evil forces were fighting against the other. Revenge, anger, and hatred were on one side while mercy, repentance, and transformation was on the other. Satan, evil, and lies were on one side while Jesus, light, and rest for my soul was on the other.

A storm of emotion wanted to explode out of me, but I held it in. Instead, I did something else: I prayed. I closed my eyes, folded my hands together, and bowed my head. I prayed like I hadn't prayed before; I prayed like a man torn between two opposing sides.

This time of prayer I'm keeping between God and me. It's nothing against you personally, but some prayers are just meant to stay between God and the individual. This privilege - prayer - God has given to all of those created in His image; it's that telephone call, that connecting link that too many people pass up on, but it's something I found myself doing at the present when I felt that all hope was lost.

It must've been ten, fifteen minutes before I concluded. When I was done, I opened up my eyes and looked at the day before me.

The day was overcast with cloud joined to cloud, like a continuous rolling white wave that had no end. I loved days like these; they reminded me of autumn. A soothing breeze came from the west and leaves rustled on the nearby trees. Birds of different species feasted from a bird feeder that I'd suspended on one of those trees. My neighborhood was quiet and all was peaceful in it.

Why couldn't life be just like this? I thought. Peaceful and quiet with people treating others well. Where a helping hand wasn't pushed away, or complimenting words weren't thought of as anything more, or a kind act didn't imply something further. Why couldn't the race of human just get along in harmony and build one another up instead of tearing one another down?

*Amen brother.*

Instead, this world was filled with lust, drugs, lies, deceit, murder, rape, theft, death, and so much more. There were people who'd rather crash planes into buildings than find ways to grow together, people who would much prefer to find their identity in the things of this world rather than in that which is everlasting, and there were those who clung to this life and lived it as if this were the only life that they had.

There was so much more to life, I thought, than what this world offers and what's going on in it. Unfortunately, I had become a part of the problem, though not to many of these degrees. Like all humans, I struggled with temptation and my weaknesses; and, sadly, I had allowed my weakness and temptation of revenge to outdo anything else in me.

183

Standing up, I went inside to get something cold to drink.

After downing two glasses of iced water, I began walking around my house to look at all the family pictures of Naomi, me, and Manhattan that were hung on our walls. They were memories that seemed to be lived so long ago.

Starting in our bedroom, there was a large framed facial picture of Naomi and I, both of us smiling, hung above our bed's headboard. Naomi had changed it into a black and white picture before hanging it up; the "selfie" had been taken in our backyard while we sat on the grass and I held Naomi from behind.

In the hallway before coming to the top of the stairs, another picture featured Naomi, Manhattan, and I on a canoe trip that we'd taken last summer on the wall above a decorative table that I'd built. We had a family who was also canoeing on the same river snap the picture during a break. Manhattan's teeth shined white and her body was soaking wet from jumping in the river all day. Naomi and I held up our oars smiling, making it look like we were about to clobber one another with them.

It must've taken me a half hour or maybe even longer to look at all the pictures that attired our home. Finally, I'd come to the picture in the living room that I treasured most of all.

The picture was of the three of us - Naomi, Manhattan, and me - standing in our front yard. To many it would seem like an ordinary picture, but to me it meant something much more. It was also the last family picture that we had taken together; matter of fact, it was just taken this spring when the leaves were budding and the flowers were starting to bloom. The sun was just about to set and the sky was filled with sharp and lively colors. Everything was captured in this last picture that we'd taken together.

With our two story brick house behind us, I stood to the left and Naomi to the right. Manhattan stood perfectly between us in front, and I held Naomi tight with my arm around her waist. Smiling - it even seemed Manhattan was too - there we stood in front of our home.

As a family.

As one.

Good Lord I missed these days.

All of that was now destroyed, eradicated from existence, burned to the ground.

With anger and sorrow mixed together within me, sorrow won me over this time. So help me God I wanted to cry like I'd never cried before, I wanted to bawl my eyes out, I wanted to fall on my knees and weep until I had no more tears left; but, in the end, I had only three silent tears fall from my eyes and make their way down my face.

184

Three, I thought, with significance. One for Naomi. One for Manhattan. And one for me.

I missed my family.

Abruptly, like awakening from sleep before the end of a dream, there came several knocks on my front door. It caught me off guard because I was so engrossed in the past with my family that it made me involuntarily shake.

Wiping my face dry, I didn't want my guest to see that I had cried. There came more knocks on my door, this time louder. Taking a deep breath and getting my bearings together, I headed toward the front door.

Who could it be? I thought. Figuring it was Jehu Bridges or a member of my family, I didn't know who else would be visiting me at this time.

My shotgun stood up, off to the side of my front door. I kept it there just in case. Plus, with all that had gone on, I wasn't going to be unprepared.

Unlocking and then opening the front door slowly, I beheld my guest.

*Whoa. I definitely wasn't expecting this.*

It wasn't Jehu Bridges.

It wasn't any of my family.

It was someone who I least expected.

A rage so intense that I didn't have a name for detonated inside of me just then. Initially grabbing for my shotgun, I stopped when the person standing at my front door just stood there with a sad face. When I met his eyes, that's when he held his head down.

This unexpected guest who stood at my front door was none other than the fourth member of SSS who I initially wanted dead just as the other three; it was the same one who I came to doubt that I could do anything against, given he was young.

*Don't forget. He was also the same one who acted like he wanted no part in a lot, if not all, of what happened.*

Here he was standing nonthreateningly in front of my face. Here he was turning himself in and I didn't know what I was going to do. Here he was and....and....

It was none other than Derek Westbrook.

# 30

Flashback.

Definition: A recurring, intensely vivid mental image of a past traumatic experience.

Too many past images still haunted me the night Naomi was killed before my eyes.

Her sitting in front of me with Rufus Booker behind her, her red-stained eyes holding back tears, her saying "we will be together, but not yet," her look right after the first shot was fired, her....

Wrath overtook me to the point where I felt nothing but hate for Derek Westbrook who stood right in front of me. Of course he'd acted like he wanted no part in any of what happened, and his depressed face and watery eyes were further evidence that he felt terrible with all that had happened.

Unfortunately, for his sake, my wrath came out in a physical hurricane.

Grabbing him tightly by the front chest area of his shirt, I threw him behind me like he weighed no more than a piece of paper. Landing and sliding on the hardwood floor, Derek made no move to stand up; he just laid there.

Slamming the front door shut behind me, I marched toward him, grabbed him tightly, one hand by the collar of his shirt and the other by his arm, and stood him up. With strength like a wild ox, I lifted him up off his feet and sent him crashing against the living room wall. Tears streaming down his face, Derek was limp and made no effort to fight back as I held him against the wall.

*Job! Stop!*

Forming an iron fist with my right hand, I raised it and started swinging it behind me. Its target: Derek Westbrook's face. My left hand tightly held Derek by his collar. But something held me back as I looked into Derek's eyes and he looked back into mine. With my face red, my temper reaching Mount Everest, and sweat dripping down the sides of my face, the fist of my right hand stayed glued behind me and I froze like a statue.

What was I doing?

*Yeah. What are you doing?*

I knew deep inside that Derek was just a kid who made some bad decisions and got mixed in with the wrong crowd. And now here he was and he wasn't even fighting back against me.

That told me something.

*It should.*

It was this kid who stood at a distance unsure of the things going on in front of him the night Naomi was murdered, it was Rufus Booker's hand that had actually pulled the trigger for him when it came to his turn to shoot my wife, it was his teary eyes and ashamed face back in the courtroom that I remembered, and now it was Derek Westbrook who arrived at my front door step, sad and alone, who wouldn't fight back because he knew he'd been in the wrong.

I wanted to put a hole through his face, initially, but enough was enough.

Yelling out loud, I kept my fist raised while Derek's dispirited face shrunk, like he was preparing for a deathblow. Swinging full force forward, my fist made contact.

But it was the living room wall that already had multiple holes in it from my punches that it made contact with.

It was just another hole in the wall.

*Thank You, God. You made the right decision J.*

I felt no pain as I pulled my hand back. Loosening my grip and then letting go of Derek's collar, my anger relented. Opening up his eyes, Derek looked at me and we just stood there. Taking a deep breath, I turned my back on him and sat down on my living room sofa.

Sitting forward with my arms resting on my thighs, I slowed my respirations and wiped the sweat away from my face. Looking at Derek, I motioned with my hand for him to have a seat next to me.

Slowly making his way to the sofa, he sat down, but he sat as far away from me as he could. Wiping away his tears, he held his head down and sat quietly.

We sat in silence for about five minutes. Finally, I realized I was going to have to be the first to speak. Like I had been throughout this whole revenge ordeal, I was going to have to take the initiative.

Finally I said, "Derek, it's time we talked."

# 31

We started out slow like turtle's pace, but the more we talked, the more comfortable we got with one another. It was like we were at first soldiers of opposing countries fighting against the other; but now, somehow through all the chaos and madness, we unexpectedly came to find a peace with each other that can't be explained in words.

With tears falling from his eyes several times, he kept apologizing at the start of the conversation, and at one point Derek said he'd repay me whatever.

I never gave a reply. There was nothing no one could pay me back for the loss of Naomi and Manhattan. Not all the money in the world. Not all the material possessions in their abundance. Not for all the kingdoms in the world and their glory.

Nothing.

Instead, I said after a long, quiet moment, "If you wanna be of use, help me by telling me where Booker is and how I can get to him."

Derek said he would.

He told me that he fell in with the wrong group of people, that he'd been raised differently, and that he never agreed with what he had partook in. It was like a "rebellious stage," a "trying to fit in" at the time phase that he went through with SSS; but as vandalism and theft grew into home invasions and murder, he told me, he knew he had to get out, and quick. My wife's murder, his first real experience, sped the process to get out quicker.

After what happened in court, he said, he had a falling out with the gang, though some of the other members tried to persuade him to stay in bed with SSS - and some still kept in touch with him about SSS and what they were doing. Going through an identity crisis and trying to make sense of life and right and wrong, Derek said he finally was over that youthful recklessness and wanted to get himself and his life straight.

Traveling into the past, Derek said he and DJ Booker were best friends growing up; but that that childhood best friend also had a twisted, out-of-control older brother who had no respect or tolerance for people or the law. Eventually, that older brother, Rufus, mind-washed his younger brother and his best friend into teaching them the gang life and what all that incorporated. Whereas DJ sunk deeper and deeper into the gang life, Derek had told me, he didn't sink quite as fast, though the gang life seemed the life for them at the time.

Derek had gotten to see firsthand a lot of what Rufus Booker and SSS did with being best friends with DJ Booker. There were things he wasn't supposed to know about, he told me, that Rufus thought he had no clue about, and some of those things were very secret things. He still knew SSS's operations and how things went with being involved for so long, and he still knew about many other things - thanks to some of its members - who tried time and again to pull him back into the gang life.

And now here we were. Continuing in on the conversation.

With already knowing why they came to my house in the first place and all that happened thereafter and other information that came from Taylor and Durgess, we skipped a lot of what I already knew and got to other points.

"What can you tell me now about Rufus?"

Derek sat forward on the sofa. "I can tell you he's currently hiding out at The Kingdom cause he knows he's safe there." Derek looked at me, having more to tell. "Rufus, Tyrese, and Kevin haven't been talking or seeing each other much, I was told, cause they had heat on them and were told by someone to lay low and not have communication for a while."

I knew who that someone was; I didn't know if Derek did though.

"So they, Taylor and Durgess, stuck to their dirty business for SSS at Ricky's arcade and Bottom's Up while breaking off with Rufus for the time being until the heat cold down some. The only reason I know certain things is cause I left the gang and a few of my good friends who are still part of SSS have kept me in-the-loop, even though I'm working on them with trying to get out like I did."

"Does Rufus think or know anything that I should know about?"

"Yeah," Derek started to say, nodding his head, "Rufus isn't dumb, and he's always been skeptical about everyone except for Taylor and Durgess and this secret someone who I know nothing about."

That answered that question. Derek didn't know who this secret someone was, but I did, and I didn't want him to know, at least not at the moment.

"Rufus has you pegged as being the person responsible for why Tyrese and Kevin have gone missing."

"Why's that?"

"Given it's only those two missing and with what happened to...." Derek paused, but I knew he meant with what happened to Naomi. "He put two and two together and that's what he's figuring. He just doesn't know how you're doing it and getting away with it."

Standing up, I walked to my right until I leaned my back against the wall, facing Derek.

"So," Derek started to ask, "is it true?"

"What?" I said, but I already knew what Derek was getting at.

"Are you the one, you know, who did Tyrese and Kevin in?"

I stood with my back against the wall in silence. To Derek, my silence meant "yes."

"What'd you do to them?"

Inhaling, I then followed with, "It's better that you don't know." Derek didn't push further. After a quiet moment, he had something more personal to ask.

"Did you ever want to...." Derek hesitated at first, "you know, do me in too?"

Letting that sink in, I answered the kid honestly. "I did at first but," I paused, not sure what to follow with. "But you're young and I could tell you wanted nothing to do with it. Your tears, scared look, and held down head at court that day told me a lot too. But," I stopped and then started again, "you're just a kid."

Derek sat there quietly looking at me. He understood where I was coming from. "Thanks," he finally said with a sad look. I didn't respond, but I knew what he was thankful for.

"So how do I get to Booker?"

Derek scratched his head and then started to talk. "It's not gonna be easy, Mr. McCants, but it can be done." Nothing had been easy, even with Taylor and Durgess, I thought, but I didn't interrupt. "Rufus has an office on the topmost floor at The Kingdom, so bypassing all the others will pretty much be impossible. Wednesdays are the busiest days cause that's when the drug shipment for the week goes out, so you won't wanna go in that day. The remainder of the week is spent cooking, money counting, watching over The Kingdom, you name it."

Going on, Derek explained the layout of The Kingdom and what I could expect. Getting to Booker was going to be my most difficult test by far, like a student preparing for the SAT, only much harder. I wasn't even sure how I was going to find a way to get to the man.

The multiple floors of The Kingdom, the stairways, the protection it had, the gang members who I wouldn't be able to get by it sounded like, the....the....it was like trying to get to a destination that had no way of being entered unseen.

Trying to create some kind of an idea in my head to get to Booker, my mind remained blank. Of course, I had no real plan of getting to Booker in the first place - thanks to not knowing where he was - but with Derek's unexpected visit, things took a change. While I continued to try and come up with some plan, Derek went on talking.

"Rufus keeps things, secret things, like telephone recordings, written dates and times in notebooks, and other things that I'm not supposed to know about but I do, Mr. McCants."

"Hey Derek."

"Yeah."

"You can call me Job. I'm only thirty-three."

"Yes sir. Just a respect thing."

With a slight smile, I asked some questions. "What's on the phone recordings? What's written in those notebooks? And where does he keep these things?"

"I don't know anything on the recordings or what's written down; I only know he keeps them secretly stashed in his office from times past with DJ. Rufus would tell us to look the other way sometimes and DJ and I had no idea why, but one time I turned around to see him put tapes and notebooks into a bag and then hide them where no one else would know."

"Where's this hiding place where he keeps these things at?"

"Up in a chimney flue in an old fireplace which is in his office. He obviously never uses it and no one would ever know."

I nodded my head. What was on those phone recordings? What was written down on those notebooks? And what else was in that bag in the chimney flue of Booker's office?

I hoped to find out.

"So Derek," I started to say, "there's no easy way to get to Booker?"

He shook his head.

"There's no getting by his gang unseen?"

Again Derek shook his head.

"And I have to get to his office to get to him?"

Derek nodded his head this time.

I thought on that. The odds were by far against me and it seemed like getting to Booker was a suicide mission. From listening to Derek, it sounded like I couldn't get past Booker's guys to get to him, it sounded like I had quite an area to travel through before getting to his office, and it seemed like the objective that I was starting to form some kind of an idea for was nothing short of impossible to accomplish.

That's when I smiled and Derek looked at me confusedly, wondering why.

"Keep talking kid. I'm starting to figure out how I'm gonna get to Booker's office."

*You plus making plans equals scary.*

"Well," Derek cleared his throat, "there's guys on every level, armed guys that is. I think The Kingdom is two," Derek stopped, "no three stories and the second floor is dedicated to nothing but cooking. The first floor is for packing and shipping out the drugs, and the third floor is mostly a hangout with Rufus's office being at the end of the hallway."

"Cameras?"

"No."

"Lookouts?"

"Yes."

"What surrounds The Kingdom?"

"Old broken down cars, unused sheds, and storage buildings with nothing much in them."

I nodded my head, like I was happy about something.

Walking away from the living room, I went and grabbed the bag from my visit with Rex at Lucky 7's bar, which seemed so long ago.

Dropping the bag onto the living room floor, I opened it up.

Removing the Sig Sauer, I took out the magazine, emptied the bullets, pushed up the empty magazine, and handed the gun to Derek.

"You'll be needing this," I said.

*Really? You're giving the kid a gun?*

I'm sure he's handled one before. He used to be SSS, remember. Plus, it's empty.

*Still.*

"Why? Especially with no bullets?" Derek said giving me an odd look. Taking the gun, he held it in an unsure and nervous manner.

"Trust me kid. With what you'll have to do, you won't need a single bullet."

"With what I'll have to do?" Derek looked puzzled, like he was the worst player available for a pickup football game who'd been chosen first when everyone else thought for sure he'd be last.

*I'm agreeing with the kid here. You're gonna make him part of your plan?*

Pipe down, would ya?

My plan for taking Booker down was growing, and the more I thought about it, the more successful it looked in my mind. "You said you'd repay me whatever, right?"

Derek slowly nodded his head.

"Then this is it." I assured him with, "Trust me, Derek, I'm making it so it'll look like you're on their side and not mine. You're gonna look like a golden child to Booker."

Sighing deeply, like a load had just been removed from him, Derek relaxed and was more comfortable.

I wasn't going to put Derek at all in harm's way. He was just a kid, but I needed him desperately for the part I needed him to play. He would be the key.

"Mr. McCants, I mean," Derek paused and then started again, "Job, Rufus knows you're coming for him."

The plan in my head seemed all right and nearly completed, but I knew that there were some minor parts that still needed filled in. I think it's going to work, I told myself, but Wednesday night would tell. The day that Derek said was the busiest, and the same day that I shouldn't go into The Kingdom.

I wanted my last and final plan to go out with a blast.

*With what I'm seeing, this plan looks absolutely insane.*

Smiling, I replied to Derek, "I'm counting on that." The smile gone from my face, I followed with, "We're going in Wednesday night."

Raising his eyebrows, Derek said, "Wednesday? But Job that's the...." but I cut Derek off.

"I know. I'm not ignoring you but," I stopped, wanting to give an explanation. Instead I said, "Just trust me. I got Taylor and Durgess outta the picture, didn't I?"

With nothing to say, Derek just nodded his head and said, "Yes sir."

I just needed to go to the local hardware store to grab some supplies to finalize the equipment I would need to carry out this plan. I'd do some quick research on the Internet first to make something in my plan look as real as it could get.

This part I would need to really sell.

Taking a deep breath, I said to Derek, "It's not one-hundred percent just yet, but you ready to hear the plan for Wednesday night?"

Shrugging his shoulders, Derek returned, "I'm as ready as can be."

Beginning to tell him, I stopped. "Oh, by the way, Derek." Derek sat quietly, wondering what I was going to say next. Opening the bag that Rex gave me even wider, I gently grabbed the two grenades that I initially thought I had no clue what I would do with.

They would serve a purpose now.

"You're gonna have to learn how to use these."

*REALLY? Now you're gonna give this poor kid grenades?*

It's going to be just fine. Trust me.

*Trust you? God love and help this kid.*

Derek's face seemed to fall; I felt bad about this, I really did - first the gun and now grenades - but it had to be done. If I wanted my plan to work, then Derek would have to do what I was about to tell him.

"Don't worry," I said, "I'm gonna show you how to use them."

# 32

After going over the plan in its entirety with Derek, we got in my vehicle and drove to R and D's Hardware, the nearest and most popular hardware store. Derek had walked to my house, so I told him I'd drop him off at home after getting the supplies from R and D's.

While filling Derek in on my plan, he would look at me at times with mass confusion, and yet at other times like I was out of my mind. I could tell he questioned me several times by the look on his face; but, when I was finished, he nodded his head and even acknowledged that this was probably my best chance of getting to Rufus Booker and getting him out.

He also shook his head, smiled, and said, "How'd you think of all this?" He also added, "You're crazy" - in a nice sort of way - "but you're a genius too."

My I-got-your-back-bro kinda being had said to me after Derek's comment, *Derek may be joking about you being crazy, but to me you kind of are. But I love you, and I'm still here J.*

I reminded it that I wouldn't be doing any of this if it weren't for what happened at my house months ago. I also told my counselor that it forced my hand to do something, though I never imagined it would be this.

It's ironic how we humans tend to think that we'll never do something, or go somewhere, or be around a certain person in all our lives, but then we find our very thoughts pierce us, and the things we thought we'd never do somehow make their way into our lives.

Derek knew what I expected of him and he knew what his job was. He felt more confident about the grenades after I'd showed him how to use them, and he felt even more confident about how he would look in Booker's and SSS's eyes with what he was going to do.

I prayed that this final plan would be successful. Of all the plans thus so far, this was the most important and also the most crucial one I was hoping to pull off. Unfortunately, it was also the same one that could easily get me killed and ruin all that I'd worked so hard on.

Hoping to the maximum, hope was all I had.

Pulling into R and D's, I told Derek to stay in the vehicle and keep his head low. I didn't want to take the chance of him being spotted with me, which would be bad news for him.

R and D's Hardware sign shined bright and large above my head. Also on the sign in smaller letters was Plumbing + Paint + Electrical + Supplies + Tools + LIC. Locksmiths.

Walking into R and D's, the *ding* sound followed after pulling the door open and Barry Manilow's *Can't Smile Without You* played softly overhead. The hardware store still carried that country feel about it, even though it was in the city.

An employee with a nametag that read Roy walked up to me and said, "Good evening, sir. Can I help you with something?" Roy was short, had brown hair, and wore glasses that looked too big for him, but he appeared to be one of those older guys who you just liked right off the bat.

"Just looking, but thanks." I walked further into R and D's.

"If you need anything, just holler," Roy said behind me.

"Appreciate it."

Looking right to left down the aisles, I walked all of R and D's. One aisle was dedicated to painting supplies, another to a plethora of nails and screws, one to hand tools, another to plumbing supplies, and so on and so on.

I love hardware stores, especially R and D's, because they have that homey feeling about it and they usually have just what you need to get the home project done.

Or, in my case, having just what I needed to get another kind of project done.

Grabbing a carrying crate, I walked through the aisles and started putting in it the exact supplies what my research on the Internet had told me I would need. There were a couple of minor things that I hadn't heard of that R and D's didn't stock - not that I could blame them - so I substituted those things with something similar.

"Whatcha building there, sir?" asked Roy at the cash register as I was unloading my supplies and putting them on the table between us.

Not sure how to answer, I said with truth, "Something new. Gonna give'er a shot."

After paying and watching Roy bag my purchases, he said, "Hope all works out sir. Have yourself a good evening," he ended with a smile on his face.

"Me too," I said to Roy's first comment. "You too, thanks," to his second.

196

Pushing the door open to go back outside, the *ding* sound followed. I'd shopped at R and D's many times but I'd never seen Roy before, and I knew most of the guys who worked here. I liked Roy. The world could definitely use more Roy's.

Opening my truck door, I started to say something to Derek, but when I looked toward the passenger seat, he was gone.

That's when I heard several voices to the right side of R and D's, the side that was dark due to the night and the side where the large garbage container stood.

One angry voice said, "This mother...." he then cursed, "is SSS! I've seen him before with them."

Another voice said, "If he's SSS, you know what to do!"

Hearing a gun's *clicking* sound, the hairs on the back of my neck tried reaching for an inch. "Oh no," I said inside.

*They got Derek, Job.*

No kidding. But who?

*I don't know. What're you going to do?*

"Please!" I recognized the voice as Derek's. "I'm not with SSS any longer. I swear!"

The angry voice that I first heard said, "You shoulda stuck with SSS." He paused and then followed with, "Now I'm gonna show you what North End Boyz do to South Side Soldiers."

*Guess we know who has Derek now.*

Yeah. NEB. SSS's rival gang. This isn't good.

"PLEASE!" I heard Derek's voice scream. I could tell by his tone that he was close to crying.

*Job, do something!*

I'm going to!

I didn't care anymore about my plans for Derek with helping me take Booker down. I didn't care about the plan at all in contrast to what Derek was now going through. And I didn't care if trying to help save this kid meant my earthly death.

I hurriedly thought some things about Derek just then.

Derek had been sorry, penitent about what had happened. He was changing his life and showing signs of it by leaving SSS and steering it into a straighter path. He was the only one of the four SSS members who had the guts to face me, even though he was just a kid. He was someone who I started to like after talking and spending some time with at my place.

And he was now the one who I was going to try and save.

Tossing my R and D's paper bag into the backseat and closing my driver's side door, I ran toward the right side, unarmed and no weapon, of R and D's Hardware.

I had no clue what I was going to do, but I had to do something; I just couldn't listen to a gun shot go off, killing Derek, when there was something that I could've done to prevent it from happening in the first place.

*Job, I feel bad about yelling at you to do something. I'm not even sure what you can do to help in this matter. I'm sorry.*

No time for apologies. Pray that Derek and I can make it outta this mess alive.

*Will do.*

I turned the corner, and that's when I saw the sight before me.

# 33

After I turned the right corner of R and D's, Derek's face looked horror-filled and his eyes were watery from tears filling them. There was some relief on his face when he initially saw me, but then it turned dismal again because I'm sure he was thinking what could I possibly do in this situation to help.

Two younger men, dressed in black - I came to find out this was NEB's gang color - had Derek pressed against the brick wall and one of them held a gun to his head. The pressure from the gun against his head made Derek grimace.

Both men were startled as they saw me running around the corner, stop, and then walk toward them. One of the NEB members was extremely thin and the other wasn't much bigger; I'm sure I could break both of them in half, I thought, but the gun made me think twice with trying to do that.

They both wore black bandanas, which shielded them from the nose down, and they both had hats on, one an Oakland Raiders hat on backwards and the other a black Ohio State University hat on frontwards - he was also the same one who held the gun to Derek's head.

*Be safe Job.*

I'll try.

"Homies," I started to say, "that's my friend." I wanted to talk to them on level ground, but also get my point across that I didn't want who they had messed with.

The angry-voiced NEB member, who happened to be the one holding the gun to Derek's head, said, "Who you calling homie, white boy?" He lowered the gun from Derek's head and focused his attention on me.

*Good. The gun's off Derek.*

There's one step achieved.

"Just showing some respect," I said. "That's my boy, and he's with me," I added, nodding in Derek's direction.

Angry - my nickname for this member - then pointed the gun at me while the other NEB member let go of Derek and turned toward me.

Derek stood frozen. His look said to me, "What are you going to do now?"

"He's your boy, huh?" said Angry. He then laughed softly and said, "Ain't too many white boys running with SSS. I guess we get two of you tonight instead of just one."

I'm sure Angry was grinning from ear to ear under his bandana after saying this.

Think, think, I said to myself.

*Make it fast too.*

I'm trying.

Just then, it was like something took a hold of me. My face turned deathly serious and my attitude said I wasn't going to put up with none of this tonight. It was like I wasn't even myself as I stood surefooted and valiant.

I said boldly, "Put your toy down before I take it away from you and beat you with it." I instantly was mad that this punk thought all of a sudden he could just point a gun at me.

Keeping the gun pointed at me, Angry looked toward his fellow member. They both looked at one another for a long moment; I'm sure probably nonverbally saying, "Is this guy outta his mind?"

Starting to walk slowly toward Angry, I went on, "I hate SSS just as much as you North End Boyz do. And this 'white boy' has nothing to do with your rival gang. And neither does he," I said, nodding again toward Derek.

With the gun staying pointed at me, Angry took a step back while his partner stayed put. Derek stayed glued against the brick wall and gave me an insane look like I was out of my mind.

*You know what you're doing J?*

Not really, but hopefully it works.

*Godspeed then.*

"Stay back!" yelled Angry.

Continuing forward, I said, "You shoot and kill the both of us, let me tell you, you'll be making a big mistake."

Taking another step back, Angry yelled, "Dude, stay back!" Angry's partner took a couple steps closer to the brick wall of R and D's.

"I took care of Tyrese 'TT' Taylor," I said, closing the gap between Angry and I.

Angry quickly looked to his partner and back toward me.

"I took care of Kevin 'K-Dogg' Durgess," I continued, about ten feet separating Angry and I.

Again, Angry looked at his partner, but this time he squinted his eyes. Something apparently hit him just then with what I said. His partner stood motionless, giving him an odd look in return.

With Angry's gun sticking into my chest, I stood in front of him with no fear. "And me and him," I looked over to Derek, nodded, and looked back into Angry's eyes, "Are about to take care of Rufus Booker, your gang's number one enemy. Unless," I added, "you wanna screw that all up by killing us."

Although it would be normal for a person's pulse to become highly elevated at a time like this, mine didn't go up at all. I kept my face serious and my stature unwavering. I couldn't even feel one bead of sweat form anywhere on my body.

"It's your choice," I said to Angry. "Make it."

*Job, what you just did was like something taken right out of a Western movie. Hopefully you - this cowboy - makes it out alive.*

That's what I'm praying for.

Angry hesitated as the gun shook against my chest. If this was it, I thought, at least I was willing to lay down my life for the sake of another. If I lived, then I lived.

Finally, Angry removed the gun from my chest, tucked it behind him, and said, "That was you?"

I didn't respond. My quietness and slow nodding said "yes."

"At first I thought you were bluffing," Angry went on, "but I can tell by looking at you and with the way you just acted that you're the real deal man."

Pulling his bandana down so his face was revealed, Angry went on, "You got some guts man. We've been hearing about this bad white dude who's been taking on SSS supposedly single-handedly."

I stood in silence. Angry's partner pulled his bandana down too and both he and Derek stepped to where Angry and I were. I'd say Angry and his partner were both in their early twenties judging by their faces.

"So what are you two planning on doing to Rufus, and how do you know where he is?" said Angry.

Finally, I spoke, with Derek standing close to me. "That's our business. You just sit back and wait to hear about the show."

Angry and his partner didn't say anything. They knew I was as serious as serious can be.

"You tell your boss and friends that I'm taking care of Rufus Booker; I've had enough of this gang feud. Its ending has arrived." I paused, looking to Derek. "And another thing," I said, looking back to both the NEB members, "you tell your peeps to lay off of him," I said nodding in Derek's direction, "he's left the gang and wants nothing to do with gang life anymore."

Angry and his partner just looked at me.

"Understood?" I said with authority.

"Yes sir," both of them, even Angry's friend replied.

Looking back at Derek, I waved my head behind me, telling him that it's time to leave.

"Before you leave," said Angry, "when can we expect to hear news about Booker?"

I smiled. Both NEB members wondered why. My smile disappeared. "If not Wednesday night, sometime soon after that."

Derek and I turned our backs on them and started making our way back to my truck. We got to the corner when I heard Angry's voice behind us.

"Hey man." I turned around to face Angry and his partner. "I'm gonna put in a good word for you on our side, all right?"

Without saying a word, I slightly nodded my head and turned back around. Derek and I turned the corner.

"What's your name anyway?" came Angry's voice again, but I acted like I didn't hear him.

Sitting behind the wheel with Derek in the passenger seat, we sat with R and D's Hardware still shining brightly in front of us. When we had started walking away from the NEB members, Derek was still shaking and had a head full of perspiration. Finally, he was calmed down and could breathe again.

"What happened when I was in the hardware store?"

Derek didn't speak. He was still shaken up a bit.

"Derek?"

Sniffing in, Derek finally spoke. "Thanks Job." He sniffed in again. "You saved me back there, and to think what I've done to you and you still came for me." That's when a few tears trickled down his face.

Emotion hit me pretty hard just then. Derek was actually a good kid. And he was an appreciative kid. Inside, I didn't have the words, but me and this kid were connecting. Months ago - and not that long ago - I wanted to kill him, but now I was far from thinking that about him. Never did I think we'd be in the current position we were in.

But here we were.

"I wasn't just going to stand around and do nothing when I came out and heard." There was a short moment of silence. "Now dry those eyes young man." I then added with some humor, "You're getting the interior of my truck wet."

Derek smiled and gave a short laugh after that.

"So what happened?" I inquired again.

Wiping his eyes, Derek answered, "When you were in the hardware store I heard a knock on the window on my side. I didn't even see them. When I looked over, I saw those two NEB members and the mean one nodded his head, pulled a gun out, pointed it at me, and told me to get outta the truck."

Derek paused and then went on.

"So I got out; I didn't know what else to do. I guess the mean one must've seen me sometime running around with my old gang. That's how the gang life goes Job. See a rival gang member on his own, do him in."

Derek shook his head. "When they pushed me up against the brick wall and the mean one said I was SSS, I thought for sure I was dead. But," Derek paused, looking over at me, "but that's when you showed up. Thank God."

*A young man thanking God. Now that's a good thing.*

Sitting quietly for a minute, Derek and I both reflected on the incident that we just walked out of. Derek was right when he said, "Thank God." I had no one else to thank but Him.

After all that I'd been doing and still God kept some form of security over me, like He was keeping me under the protection of the shadow of His wings.

Even through all that had happened and was happening, I still maintained my faith in God, though it was small; however, it was still there. Yes, I know, it seems very messed up and backward of me to claim to be some sort of faithful man in God with all that I did and was about to do.

But many things I will explain to you later.

I had prayed to God many times throughout the past weeks, and I still leaned on Him when I was at my lowest and weakest. As the Lord says in the Word, "*My grace is all you need. My power works best in weakness.*"

I had been weak, exhausted, tiresome, you name it. To me I was the lowliest of all humans ever created because I had fallen extremely short of His perfect standard with being a believer. I should've known better. I had believed, and still did, but I allowed the power of sin to take root within me to the point where I thought I could never turn back from what I was doing.

*You still can Job."*

Like Job from the Bible, I wanted to know why I had suffered so much. I wanted answers to so many questions. Why? Why? Why? But, I also understood from reading the book of Job a long time ago that it's better to know God than to know answers.

I still believed yes, but I still had work to do. It was too late to turn back now.

*No it's not.*

I ignored my buddy.

Everything would be made clear when all was said and done and the smoke dissipated.

Looking over at Derek, I said, "Let's get you home."

Before starting the vehicle up, Derek rested his hand on my shoulder.

"Job."

"Yeah."

"I got your back Wednesday night. You won't have to worry about me messing up or changing my mind about the plan."

I didn't respond. I sure was glad to hear Derek say this though. I wouldn't be able to pull the plan off without him.

"I'm all in," he said.

I started the truck up.

"Good," I said, "me too."

# 34

Wednesday.

The day Derek and I were going after Rufus Booker on his home turf.

It was early in the morning; I couldn't fall back asleep, so I decided to sit outside in the screened-in back porch area and watch the morning sun arise.

Too many people just didn't appreciate the simple things in life. Awakening to a new day, sleeping in a comfortable bed while others in the world went without, having the blessing of sight, hearing, taste, touch, and smell, using clean water, and I could go on and on.

*Amen J.*

My point is that we should be grateful with what we have instead of what we don't have. We shouldn't compare our lives to others, wishing we had other things or more, especially while so many in the world didn't have much at all. If there was food on the table, clothes on our backs, and a roof over our head, then we should learn to be content.

*True, true.*

I'm not trying to lecture you, but this morning has me looking at things differently that I hadn't thought of for a while, especially with taking the risk of possibly dying tonight.

It was mornings like this when I usually had my sidekick Manhattan right at my side. It was mornings like this when Naomi would eventually come out, sit on my lap, and we'd talk and enjoy the morning together. It was mornings like this....

Those mornings, unfortunately, were buried.

I don't remember what all I thought that morning, but I thought deeply, spiritually, and emotionally, like I was a man on death row whose day had finally arrived, trying to get my heart in order before I walked to my execution site.

I thought about God, Jesus, Naomi, Manhattan, my family, my coworkers, Jehu, Al, Wendy, Derek, and others. I also thought about Rufus and DJ Booker, Tyrese Taylor, Kevin Durgess, and the others, including the situations that I found myself in a little over the past two months ago now.

And I also thought about this secret someone who I haven't yet told you of who had been working with Rufus Booker. It was no wonder why Rufus was able to get away and never get caught time and time again.

This collage of people I'd been thinking of and all that I'd done spun around and around in my head. But I had to believe that I was doing these things and was around these people to fulfill an important purpose. Yes much of what I'd done had been wrong and was against God's ways; and, against my better judgment, I went along with these things anyway.

With all these things filling my head, I finally took a deep breath, let it all go, bowed my head, closed my eyes, and prayed one of my final prayers to God, possibly.

In all honesty and truthfulness, prayer was that thing that made me feel better afterwards, like the burdens that I carried were no longer mine.

"Heavenly Father, in Your Son's Name, I have no good reasoning for all that I've done. I have no excuses. I've went against Your ways, I've allowed wrong to take birth in me and continuously grow, and I've done things I'm not proud of."

I took another deep breath. This was a hard prayer to pray; the words I didn't know how to make sense of.

"I have not once thought nor expected for You to watch over me or be behind me with what I've been doing, God. And it's not that You're agreeing with what I'm doing, but for some reason You're keeping me alive. Honestly, I'm surprised I'm still living and You just didn't seal my fate long ago back when I was in my coma."

The morning sun felt warm against my face and birds sung their songs, welcoming the new day that had dawned.

"You know God my purpose for what I've been doing. I ask, though it seems messed up of me, for You to help Derek and I tonight. I don't intend for anyone to get hurt; but if anyone does, then it's going to be me."

I prayed probably for about a half hour, but I'm obviously going to spare you the words and the pages that would take up.

I lastly said, "Your will, God, it will be done. I love You Father and I believe in Your only begotten Son. Help me to make what I'm about to do right. I will accept the punishment and disciplinary action that I deserve if it comes to that, if I live, but help me to get through this.

"You know my heart and You know all things, God. Nothing is hidden from You. Please be with me this last time. Thank You for hearing me." I then prayed how Jesus teaches believers to pray: with the Lord's

Prayer. I ended with, "It's in Your saving Name I pray in Christ Jesus. Amen."

Lifting up my head and opening my eyes, God had truly blessed His creation with a beautiful morning. The sun was a yellowish-orange and thin clouds hung next to it. There was a friendly breeze, and it felt like not a thing could go wrong today.

Before I knew it, it was almost noon, and still I sat out back in the screened-in porch area. I told Derek I'd pick him up later this evening. Everything was ready; I made sure of that last night, but I'd double check just to make sure.

I was as ready as I could be, and I knew Derek was too.

If this was the last morning I saw as a human being, then it was by far one that I was truly grateful and appreciative to have woken up to and witnessed.

It made me think of something that I already told you.

Too many people just didn't appreciate the simple things in life.

# 35

Driving on the bridge that was nearby The Kingdom that Tyrese Taylor had told me about, Derek sat in the passenger seat while I took a glance to my right. Besides passing a couple vehicles on the opposite side, the bridge was mostly empty and this side of town seemed dead.

"That's it right there," said Derek pointing with his finger.

Below us on the right hand side was an old, three-story brick building that had chain link fencing around it, and wrapped around the fencing was faded and torn yellow police tape. The Kingdom was surrounded with exactly what Derek had told me of: unused sheds, storage buildings with nothing much in them, and old broken down cars that screamed antique and long out of use.

The only reason we could see the site below us and its characteristics was because of street lamps that shown on the building and its surroundings.

Dim lighting could be seen coming from within The Kingdom. The building reminded me somewhat of a haunted house, but there was something worse than ghosts haunting this old building.

*I'd have to agree.*

I wondered what I'd be seeing soon. Thugs, guns, drugs? What else? Just as Bottom's Up had been to me, so going into a gang's base of operations was a first for me too.

I guess I'd be finding out soon enough.

"There's where you'll wanna park," Derek said pointing with his finger again. "That's the building." Derek had already told me where to park so we'd be out of sight. It was a building that was out of service in front of The Kingdom. "No one, not a soul is in that building," Derek had told me.

Parking in front of that building, out of The Kingdom's sight, I killed the engine. Unclicking my seatbelt, I removed it from around me. "You got what you need?" I looked over at Derek.

Derek pulled out the empty Sig Sauer. "Yes sir." He then grabbed the small Nike gym bag that was at his feet. It had the grenades in it. "And yes sir."

"Any questions?"

Derek shook his head.

"You remember exactly what you gotta do?"

Derek looked into my eyes, nodded his head, and said, "How could I forget," he smiled at me.

I smiled back. Derek was a good kid.

*I can't believe this is about to happen.*

Yeah, I know. We've come a long way partner. You've stuck with me when most would've turned away.

*I've not agreed with a lot of what you've done Job. But what kinda friend would I have been to leave you? I'm with you J, even through the good, the bad, and the ugly.*

Thanks buddy. I love you, whatever you are.

*Love you too man.*

Bowing my head and closing my eyes, I started to silently pray one last prayer.

"What're you doing?" said Derek.

I stopped, but I kept my head down and eyes closed. "Saying a short, quiet prayer. I suggest you do the same."

Not knowing if Derek did or not, I opened my eyes, lifted my head, and looked at the night in front of us. This was it, I thought. The time for taking down Rufus Booker had finally come.

I just hoped and prayed that success laid in my path.

I had everything that I needed; I didn't need to go over myself a final time. Hoping with all my heart, I just hoped that everything fell perfectly into place; well, at least I hoped most of everything fell perfectly into place given the situation and who I was dealing with.

Taking the deepest breath that I had probably ever taken, I looked over at Derek, our eyes met, and I said, "You ready?"

Replying how he had back at my house, Derek said, "I'm as ready as can be."

Turning my head in front of me, the night was starry and the moon's white wheel shined brilliantly. Thick pale clouds hung high in the sky, and there was a peaceful serenity in the atmosphere.

If this was the last night I saw as a human being, then it was by far one that I was truly grateful and appreciative to have stepped out into and witnessed.

"Then let's do this," I said to Derek.

# 36

For the purpose of making it easier for you to differentiate between the past and present, I'm going to reveal my plan that I came up with at my house the same time I presently was a temporary resident at The Kingdom. I'm going to use italics to explain the past, something similar to how TV shows show a younger version of an older character or how they oftentimes will show a scene more paler than the present one so they know the viewer will understand the difference between the past and present.

The italics are also not to be confused with my counselor/buddy/guide/I-got-your-back-bro kinda being's voice.

Closing our doors, Derek and I started making our way toward The Kingdom.

When The Kingdom opened up into view, I said, "All right Derek, go ahead." We stood just outside the light of the street lamps, still in the darkness.

Derek took the Nike gym bag and tied one of its strings tightly around a sewer drain, you know, the kind that's just off the street that you often see raccoons run into? The bag hung down the drain so only Derek would know it was there when the time came.

*"Before we go in, make sure you put the grenades somewhere close but outta sight."*

*"All right," Derek replied.*

Before we stepped into the light, I then said, "Let's make it a good show young man."

Derek pulled out the Sig Sauer, walked behind me, and stuck the gun into my back. I went to walk under the light, but before I could, Derek grabbed my shirt tightly and held me back.

"Job," Derek started to say, but he stopped. He didn't have the words, so he patted me on the back several times instead. I knew what he was meaning and getting at though.

"Thanks kid," I said. "Don't be afraid. You have no reason to be."

"I know," Derek returned, "it's....it's you who I'm afraid for."

*"We're gonna make it look like you got me and you're handing me over to Booker. With as impossible as you say it is to get past his guys, we're gonna walk in and right through The Kingdom instead doing this. I think it'll work."*

*"You think?" asked Derek.*

*"You got any better idea?"*

*"No."*

*"Then let's make this one work. You're gonna bring me in like I'm your prisoner. The rest of the gang will look upon you with praise, and you'll lead us right to Booker and his office."*

*Derek's initial puzzled look turned less puzzled. "Dang man, that's actually pretty good. If I'm Rufus, I'm not expecting a thing."*

*I looked into Derek's eyes. "That's what I'm hoping for."*

Walking under the street lamps, I could see members of SSS looking out the broken windows of The Kingdom. A couple of them turned around and yelled something below them, like they were telling their fellow members on the floors under them what was going on.

Coming to the first of many cracked concrete steps leading up to the large door of The Kingdom's entrance, Derek kept the gun glued to my back and shouted for the SSS members to hear, "Keep moving sucker!"

One of the members looking outside yelled happily, "Hey, it's Derek! Hey ya'll," he turned around and hollered, wanting the message to be passed along, "it's Derek! He's bringing in some dude!"

*"What happens if the guys don't care and they wanna do something bad to me too with leaving the gang?"*

*"Trust me kid," I smiled, "they're gonna love you with what you're gonna do. They'll totally forget about you leaving once they see you bringing me in."*

*"You think?"*

*"Derek, even corrupt tax collectors love one another. And even pagans are kind to their friends."*

*Looking like I totally lost him, Derek said, "What the heck does that mean?"*

*"Forget it. Just know that Booker and his gang won't have any hard feelings. Trust me, they're gonna love you."*

*Derek partly smiled. "If you say so."*

*"I know so."*

When we got halfway up the stairs, The Kingdom's front door opened with the most annoying, ear-irritating creaking sound. It desperately needed WD-40. Stepping out were two SSS members with guns in hand.

One said, "Well well, look who it is. Little Derek Westbrook. We knew you'd be coming back around. Good to see you little brother."

We made it to the top landing with about five feet separating us from the two members.

The other member walked over to Derek, patted him on the shoulder a couple times, and said, "Welcome home. Who's this punk?" He then backed off a few feet and looked at me.

Dressed in a buttoned up, short sleeved flannel shirt with jean shorts on, I had a five-day beard going and my fast-growing hair was a little more than a crew cut. With tennis shoes completing my attire, I stood before the two SSS members.

"Wait a minute," the second member who spoke said, "is this...." he paused. "It is, isn't it Derek. It's that dude who killed DJ."

The first member who spoke said, "Job it is, right?" I didn't say a word. "Rufus has been expecting you, but not like this," he smiled boastfully. "Derek," he then said looking at him, "you did good, real good. Rufus will be pleased."

*"If they ask me, should I say how I got to you? You know, make something up? Or if they don't ask, should I say something that would make me look better to them?"*

*Thinking for a moment, I finally said, "You say or do whatever you think will sweeten the scene. You know these guys better than I do."*

The second SSS member who spoke said, "And little Derek got a hold of a piece too." He smiled and gave a short laugh. "You bad man, real bad."

With the gun in my back, I grimaced and acted like it was killing me. That made the two members laugh. I wanted them thinking that Derek had complete control.

"I felt bad for leaving," Derek started to say. "I had to make sure my coming back meant something big." Derek gave me a little push from behind. "I think Rufus will forgive me when he sees him."

"And then some," said the first member who spoke.

That first member who spoke then grabbed a cell phone out of his pocket, pressed on the screen a couple times, and then put the phone to his ear. "Hey boss," he said shortly after, "we have a couple visitors. One of which you'll be thrilled to see, and the other you won't believe." He then went on to explain what had happened from the time The Kingdom's door opened to Derek and I until now.

So it was Rufus Booker he'd called. Was he here or was he somewhere else? I hoped Derek was right and he was here instead of leaving for some reason.

But I didn't worry; there would be no need for that anyway.

Rufus said something on the other end while the SSS member stood and listened.

"All right," he said after a long moment, "I'll send 'em both right up. We'll let little Derek deliver him to you. He's the man boss. You'll be proud."

Good, I thought. Rufus was here. No doubt I'd be seeing him soon. I couldn't wait.

*"What if they check you before we go in?"*

*I thought on that. "If they do, you gotta step up and say you already did. Show them if you have to, but don't unbutton or lift up my shirt, or the plan will be ruined. I'll keep a few buttons undone so they see my chest and won't think I'm hiding anything."*

*"All right," Derek nervously replied.*

*"Hopefully they'll be too excited and into the moment to remember to check. The element of surprise has its ways."*

*Derek didn't return with a word.*

"Go on up," said the member who talked to Rufus.

Thank God, I thought. They weren't going to check me.

Derek nudged me forward. We got to the door when the second member said, "Wait."

Oh no, I thought. So much for not checking me. I'm sure Derek's pulse was rising and he was getting nervous inside as we came to a standstill.

"Don't check me. Don't check me," I whispered to myself.

The second member walked over to us, standing beside Derek. He put his arm around him and rocked him a little. "I'm glad you're back little Derek." He removed his arm from around him and said, "Now go on."

Phew, I said inside. I'm sure Derek was saying the same thing. That was too close. We made the few steps through the door, and there we were.

Inside The Kingdom.

&#8224;   &#8224;   &#8224;

Poking his head in, the member who just had his arm around Derek shouted for all to hear, "Hey boys, guess who we got!? The guy who killed DJ! Here he is!"

There to greet us were probably about twenty SSS members, half of them lining on the right and the other on the left. I felt lonely and naked as all eyes were on me. Keeping deadly silent, Derek pushed me onward, passing through this sea of SSS members.

"Got you now," one of them said to me.

Another said, "SSS forever mother...." he cursed.

And then many others just gave me impassive stares, but I thought I could feel hate while passing through them. Was there any one of them who cared about me in my present situation? Was there not a single one who felt sorry about what had happened to me? Or did they, like Rufus, not have a care in the world? Or did Rufus keep certain details from them, making them believe a lie? So many questions circled around in my head just then.

But I erased the questions from my head quickly. I didn't come here for questions or answers; I came for revenge. These guys would think what they wanted to, and there was nothing that I could control or do about it.

We humans had no control in this world when we really thought about it.

On a good note, for Derek's sake, I heard some of the members say comments such as, "Way to go Derek!" or, "You the man little Derek!" or, "He's back ya'll!" Some of them patted him on his back as we passed by and I even heard hollering and clapping at times.

Right then though this also made me sad. Here were people who were celebrating, even praising that something bad was about to happen to me. And why? Naomi and I had been the ones wronged. I was the one whose wife was murdered. Here was a gang of people who were ready to have me executed and they didn't even know me. Why? Here was SSS, the most notorious gang in Columbus, sending me into a deep dark pit and they didn't even care. Why?

I could ask "why" all day and still not receive an answer. Unfortunately this was the world we lived in and, as sad as it is to say, it's the way it operated and revolved. It's such a crooked and ungodly world that we live in.

But I knew that light would eventually break through the darkness one day and make all things new; that truth kept me going.

Pushing me again from behind, Derek had me turn right toward a door. When he had me open it, it led to four flights of stairs. Climbing the stairs, he had me push open the next door which opened to the second floor: the floor where everything was cooked.

*"As we make our way from the first floor up to Booker, just act like you have control of me. Push me, order me around. The better you do this, the better your old gang will buy what we're selling."*

*"I'm gonna hate treating you like this."*

214

*"Well," I started to say, "learn to love it. If you're soft it could ruin us. If you're hard, then we'll make it."*

*"Whatever you say Mr. McCants...." Derek paused. "I mean Job."*

It looked like a science laboratory; however, the equipment being used was for a much different purpose, and it currently looked like SSS had closed up shop for it this evening. The lights were dimmed down on this floor and none of the equipment was up and running; there was also not a soul cooking.

As we walked through this floor, I looked at the equipment that I now had a better view of. There were glass bottles, weight scales, tubing connecting bottles to devices that I hadn't seen before, containers that held white powder in them, and much more.

Drugs, I thought. It was both sad and disastrous with how they seemed to be taking over the world. Even more so with the lives they were ruining and the people they were killing. Drugs just never made sense to me. I had never tried one, and I didn't see why anyone ever would.

Derek led me to another door at the opposite side from where we entered and said, "Open it, now." Looking behind him, it looked like the entire gang from downstairs followed us up, like I was a celebrity making my way to see another one.

Opening this door, it led to another four flights of stairs. After climbing the flights, Derek had me open to the third and final floor; the floor where Rufus Booker was waiting for me, I assumed in his office.

Derek was right. This floor was nothing more than SSS's hangout. A room the size of a very large living room had several big-screened TVs, along with gaming systems and speakers to add to the entertainment. As we started walking toward a closed door at the end of the hallway, I noticed about a half dozen rooms were dedicated to living quarters, some of which held multiple beds. A kitchen-like room contained two refrigerators, two large tables that were joined together as one, a plethora of chairs, and cooking appliances that were in desperate need of being cleaned. Besides a door that had 'bathrooms' written on it in black ink, that seemed to have summed up the third floor.

For being an old and abandoned toy store building, this was actually a really neat building. I felt like I was walking through ancient history; I'm sure in the mid 1900s this place was better taken care of. Too bad it was being used for this now.

I'd say about twenty more SSS members were on this floor. Like vultures hanging around a dead carcass, they congregated outside the closed door at the end of the hallway. Similar to the members down on the

215

first floor, about half lined the right side and the other on the left, like it was some formation they were to practice with the presence of visitors.

*"You said Booker's office is on the top floor at the end of the hallway, right?"*

*"Yeah,"* Derek replied. *"Hey Job."*

*"Yeah."*

*"What if Rufus isn't there when we show up?"*

*That never once crossed my mind, but I didn't see a need for concern. "If he's not, then I'm sure his crew will quickly tell him what's up. He'll make it to The Kingdom in a hurry shortly after that. Tru...."* but Derek broke me short.

*"Trust you,"* Derek said with a smile. *"I know."*

Passing through this new sea of SSS members, not a single one of them said a word. They just stared at me with hard looks, but for some reason I didn't feel as threatened by them as I had with the first twenty members downstairs. Maybe it was because I was just getting used to these guys and this place, but I don't know.

There I stood at the closed door at the end of the hallway knowing that my number one enemy was just behind it.

He was the one who forced me to kill his brother in self-defense by allowing DJ to partake in this kind of lifestyle in the first place. He was the one who returned to my house with revenge in his mind to kill both Naomi and I; but miraculously, by the grace of God, I had been spared, though I still wasn't sure why. And he was the one who I despised more than anyone else in the world.

The time had come to finally meet again.

Face to face.

Man to man.

Revenger against revenger.

"Go in," said the SSS member closest to the door, "Rufus is expecting you." Looking me over, he didn't feel the need to search me. He added, "You too," looking to Derek. He ended with, "Rufus is happy with you Derek. Welcome back."

I took a deep, quiet breath and stared at the wooden door that had pieces stripped away. Extending my right hand, I turned the doorknob and pushed on it. The door opened slowly, fully opening until the back of it gently hit against the wall.

*"What do we do when we reach Rufus's office?"* asked Derek.

*I shook my head. "Honestly, kid, this is where I'm hoping for some good fortune. You're gonna have some work to do. At some point you gotta try to convince Rufus to let you go somehow."*

*"How?"* I could tell Derek was a little nervous.

*"Just speak when you're spoken to at the start. You don't wanna act like you're wanting to get out of his office in a hurry or he'll think something's up. But at some point you gotta give him a good reason to leave. Say...."* but I stopped, trying to think of something convincing.

Derek stared at me, looking for an answer to this potential problem.

A smile shined on my face. *"I got it."* Derek seemed to light up too, happy that I found something, even though he hadn't heard it yet.

*"I'm gonna make you look like a genius."* I paused and then told him his solution to getting out so he could carry out the rest of the plan. *"Tell Rufus that you had me drive you there and that you need to dump the vehicle so it's away from The Kingdom so that nothing will come back on them."*

Derek listened, and the more he heard me out, the more he loved my idea. *"You ought to be an author or something man. You're good at coming up with stuff."*

I didn't bother telling him I had a voice that told me my plan making was scary.

Sitting behind a desk was Rufus Booker - the number one man who carried out killing my wife.

His dreadlocks looked like they had grown since I last saw him. He wore a t-shirt with a gold chain hanging from his neck. On either side of him on his desk were guns. His office was dimly lit, had windows on three sides, and to me it felt more like a prison cell than a drug kingpin's office.

Leaning back on his chair, he said, "Job McCants." There was that awkward silence that followed when two rivals finally meet face to face. "I've been waiting for you."

Sitting upright with his hands folded in front of him on his desk, he then said looking to Derek, "Derek, my little soldier, you've proved yourself." He smiled a white smile to Derek, but there was something hideous in that smile.

"Both of you," Rufus started to say, "come in and close the door behind you."

Derek pushed me forward with the Sig. I came into the office. The inside of Booker's office was exactly how Derek had explained it to me. Standing on the left hand side of his office was the fireplace that held pertinent, secret information.

Derek made his way in behind me and shut the door.

We both were inside. So far, so good, I thought. The plan was going just as planned. Hopefully the rest of it would too.

But time would tell.

And soon.

*"Job, if we pull this off, what do you plan on doing to Rufus?"*

*I'd had something drawn up in my head for Rufus Booker for sometime now. Of Tyrese "TT" Taylor, Kevin "K-Dogg" Durgess, and Rufus "D-Locks" Booker, my plan for Rufus, to me, seemed the most fearful of all.*

*Though the fake out paralytic with Tyrese Taylor was pretty scary too, I had to admit.*

*I shook my head, not wanting to tell Derek.*

*He understood.*

218

# 37

I stood before Rufus Booker's desk with him sitting behind it. Without saying a word yet, I acted like defeat was written on my face. Rufus looked me up and down, and then he shook his head slowly.

"You've been a busy man Job McCants," he started to say. "When Tyrese went missing," he said arising from his chair, "I didn't think a thing about it, but," he then walked over to the fireplace and then faced me, "after what happened to Kevin, that kinda got me thinking.

"First I'm told that some fancy dressed white businessman was at Ricky's arcade the night Tyrese went missing, and then I'm told some regular white Joe Schmo was at Bottom's Up the night Kevin was taken who'd never been seen there before." Booker then smiled and nodded his head, like something was making sense. "That's when I started to really do some thinking and put two and two together." His smile seemed to widen.

He opened one hand and said, "Tyrese Taylor. Why?" He opened the other and said, "Kevin Durgess. Why?" Rufus then clapped his hands together. "That's when I knew it was you Job. I still don't know how you did it all, and right now I don't care since you're here; but, somehow, someway, you made things happen."

Rufus then walked toward me, came to a stop about two feet in front of me, and then said, "Unfortunately for you, your road to revenge has come to an end." The smile that he just had not too long ago faded away and he stared at me like I was dead meat.

Inside I smiled. This road wasn't ending; it was still carrying on, but Rufus didn't know this.

Looking to Derek who stood behind me with the Sig still dug into my back, Rufus said, "I can't tell you how proud I am of you, Derek." Booker seemed to speak to him with a brotherly concern, I thought; but they also had a long history, especially since DJ and Derek had been best friends.

Passing out of my sight, Rufus walked to Derek. I could hear patting, which I figured was Rufus patting Derek on his back or shoulder, and then Rufus returned to his desk, sitting down.

"So, little Derek," Rufus started to ask, "how'd you get to this fool?" Rufus leaned back in his chair, waiting for Derek to respond.

Within me I said, "This is your time to shine Derek. Don't panic, just stick to the plan." I was nervous and scared for him.

Confidently, Derek said, "After I'd heard about Tyrese and Kevin gone missing, I'm sure like you had," he said looking to Booker real quick from behind me, "I knew it had to be this clown involved." Derek then pushed me from behind. I let out a long sigh with pain written on my face, acting like it hurt more than it really did. Derek then stood to the side of me so Booker could now see him; he kept the gun pointed at me.

Derek was surprising me. His initial nervousness had turned to bravery, his fear to gallantry.

"I knew it was just a matter of time," Derek went on, "before he came looking for you and me." He pushed me again from behind. "I couldn't let that happen." There was something both bold and eerie in his voice when he said this.

"So I kept an eye on him until I saw my opportunity to take him down." Derek looked at Booker with a smile. "Now, here he is."

My counselor butted in real quick just then. *He's kinda starting to remind me of you.*

That's what I was just thinking too.

*That's not good J.*

Yeah, I know.

Derek had done a superb job, I thought. If I was Rufus Booker, he definitely just sold me a story that I would believe. I just hoped Rufus bought into it too.

Rufus leaned back further in his chair, smiled, and filled the room with his laughter. "When did you get so bad kid? I love it!" Rufus then sat more upright, his smile and some laughter still following him. "I don't even care about the details. You got him here and that's all that matters."

Rufus bought it. Good job Derek, well done.

"Anything else I should know about?" inquired Rufus.

"Actually," Derek said, "there is."

Rufus sat behind his desk serious faced without saying a word, waiting for Derek to tell him.

Derek told him what else there was, and I couldn't have been more happier with him after he was done speaking. "I gotta dump his vehicle somewhere far from here." Derek went on to explain. "I had him drive me here in his own vehicle and we don't need anything coming back on us if it were to stay here, especially any heat." He stuck right to the plan.

"With your permission," Derek went on, "I'd like to drop it off somewhere now and quick in the city where it won't be found for a while."

Rufus sat in his chair not sure what to say. Honestly, judging by his face, he looked to be impressed and taken aback.

Finally he said, "Not only did you get bad, but you also got smart." Pausing and nodding his head like he agreed, he added, "Good point. Since you know where it is, get outta here and go dump it, but come back tomorrow. We have some partying to do." Rufus smiled at Derek and then waved him to go ahead.

Perfect. The plan was going smoothly and Derek had only talked when he was spoken to. And now he even got Rufus to let him go so he could continue on with the next phase of the plan.

I was impressed with Derek. He did outstanding.

Opening the door behind me, Derek started to make his way out. Rufus shouted for his entire gang to hear out in the hallway, "Derek's got business to do for me! Alone, by himself! All of you will let him go!" He smiled and looked at me. "He's with us boys! Derek's one of us! Be proud and look after him!" he ended boastfully.

Out in the hallway I could hear Derek being praised and gladly accepted back into his old gang, but unknown to everyone except Derek and I, the kid was really on my side.

This plan promised for an exploding ending. So far, so good still. I just hoped the rest of it went as well as it had been going.

*"What do you want me to do after I walk outta The Kingdom?"* asked Derek.

*"Quickly, grab the bag of grenades and get close to one of those unused sheds behind the building. You can get to the unused sheds and storage buildings without being seen, right?"*

*"Yeah,"* said Derek, *"the lights only shine on The Kingdom and some of the area surrounding it. I can keep in the dark. What do you want me to do next?"*

*"I'll keep Rufus talking for a little, but when I call make sure you pick up. Rufus won't know it's you on the other end and we won't be speaking to each other anyway. He'll think it's part of something else."*

*"Part of the....the...."* but I cut Derek off.

*"Yes Derek,"* I started to say, *"part of that."*

"Shut the door," said Booker to the SSS member closest to the door. With the door now closed, it was only Rufus Booker and I. He had guns on his desk, so he knew I couldn't try for anything.

"Now it's just you and me, Job." His face bragged victory and exaltation. "You haven't said a word. You can speak now. It's just you and I." Soon his elated state of mind would be humbled.

I hoped.

Finally speaking after being silent for the longest time, I said, "What's there to say?" I let that sink in. "One of your goons got me and brought me to you. I shoulda killed him when I had the chance, but he's only a kid." I spoke making it seem like I despised Derek. I wanted nothing to come back on him just like I wanted nothing coming back on Wendy when it came to Kevin Durgess.

That was also a reason why I didn't take the chance and risk of bringing in a gun. I felt it would've been too obvious. Plus, trying to get outta The Kingdom with one gun against many men was just insane and out of the question.

"He made the right choice if you ask me," said Booker with a partial smile.

I stood saying nothing.

"So," Booker went on, "how exactly were you able to pull off all the things you did?" He paused and then said, "Man to man, I'm highly impressed."

Looking around his office and then back to Rufus, I said, "You SSS guys aren't all that hard to figure out. It was actually quite simple" - really it wasn't - "I mean," I added with some sarcasm, "I probably could've taught a monkey the things I did and he would've been able to pull them off with ease too."

Not liking my comment at all, Rufus returned with, "You're talking quite the talk for someone who's a dead man."

He then added, "And also for someone who can't protect his own wife."

Like someone reaching into my chest and squeezing my heart, pain filled my entire being just then with Rufus Booker's cutting words. My body tensed and I was driven back to the past. Flashes of the night Naomi was killed in front of my eyes shined like lightning in the sky. It penetrated me to the core, but I had to maintain my composure in front of Booker; I couldn't allow him to think that he'd gotten to me in any shape or form.

"It hurts doesn't it," carried on Booker, standing up with a gun in his hand. "I can tell. But don't worry, you'll be joining her soon." He then said, "And I won't be making a mistake like I did last time."

If he had his way, which he was, I thought, Booker would probably waste an entire clip on me just to make sure I was dead this time around.

"That's the thing, you know," I said to Booker. He looked at me wondering what I was getting at. "I was prepared...." I stopped and then

222

started again, "I expected to die the very first day I started my revenge." Rufus squinted his eyes and listened closely to what I said. "You think I fear death, Rufus Booker?" He didn't have an answer. I went on, "I've been welcoming it for so long now, but it hasn't found me yet."

"Yet," said Booker smiling and pointing the gun at me. He then lowered the gun, making sure he got his point across.

Letting Booker know he didn't instill any kind of fear in me, I said, "You see, if I lived, I thought at the time, then I lived; but, if I died, then I'd be with my wife. You get me?"

"Yeah I get you Job McCants." I honestly think Rufus Booker understood me, even if it was just for one second.

"We both lost loved ones," Booker went on, "but tonight this all ends." He sniffed in and then said, "Matter of fact, it's about to end right now." Rufus started to raise the gun at me. "You got any last words, Job McCants?" I was just getting ready to unleash the next step in my plan, but something else happened instead.

Booker's cell phone sang its tune just then. He lowered the gun again, dug out his cell phone from his pocket, looked at the screen, and then said, "Well aren't you lucky," he said looking at me, waving the cell phone at me with his left hand, "saved by the bell."

Rufus answered the call. "Yeah."

Someone on the other end spoke for about a half a minute before Rufus spoke again. "We'll deal with that later. I got something more important happening right now," he said beaming a smile. "You'll never guess who's standing right in front of me."

The person on the other end must've asked. Rufus followed with, "Job McCants. One of my boys got him and brought him to me. I was just about to waste him before you called. Guess God gave him a few more minutes to live," he said with a laugh.

Rufus paused to listen to the voice on the other end. He replied with, "Don't worry boss. I'll make it fast and get rid of him quick. His vehicle's already being taken care of too."

Boss? I couldn't be certain, but I was pretty sure I now knew who Rufus Booker was talking to. It was the secret someone who'd been helping him for I don't know how long, it was the secret someone who would be looked at as a traitor by society if information leaked about him, and it was the secret someone who'd be exposed if I got outta The Kingdom alive.

Secret someone was saying something to Rufus. Booker returned with, "Yes sir." He then ended the call and stuck the cell phone back into his pocket.

Hoping and praying, I figured enough time had finally elapsed to allow Derek to grab the grenade bag and get to where he needed to.

It was time.

"Sorry Job," said Booker, "that was my partner in crime," he ended with a smile. "You'd die if you found out who he is."

I already knew. And I wasn't dead.

"Where were we?" Rufus paused. "Oh, that's right, we were here," he said raising the gun at me. "You have anything you wanna get off your chest before you die, Job McCants?"

Like what I was about to do was meant to be, I smiled and laughed. Rufus wondered why as he looked at me with bewilderment and surprise.

Starting to unbutton my flannel shirt, I said, "Actually, Rufus, there is something I've been wanting to get off my chest. Funny you should ask."

Unbuttoning the final button, I grasped my flannel shirt with both hands and opened it up for Booker to see, exposing my chest.

With fear, horror, and gloom filling Booker's face, he just stared at my chest like he couldn't believe what he was seeing. Lowering the gun, his mouth actually opened, like he was seeing a ghost or something.

Strapped to my chest was a fake homemade bomb that I'd put together using supplies from R and D's Hardware. It was what I spent time doing research on to make it look as real as I could the day Derek Westbrook arrived on my front doorstep. And, by the look on Rufus Booker's face, it was something that I'd sold successfully and pulled off.

It wasn't real, but Booker didn't know that.

I did though.

And it wasn't thick either, which made it not stand out under my flannel shirt. I tried to plan accordingly, and it had paid off.

To try and pull off the fake bomb stunt even more, I used electric tape to secure my phone to it and I tore off and held in my hand what looked like a small handheld detonator, you know, the kind you see bad guys hold in the movies. The kind where if the good guy makes one wrong move the bad guy will push down on a small button which will in turn blow something up.

It's amazing these days what you can put together using the Internet and your local hardware store.

When I looked at myself in the mirror earlier, I had to admit, the fake bomb looked authentic even to me. From several colored electrical wires, to lots of plumbers putty being formed into rectangles and then wrapped in thin cardboard paper, to drill bits buried into the wrapped plumbers putty with their ends sticking out attached to electrical wire, to

224

wires being connected to a gold wristwatch that was super glued to my fake bomb, to....to....you get my point. I used a handful of other things, but quite frankly I don't feel like explaining the whole fake bomb or what I made it of.

*"What're you gonna make the fake bomb out of?"*

*"I got some ideas," I replied, "but I'm planning on the Internet's help and some of my own thinking.*

*"Now listen," I said to Derek, "my iPhone's gonna be taped to the fake bomb just for looks. I'm gonna call you, don't worry, I'll save you as multiple numbers in case Booker can see the display screen, and I'm gonna put you on speaker phone. That way we don't have to talk and you can hear exactly what Rufus and I say in his office. That way you can hear what I say and know when to play your part."*

*"Then what?" asked Derek.*

*"Then," I said with a smile, "then the fun begins."*

"What....what're you planning on doing?" Rufus asked with fright tattooed on his face.

With my right hand clenching the fake handheld detonator, I smiled widely at Rufus Booker. I had him just where I wanted him, believing in every part of my plan that was working to perfection.

Smiling wider I said, "You'll see."

# 38

*"Derek,"* I started to say, *"you're gonna have to really listen closely to when I talk. When I tell Booker to look out back at the unused sheds, you throw a grenade in that direction, get away, and take cover, you hear?"*

*"You got it Job."* Derek then added, *"How you gonna sell it with the detonator?"*

Pausing to think, I then said, *"I'm just going to try and time it right. With looking out the window and seeing the explosion, I'll just press on the detonator with Booker thinking I was the one who caused it."*

*"He's gonna crap his pants you know."*

I laughed at Derek's comment. *"If he does, I don't wanna know."*

Rufus Booker still stood lost and shocked, like he had just landed onto some planet unknown to man. I never thought I'd be able to wipe away his sly smile or silence his boastfulness.

He proved me wrong.

I could see circles spinning in Booker's head. He was wondering how this could be, he was wondering how in the world could I, Job McCants, pull this off, and he was probably wondering, though I was unsure, how it was possible that I could carry this out alone.

So before Rufus Booker could jump to assumptions or point fingers - especially at Derek - I said, "Guess your boys, including young dumb Derek, isn't good at patting down and making sure visitors aren't booby-trapped first." I said this so Derek would be in the clear and Rufus wouldn't think him guilty of assisting me.

"How'd....how'd you...." Rufus started to say, but he stopped, still in awe of how this could be.

"It's a long story," I started to say, "but I don't feel like explaining it, especially to you." I wanted to leave him puzzled and confusedly thinking "how?"

Carrying on, I said, "I've been wearing this" - I was referring to the fake bomb - "most days just in case you came for me. That way I could take you with me." A lie, I know, but I needed to make Booker think this. I needed to make him think that I turned into a complete psycho. Plus, with catching him off guard and fearfully surprised, I figured he'd buy just about anything I said right now.

Not giving him anytime to think, I then fired up the display screen on my iPhone, punched in my password, and went to my favorites screen. Clicking on a ten-digit number which I had saved as a favorite - which was really Derek's pre-paid cell phone - I pressed on it and then pressed on the speaker phone option. I heard ringing on the other end.

This was kinda hard to do with my iPhone being taped to my chest, but I got it done.

"What....what're you doing?" asked Rufus nervously.

I didn't answer him.

*"Just answer when I call. Don't say anything on the other end," I told Derek. "You'll be on speaker phone, so press a button to acknowledge that you're on the other end. Then just listen after that. You'll know what to do and when to do it."*

*Derek shook his head. I didn't know what to think of that.*

*"What kid?"*

*Looking me in the eye, Derek said, "You're good Job. Real good."*

*I sat quietly, not replying back.*

With Derek on the other end - this was confirmed by the sound of a button that had been pressed - he was now in the office, just not physically.

"WHAT ARE YOU DOING!?" Rufus yelled, more out of worry than anger. He then lifted his gun up and pointed it at me.

I softly laughed, looking him right in the face. "Go ahead, shoot me. You do that," I said, "then we all go boom." It was something else I was making up, but I was pretty sure Booker would believe me.

He lowered his gun not sure what to do or think.

He bought it.

Just then the door behind me opened. I didn't bother looking back; I just stood still, staring at Booker.

"Boss, everything all right?" an SSS member said.

With sweat starting to form on his forehead, Rufus looked at me in desperation. I moved my right hand in front of me so the SSS member behind me couldn't see. Threatening to press down on the fake detonator, Rufus chose wisely and said to the SSS member who opened the door, "Get out! Did I say you could come in? Don't you or anyone else come in unless I say so!"

I heard the door behind me close with a slam.

Once again, it was just me and Booker.

227

I was ready, and I knew that Derek was also ready.

It was time for the bombs to start bursting in the air.

"You wanna know what I'm doing?" I said to Rufus. He didn't answer; he just stood in despair. "If you wanna know, then look out that window behind you." I walked toward Rufus and stood off to his left side about ten feet.

Turning around, Rufus looked out the large window behind him.

I quietly inhaled deeply through my nose and let it out.

"Look over at those unused sheds." I held up the detonator in my hand.

That was Derek's cue.

Rufus focused his sight on the sheds. Sweat was falling down the side of his face.

"Come on Derek, come on," I said to myself inside. "Throw the grenade, get outta there, and take cover."

It seemed like it was taking more time than it should have. Something was wrong, I thought, but then that's when it happened.

Rufus wasn't looking at me, but I pressed down on the detonator as soon as I heard the explosion and saw the bright orange cloud of fire.

BOOM!

Derek must've thrown it just right because there was nothing left of the shed. What used to be an unused shed was now nothing more than a vacant spot.

Rufus looked over at me wide-eyed.

I smiled like a maniac and said, "Impressive isn't it? Wait until you see what's next."

A couple of other sheds that were next to the one that was no longer there started to burn as well. From where Booker and I stood they looked like huts caught aflame.

*"Now, after the explosion from the first grenade, you gotta next get to one of those storage buildings out back. As with the shed, wait for my signal and follow suit."*

*"All right," replied Derek. "What do I do after that?"*

*"Next kid," I started to say, "you get rid of the pre-paid cell phone and get outta there." I was going to make sure that Derek had a way out. "You get in my vehicle, drop it off back at my place, and stay at my house if you have to."*

*Derek at first didn't say anything, but then he spoke. "My mom will be worried about me Job. I gotta go home."*

*I smiled. "Sounds like you have a good mom. In that case," I went on, "drop off my truck at my place and get on home."*

*"What about you?" Derek asked.*

*"What about me."* I returned.

*"What if what happens isn't enough for Booker? Or what if, what if...."* but I stopped Derek.

*"Derek, this is my fight. You will have done your job. I hate asking you for all this, but I won't be able to pull it off without you."* I said to reassure him, though I couldn't be certain, *"I'm walking outta The Kingdom with Rufus Booker. Everything's gonna be just fine."*

*"I hope,"* said Derek.

With Rufus wetting in his pants, I then said, "Now look over at those storage buildings to your right." Looking to his right, Rufus waited in fear as I moved closer to him, the detonator raised in my hand.

Again, that was Derek's cue.

The storage buildings were closer to The Kingdom than the sheds were. I was glad; it would make for a better final scene.

"Come on Derek," I said again to myself inside, "one more. You can do it kid."

I clutched the detonator in my hand, ready to press down on it. BOOM!!!

Pressing down on the detonator, this was a much bigger explosion than I had planned for. So much bigger that it even made me jump and stare in amazement.

Derek had said there wasn't much in those storage buildings; but whatever was in that one, I thought, it made for one heck of an explosion.

Like a tidal wave on fire, pieces of the storage building that Derek just blew up hung in the air and made their way down, collapsing onto the ground below. Orange and yellow painted the sight before us and the fire seemed to fill our eyes, making them squint. It was like a magic trick: the building was just there a minute ago, and then it was mysteriously gone. Only this magic trick ended in being blown to smithereens.

Outside looked like a miniature warzone. At first I couldn't believe that Derek and I had just pulled this off; it seemed like a goal that was so hard to reach, but we made it.

We'd done it.

I knew Derek was now on his way to my truck and getting out of here.

Shaking, I mean actually shaking, Rufus Booker slowly turned toward me. I took no joy in this, but if I wanted Booker, then I had to continue on.

Resting my right detonator hand down to my side, I wide-eyed looked at Booker and laughed. "First the shed, then that storage building," I said looking into Rufus's watery eyes. "Would you like to take a guess what's next?" Knowing that he knew what I was getting at, I said anyway,

"Let me give you a hint. It's a much larger building and about forty people are inside of it right now." I then smiled a creepy and terrible smile.

I wasn't sure what Rufus Booker would do. Of all SSS, he was by far the hardest and I was sure the most difficult to break. I was pretty sure I'd gotten my point across both clearly and explosively, but what would Booker do?

Time would tell.

And very soon.

Standing in defeat, Rufus hung his head down with his dreadlocks sagging. Walking over to his chair behind his desk, he plopped down, like his kingdom had just been stripped away from him.

Shaking his head incredulously, he leaned back in his chair, looking at me. "How? When?" he asked. "How and when did you do this?"

His head had too much going on inside of it. He wasn't going to figure any of this out; it was all too much to take in. I kinda thought it would be similar to amnesia with him: whenever he'd remember Derek and I first walking into his office, there would be nothing he'd be able to remember after that. None of it would make sense.

It was the perfect plan.

I said what I had said to him not too long ago, "It's a long story, but I don't feel like explaining it, especially to you."

Realizing he wasn't going to get anywhere with me, Rufus said, "What....what do you want then?" He sat more upright in his chair.

I stood silent for a long moment. Finally, I spoke. "All I want is you."

Nodding his head like he was agreeing to something, it seemed Rufus Booker understood me again just then, even if it was only for a second.

"I'll let your gang live," I went on, "all you gotta do is come with me."

"Or else?" inquired Rufus.

"Or else we all burn up in flames." I let that sink in. "Honestly, it doesn't matter to me." I held out my last dollar in this plan; I hoped Booker would reach out his hand and take it.

Without his gun in his hand - he'd dropped it after the second explosion - Rufus looked away from me for the longest time. Finally he said, "All right."

"All right what?"

Swallowing hard and still blown away by what just happened, Rufus said, "I'll go with you. I'm not gonna let you kill all of us." Mmm, I thought, even drug kingpins can make wise choices at times.

"Phew," I said inside. Thanking God that he bought this, I had nothing left to offer.

Walking over to his desk, I put the fake detonator in my left hand and grabbed a handgun off of his desk with my right. "You're gonna walk us right out of here. Anything funny, this place goes boom. You got me?" Without saying a word, Rufus nodded his head.

"Good," I said, "now let's get going."

This gun I grabbed wasn't the one I had intended for Booker. That gun was the Sig Sauer that I bought off of Rex at Lucky 7's bar that resembled similarity to the one Booker shot Naomi with. But, with a change of plans and that gun going to Derek instead, it still served a significant purpose.

Standing up, Rufus started making his way to his office door. Suddenly, I remembered something just then. In the midst of all the action, I'd forgotten about it.

"Wait," I said. I looked over to the left side of his office. Rufus's eyes followed mine to the fireplace. Walking over until I stood in front of it, I turned around, looked Booker in the face, and said, "We're forgetting something."

I smiled after saying this.

Bending down and reaching up into the chimney, I felt the bag that Derek told me would be here. Pulling down on it, it was about the size of a book bag and had some weight to it. Putting its long strap around my shoulder, I turned back to Rufus.

Rufus's face again was shocked, like it said, "How on earth did you know?" The look on his face was priceless. It was like I had just taken the most valuable thing away from him that held secrets that even the world didn't know about.

"There," I said smiling again, "now let's get going."

†　　†　　†

Rufus opened the door to his office and there stood the entire SSS gang - at least all that were at The Kingdom - on both sides of the hallway, some black and some white. With shock and dismay written on their faces, they just stared at us.

Rufus stood in front of me. Looking back at me, he looked into my eyes, and then he looked back to his gang in front of him. "Listen up!" he said aloud. "Me and the white boy are gonna walk outta here, and if you do anything stupid," he paused, "he's gonna blow this building up!"

That's when I moved to the side behind Rufus and let SSS see my chest. The faces that were initially hard before I walked into Booker's office had turned soft and worried, the celebrating and praises had ceased, and the hate that I first felt had relented some.

In their minds, I thought, now they knew who had caused the explosions. Now they knew who meant business. Now they knew who had control.

Obeying me, Rufus then said, "And don't follow us as we're leaving! Got it!?"

The silence of the gang members told us that they understood.

Making our way, Rufus and I slowly passed through them until we got to the door that led to the second floor. I kept quiet the entire time; people knew to watch out for the quiet ones.

Opening to the second floor that was dedicated to cooking, we walked through it until we got to the door that led to the first floor. Finally on the first floor, we made our way out of The Kingdom the same way I had entered.

SSS obeyed orders. Not a single member was behind us.

A lot of planning went into this and I had my moments of concern at times; but, finally, here I was.

Walking out of The Kingdom.

The air I breathed in just then was probably, to me, the freshest and cleanest air I had ever breathed.

"What now Job?"

"Take me to your vehicle."

After walking down the cracked steps of The Kingdom, I looked behind me. SSS members were packed in front of the windows on the third story so thickly that I thought a few of them might fall out.

Looking in front of me, Rufus led us to his vehicle: an older black Dodge Charger with black rims.

"Nice ride," I said to myself inside, "guess drugs buy nice things. Too bad."

We stood at his vehicle in silence. Breaking the silence I said, "Keys." Digging into his pocket, Rufus grabbed his keys. "Now open the trunk," I said.

"Why?"

"Just do it."

Walking over to the trunk of his Dodge Charger, Rufus unlocked it and opened it. "Now what?"

With Rufus's back to me, I made my way behind him.

The night they killed Naomi came back to me like a memory I would never be able to forget. Remembering what Rufus Booker said right before he pulled the trigger on me, I said, "Now say good night."

I then hit him hard on the back of his head with the gun in my hand. Falling forward unconscious, his body landed in the trunk with the keys falling from his hand onto the ground. Picking up the keys off the ground, I stared at Rufus Booker's body lying in the trunk of his Dodge Charger.

It was tempting at first to tell him to get into the trunk, take off my fake bomb, throw it and the false detonator into the trunk with him, and tell him it was all a hoax; but, then I thought, I didn't want him knowing it was fake. For all his days I wanted him to think that Job McCants was a crazy, bombing lunatic who devised an unthinkable plan that would keep him up late at nights trying to figure out how I pulled it off.

He could try, but he'd never figure it out.

Shutting the trunk door with a slam, I made my way to the driver's seat and started the car up. It roared as I pressed on the gas.

We did it Derek.

Putting the Dodge Charger into drive, I peeled out, loudly driving away from The Kingdom and making my way toward the old Mount Vernon High School.

# 39

On the drive to Mount Vernon, Derek had called from a payphone, telling me that he'd made it home. I'd asked him how in the world had he made the shed and storage building blow up so big - I knew grenades alone wouldn't have been able to do what they had done - but Derek just laughed and said, "I'll tell you how some other time." Ending the call shortly after, I was still impressed with how the kid had handled himself the entire time.

Now that all is said and done - as I'm writing this - I never did remember to ask him about those explosions the night we went to The Kingdom.

Finally making it to the abandoned Mount Vernon High School, it had taken an effort, but while Booker was unconscious I'd gotten him to another room located downstairs. This room I had set up not too long ago, and everything was ready.

As with Taylor and Durgess, Booker was tied down - arms and legs - to a chair. Unlike Durgess there were no rats in this room; but, unfortunately to Booker's mind, there was something else prepared for him on the ground.

I wasn't going to wait and deal with him tomorrow; he was going to be dealt with tonight.

Unable to see his face due to his head hanging down with dreadlocks adding coverage, Rufus sat motionless. I could hear his soft breathing as I stood before him with a bottled water.

It was time.

Dumping the entire bottle of water on top of his head, the liquid sprinted down his dreadlocks and face onto the ground, like rain falling from the sky.

Throwing the empty bottle to my side, I took some steps back as he started to wake up.

Lifting up his head with his eyes opened, Rufus Booker and I stared at each other: eye to eye. His body language looked calm and he sat still, but his worried look told me that he was wondering what I was going to do next.

Sniffing in several times, he had finally become aware that something wasn't right and out of the norm. "What....what's that smell? And why are my clothes wet?" He sniffed in a couple more times and then said, "Is....is that gasoline?" The look on his face had grown from worry to panic.

Rufus then looked around the room, like he was a lab rat observing his surrounding before being experimented on. When he looked down at the ground, that's when his face fell lower than any humans I'd ever seen.

Like a moat encircling him, wetness covered the area in front of him and to his sides. He couldn't see, but it also soaked the area behind him. He sniffed in again, looked around him, and put two and two together.

That's when his panic came out verbally.

"Job, I'm Rufus Booker. You....you know me. I'm the head of SSS. I....I can get you whatever you want." Seeing that meant little to me, he carried on louder. "Job!....Job!...." he stopped. Starting again, he said, "I'm sorry for killing your wife! If I could...." he paused, "I'd take it back! Do you hear me!? I'd take it back!"

He continued on in his frenzied state. "Job! Come on! I don't wanna burn alive! Please! I'm sorry!" Ironic how this man had always seemed so hard, but now he was soft. So cocky and tall, but now panicking and low.

*Mercy, J, mercy.*

I'll show him mercy all right.

Without saying a word, I just stared at Rufus. I had already gotten what I wanted out of him - thanks to him and his mouth - and now it was time to wrap up this short show.

I pulled out a rag out of my back pocket, removed a lighter from a front pocket, and struck the lighter so a flame was born. Holding both the rag and lighter close together, I didn't set the rag on fire just yet.

"I messed up Job! I'm sorry!" Rufus yelled. "I'll do anything! ANYTHING!" He started to shake in his chair but that was futile; he wasn't going anywhere. Almost in tears, Rufus shouted, "I was wrong! Please, don't kill me! Not like this!"

Touching the flame to the rag, the fiery path started to make its way closer to my hand. I could now feel the heat against it and a few of my hand hairs started to singe.

*Haven't you ever heard the saying: if you play with fire, eventually you're gonna get burned?*

"JOB! I'M BEGGING! PLEASE STOP!"

Tossing the rag into the air in Booker's direction, the moment seemed to go in slow motion.

*Oh my.*

"NO!!!" screamed Booker.

Rufus shouted other things, but I wasn't listening to his words.

I watched the burning rag as it fell closer and closer to the wet floor that awaited its presence.

This old furnace room we were in was muggy and outdated. Rusted pipes hung overhead and the concrete floor had numerous cracks in it. The glass that covered gauges of other equipment was damaged, and there was a stink in the air that at least wasn't too offensive.

The room was definitely one I wouldn't want to spend my last moments in.

Looking at Rufus, he closed his eyes tightly and tensed his body as the rag touched the wet floor in front of him.

He waited for the flames to reach his feet and go on up until they reached his head and finally consumed his body. He waited for the overbearing heat that would leave him well-done. He waited to be burned alive.

He waited and he waited.

But the flames were never created, the temperature never increased a degree, and his body was left unburned.

I stood there in silence, waiting for him to open his eyes.

When he finally did, he opened one eye first and the second followed suit after that. Realizing nothing had happened, he stared at me scared and in a state of confusion. He didn't know what to think.

"What....what happened?" he said softly.

Finally speaking, I said, "What happened is you're alive." I let that sink in before I said my next words. "It's hard for water to catch on fire Rufus."

Puzzled with a lost look on his face, I could see Booker thinking inside of his head. For about a half a minute he turned his head from one side to the next and looked down at the ground below him and at his clothes.

Looking at me enraged, it finally made sense to him.

"You son of a...." he cursed. "It was just water?" He stopped, but something else just clicked with him. "But the gasoline....I smelled gasoline. And I still do." He looked at me waiting for an answer.

Trying not to smile, I said, "A little gasoline to the nose and upper lip never hurt anybody."

Madder than a hornet, Booker gave me a look that wanted to bore holes through my body.

Just then, I thought I'd heard a sound. It was still a little distance off, but I was sure I had heard a sound. I just wasn't sure what.

"You're gonna pay for this Job. You're gonna...."

"Shh. Shut up," I said to Rufus.

*I think I heard something too.*

After Rufus shut up, I stood still and listened as best I could.

There came another sound, like a footfall.

Someone was coming down.

Pulling the gun from Rufus's desk back at The Kingdom from behind my waist, I pointed it at Booker and said, "You shut up and don't say a word," I added, "or you're dead." I really wasn't going to shoot him, but Booker didn't know that.

Standing to the side of the door of this old furnace room in the dark, I waited to see who was coming.

Who could it possibly be? I thought.

A homeless person?

Kids screwing off?

Who?

*I dunno, but you're about to find out.*

The footsteps were approaching and coming closer.

Quietly pushing down the hammer of the gun, I raised it so it'd be about head level. I didn't know who it was, but with all that had and was going on, I wasn't taking any chances.

Closer the footsteps came....closer....closer....

*Job, whoever it is, they're here.*

I know.

The footsteps stopped right in front of the open door. One more step and whoever it was would be inside the furnace room with Booker and I.

"Rufus Booker," said a man's voice.

To me the voice sounded familiar, and whoever it was, he also knew Booker.

Not listening to me telling him not to say a word, Rufus said, "What're you doing here?"

"Look at you now," said the unwelcome man.

To me the voice sounded very familiar.

Taking another step, the man whose voice sounded very familiar made his way inside the room with us. When he stepped in front of me, that's when I put the gun to his head.

I didn't see it at the time, but the man held a gun down to his side.

"Who are you?" I said. "And what are you doing here?"

The man stopped and didn't move. Then, turning his head as best he could, he started to slowly look over at me with a toothpick in his mouth. His cornrows and face started to shine some in the dim light.

That's when I knew who the unwelcome man with the very familiar voice was.

Slowly lowering the gun down to my side, I stared at him in disbelief. What was he doing here? How did he....? Questions circled around in my head just then.

Facing me, Jehu Bridges and I stood face to face.

*Like it had been with Derek at your front doorstep, I wasn't expecting this.*

Yeah, me either.

"Job, it's me, Jehu."

What was he doing here? I continued to ask myself.

With the questions rotating in my head and with all the bad that had happened, I hadn't trusted a soul. I thought Jehu Bridges was someone I could trust, but with him being here I wasn't sure anymore.

Lifting the gun back up and pointing it at Jehu's heart, as much as I hated to acknowledge, I actually had to agree with Rufus Booker.

"What're you doing here?"

238

# 40

Keeping the gun pointed at Jehu, I waited for him to give an answer as to why he was here. It made no sense to me why he was, and I started to get a bad feeling that this detective who I'd trusted was now betraying that trust right in front of me.

But before Jehu could speak, Booker spoke instead.

"What's going on?"

With my free hand, I took Jehu's gun away from him. "Back up, Jehu." The detective took a few steps back.

"Job, you're making a big mis...." Bridges began to say, but I interrupted.

"Not now Jehu. Not now."

"Hey, did you hear me!?" yelled Booker.

With some distance between Jehu and I, I turned the gun on Booker. "I thought I told you to shut up." I thought that would silence the man, but it did the opposite instead.

"Forget that," Booker said. "Let me go. Now! Or kill me!"

"Rufus," I said, shouting at the top of my lungs, "SHUT UP!"

It's amazing what we humans can say when our tempers start to rise. Rufus's next words I'm sure he wished he could take back.

Looking at me, to Bridges, and then back to me, Rufus started to shake back and forth in his chair, like he was trying to free himself from his trap. "I don't give a...." he cursed, "anymore!" Shaking wildly, he exclaimed, "Since you're not gonna kill me, I'm gonna get outta this chair, take that gun from you, and kill the both of you just like I did your wife and his brother!"

Bridges and I stared at one another for a few long moments and couldn't believe what we had just heard. A boiling wave of wrath and anger came alive in me just then, and I could tell something similar was coming over Jehu as well.

Jehu started walking toward Booker. Pointing the gun back at Jehu, I yelled, "Bridges! STOP!" I was in a world of confusion and pressure with too much noise and action going on right now. Like a man gone crazy, I wanted to pull my hair out as I still couldn't believe what Booker had just said.

Reluctantly - and I'm sure with great difficulty - Jehu came to a halt. With fury eating at my heart, I marched toward Booker. I'd had enough of his mouth. When I got about five feet from him, he started to say, "Yeah, go on, it's about...."

But before Booker could finish, I lifted the gun in my hand and pistol-whipped him across the face. It only took me one hit, but finally, Booker was shut up and he hung his head down, out cold.

*Ouch! That had to hurt.*

There was one problem fixed, I thought. Now I turned back around to face my second: why was Bridges here?

Jehu Bridges stood before me breathing heavily as his chest rose and fell with each breath. The toothpick in his mouth he must've thrown or spat out because it wasn't there anymore. And I was pretty sure I saw him wipe away a tear just then.

I remembered the picture of the detective and his brother, Jerome, in his office. I remembered the article about Jerome's murder in the paper that I happened to find on the computer. And I also remembered Booker's penetrating words he just spoke maybe a minute ago.

Now knowing for sure who Jerome's murderer was - though this is who we assumed anyway - I said to Jehu, "I'm....I'm sorry about your brother."

But then my attention came back to the present and I wanted some answers. Sitting Bridges' gun down on a desk, the other one was lowered at my side. "Jehu," the detective met my eyes, "what are you doing here?"

Slowing his respirations and wiping sweat away from his brow, Bridges leaned up against an old furnace. He stood there like that for about a minute before he spoke, but finally, he did.

"I was following you." I didn't say anything. Going on, Bridges said, "Why else do you think I'm here?"

"You on their side?" He knew I was referring to SSS.

Jehu's face changed, like I had just insulted him in front of a crowd and now he was upset. "Are you serious right now Job? Are you stupid? Have you lost it?"

*Can't blame Jehu. You kinda have.*

Wouldn't you in all this mess?

*I see your point.*

Jehu had always been a friend toward me and I hated asking my last question, but nothing was making sense right now and I was like a lost sheep without a shepherd.

"I had to make sure." Thinking more, I asked, "How long you been following me?"

Looking down like he'd been caught in a lie, Bridges said, "Since after the night Kevin Durgess went missing at Bottom's Up." He paused and then said, "The same night you were there."

I thought on that. "You said after, so how'd you know I was at Bottom's Up?" I was growing very curious with what Bridges was saying.

Sniffing in and picking at a fingernail, Bridges was postponing answering my question. I could tell he was hiding something.

"Any day now Jehu."

Bridges finally looked at me and answered, "I used a GPS tracking device. Similar to what you see people using on TV shows and movies with bugging equipment, but without actually hearing your conversations."

GPS. Bugging equipment. Conversations. These were words that Bridges just used. Trying to piece things together, that's when it finally hit me.

The day he visited me at my house came back to me. It was the same day when I came out of my restroom and he had to go because he said, "Work calls." It was the same day I knew he didn't fully believe me when Ricky's arcade got brought up. And it was the same day I thought my cell phone had been moved on the kitchen island.

Putting this puzzle together, I looked at Jehu. "My phone."

The detective nodded his head. "I didn't listen in on your conversations. It was just used to show your location."

"Yeah," I started to say, "and anywhere, anytime."

Jehu's silence confirmed what I had just said.

I stood quietly with anger again rising in me. This was illegal, right? This wasn't right. This was backstabbing. This was....

*Job, come on.*

I know.

Illegal or not, I wasn't going to blame Bridges or tell the authorities what he did. Jehu did the right thing. He wasn't betraying me, though for a split second I thought so. The detective did what he believed to be the right call. And....he was right.

It was right. No matter what anybody else thought.

Looking back, I'm glad Jehu did what he did.

I'll explain that later.

"You changed Job," Jehu started to say, "I could see it on your face and in your eyes both at the courthouse and at your home the day I put the tracking device in your phone while you were in the bathroom.

"I'll admit," he stood straighter, "you kinda talked me out of believing you had anything to do with Tyrese Taylor gone missing, but not enough. I had my thoughts. But before I visited you that day, I had this gut feeling that something was going on with you, so I secretly put that GPS in your phone."

I sat down on a desk, taking in everything Jehu was saying.

"And then Kevin Durgess went missing. You were there that night and headed to this city afterwards. I had no clue why. Then I thought to myself, first Taylor, and now Durgess."

Bridges knew exactly what I had been doing. He read it off to me like I was a little child listening to his mother read him a bedtime story.

"Why those two, I asked myself." He stopped and let that settle in. "That's when I knew for sure you had something to do with Taylor and Durgess disappearing. Your behavior, you changing, something just clicked with me. I just couldn't believe you were actually pulling these things off.

"That's when I started to follow you at times and keep an eye on you. Lately you've just been home and running regular errands like anybody else. It was obvious to me you were spacing taking your victims out. I didn't know much about the really young member of SSS, but I knew for certain you'd try somehow to get to Rufus Booker."

Taking a break from story time and looking at me curiously, Bridges asked, "Job, how did you do all this? And how did you possibly get to Rufus Booker and capture him?"

I sat without giving any answers. Some things were best left untold. The least Bridges knew, the better. Plus, I wanted to keep Derek out of any of this; I hoped all of it.

Realizing I wasn't going to talk, Bridges carried on, "And then there came the grand finale. I was at the station when I noticed you were heading toward the way south side of town. The side of town where most cops won't even venture into and where most people know to stay away from.

"The side that's inhabited by SSS and supposedly where their base of operations is. Across Cana Bridge is nothing but SSS trouble.

"I've seen and heard about The Kingdom, but with orders that we're to stay away from there, there's little I can do. But," Bridges pointed to his own head, "I knew where you were going when you were crossing that bridge. I don't know how you knew for sure Booker was there or where you got your information from, but I knew somehow, someway, you'd gotten what you wanted and were setting off to finish business."

Bridges was piecing this thing together very well. I was impressed. I tuned back in to hear him say, "That's when I left the station to come after you to make sure you didn't get yourself killed.

I don't know what happened, but I was too late. The back of The Kingdom looked like a bomb had destroyed it; and when I pulled to the side of one of the old buildings across from The Kingdom, there you were with Rufus Booker."

Laughing softly and shaking his head, Bridges went on, "I was actually gonna let you go and do nothing. I mean," he said with a slight smile, "here you were with the worst guy, SSS's drug kingpin, under your authority, and you had him. You were taking care of who we longed to have in our custody, and, speaking on behalf of the citizens and authorities of Columbus, who we wanted to see put away, and I'm sure, for most, even killed."

I took no joy or pride in what I had done, but for many, I'm sure they would've agreed with Jehu Bridges just then.

"That's when I started following you to this city called Mount Vernon where you came to after you'd taken Kevin Durgess, and I have no doubt where you had taken Tyrese Taylor. I lost you at one point and had to pull over to see where you went, and when I finally did, I came to this old brick building."

Looking around he said, "What is this place anyway?"

"It's an old abandoned high school," I replied.

"How'd you find out about it?"

I didn't answer.

Going on, Bridges said, "I know you're not gonna tell me if I'm right, but I believe I got you down Job." Taking a breath, Bridges said, "My guess is that you found out ways to get to Taylor, Durgess, and Booker, which is beyond my imagination, and brought them back here to…." Jehu paused and then said, "to have your way with them and then kill them.

"If revenge was the name of this game, then you excelled in it. I don't know why you didn't go after the young member of SSS, Derek…." he tried to remember his name, "Derek whatever his name was, but I'm sure you had your reasons.

"And now we're here, and I'm wondering what I should do next."

He stood and I sat in silence for about thirty seconds before one of us spoke.

"In one hand," Jehu raised a hand, "as a cop I'm supposed to arrest you and turn you in with all you've done. And you've done some bad things Job." I didn't disagree. "But in the other hand," he raised his second hand, "I have this feeling I should just let you go, say nothing, and act like I found nothing out with you wiping away so much filth and poison off of our city and streets."

Jehu lowered his hands and sighed. "I'm torn between two options. To me, I'm fully on board with option number two and letting you go, saying and acting like nothing was found out; but, by law and as an officer of it, I should uphold that cause that I swore to for the city of Columbus and arrest you."

While Jehu decided what option he was going to take, I drifted off into my own world.

I had come this far and gotten what I wanted. Yes I had done some bad things, things that people only say they would do but never actually go through with. I'd plotted and planned precisely so that every mission was carried out with success. I had never been caught until now; but everything, at least to me, was completed, and it would be up to others to decide what to do with me next.

That's when I finally realized: the race had come to its close, and it was time to turn myself in.

*You're making the right choice J.*

I couldn't allow Jehu to hold all of this in and later down the road regret his decision and wish he had turned me in. I couldn't possibly let him carry this untold burden around like a thorn in his flesh for the rest of his life. I couldn't permit Jehu Bridges, my detective friend, to succumb to a low depth when righteousness and justice needed to shine.

*I'm proud of you for doing the right thing J.*

Making the decision for my friend, I picked up his gun off the desk, walked over to him so we stood face to face again, and held out both guns for him to take.

"You do what's right, Jehu." He took the guns from my hands, understanding me completely. "Always."

Detective Bridges tucked both guns behind his waist. He held out his hand and we both shook and held the firm grip for a long time. Pulling me in for a hug, he said, "Thanks Job."

I didn't know what would happen from here; but, I have to admit, I felt like the world's heaviest weight was being removed from me just then.

*We'll be all right J. Doing what's right can cover up many wrongs.*

All of a sudden we heard a loud sound upstairs somewhere, like a door being kicked in. It was followed with, "POLICE! POLICE! THIS IS THE MOUNT VERNON SWAT! STAND DOWN! STAND DOWN!"

Separating myself from Jehu, at least he'd done the right thing before walking into the old Mount Vernon High School: he'd called in the local authorities.

"What the...." Jehu said. "Job, I didn't call anybody." His shocked look confirmed this.

And he didn't call. I found out later that a close-by neighbor of the abandoned MVHS - outside sitting on his front porch - heard sounds coming across the street from the old school. Eager to find out more, the neighbor made his way through some pine trees to find me getting Booker out of the trunk of the Dodge Charger and taking him into the school. Some time awhile later, the neighbor said, he saw another man with a gun - detective Bridges - walk into the school, and that's when he called the police.

Not only had the SWAT division from Mount Vernon's Police Department been on scene, but also present were PD units, as well as almost the entire Knox County Sheriff's Department.

We didn't have much time, and I knew Mount Vernon's SWAT would be down here where we were any minute now.

"Jehu, listen."

"Job, I'm sorry."

"It's not your fault, just listen. We only have another minute or so."

Bridges listened closely, realizing I had something important to tell him.

Running over to the desk I sat on, I reached under it and grabbed the bag from Booker's office at The Kingdom that had all kinds of secrecy in it. I didn't have time to open it, but at least I knew the bag and its assorted material was going into good and trusted hands.

Hurrying back over to Bridges, I handed him the bag and said, "Here, take this. I'm not fully sure what's all in it, but I think it's Booker's deepest and darkest secrets that he didn't want anyone to know about. Maybe some things in it will be of use."

Taking the bag from me, Jehu said, "Thanks Job. We'll see."

Bridges shook his head. "I hate to do this," he said taking out handcuffs, "but let's make this easy. That way they won't come in here and take you down."

Turning around, I allowed Jehu to cuff me. "Thanks Jehu."

"Job."

"Yeah."

"Sorry that it's ending this way. If you ask me, you've removed some very bad people from Columbus, as well as countless amounts of drugs. Also, who knows how many future lives you saved because of what you did." He paused and sighed, "Hopefully that means something down the road."

I didn't say a word; I just nodded.

"Most likely," Jehu started to say, "we'll be taking you to Mount Vernon's station since we're in their jurisdiction. I'm hoping to take you back with me soon to Columbus, but since crimes have been committed in two places, these sorta things can get complicated. But," Jehu said lastly, "it'll all get figured out."

He patted me on the shoulder several times.

"Job."

"Yeah."

"How'd you go through all you did, get this far, and not get yourself killed?"

I wasn't going to answer him at first. Some things were just better left untold. But then I said, "Maybe one day, friend to friend, not police officer to friend, I'll tell you."

Patting me on the shoulder one final time, Jehu said, "Sounds good to me my friend."

Just then, "DOWN ON THE GROUND! DOWN ON THE GROUND!"

SWAT members, just as you see them on TV, swarmed into the room as thick as locusts. I don't know how many there were, but there seemed to be plenty. Beams from flashlights bounced off the walls and into my face, multiple guns were pointed at both Jehu and I, and the old furnace room hurriedly filled up.

Holding up his badge in one hand and his identification in the other for all the SWAT members to see, Jehu yelled, "Police officer on scene! Police officer! The situation is controlled! I have the suspect apprehended! Stand down!"

The in-charge of the SWAT team approached Jehu, took his badge and ID, studied it, and said, "Everyone, stand down!" Looking over the badge and ID some more, he said, "Columbus? You're a little ways from home, detective Bridges."

"Yeah, I know."

"What the heck's going on here?" inquired In-Charge. "We got a call that some neighbor saw a man being dragged in here from the trunk of a vehicle by someone, and another man coming in sometime after with a gun."

Putting a hand on my shoulder, Jehu answered, "It's a long story. I'll tell you when we get outta here."

"Very well," said In-Charge, "anybody else down here besides you three?" he ended, looking over at Booker unconscious on the chair.

One of the SWAT members checked Booker for a pulse and nodded his head, signaling that he was still alive.

Jehu cleared his throat. "Job?" I didn't give a reply, but the detective knew he had my attention. "Where are the bodies at?"

"Down here."

"How many?"

"Just the two."

"Where?"

"Just outside this room. Taylor's in the room behind the closed door on the right and Durgess is in the one to the left."

"Jenkins," said In-Charge, "you check out the room on the right. Flowers, you take the room on the left." Both SWAT team members started making their way out of the furnace room. "The rest of you," continued In-Charge, "fan out and secure all rooms. Give me an all clear when you're completed."

Soon after In-Charge had given orders, it was only he, Jehu, and I left in the room. Oh, forgive me, and unconscious Booker still in the chair.

"Who's that in the chair?" asked In-Charge.

"That's Rufus 'D-Locks' Booker," answered Jehu. "He's the leader of our big bad gang in Columbus, SSS."

"You're kidding me," In-Charge said. "We've heard of them. They're talked about in this state like they were the President himself."

"Yeah," Jehu said, "hopefully this settles them down some. Thanks to this man," he obviously was referring to me, "their ringleader's outta the picture, and for a long, long time." Jehu added, "This man here is a good man."

"You mean," In-Charge started to say, "he took care of this scumbag who everyone will be happy to hear about, and we're gonna put him away?" He let that sink in. "Seems upside down if you ask me."

In-Charge looked me up and down. I stood quiet and unmoving.

"Off the record sir," In-Charge said to me, "sounds like this Booker got what he had coming. Sorry you gotta be punished too."

I didn't reply, but I appreciated In-Charge's comment. But, in contrast to what he said, I deserved to be punished for my actions.

I needed to be punished.

"What's that bag you got there, detective Bridges?" asked In-Charge. With the light shining on him some, In-Charge was a burly white man who had a thick mustache and sideburns that went down past his ears. He looked to be a man who one wouldn't wanna mess with.

I liked him.

"Not quite sure yet," replied Bridges. "Supposedly, according to Job here, it's possibly a lot of dirt on Booker. Who knows what else we'll find."

"Let's take a gander," said In-Charge, shining his light on the bag.

Moving in front of me, Jehu stood next to In-Charge and kneeled down. Shining his light down, In-Charge made it easier for Jehu to see.

247

Just then the SWAT team came back into the room. "We're all clear, sir," said a member.

"Where's Jenkins and Flowers?" inquired In-Charge.

I could hear the unzipping sound come from the bag that Jehu was opening.

"We don't...." the member who gave the all clear started to say, looking behind him. "Never mind sir, here they come."

Jehu was just getting ready to open the bag wide open when Jenkins and Flowers entered the room.

"Well," said In-Charge, "what'd you two find? How dead are they?"

Looking at each other and then to In-Charge, Jenkins and Flowers had looks on their faces that I can't explain. Like they had seen something they weren't expecting.

I knew why they had those looks.

*Me too.*

"That's just the thing, sir," said Jenkins, "they're not."

Jehu stopped what he was doing; the bag remained unopened. Everyone's attention was on Jenkins and Flowers.

"You mean they're alive?" said In-Charge.

"Yes sir," replied Flowers, "they're alive as alive can be."

That's when all eyes in the room turned to me, wondering what in the world was going on. The last set to look at me was Jehu's. His face was trying to understand, trying to figure out this new piece of information.

"Job," he said, "you didn't kill them?"

Shaking my head, I stood quiet and unmoving.

With all eyes on me.

# 41

Travel back with me into the courtroom some months ago. You know, when I said I couldn't remember anything to Judge Porter due to my coma and Tyrese Taylor, Kevin Durgess, and Derek Westbrook walked free.

No doubt I wanted to kill all three of them, including Booker, at the time. So much anger and hatred was stored in my heart at that time that I thought I was just about capable of anything.

I flirted with thoughts of killing them for days, just like a man flirts with a woman who he likes; however, the more I walked the streets of Columbus and the more I saw how ugly people and situations can be during those two months of planning, the less and less my flirtation with killing all four SSS members grew.

Though I thought for sure I could kill them with no hesitation in the beginning, I soon realized that death was too good for them and, if I ended them, I'd be no better than they were.

If I went through with what I initially wanted to do, I would've been someone who I never wanted to be.

One of them.

And though I was confident I couldn't have killed Derek - if I would have - then that would've meant he couldn't have said, "I'm sorry," to me. Which meant I wouldn't have been giving one of God's creations the opportunity to change his way and life. Which meant that Derek wouldn't have knocked on my door that day, apologizing for his transgression. Which meant that I probably wouldn't have been able to get to Rufus Booker.

God works in mysterious ways is what I'm saying.

It took some time and inner labor, but I finally realized I had something better in store than death for these men.

Seizing them.

Breaking them.

And, most of all, getting them to confess.

From that point on, I knew exactly what I was doing and wanted to achieve. I just wondered if I'd be able to pull everything off. In the end, I actually did, and sometimes it's still hard to believe.

I knew what I was doing when I raised the .357 and shot wide left of Tyrese Taylor's head, hitting the wall behind him instead. I knew what I was doing when I stopped at my station that day when I ran into Leo Watson and gathered trauma supplies just in case; I didn't think I was going to actually shoot Kevin Durgess, but with my paramedic skills, if I did, I knew it would be an easy wound to fix by shooting him in a minor spot, making sure the bullet passed through. Also, I knew what I was doing by keeping him alive - like Taylor - by shooting wide right of his head, also with the .357. Finally, I also knew what I was doing by not having Rufus Booker engulfed in flames.

I'd fed and gave clean water to Taylor and Durgess, I cared for their wounds, and I treated them, my enemies, with compassion. It was the hardest thing I ever did, trust me, but I remember something in the Bible that says: *If your enemies are hungry, give them food to eat. If they are thirsty, give them water to drink. You will heap burning coals of shame on their heads, and the Lord will reward you.*

Yes I may have placed duct tape over their mouths when I was gone and kept them tied tightly to their chairs and kept them mostly warm in the dim light of those scary rooms; but I'm sure I'd acted better than most would have, given with what they had done to Naomi and I.

With extra visits to Mount Vernon, I'd also untied Taylor and Durgess at times and allowed them to stretch, eat, and relieve themselves inside of buckets. Always a gun was pointed at them, and never once did they try any funny business. Before I'd leave, it was back to the chairs, duct tape, and lights out.

By keeping them alive I'd broken them down, I'd gotten them to turn on one another to reveal their inner cowardice and watch them rat each other out, and I'd gotten them to confess to murdering my wife, as well as to their identity.

Now, you may ask why all this was so important.

Let me tell you why.

What seemed like long ago now, when I was first setting things up in the old Mount Vernon High School, I placed within all three rooms where Taylor, Durgess, and Booker would be, cameras and recording equipment to take everything in - thankfully I'd turned everything off before Jehu came down. It was all hidden from their eyes and they didn't have a single clue. Of course, I knew I'd also be starring on these cameras and my words would also be recorded, but I didn't care about the trouble or punishment it would cost me. The truth would be known, even if I had to go down with it.

Did I put these men in deadly situations, having them confess while their lives were threatened? Yes. Did I think because of my actions that maybe this evidence wouldn't matter in the end in the court of law? Yep, but I didn't know how the law totally operated; it seemed there were many loopholes in it anyway. Did I know I'd go down with these three? Absolutely, but to me, it was totally worth it.

Oh, and did I think that I might die with carrying out each and every plan?

Everyday.

So you see, after much time and inner labor, I knew exactly what I was doing.

Thinking into it now, maybe this is why God spared me and allowed me to live through the gun shot to my head and to awaken from my coma. Because He knew I wasn't going to end up killing them. Of course, I knew it was against God's way with what I did and that He didn't agree with my actions; and I'm not saying this as an excuse for Him to condone my doings, but for some reason He let me live and I still at times wonder why.

All I know now is that I'm glad I don't have blood on my hands, I'm at peace that the truth has been set free - even though it was gained by crooked ways, and my conscious is clear now that all is said and done.

I often ponder on this experience and the individuals involved, from when it all first started until where I was now.

Jehu Bridges came into my life and I gained a true friend, even though I'd had my times with him. Al was a loyal partner who had a heart for helping out - with money being in the mix - especially if it was against bad people. Wendy turned away from a hated lifestyle and was walking a straighter road with her son, Stephen, and making huge strides for a better life for both of them. And Derek Westbrook, who I once looked at as an enemy, became an unexpected ally who was really a good kid.

*Don't forget about me!*

I could never. You're a part of me brother.

*Thanks J.*

Even though this experience had its moments of various emotions, inner struggles, and craziness, I had at least done some good. I'd had a hand in touching the lives just mentioned somehow in a positive way, and some good and right had been done.

As to the original six:

Rufus Booker, Tyrese Taylor, and Kevin Durgess lived, though I could have easily killed them. One young man named Derek Westbrook

251

repented, helped me, and was living a changed life as a result of his past mistakes. My wife resided with The Lord, which brought comfort to my heart. And me, Job McCants, could move on - not forgetting - knowing that some right had been done.

God is good.

No, let me rephrase.

God is great!

# PART 4

"There is forgiveness of sins for all who repent."

*Luke 24:47*

# 42

Walking out of the old MVHS - handcuffed - the entire area was lit up red, white, and blue. One would've thought a bomb threat had been called in by the look of all the police officers on scene, as well as the Mount Vernon Fire Department, which included two fire trucks and two ambulances.

To me it seemed like every police officer in the county surrounded me.

Making the last few steps down from the old high school, Jehu Bridges headed me in the direction of what was the command center. Located here was the police chief of Mount Vernon, as well as the Knox County Sheriff.

I felt like a model making my way down a stage with viewers all around me; however, there was nothing pretty about me or my clothing, and the spectators, I'm sure, found nothing entertaining about me.

*Have no fear, Job.*

Coming to the command center, the overweight Knox County Sheriff looked me up and down. The police chief did the same, but he shook his head, walked away, and joined others from within the command post. Jehu patted me on the shoulder and walked over to two other police officers who were nearby the command center.

"Mr. McCants," the Sheriff started to say, "I'm Sheriff Wallace of this county of Knox. You've made quite a scene and mess tonight."

I wasn't sure if this Sheriff was expecting a reply, so I just stood quietly.

Sheriff Wallace had a thick brown mustache and he looked like a Wild West Sheriff with his hat on. His gut hung over his belt buckle and he looked like he needed to start working out, but he looked like a nice man and a Sheriff who took his job seriously.

"I haven't received the full story yet, Mr. McCants," Sheriff Wallace went on, "but from what I've heard you took down a few big members from a notorious gang in Columbus, including their head honcho."

The Sheriff waited to see if I would say anything. I didn't, so he continued.

"You'll be heading to the Knox County Sheriff's Department. Two of my detectives will drive you there, along with this detective Bridges from Columbus."

Looking to my right, Bridges was talking to who I assumed were the two detectives who'd be taking me to the Sheriff's Department. Both were Caucasian. One looked younger with thick, puffy brown hair, and he also appeared fit. The other looked older than his partner; his hair was balding but he had decent sized arms. The younger one had his badge attached to a necklace wrapped around his neck, and the older one had his connected to his belt.

Bridges seemed to be in deep conversation with them. At one point all three of them looked my way, and the two detectives who I didn't know had concerned looks on their faces, like they were trying to understand me more than judge me.

Turning to Sheriff Wallace, I said earnestly, "I'm sorry, Sheriff, for causing all this trouble tonight. I have no good excuse; I just hope that the truth will be known now."

Seeing and hearing my sincerity, the Sheriff relaxed his stance a little and nodded his head. "Thank you, Mr. McCants." Pausing, he then said, "I'm not sure what all you did, but I'm gonna find out soon. I hope it was all worth it."

Not answering him, I said inside, "Yes and no." Yes because the truth had come to light, and no because I finally realized - in the end - that revenge is in God's hands, not ours. We, as humans, shouldn't claim it for ourselves, but leave it to the righteous anger of God.

*Amen!*

"Detectives," Sheriff Wallace said, looking to his left. Coming toward us were Bridges and the two Sheriff's Department detectives.

"Mr. McCants," the Sheriff said, gesturing with his hand toward his two detectives. "This is detective Jennings." The younger looking one nodded his head in a friendly manner. "And this is detective Woodson." The older looking one followed his partner's suit. "They'll be taking you to the station." Sheriff Wallace paused. "Detective Bridges," he said looking at him, "you're going too. I want somebody who knows what's going on to be present.

"Anybody have any questions?" finished Wallace.

No one said a word, which signaled all was understood.

"Very well," said Sheriff Wallace. He then said to the detectives, "We have personnel, including crime scene investigators inside. Once things settle down some, I'll meet you at the station."

The Sheriff nodded his head at me and then Bridges grabbed my arm. Next, Bridges, Jennings, and Woodson led me to a Ford Explorer, which had the Knox County Sheriff's Department logo painted on its sides.

Opening the driver's side back door, Jennings said, "Watch your head, sir." He gently placed a hand on my head, making sure I didn't hit it on anything.

Bridges made his way into the vehicle from the other back door and sat next to me. Detective Woodson took his place in the passenger seat. Once everyone was belted in, Jennings started the Ford Explorer up, and we made our way.

To the Knox County Sheriff's Department.

Ɨ   Ɨ   Ɨ

Sitting in the backseat of the Ford Explorer, it seemed everything hit me just then like a punch to the stomach. Emotions flowed through my blood and I felt like I was myself again, like I had been a different person for the past few months who had finally woken up from a terrible curse.

It was over.

I'd done it.

I still couldn't believe it all.

*Yeah, me either.*

Detective Jennings turned on the windshield wipers as a light rain wetted the glass. No one had said a word so far. But, in all honesty, what were we to talk about, especially with me in the vehicle?

Something else came into perspective as well. What would I have done if I didn't get caught? I thought on that and everything that would've meant.

What would I have done with Taylor, Durgess, and Booker? When and where would I have set them free? What would I have done with all the information that I'd found out, which included the secret someone who'd been helping Rufus Booker? How could I have gone on with a guilty conscious over all the things that I'd done? The What's and How's piled up in my head until there was no more room.

But it didn't matter anyway; I'd been caught and I'm actually glad I had, because I don't know what I would've done or how I would've felt if I didn't.

What I had done was now the past. Yes I would have to face the consequences of my actions - which I wasn't sure what all of them would be right now - but I knew, whether it was behind bars or somehow getting free, I had a future and could start anew.

As people, we have to make the most of the opportunities we have, whether that's from making wise or bad choices, whether that's being in a comfortable place or somewhere unpleasant, whether we had been in the right or wrong, whether we caused misfortunes to befall us due to our own actions or those of another, whether....

You get my point.

Of course I'd never forget this whole entire ordeal; it was a part of me now, however, there was light at the end of every tunnel if one searched for truth, remained hopeful, and turned to the way of faith.

Inside, I prayed. I prayed hard. I prayed as I remembered Naomi and Manhattan. I prayed for the lives I had put in jeopardy. I prayed to God that my path of revenge was a mistake and that revenge belonged only to Him. I prayed....

I prayed to the point where I unknowingly was crying. It took Jehu's hand resting on my shoulder to wake me up from my trance.

Opening my eyes, I continued to cry. Detective Woodson in the passenger seat looked at me with a sad face, and I saw detective Jennings' caring eyes looking at me from the rear view mirror.

As if God perfectly planned this moment - I know He did - my eyes fell on a brick building to my left that shined brightly in the night. There was a stone monument of Jesus in the front yard of it holding out His arms, and a large cross held tight toward the top of the building, sparkling in the darkness.

*Go to Him, Job.*

Whether it was a Baptist, Nazarene, Methodist, Catholic, or whatever church, I do not know; but I didn't care and that didn't matter at the moment. All that mattered is that I felt God drawing me closer, and I knew what I needed to do.

*It's time J.*

"Please," I said with urgency, "stop the vehicle. Please."

Jennings started to slow but he wasn't sure about my request, not that I could blame him.

"What is it, Job?" asked Jehu.

"You have my word," I started to say, "I won't do anything funny. I just need to...." looking at the church, all the detectives' eyes followed mine. "Please detective Jennings. Please."

Realizing what I wanted to do, Bridges said, "I'll be with him guys," he said to both detectives. "I know this man. He won't do anything inappropriate."

Jennings looked over at his partner in the passenger seat. His partner in return looked at him and then they both nodded their heads. All men in the vehicle must've understood my intention. My pressing request, the church on our left, and my crying I believe summed it all up.

Pulling off to the side of the street, Jennings put the Ford Explorer into park. Without any words being said, Bridges got out of the vehicle, opened my door, and there I stood with the church across from us.

The night was overcast, dark, and rainy, but there was something friendly and kind about this street. Rain started to come down harder and some of the homes around here had candlelight's glowing in their windows. It reminded me of one of those neighborhoods you see in movies or in a magazine that has everything going for it.

From growing up here, this was East High Street, unless they changed it for some reason; but the church was new and I hadn't seen it before.

Crossing the street, Bridges and I climbed many cemented steps until we stood at the top with the front of the church largely in front of us. The cross seemed to shine even brighter now that we stood in front of it.

*Job, it's been quite a ride.*

What? You're leaving me?

*I'm sorry, yes.*

But why?

*You don't need me anymore. You finally figured it out.*

Figured what out?

*That revenge is in God's hands, of course, not yours.*

But, but....

*You're gonna be just fine. Trust me.*

Will you ever come around again?

*You just never know. I'm winking at you now.*

Will you finally tell me what you are?

*What I am isn't of utter importance. I will tell you this though. God is alive, though many people say He is dead, and He sends messengers oftentimes when people need Him the most.*

Thank you. Thank you so much for everything. I'm gonna miss you.

*I'll miss you too, but you're gonna be all right J. You have God.
Now go to Him. You know what you need to do.*
You better visit every once in a while, you hear?
*HaHa! All right J. I'm fist pumping you right now.*
Back at you brother!
*God bless. Never leave Him.*
I won't. Goodbye.

And those were the last words my I-got-your-back-bro kinda being said to me. We'd been through a lot and I wouldn't have been able to get through everything without it. Matter of fact, I probably would've done a lot of regrettable things if it weren't for it. I sure was going to miss it.

But I knew what I needed to do now.

Falling to my knees, I lifted my arms Heavenward and tears fell from my face, mixed in with the rain beating down on it. For a split second I felt bad that I was making Jehu stand out here with me, but this I needed to get off of my chest.

"God," I exclaimed, "I'm sorry." A crack of thunder pierced the sky just then. "I was wrong; it wasn't worth it." My clothes were soaking wet now. "I thought it would be, but revenge is Yours, not ours.

"Forgive me God," I said, trying to keep myself together. "I'm so, so sorry. I was so wrong." I could barely keep my voice from cracking. "I'm here before You as a confessing sinner, a repentant debtor. I," the rain was really coming down now, "I was a lost sheep, but now I'm returning to You, my Shepherd. Cleanse me from my unrighteousness and make me whole again."

With the rain pouring on me, I felt like I was being re-baptized, like my heavy sins were being washed away. Again I was identifying with the Father and His Son through His Spirit. It was a feeling I can't give words to, but I felt set free with the weight of sin being removed from me.

Taking a deep breath, I said, "I pray all of this in Your Son's saving Name, Jesus Christ." Opening my eyes, I looked up to the dark, rainy sky and said, "Amen."

I truly was sorry for my sins and mistakes. Whereas many people confess and say they repent, only to go out and repeat their sins and mistakes again, I actually felt terrible about mine and wasn't going to repeat them.

True confession and heartfelt repentance can lead to a changed life if one really works at it. It's not always easy, but it's also not always hard. It takes work, but when it's accomplished, it brings inner peace and produces wonderful results.

The rain suddenly relented and was no more than a sprinkle. The thunder had ceased and there was a tranquility in the atmosphere that I can't give a name to.

I stood up and looked at the cross. I had a Savior named Jesus who gave His life for me and made it possible for me, a sinner, to be forgiven of all my sins and have everlasting life if I believed in Him and lived how God wanted me to. I wasn't going to live in violation of His ways any longer.

With the last couple of tears flowing down my face, I said, "Thank You, God."

Just then I felt a hand on my shoulder. I was just getting ready to turn around and thank Jehu when I felt another hand on my opposite shoulder. Following quickly was another hand on my back.

Whose hands were all these? Most humans had two, so I knew one of them didn't belong to Jehu. Handcuffed, I turned around, and that's when I knew who all the hands belonged to.

Standing to my left was detective Jennings, on my right was detective Woodson, and standing in front of me was Jehu Bridges. All of them were as soaked as I was, but I knew they didn't care by the looks on their faces.

Detective Woodson wiped water away from his forehead. "He heard you, Job, and knows you're sorry." He paused and then said, "We also could tell."

With a hand Jennings brushed his hair back, removing a handful of water. His thick, puffy hair not too long ago was now a watery mess. "And He forgives those who sincerely seek Him," he said, looking at me. He paused and then said, "Welcome home, sheep."

Jehu Bridges didn't have a toothpick, but he fought back tears from his watery eyes. "And," he said, emotional, "Jesus knows you pray in His saving Name, Job." He paused, looked at me, and then said, "Amen."

I didn't have the words for what was going on right now. Here were three men - two who didn't even know me - standing by my side as broken as I was, hearing every word I said and were there for me as if they were my very own brothers.

Perhaps they went through their own trials that brought them closer to the Lord. Maybe they too committed great sins that caused them to turn from them and seek forgiveness from God. Whatever it was, I don't know, but right now it didn't matter.

Wanting to break down in tears, I instead looked each man in the eye and said, "Thank you. Thank you all for what you did, and for being here."

How does one explain such compassion and kindness? Why did these men gather around me and care as if I were family? What was going through their minds right now?

One: I can't explain this, but it was obvious that God's love was working through them. Two: I have no clue what made them get out of their vehicle and stand by me, but it was apparent that these were Christian men. Three: I didn't know what they were thinking. What mattered is that we were four men of different backgrounds, color, likes, pasts, dislikes, childhoods, and so much other things, but still we could come together as God's children.

Not knowing how to sum this up, I didn't. Instead, I turned back around, and there detectives Bridges, Jennings, Woodson and I stood, staring up.

Up at the cross that shined so brightly.

# 43

The following afternoon I found myself back at the Columbus police station with Jehu Bridges. After what was found inside the bag in Rufus Booker's office, Jehu told the Knox County authorities it was imperative that he gets back to Columbus, with me tagging along with him. When Sheriff Wallace saw the bag's content himself and went over it, he also realized the necessity of both Jehu and I getting back to Columbus.

I'll never forget the generosity Sheriff Wallace and detectives Elijah Jennings and Thomas Woodson - I found out their first names - showed me. It was cops like them who gave the force a good name. Hopefully there were many watching and following their examples of leadership.

Sitting in the deputy chief's office, Haman finally showed up and sat behind his desk. Jehu and I sat opposite him.

I looked behind me. The entire department had their eyes glued to the large window that showed the inside of DC Haman's office. With the curtains not being drawn, most made their way closer.

I turned back around.

"Detective Bridges," he said looking at Jehu, "Mr. McCants," he then looked my way. Neither one of us said a word; we just sat there staring at him.

"You've caused quite a storm," Haman said to me. "I haven't heard the full gist of it all, but you're in some serious trouble." He seemed to look at me condescendingly, like I was lowly to his highness.

"You have anything to say, Mr. McCants?" He opened up his hands, palms up, on his desk and waited for me to say something.

I didn't reply.

"Figures," said Haman. "Most don't."

Sitting, still handcuffed, Haman focused his attention next on Jehu.

"And how'd you find out about all of this, Bridges? You traveled all the way to the city of Mount Vernon to nab him. How long did you know he," Haman pointed at me, "was up to no good?"

I could tell Haman had questions circling around in his head like a merry-go-round. He wanted so many answers, but he wasn't going to get a single one.

Jehu sat there at first quiet, but then he grabbed the bag from Booker's office at his feet and sat in on top of Haman's desk, knocking over a couple picture frames, as well as Haman's gold desk plate.

"BRIDGES! What do you think you're doing!?"

Looking behind me again, some of the department stood inches away from Haman's window and others crowded behind them. I noticed one of them was detective Goodwin, the detective I'd met the one day in here.

"All of you," Haman yelled, looking at the crowd that was piling outside his window, "get back to work!" Not moving, not one person in the crowd behind me moved. Red faced, Haman was getting ready to yell something else, but Jehu broke him off instead.

"I think you'll be interested with what's in that bag, chief." Haman gave Jehu a puzzled look. "While Mr. McCants was at The Kingdom with Rufus Booker, you know, the place where you," he emphasized "you", "told us to stay away from and have nothing to do with, he," Bridges pointed to me, "happened to find this bag."

"Yeah, so," said Haman, still none of this making sense to him.

"So open it," said Bridges.

Haman made no move to.

"Okay, be that way," Bridges said, standing up. "I'll do it for you." Opening the bag, the detective removed a tape recorder that had a tape already in it. Putting it in front of Haman, Bridges said, "Just push play, chief."

Sitting back down, Jehu and I just stared at Haman. With beads of sweat starting to form on his forehead, Haman hesitated at first, but then he pressed the play button.

*"Come on Mr. Deputy Chief of Police Charles Haman, work with me here."*

The voice belonged to Rufus Booker.

*"What did I tell you about using my name you idiot!"*

Seemed that Haman had a temper problem like I had.

*"Aw calm down,"* said Rufus. *"We've been working together for how many years now?"*

*"Calm down? Do you know how much trouble I could get in, Rufus Booker?"*

A pause on the other end. Then, *"All right, enough with the names,"* said Rufus.

*"Yeah, how's it feel?"* picked Haman.

*"Back to business," Rufus said. "I heard Job McCants woke up from his coma. Is that true?"*

Another pause before Haman said, *"It is."*

*"I want him dead. I'm going after him."*

*"No. At least not yet," said Haman.*

*"Why the...." Rufus cursed, "not?"*

*"Because," Haman started to say, "I have enough going on right now and I don't need that. Plus, you need to lay low for a while."*

*"But he," Rufus began to say, but Haman cut him short.*

*"I know he killed your brother, but just give it some time, would ya?"*

*"If you don't let me have my revenge, Haman, I'm gonna sing like a bird, and you know what I'm referring to."*

A pause followed. Haman realized Booker was going to expose him if he didn't give Booker what he wanted. Seems Booker didn't care if that meant going down with him, but who knows. It was a true case of blackmail.

Reluctantly, Haman said, *"You'll get what you want. Just give it some time. Understood?"*

*"Crystal," replied Booker.*

Jehu stood up, reached over, and pressed the stop button. Removing the tape, he grabbed another one from the bag and put it in. "Or how about this one, chief." Pressing the play button again, Haman was as pale as a white sheet and now had sweat dripping down the sides of his face. Sitting stone cold still, he listened.

*"I met Job McCants this evening," said Haman. "He came into the station with Jehu Bridges."*

*"Really."*

*"Yeah."*

*"So?"*

*"So," said Haman, "he remembers everything. I mean everything."*

*"Yeah so what," Rufus said snobbishly.*

*"So what?"* There was a long, quiet pause. *"Rufus, you gotta give me something."*

*"Watch the name thing, Haman. And what do you want me to do about it? You're the genius who's kept us from getting caught for all these years. Figure something out like you always do."*

*"I got so much heat on me. I gotta give the city something to appease them with all you and your gang are doing. I've received so many complaints about lack of police work. I'm asking a favor then. Please take some pressure off me."*

*"Is Jehu Bridges gonna be a problem?" inquired Booker.*

*"No. I'll keep him busy with other things."*

*"Good. Cause unless he wants to end up dead like his brother, he better stay outta my way."*

*"Back to business," said Haman, "you gonna do me a favor?"*

A long pause followed. Then, *"I'll give you Taylor, Durgess, and Westbrook. That should take a lot of pressure off of you and make the city feel better."*

*"Great. How?"*

*"I'll send 'em downtown, telling those three I need them to pick up a decent sized shipment for me. Better yet," Rufus went on, "I'll send 'em in the Ford Expedition we drove to McCants house to sweeten things up. You just say someone called in a suspicious vehicle that looked like it was making a drug trade-off or something."*

*"Genius," said Haman. "When do you want to set this up?"*

*"I'll call you soon."*

Bridges stood up again and stopped the tape recorder.

If Haman was pale, he was dead pale now. Fear was in his eyes and he had finally been caught.

This was the secret someone who'd been helping Rufus Booker. He was the one whose name was said to me when I had the barrel of the .357 buried in Kevin Durgess' mouth. This deputy chief of police was the reason why Rufus Booker had never been caught. Charles Haman was the one who'd be looked at as a traitor and who had finally been exposed.

Haman was also the one on the other end of the line talking to Booker back in Booker's office when Rufus had called him "boss" before the explosions started at The Kingdom. Haman knew what was happening, and he just went along with it anyway.

Back in Mount Vernon at the Sheriff's Department, Jehu had let me listen to most of the tapes because some of them had my name in them. I came to find out many things on those phone recordings in addition to what you just heard. Some of them I'll tell you.

I found out that Haman and Booker had been working together for years. They had an agreement that Haman could keep a large sum of the drug money if he kept heat and the cops off of Booker. It now made sense to me why Haman could afford the white Cadillac Escalade EXT he drove.

I found out that the reason why Booker didn't come after me for the two months after I got out of the hospital was because Haman had told him to let things cool down some; however, even though it was said in a recording that Haman didn't want Booker to kill me or my wife, and then me after my coma, threats of blackmail forced Haman's hand and he eventually let Booker have his way.

266

I found out that Haman, with being the deputy chief of his department, had responsibility for a certain area, which included The Kingdom. Which now made sense why Bridges and their department was to "stay away" from this area. Bridges had also told me that Haman's excuse for this was because he didn't want any of his officers killed - which I'm sure was true - and because he didn't want any of his department putting themselves in harm's way with what went on across Cana Bridge. However, allowing The Kingdom to operate meant Haman's pockets stayed filled.

There were so many things I found out on those tape recordings, but I don't have time to mention them all. At least I told you some of the key ones.

When I first found out about Haman, I wanted to get to him somehow to reveal what had been withheld from everyone else, just like I had with Taylor, Durgess, and Booker. But thanks to the way things went down, that part had been done for me.

"You're a piece of work you know that!" Bridges yelled at Haman. "You abetted a criminal for years! Someone who'd killed people! Someone who made and handed out drugs! Someone who committed all kinds of heinous acts! Someone...." Jehu, angry, paused for a few long moments. He then said, with his voice lowered, "You helped someone who took the life of my brother and the life of this man's wife."

With that sinking in, Haman sat motionless. I wasn't even sure if he was breathing.

Putting his hand in and out of the bag continuously, Jehu began tossing tapes, photos of Haman and Booker meeting together, and written notebooks with dates and times of drug trades, meetings, crimes, and other things at Haman.

"Booker made sure if he went down, you were gonna go down with him!" When the bag was finally empty, Bridges said, "You have anything to say, deputy chief Haman?"

Haman didn't reply.

"Figures," Jehu started to say, "most criminals don't."

The whole entire time I just watched and didn't say a word. Jehu, I thought, handled the matter better than most would have. With my temper, who knows what I would've done. There's a time to be quiet and a time to speak.

This was a time for me to be quiet.

Swallowing hard, Haman grabbed a desk drawer quickly and pulled it out. When he went to grab what he wanted, it wasn't there. His face dropped.

"I already removed your gun if that's what you're looking for," Bridges said impassively, standing before Haman's desk. "If you planned on shooting us, sorry about your luck." Jehu paused while Haman stared incredulously at him. "But I doubt that's what you were gonna do anyway. I'm sure if that gun was in there you would've taken the coward's way out."

Putting a toothpick in his mouth, Jehu said, "Again, sorry about your luck."

Turning around, Jehu nodded to detective Goodwin. Opening the door, Goodwin made his way in - as did several others - walked over to Haman, and read him his rights. Standing up, Haman, as well as his treachery, was defeated.

"Get him outta here," Bridges said, "before I put a bullet in him." Looking at me and back to Haman, he added, "Or before I let Job put one in him."

Cuffing DC Haman, detective Goodwin grabbed him by the arm and he, as well as the others who'd walked in, led Haman out of his office.

Turning around, the crowd outside Haman's office didn't move. Some shook their heads in disappointment, others gave him an angry stare down, and some just stood, staring at him.

Leaving just Jehu and I in the room, the detective said, "You all right, J?" Him calling me "J" reminded me of my counselor and guide.

I nodded my head. "I'm just glad that it's now all over. Everyone who had a part has finally been caught."

Jehu sat down in DC Haman's seat. "Nice comfortable chair. Maybe this'll be my office one day."

I smiled. "Yeah, maybe."

The room got quiet for a short time. Bridges then broke the quietness. "Everything's gonna be all right Job. I don't know what's all going to happen from here, but everything's gonna be all right."

I didn't know what to say, so I said nothing. But one thing still lingered in my head.

What was going to happen to me?

# 44

In the state of Ohio, kidnapping is a first-degree felony and aggravated assault with a deadly weapon is a fourth-degree. Kidnapping in the first-degree carries anywhere between three to eleven years in prison, and aggravated assault with a deadly weapon in the fourth-degree can get you anywhere between six to eighteen months in prison.

If you do the math, I faced a potential maximum of thirty-four and a half years in prison - kidnapping of three men - and a minimum of nine and a half years.

My case was made a big deal. News channels on TV, newspapers handed out all around the city, and the Internet broadcasted it far and wide.

Now, I'm not the wisest man when it comes to law, court, district attorneys, lawyers, deals, and things like that, so I'm not going to even act like I have an ounce of understanding in these areas, because I don't. To me it's a world of mass confusion and mazes that have too many alternatives if words are said a certain way and things being presented are given a little twist.

However, with all that being said, this is what happened to me.

Many things came into play, such as the following: (1) I had no past record, (2) I didn't kill my victims, (3) I had been a public servant serving the city of Columbus as a paramedic for years, (4) I had been psychologically traumatized - I didn't say this, others said it about me - as a result of Naomi's murder and with me witnessing it, (5) the city's crime rate and gang tension - both SSS and NEB - started decreasing, and (6) I had the support of what seemed like a numberless amount of Columbus citizens who publically stood behind me, thrilled that somebody took action against SSS.

Oh, and (7), I also had a sensitive and compassionate judge who, at my sentencing, lessened my punishment way more than I ever would have expected him to.

I was very thankful that many other laws that I'd broken didn't come up, which would've had me doing more time; but something tells me that the judge and those taking on my case looked the other way more than once.

Finally, after being convicted of both kidnapping and aggravated assault with a deadly weapon, I was sentenced from one to four years in prison. When I thought of how many years it could've been, I was immediately overcome with gratitude.

But things didn't stop there.

After sentencing me, the merciful judge motioned for me to approach his bench. When I did he said, "I'm going to write a personal letter on your behalf, Mr. McCants, pushing for an early release. With good behavior, you should be out in a year."

Almost in tears and taken way aback, I didn't know what to say. Finally I said, "Thank you, Your Honor."

"You're welcome, Mr. McCants," the judge said with a nod of his head.

But I wasn't just thankful for that. I was glad that the judge gave me time to serve, because I deserved it and I needed to suffer some kind of consequence for all my actions.

That's why I was glad Jehu did what he'd done to me; that is, placing the GPS device in my phone and catching me. I needed to get caught to see more from the right perspective.

A year?

A year was nothing compared to what it could've been.

One might say that the law had been made a mockery of given that I only received a year for all I'd done. Could I blame that critic?

No.

Did some in our nation's judicial system get less time when they should've gotten more, or others got more time when they should've gotten less?

Yes.

Was I the one taking on my own case, trying to persuade the judge to go easier on me? And was I the one who gave myself a lesser sentence?

Absolutely not. Others had done that for me.

I guess what I'm saying is that I had no control over any of these things, including the decisions and the individuals involved in my case: the judge, the lawyers, you name it. I didn't have a say, and others couldn't blame me or point the finger. Like I had in Haman's office with Jehu when the deputy chief had been caught red-handed, I sat back, watched, and didn't say a word.

Would someone blame a young child for stealing a loaf of bread when his drugged-out parents laid around at home ignoring his physical needs?

So I kinda felt something similar with my situation; I couldn't be blamed when others held my future in their hands, with me having no part in it whatsoever.

What I've found out is that we humans have no control in this life. When we think we do, we really don't. After I'd been sentenced and with the way all the chips fell, all I know is one thing.

God is in control, and I was by far a very fortunate man.

&#8224;  &#8224;  &#8224;

Though crimes had been committed in both Columbus and Mount Vernon, I ended up serving my time at Franklin County Corrections Center II. It didn't house as many felons as F.C.C.C. I did, but it was still a prison.

F.C.C.C. I was where Taylor, Durgess, Booker, and Haman were. I was told that the three SSS members, in exchange to have the death penalty removed, gave out years' worth of valuable information, leading to their gang's long-awaited and celebrated end. For aiding and abetting, Haman could've received the same punishment as the three just mentioned; however, with being an officer who did do some good throughout his career, he received a lesser punishment. But from what I've heard, all four of them will spend the rest of their days in prison.

Because the truth came out - I'm sure from Taylor, Durgess, and Booker, because it sure wasn't me - Derek Westbrook was punished as well. However, I'd spoken up for him and said it was Booker's hand over his when the trigger was pulled; and I had also said he was forced to do things he didn't want to. As a result, Derek was treated as a juvenile and was placed on a year's probation and community service. I knew the kid learned his lesson as well.

Life isn't actually all that bad here at F.C.C.C. II. Some of the prisoners are North End Boyz and have had my back while I'm here. NEB member Angry from R and D's Hardware - if you remember - did keep his word in putting in a good one for me. Word of mouth about me spread into this prison and I've won the respect of the NEB members incarcerated here. They've taken me in as one of their own, though I don't act at all like any of them.

The guards here at F.C.C.C. II have also been compassionate, because they too are like the judge. They don't let anyone mess with me and they watch over me like an eagle. Though they don't have to, they give me additional privileges that many of the other prisoners don't receive.

THE DEAD WILL RISE

Besides my family and Jehu Bridges, I've also been visited many times by my paramedic brothers and Al. Heck, even detective Jennings and his partner detective Woodson have driven down several times to visit. I've been blessed to have so many visit me in my current condition, unashamed to still call me their son, brother, or friend.

One day when I was reading the Bible in my prison bed, I happened to read the following passage: *I was in prison, and you visited me.*

That really hit home with me after reading this and thinking about those who had visited me.

Someone who visited me at least once a week was Wendy. I was surprised, and then I wasn't. I could tell that Wendy had a thing for me a while back, but not in a pushy or extreme way. Something had definitely clicked with her toward me back when I first got to know her, and she didn't want to let that escape. We got to know each other very well and she too was a changed woman living out her faith.

She'd started attending church again and said she was doing her best to set a good and godly example for Stephen, her little son. Currently in nursing school, she was excelling and was the top student in her class. During one of her visits, she got a little emotional and began crying over her past life that she was ashamed of. From getting pregnant out of wedlock, to having a son whose deadbeat dad left and wanted nothing to do with them, to her old job as a dancer at Bottom's Up; she let it all out, and I also realized she didn't really have anyone else to talk to. But, with much joy in her eyes and a smile on her gorgeous face, she said a personal relationship with God through her Savior Jesus Christ made all things new.

No one could ever rob her of that saving grace.

It's absolutely amazing what God and Jesus can do with a human life.

Before I stop talking about Wendy, there was one more thing. She made it a point to quietly tell me often - though I obviously got the point - that she wasn't seeing anyone, hadn't since having Stephen, and didn't have any plans to. Finally, after about the third time, I asked her, "What are you getting at, Wendy?" with a smile on my face.

Smiling an all-white smile, she said, "You know what."

At the time I said seriously, "I still have half a year in here. That's a lot of time to wait. Plus, I don't know if I'm ready to...." but then I stopped. She knew what I was getting at: I wasn't sure if I was ready to move on from Naomi just yet, begin a new relationship, and marry again.

Not allowing this to collapse her dreams, Wendy just smiled. She then said something similar to what I'd told her about leaving Bottom's Up when we'd first met at her apartment. "This opportunity may not ever present itself again."

Smiling brighter, she ended, "Think about it."

I have been lately, and a lot.

With not too much time left to serve, I've also thought a lot about what I'd done. It still seemed like it was all an unbelievable dream, but it happened. I had nightmares my first few months here, but thankfully they've passed away.

As human beings we are capable of just about anything; and when we think we're not, trust me, we are. I never thought I ever would've done the things I did, as well as be in certain places or around certain individuals. This world can steer us in the wrong direction and have us do bad things if we allow it to. Violence, pornography, lying, murder, slander, hate, revenge, lust, drugs, alcohol….you get my point. If you let the things of this world consume you, they eventually will.

My exhortation to you is: DON'T LET THEM!

In contrast, God created us for so much more than to settle for the things which this world offers. He's still in the business of forgiving, He's slow to get angry, He's merciful, and He loves; however, it's up to you to make that change that He's waiting for you to make and to invest in the greatest gift of His life-saving and changing business.

I still often think about that minister on TV preaching the Gospel when I laid in the hospital bed after awakening from my coma. The power and conviction in his voice I will never forget. The belief that he held so strong to we both share, and I will never forget him or The Word he boldly preached.

Also, I still think about that world of blackness I was in when I was in my coma and the divine, roaring lion voice that said, "*When you have repented, return to me.*" Every time I think of this, it touches my heart. I have repented, and I have returned to Him.

God sent a Savior and Redeemer named Jesus for people like you and I. If I can make that change, trust me, so can you. It takes a change of heart and some work, but it's the most significant and cleansing change you'll ever experience.

So, I leave you with this and ask you.

Will you make that change and turn to Him?

✝     ✝     ✝

273

After applying the finishing touches of my detailed account and some of my life story, my hands finally stopped typing. It was finished. Maybe you learned something or got something out of this, or maybe you didn't.

I hope you did.

Today is also the day that I'm being released from F.C.C.C. II, and I couldn't be a happier man. I served my time and now I was being set free, like a caged bird whose broken wing was finally healed and who was ready to be released back into the world.

The NEB members fist pumped me by holding their fists against the window in the door of their cells. Many of the guards shook my hand and some even hugged me. The main secretary of the prison, Holly, who had blond hair and a welcoming smile, also hugged me and said, "I'm going to miss you, Job."

As I passed through the main gate outside of the prison, the day was sunny and pleasantly warm. White puffy clouds hung above my head and the air gave life to my lungs as I took in a deep breath. Before too long autumn would arrive, and I couldn't wait.

When the last guard shook my hand and said, "Good luck, Job," that's when my attention focused on the crowd waiting for me, ready for this day as much as I had been.

Standing and smiling in front of several parked vehicles was my mom, pops, my brother Cyrus and his wife, Wendy, Al, Jehu, Derek Westbrook, and detectives Elijah Jennings and Thomas Woodson.

I didn't have any more room for tears, but some standing in front of me made up for me. Embracing me like a prodigal son, my mom and pops held me tight. My brother's wife hugged me, and Cyrus shook my hand and then pulled me in for a hug. I never did ask him if he wondered why I'd asked him about specific information about the old and abandoned Mount Vernon High School - I'm sure he knew why now - but it didn't matter at the moment anyway.

Wendy hugged me tighter than anyone else and landed a pretty good kiss on my cheek. When I looked into her eyes, I believe there was something there; I just wasn't sure what yet.

Al patted me on the shoulder and firmly shook my hand while Derek - with a big smile - fist pumped me and then hugged me. Honestly, I loved the kid as if he were my own, no matter what we'd been through.

Jehu, as usual, with a toothpick in his mouth and cornrows neatly parted, hugged me and held it the longest. "You're free brother. You're free," he quietly said. "I love you man." Letting go of me, he said with a smile, "Now stay free." We both laughed after the comment.

Turning to the two Knox County Sheriff's Department detectives, I embraced them before they could me. They didn't have to be here and it meant a lot. I was still taken aback by their compassion and kindheartedness.

*You are free, J. But the greatest freedom you have is in Christ.*

Hey buddy! You did drop in to visit.

*I wouldn't have missed this. Now go, J, and live your life with God.*

I'm going to. Thanks brother.

*By the way, I see Wendy's here. I told you she liked you.*

Yeah yeah. Don't you have someone else to help?

I didn't receive a reply. It was gone. And unless it planned on visiting me sometime in the future, that was the last time I ever heard from my I-got-your-back-bro kinda being.

I felt in a way that cannot be put into words. My heart was glad and my soul was rejuvenated with the presence of all those before me. There are good people in the world. Sometimes they're hard to find, but they're out there.

I was thankful, appreciative, grateful, and blessed all at once. But there was One in particular Who I was thankful, appreciative, and grateful to the most.

Looking up into the sunny, cloud filled sky, I said, "Thank You, God."

275

# EPILOGUE

## ONE YEAR LATER

With being a year out of prison, I am most definitely living a changed life, and there's been a lot of new in it. I am both a very happy and fortunate man.

I ended up moving back to Mount Vernon. I wanted to be closer to my family and friends - my parents also moved back from out of state - as well as make a new start in life. The house I live in is situated in the country. It's quiet, peaceful, and I get to see the sun set beautifully in the west every night from my front porch. With living in my hometown, I feel like I'm growing up in it all over again. The feeling does my heart good.

I don't live alone either.

Wendy and I got married about nine months after I got out of prison. We took things slow, got to know each other as if we'd been together for years, and finally tied a committed, faithful, and romantic knot. In all honesty, I never thought I'd marry again; however, Wendy was that very, very rare exception.

Her and I both had pasts we weren't proud of. We'd done things we regretted and wished we could take back. But, in contrast to our pasts, we were not defined by them, and we both started new, on a clean slate. The three of us, my stepson Stephen being the third, attend church regularly, pray as a family, and try to live everyday how God wants us to.

Speaking of Stephen - who I plan on adopting soon - he looks way up to me and treats me as if I were his birth father. I'm going to love him as my son and raise him to the best of my ability. I'm gonna be there for him during the hard times as well as the good, I'm gonna discipline and love him at the same time, and I'm gonna raise him how children should be raised instead of how many parents were raising theirs today.

He and I have a tight, fun relationship.

I'm blessed.

My wife and I both agreed on not bringing our own children into this world. Each to their own, but with the way the world and people were, we just didn't want to bring children into this place with all that we'd seen in our lives and with what was going on in this present day.

I'm enjoying my life, and I love what Wendy, Stephen, and I have. And that's just perfect with me.

Like I said, I never thought I'd marry again after Naomi. But I didn't want to spend the rest of my days alone, one day looking back wishing that I'd married Wendy. I was still young and believed that I could make a woman a happy wife, that woman being Wendy. In my heart I made the right choice, and I love Wendy just like I had Naomi.

Yes Wendy is about as gorgeous as they come, but that's not what I was attracted to the most about her, though, I'll admit, it still had a part. Her godliness, loyalty, and inner beauty are what I found most appealing. She dressed modestly unlike most women today, she was there for me when others would've said, "Forget you," and walked away, she was genuine, forgiving, and loving, while so many other women were promiscuous, deceiving, and unfaithful. She was so much more, but these are just a few of her attributes that I love the most.

I most definitely made the right choice in marrying her; I love her with all my heart.

With that being said, not a day goes by that I forget about Naomi. She's still a part of me and I know she sees me. In my heart I believe she's pleased with my choice of wife. She'd want me to be happy, not sad; together, not alone; and sharing my love, not withholding it. I pray to her everyday and still talk to her. To me, she will never be forgotten.

I still end our conversations with, "Too me."

But life does go on, and I know my first wife smiles upon me.

Jehu Bridges and I are best friends and talk on a weekly basis. Our wives have also gotten close and we have cookouts, get togethers, and things like that quite often. Only about an hour separates us, after all.

Oh, and how could I forget. I rarely have a drink, but during one of our cookouts, Jehu and I sat in rocking chairs out on his back deck each drinking a Coors Light while I told him everything I could remember about what I'd done when I went after Taylor, Durgess, and Booker.

Simply put, Jehu was blown away. I won't say anymore.

I visit Derek Westbrook every once in a while when I'm down his way. He got his license and is working for a landscaping company. Manual labor. That's something most young people don't know a thing about these days. I'm proud to see him grow maturely. He's walking a good path in life and I keep him in my prayers.

With living in Mount Vernon, detectives Jennings and Woodson and I have become good friends. Sometimes we'll meet up for lunch or do a guy thing together. We also happen to serve in the same church. They're the ones who talked Wendy and I into attending the same one they do.

Also, Wendy got a job working as an RN for Knox Community Hospital, which is located in Mount Vernon. She brings home good pay and I'm so proud of her for pursuing a career that she studied and worked hard to get to. One of her fellow RN coworkers happens to be Fiona Jennings, the wife of detective Jennings.

Now we're all pretty good friends.

It's such a small world, isn't it?

At first I didn't know what I was going to do job-wise for the rest of my life. With doing what I'd done, that kinda kept me from working many jobs. But, as God works in mysterious ways, He was preparing me for something else.

It seems I've impressed many people with my writing in prison. How? I don't know, but somehow it got out. Maybe it was the guards. Again, I don't know; but I've impressed certain individuals so much that a traditional publishing book company sought me out and wanted to know what I could further write about.

Now in a long contract with a publishing company, my prison story has become a best seller, and it even sits on the shelves at Barnes and Noble. Furthermore, I now write fiction, whether it's thrillers, mystery, or suspense. I'm no James Patterson, but I'm me, and I'm not doing too bad.

I sure do miss being a paramedic though. Everyday was different and I just never knew what I was going to get into next. It's not everyday you get to ride in an ambulance, start IV's, push medications, shock people, hangout with the guys at the station, help save lives, and see all sides of people and places; and trust me, many of them weren't pretty.

I've also controlled my temper problem that I'd suffered for so long. I now channel my anger toward writing, working out, and spending time with my family. It was a terrible habit, like biting your fingernails too much; but, with time and work, anything's possible.

Anger no longer weighs me down as it once did.

Thank God.

So now I, Job McCants, am a stay-at-home author/stepfather who's living a peaceful and happy life, married to a beautiful and faithful wife in the country of my hometown.

Life is good.

Right now Wendy and I are sitting at a red light on East High Street in Mount Vernon in an older black Cadillac convertible that I'd bought at a very low price. It's the furthest thing from being top-notch and needs a lot of work, but I was never one for high-priced vehicles anyway.

Looking to my left, there was the church that I had fallen on my knees in front of before God as I was being transported to the Knox County Sheriff's Department. I stared at it for a long time.

"Honey," said my wife, who was nestled up against me, my arm around her shoulder, holding her close to me, "the light's green."

Shaking my head and focusing on the street before me, I said, "Thanks babe."

Pressing a long kiss on my cheek, Wendy said, "I love you; I'm so blessed."

Smiling I said, "I love you too wife."

Driving down East High Street, the trees on our sides had branches that reached skyward, somewhat forming a ceiling over us. The sun peeked through their branches and the grass was a brilliant green. People were either out sitting on their front decks in conversation, grilling out, or just enjoying the passing people and vehicles go by.

Suddenly, a sign in one of the yards caught my attention.

Passing it, I turned into a side street, put the car in reverse, and made my way back.

"What is it honey?"

I didn't answer my wife.

Parking across the street to the side, I looked over at the handwritten sign in big black Sharpie ink. I had read it right. A smile spread widely on my face just then.

"Job," Wendy said, a smile now also coming across her face. "What is it?"

Giving her a kiss on the lips, I said, "Come with me."

Taking her hand, we got out of the car and made our way into the yard that had the sign in it. She looked at the sign and read it aloud, "Black lab puppies for sale."

Putting two and two together, my wife squeezed my hand and said excitedly, "Job, we're getting a puppy!?"

I nodded my head and smiled at my wife. "We are today." Inside, I couldn't help but think of Manhattan. I still thought of her too, and I had to turn around when I saw that sign.

"We need a dog," I started to say. "Plus, it'll make Stephen's day and give him some responsibility." Inwardly this warmed my wife's heart. "Thanks babe, you're the best," she said, giving me another kiss on the cheek.

Making our way to the backyard, there was a small fenced-in area where a mother black lab laid with her five babies. How ironic, I thought. That's exactly how many babies there were when Naomi and I had picked out Manhattan.

God has His ways.

The people giving the puppies away were extremely nice and I just watched as my wife's face was lit up. I told her to pick out the puppy. It didn't matter to me; I was too engrossed in my wife and her happiness at the moment anyway.

I really loved her.

Just like I had Naomi.

After paying for the puppy, Wendy and I returned to our vehicle, the puppy held gently and securely against her chest. We made our way down East High Street, back home.

"What should we name her?" my wife asked me.

I thought on that. "Why don't we let Stephen decide?" My parents were at our house watching him right now.

Wendy smiled. "Job."

"Yeah."

"Pull the car over."

Pulling over with my wife still nestled beside me, she said, "I love you so much." She kissed me several times slowly on the lips, the puppy yipping between us. After the last kiss, I pulled back onto East High Street, again making our way home.

Stephen ended up naming our new puppy Brooklyn. I wiped a tear away from my eye when he did. Naomi and I had named Manhattan after the borough in New York. I wonder what made Stephen think of that name? I never encouraged anything; he came up with it on his own. Manhattan and Brooklyn are two boroughs close together in New York. What on earth made him think of that name?

Again, God has His ways.

Smiling, I looked up to the sky, stopped again at the same red light. The sun's warmth covered us and the comforting breeze felt good. Mount Vernon's city clock chimed loudly, acknowledging it was the start of another hour.

Holding my wife close to me, everything just seemed so right as we sat in our old Cadillac convertible with the radiant day in front of us. Everyday was a blessing but for some reason something felt different on this day, but in a very, very good way. Looking ahead of me, the light turned green.

Holding Wendy tightly with our new puppy between us, I pressed down on the accelerator, and there we went.

Making our way back home.

# ACKNOWLEDGMENTS

My first thanks in everything goes to God. He and His Son, Jesus Christ, have turned my life upside down, and I haven't been the same since. He's blessed me with the gift of writing, and I'm going to continue doing it with all the glory going to Him.

CreateSpace, none of this would be possible without your professional assistance and touch. I give thanks to your organization and employees who work tirelessly.

Debi, my wife, your input and patience with my writing I always appreciate. I am a fortunate man to have a bride who is loving, faithful, and who loves God. You bring so much joy to my life. I love you.

MaMa, your motherly support and love cannot be contained in words. Besides my wife, you're the next best friend I have. How am I worthy to have you as my mother - I'm not - but I thank God you are. I love you more.

PoPs, thank you for backing me with this writing business and being proud of this man you helped raise. It means more than you know. Love you.

Grandma Arck, my love for you reaches deep down inside. Your warm hugs, soft kisses, and encouraging words uplift my spirit. I treasure our visits and conversations; they're more precioius than rubies. I love you so much my godly grandmother.

Nick, my brother, thanks for supporting and being there for me. Tierney, my sister-in-law, thank you for your help in spreading my novels. Your kindess won't be forgotten. Trevyn, you've been a good stepson and have respected and treated me well. I thank you for that. I love all three of you.

To all of my family, you are not forgotten and I love you.

My church family at Brandon Baptist, your fellowship, prayers, and love lift mountains. I am close to many of you - you know who you are - and I thank you and love you.

My Mount Vernon Fire Department family, your enthusiasm and joy over my success in writing I'm truly appreciative for. I love our job, what we do, and the times we have, both play and work. Holly, I love you sister and I can't thank you enough for your excitement over my writing and your blessings.

To all my friends, again, you know who you are. School, work, church, neighbor, serving - however we met - I thank you and love you as well.

Also, to all who help promote my novels. Whether it's by word of mouth, social media, the newspaper, etc. I am in debt to you all. You know who you are and you're not forgotten by me.

To Paragraphs Bookstore and their staff, thank you. My first book signing brought in multitudes and you made a dream of mine come true.

To the people who cried in front of me after the release of my first novel, *Marked for Judgment*, to the people I still see at the grocery store, in town, in stores, in homes, at appointments, at work, in church - you get the point - who just talk to me or ask me about my writing and say, "Keep writing! When's the next one coming out!?", to the people who pray for me, to the people who still talk about my first novel (I never thought a book could be such a huge hit), to anyone and everyone who I have touched and who have also touched me, thank you. You are not forgotten and are a strong, encouraging force that gives me strength to keep writing.

As I've said before, I could go on and on; but, as you see, this page is running short on space. Thank you all again, with all of my heart. I love you all in love's various, repective forms: for a friend, a family member, a coworker, an acquaintance, etc. May God bless and guide you.

# ABOUT THE AUTHOR

## Jared McCann

resides in Ohio and is happily married to his beautiful wife, Debi. In addition to being an author, Jared has served as a firefighter/paramedic for his hometown of Mount Vernon going on ten years. He is also the author of *Marked for Judgment*, his first novel. Jared is preparing a book of poetry at this time that should be available on the bookshelves next year. A lover of pets and an avid woodworker, the author can be found outdoors doing just about anything. Also a missionary, Jared hopes to continue traveling - both domestic and overseas - around the world, helping people and writing as much as he can in his free time. He appreciates and loves hearing from his readers, family, and friends and can be found at:

Facebook:
@jdmbook

Amazon:
amazon.com/author/jaredmccann

&

E-mail:
j_money_5@yahoo.com

Jared's author profile and books are available on Amazon (www.amazon.com) as well as Barnes and Noble (www.bn.com). Just type in his name or novels. His books can also be purchased at Paragraphs Bookstore in downtown Mount Vernon.

# ME & MANHATTAN

Made in the USA
Lexington, KY
05 May 2017